When Dreams Touch

Rosemary Hanrahan

When Dreams Touch, Published March, 2014

Editorial and Proofreading Services: Shannon Miller, Karen Grennan

Interior Layout and Cover Design: Howard Johnson,
Howard Communigrafix, Inc.

Photo Credits: Front Cover: *Escaping From the Prison*, Shutterstock
#122791417

 SDP Publishing

Published by SDP Publishing, an imprint of
SDP Publishing Solutions, LLC.

For more information about this book contact Lisa Akoury-Ross by e-mail
at lross@SDPPublishing.com.

ISBN-13 (print): 978-0-9913167-2-4

eISBN-13 (ebook): 978-0-9913167-3-1

Library of Congress Control Number: 2014930616

Copyright © 2013, Rosemary Hanrahan

Printed in the United States of America

In gratitude, this book is dedicated in special memory to Sister Marie Carmelle Voltaire—my student, my teacher, my friend—and to all the amazing individuals I've worked with in international health, my parents, and my children. With their love and support, they have challenged and inspired me to honor my dreams.

When it is genuine, when it is born of the need to speak, no one can stop the human voice. When denied it speaks with the hands or the eyes, or the pores or anything at all. Because every single one of us has something to say to the others, something that deserves to be celebrated or forgiven by others.

—**Eduardo Galeano**

AUTHOR'S NOTE

My personal experiences living and volunteering in Haiti provided me a unique perspective in writing this book. Three decades of man-made and natural disasters and the HIV/AIDS pandemic created the conflict. But the characters and relationships between them are the real story.

Much of this novel takes place in the small country of Haiti, just over 700 miles from the coast of the United States. However, similar stories could occur in a number of countries around the world, the so-called developing or third-world countries. This story is about what happens when those of us privileged to live in relative physical comfort and personal security, unite with individuals and communities in their struggle to overcome poverty and oppression. It is about the sorrows, the joys, the tragedies, and triumphs that result when our passions and sense of purpose touch one another.

When the tragic earthquake struck Haiti in January 2010, I had completed the first 200 pages of *When Dreams Touch*. I seriously considered not finishing the book. It seemed exploitative, yet essential. But friends and fellow writers encouraged me to continue. And so, with many tears, a heavy heart, and several trips to lend my hands to the many committed to rebuilding Haiti, I forged ahead to a very different ending than what I had originally conceived.

In fact, the Prologue/Epilogue was written on the one-year anniversary of the earthquake. I sat in a lopsided rattan chair on what remained of the veranda overlooking Port au Prince. This was the place I had lived, worked, and stayed many times. It had been my home, and like many homes, churches, schools, and businesses, it came crashing down in just over thirty seconds.

The streets were strangely quiet that morning of the first anniversary. People came together to grieve with friends and family, in places of worship, or in quiet solitude. I believe everyone shared the disturbing reflection about the days, weeks, and months following the earthquake when international aid and disaster relief flooded into Haiti. First hand, I witnessed the dis-coordination of medical supplies, food, water, and shelter. No one denies that more lives could have been saved and much suffering prevented. But I also recognized the extreme efforts that were put forth by so many individuals and organizations to "do something." Now, four years later, much has been done—but not nearly enough.

I hope both those who know Haiti well and those who do not will feel the *Onè*—Honor—that warms my heart and guides my efforts and the efforts of others who have come to know and care for her people. I hope the reader will share in the *Respè*—Respect—that I have for my Haitian friends and other international volunteers and collaborators.

In this spirit, I continue to challenge myself and ask my readers to do the same. What if, when our dreams touch, through tragedy, circumstance, or active advocacy, we come together in understanding and action? What positive and lasting change might result, not just for those struggling with poverty and oppression, but for any of us willing to be part of this incredible and courageous journey?

The net proceeds from *When Dreams Touch* are donated to support non-profit healthcare and education initiatives in Haiti.

Port au Prince, Haiti 2015

"Monte kap," the Sanba calls out . . .

Two dark hands envelop the lighter one that trembles just slightly as they hold the scissors. Together the three sisters who share no common blood, but who had finally claimed their common dream, cut the ribbon.

Thousands of men, women, and children enter. I feel their weight upon me. It is a good feeling to know joyful steps again—although they are different now. Oh yes, many are still shoeless; some are big and some are small. But now there are those that move with only one step instead of two. And some come on wood or plastic; a few roll in on wheelchairs. A father carries his son, missing both legs, on his shoulders. Most know only pieces of the story behind the dedication—the dedication of the new soccer field—Garden of Roses. The three women who cut the ribbon hold it all in their hearts, collectively.

No one would have imagined this five years ago . . .

The three sisters were here that day too—January 12, 2010—watching another soccer game with the young American man. The man who loved soccer and whose hair was red. Red like his mother's hair when she was younger—when she first came to me to read the wall and run around my field. Many times more she came. In her last few years, her steps changed from easy and brisk to a low and slow shuffle. I noticed even before she did. She would write in her little book and sometimes she would shout to no one but me. A few times she cried and sometimes she prayed.

On that day five years ago, there was a little Haitian boy; it was his first soccer game. The Americans brought dozens of shoes and T-shirts for the children. The little boy wore one of the blue shirts and played in the middle of the field. He was running down toward the goal when he lost his shoe and fell to the ground.

The short Haitian woman ran out on the field.

"Are you okay?" she asked, and then to others watching the game. "Didn't we bring more shoes? These are way too big for him. Can one of you check in my suitcase at Didi's?"

"I'll go," the tall American woman with dark hair and glasses offered.

"No, I got it. You stay and watch the game. I know how you *love* sports." The red-haired man teased his sister and dropped his wife's hand. He ran off to the place he and his mother had stayed so many times.

It was only across the street. I remember he jumped in the air and nearly turned upside down to face me for an instant. Then he landed on his feet again.

"Keep playing, guys," He yelled over his shoulder. "We need to finish the game. It'll be dark soon."

"My mother always held her breath when he did that," the woman with the dark hair and glasses said to the other two. "She said it would either be the death of him *or* her."

They laughed and then stayed quiet for a minute, each alone with their memories.

"It was nice yesterday," the Haitian sister said.

I remembered her kicking a ball here, too. That was many years ago. She wore pink sandals.

"I thought I would feel bad," she said. "You know, leaving her here. I guess that's silly—they're only ashes."

The tall Haitian woman whose belly then swelled with their baby spoke, "I know what you mean. But so many people came. I couldn't believe it. I hadn't seen that many people together since— well, forever." She caught her breath as the baby kicked inside her. "My mother sure loved her. She wanted to be here today. But the trip was too much." She looked across the street, to where the baby's father, her husband, had gone.

Hurry! I wanted to say. *Forget the shoes. They aren't important.* But I couldn't. No one ever seemed to hear when I tried to speak anyway. All that day, I held it together—the pressure that was building deep inside me. I waited until most of the children were out of the schools. I waited until the businesses were closed; although there were not many open those last few years. But when he went into the guesthouse and up to the second floor and into the back room and opened the suitcase, it was already too late. He wanted to find the perfect pair of shoes for the little boy.

Hurry! I wanted to say. But he didn't. And the sun was already low in the sky and if I waited any longer, if I waited for the red-haired man to come back to his wife and his sisters, so many more could have died.

"Do you think we'll ever win those Nobel and Pulitzer prizes?" the American woman asked her sister.

"Doesn't seem so important anymore, does it? Winning prizes," she answered back.

Strange, that was the last thing I heard before it happened.

At first, it was just a tremor; the plates shifted slightly, then a little more, and then there was nothing I could do.

Thirty-five seconds; that was all it was . . .

I

PASSAGES

(1984–1985)

I decided that I would make my life my argument.

—Albert Schweitzer

1

ADELAIDE DELVA

VILLE BONHEUR, RURAL HAITI
JULY 1984

The chipped, blue-and-white ceramic statue of the Virgin Mary, draped in blue satin and adorned with plastic, blue-and-red flowers, rested in a makeshift grotto of rusting chicken wire. She was bolted to a thin plywood platform for safety as four men carried her up the rocky mountain path to the church. Their bare, ropy shoulders gleamed with sweat in the late-afternoon sun.

Adelaide Delva and her mother, Yvonne, joined the thousands of Haitian peasants who followed behind, spread out like the long and elaborate train of a wedding gown. The women had white ribbons tied around their foreheads, and necklaces of brightly colored plastic beads intertwined with rosaries around their necks, the small plastic crosses dangling between their breasts. Some were dancing; others, like Adelaide, walked solemnly to the beat of the drums echoing off the mountains. They carried ivory candles in one hand and gifts in the other—offerings of food, perfume, or photos of loved ones faded to gray and framed in banana bark. A few fortunate individuals who had connections in

Port au Prince raised Haitian passports, offering prayers to both their Christian God and *Vodou lwa*—spirits—in hopes of safe passage to the United States.

Adelaide, almost six months pregnant, did not have a passport or a photograph to present to the spirits. Instead she brought a tiny pair of white socks trimmed in pink lace. These were a gift from her mother, who insisted the baby growing inside her was a girl. Her mother, the only person who knew that she was carrying the child of an already married man. The father, a visitor from Port au Prince for the New Year holiday, came and went from their small village, Petit Mirebelais, in less than three weeks. Just enough time to steal Adelaide's sixteen-year-old heart and virginity, but not long enough for her to know the price she would pay for a few nights in his arms.

Adelaide's mother had insisted they make the pilgrimage to Saut d'Eau that year. Like many of the other Haitians in the group, they were Vodouissants. As such, they were required to go at least once in their lifetime. Many believed the waterfalls of Saut d'Eau had special healing powers that banished sickness and answered impossible prayers. Their spiritual beliefs incorporated Catholic and Vodou traditions. Their God ruled from both heaven and earth, inhabited the stars and possessed their flesh. To the outside world, it might appear that they were hedging their spiritual bets. But the Haitian peasants, like Adelaide and her mother, were just hoping to escape the escalating poverty that enveloped their country.

In March, just four months earlier, their desire to make the pilgrimage took on a new urgency.

Adelaide's mother hadn't gone as far as the mother of one of her friends, inserting a finger between her daughter's legs each month to make certain she was still intact. But nonetheless she kept close track of her cycles, and after two months with no bleeding, she confronted Adelaide.

"You've been with someone and now you are carrying his child."

At first Adelaide felt great shame, and denied the relationship. But before long, under her mother's loving yet shrewd gaze, her denial turned to tears. After a few angry words and futile accusations, a covenant was made between them.

"Yes, Mama. I promise this child will have a better future—an education, a life outside this misery." She truly believed it was possible.

It was all her mother needed to hear. "I will help you," she said. And so, they began to plan.

"We will make the journey to Saut d'Eau this year, while your belly is still small enough to hide it," she whispered one April morning. She and her mother sat alone by the charcoal fire outside their two-room house, waiting for the coffee to boil. Her sisters were still sleeping, while Adelaide was dressed early and ready for school in her blue cotton skirt and white blouse, always washed and freshly pressed by her mother as soon as she took it off the afternoon before. Each day, she went to school an hour early. One of the teachers was tutoring her for national exams she would take at the end of next year.

"I'm so tired, Mama. What does it matter? I'll never finish school or take the exams." She pulled a wooden comb through her stubborn hair and instantly regretted her complaining. Her mother never had the chance to go to school. She couldn't read a simple Bible verse and only marked her name with an X. Still she was clever with money. On more than one occasion, Adelaide had witnessed her manipulate the price for her bananas so quickly that even the university educated visitor from Port au Prince couldn't counter her offer.

"Hush, child. That is why we must go." Her mother was as unrelenting on this as she was coaxing her crops out of the ground, yearning for their first spring rain. But of course there was no money for extras like pilgrimages. Most days there wasn't enough for food. "I'll go to the moneylender for a loan," her mother announced.

"But he'll charge three times what you borrow. And what if we can't make payment on time, like Madame Boule?" Adelaide's concern grew at the memory of her school friend's family who could not repay a funeral loan. They lost their home, and the children went to an orphanage in another village. Their relocation was only supposed to be temporary, until Madame Boule could find some money. But two years later, none of the Boules had returned. Although Adelaide had not even felt the baby kick yet, she knew she would rather die than be separated from her child.

"You are *not* going to be a *ti machann* like me." Her mother stood up, gathering her basket of fruits and vegetables that she would carry up the mountain and sell in the market that day with the other women from their village. She was sturdy and thick from five pregnancies and twenty years planting and tending to her fields on the steep mountain slopes. "You are the brightest of my children. There is a better life out there for you and for your child." She lowered her voice at the mention of the baby. "This loan will permit us to make the journey. Dreams are good. But it is time to pray and pray as hard as we can."

Now the day had finally come. The pilgrimage was a five-hour trek from their house and the older woman's knees ached from years of walking up and down the rocky paths. So they had taken a *tap-tap*—a small public bus—until the road ended near the Cave of Doko where Adelaide and her mother joined the procession for the final hour walk to the small, cement-block building that was both church and temple. They were mostly silent, walking among the others, occasionally greeting someone they knew from their village. As they ascended the steps to the church, the beating of the drums diminished and was replaced by the voices of children singing "Ave Maria."

After the church service, a dozen or so charcoal fires appeared and the women, most of whom were strangers, gathered around to cook rice and beans, plantains, and fried sweet dough. The men congregated around a central fire pit and roasted goats and pigs while they passed around bottles of dark Haitian rum.

That night the two women lay side by side on a bed sheet on the ground outside. Most of the others had nothing between their thin clothes and the rocky dirt but a few mango leaves. It was impossible for Adelaide to find a comfortable position. Her growing belly in front and her boney back behind left her navigating the uneven ground with her shoulders and hips. The smell of charcoal and goat lingered in the air, and even though she had eaten well, she was still hungry. The rhythmic beat of the drums joined with the rumbling of the toads so that she couldn't tell if the throbbing came from within her chest or from outside. She pondered what would happen the next day. "Mama, I'm afraid of the water. I don't know how to swim."

"It is not that deep, Adelaide. I will be there watching you. Erzuli, too."

Adelaide knew the story of Erzuli, not from anything she had learned from her textbooks, but from pieces of conversations she had overheard from her mother's friends. Very few details were ever formally recorded in Haiti. History was passed by word of mouth, embellished into legend by those who were there or knew someone who was. Shared or kept in private, the stories were powerful forces that could console or control. As the Vodou counterpart of the Virgin Mary, some believe Erzuli was impregnated without sin, a dual symbol of purity and lust. But for women like Adelaide and her mother, Erzuli was a fierce protector of women's hopes and dreams for themselves and their children.

"Thank you, Mama. I will remember that tomorrow." After a while, Adelaide found a more comfortable spot and studied the night around her.

Thousands of burning candles had been placed in the trees, and every split of the bark, roots, and trunks were alive with the flames. The trees themselves did not burn, despite the long drought; the local peasants had doused them with water. The water came from a series of shallow pools beneath the Saut d'Eau where Adelaide and the other pilgrims would bathe and make their prayer offerings the following day.

Early the next morning, the others were up and ready with the sun, laughing and singing. While Adelaide went to find a private spot to release her morning water, her mother searched for a little food. They had no money left; the trip had already cost more than planned. Her mother had to beg or they would have nothing until nightfall when they returned home.

"Here, you should eat." Her mother's dark eyes so much like her own, studied her with a new weariness these days. Adelaide regretted more than anything the extra worry she had caused. Would she be the same kind of mother? A mother who would stand beside her daughter despite the shame she had inflicted on her family?

She took one of the tin cups half filled with dark, sweet coffee and a hunk of bread from her mother, noticing that she had kept none of the bread for herself. They rested on a trunk of one of the larger trees. All that remained of the candles were lumpy mounds of gray wax.

Soon after they finished their coffee, Adelaide descended to the pools with the other bathers. The waterfall cascaded down the rocks and the splashes danced on the surface. It was the most beautiful thing she had ever seen. The Virgin Mary—Erzuli—floated, gently rocking on her plywood platform. Adelaide slid behind a bush and lifted her dress over her head. She had no bra. She looked down at her protruding belly, her swollen breasts and her nipples now a deep and rich brown, like the coffee they drank that morning. The plumpness made her look more prosperous. She touched her nipples and was surprised that they were so soft. For an instant she remembered the way it felt when his tongue moved in circles around the border where the dark part met the lighter skin of her breasts. She longed for his touch and all that followed. But that was not a thought she would allow to continue for today.

One hand still covering her breasts and the other grasping her first baby gift, the pink-laced socks, Adelaide walked to the edge of the water and stepped out of her panties as she had seen the others do. She threw them into the water as far as she could and waded in. Once immersed, she released the socks, one from each of her upturned palms. The current of the healing waters caught them and brought the tiny, white-and-pink offerings together as they drifted away from her and toward the floating grotto.

Adelaide shivered in the cool water. Her bare feet searched for solid ground, but found only rocks and mud. She did not like the way it felt. The mud between her toes and the gray water made her stomach ache. An ache that was different than the hollow feeling of hunger she had known each day for most of her life. Still she did not mind much; she understood this was only the first of many sacrifices she would make for her unborn child.

2

KATE

SAN FRANCISCO MEMORIAL HOSPITAL
OCTOBER 1984

Three covered breakfast trays had been abandoned on three chairs outside three rooms, all with closed doors. As Kate walked down the hospital corridor, the smell of lemon bleach unsuccessfully masking the odors of stale urine and soiled bed sheets, she counted the trays. She would be rounding on three AIDS patients that morning.

She picked up the first tray and noted the coffee-stained dietary slip tucked under a mug:

> Eggs: Scrambled
>
> Toast: Wheat
>
> Coffee: Black
>
> Orange Juice
>
> Patient: Reed, William

Kate opened the door and put on her best "cheerful doctor" smile for another of her twenty-something male patients with a menu of ominous symptoms—fever, cough, unusual infections and relentless diarrhea. The prognosis was always the same, even if the name for the diagnosis had changed a half-dozen times in the past three years. Today it was AIDS, six months ago it was HTLV— Human T Cell Lymphotrophic Virus—and two years ago it was GRID—Gay Related Immune Deficiency. In parts of Africa, what appeared to be the same condition was known as "Slim Disease" because of the severe weight loss common to all those affected. The end result was the same. With no cure in sight, AIDS was a death sentence without appeal, without pardon.

At first, Kate's patient, William, was somewhat of an enigma. He was heterosexual, not a hemophiliac, and never used intravenous drugs, so he did not fit into one of the major risk groups. However, several years earlier, before he had moved to San Francisco, he received two units of blood for a bleeding ulcer while traveling in South Africa. In the four months since Kate had graduated medical school in western Pennsylvania, blood transfusion had joined the list of suspects as a cause for AIDS.

"Good morning, Mr. Reed. Here's your breakfast." A quick look at his chart told her he was down another five pounds since last week.

Her patient removed the plastic lid from the mug and took a sip. "The coffee is cold—again." He commented without surprise or anger or much of anything.

"I'll ask the aide to microwave it for you," Kate offered. After that, she would call the supervisor in the dietary department and explain again that it was completely safe for them to deliver food trays into William's room and the rooms of other AIDS patients.

"I don't get it. They won't bring the food trays into my room, but the guy delivering newspapers has no problem coming in to collect his money every Friday."

Every Friday. Kate contemplated the sad significance of those two words for this patient. Her rotation on the AIDS ward began only a few weeks ago, so she didn't know exactly how long William had been in the hospital. But it was at least six weeks, which was as far back as the current volume of his medical chart recorded. "Chart Thinned" was stamped on the front of his hospital chart, indicating that the chronicle of his medical saga had grown beyond what a four-inch ring binder could hold.

Kate also suspected that he would spend the rest of his life in this dreary gray room with his potted plants on the windowsill overlooking the San Francisco Bay. William's most significant issue was that he could not be away from the bathroom for more than an hour. There was no treatment for the parasite infecting his gut. Too frail to live alone, William had lost his job, and simply had no place to go. His social situation, perhaps as much as his medical condition, had prompted him to request that he receive nothing more than comfort measures. Each day when Kate rounded on him, she fought not to feel defeated by the second and more ominous red sticker on the front of his chart:

DNR

Kate searched for the right words, but doubted they existed. "I'm sorry, William. It's no excuse, but people are afraid. And when they're afraid, they do and say stupid and thoughtless things."

"You're not afraid," he challenged her. "You don't even wear the gown and gloves anymore. "Do you realize, Dr. Rigando," he said, his hands clutching the bed sheets, "you are the only person who has touched me in the last two weeks?"

He bit his lower lip and Kate waited for his tears to follow. A few did; but not nearly the flood she expected. She watched the tears trickle down his cheek in a solitary and silent journey that didn't even warrant him brushing them away.

She unclasped her patient's hands and held one. It was covered in bruises from attempts at blood draws and IV starts. Damaged and fragile, yet warm and alive, it was just like the young man in the bed beside her. Not trusting herself to say anything for fear she'd start bawling, she didn't explain that unless she had contact with his blood or body fluid, gowns and gloves weren't necessary. She just sat beside him and listened to the muffled sounds outside her patient's door—details she couldn't make out from conversations between nurses, the rattle of the cart picking up the breakfast trays that were never delivered, the hospital paging system announcing a "Code Blue" somewhere.

Four years at the top of her med school class prepared Kate to make accurate diagnoses, answer questions, dispense cures, and give hope. But she knew William's expectations for any of these ended long before she became his resident physician.

"William, I am so sorry. Nothing about this disease is fair. We'll do everything we can to keep you comfortable." Kate knew that patients often feared the physical pain they faced at the end of their lives.

He lay still and motionless. The tears had stopped and left his face even more pale and gaunt than when she had walked into his room.

She picked up his tray with the intent to microwave the food and drink before seeing her next patient, but William stopped her. "Never mind about the coffee. It's not a coffee kind of day." He reached for the TV remote on his nightstand and collapsed back onto the bed. The hospital-issue plastic pillow sighed from the weight of his head.

"Just press your buzzer if you change your mind. I'll check in on you later." Kate wished she had more to offer.

"You know, doctor, I can't honestly say that I have good days anymore." William clicked on a morning game show.

Kate thought the audience applause and canned laughter mocked them both.

"But at least this one's been bearable. Thank you."

Kate eased the door closed behind her. She needed to take a minute before she continued her morning rounds. She leaned against the hard, cold wall. There were so many things they didn't teach her in medical school. Important details, like how to prepare for the reality that three out of four patients would be the same age as her, dying from some disease she could not diagnose or effectively treat, much less cure.

Some days she longed for a sixty-five-year-old patient with diabetes or a seventy-year-old guy with a heart attack, someone who didn't look just like her husband or one of her fellow residents. Yet she reminded herself, as she did almost every day since her international health and tropical medicine internship began, that this was why she went into medicine, to help the people who needed it most. At least for now, with a four-year-old, she wouldn't be trekking through the African jungle like a female Albert Schweitzer, as she had imagined when she was a teenager. She was lucky to be in San Francisco. The program was one of the best in the country, even if it was 2,500 miles from her home in western Pennsylvania.

As her husband, Mark, had said when he received his acceptance letter from the University of California surgery program, "This is the beginning of our dream, Kate. We can go anywhere we want to from here."

She felt it, too. When she had accepted her diploma from the University of Pittsburgh in June, she imagined that she and Mark would kick butt in their respective residency training programs over the next four years. After that, they'd pack up their books, their son Danny, and perhaps a younger sibling or two—and move to Uganda or Nepal or some other exotic place where they would be the only healthcare workers for miles. She didn't see herself exactly as the missionary type. They would bring medicine, not Bibles, and teach about clean water and proper nutrition, not about God and salvation. Not that she was an atheist. In fact, she was raised Catholic and had attended a Catholic school for eight years. But for most of her teenage years, religion was something that eluded her. Now it just seemed irrelevant.

Her father, on the other hand, was not so encouraging about her choice of residency programs. "Many people right here in your own backyard need your skills, Katherine." He called her by her full given name when he was emphasizing a point. Of course he was hoping she would settle in his backyard and join his busy family practice. To him, San Francisco wasn't much better than Africa.

"Well, Dad," she had teased him. "Then I guess instead of letting me study in your office with all your textbooks on tropical medicine, you should have encouraged me to watch *Marcus Welby, M.D.* on Tuesday nights."

He had no response, only shrugged his shoulders—a sign that he had finally given up on trying to influence his eldest, fiery red-haired daughter. Then for her med school graduation he presented her with an old, heavy black metal microscope he had found in an antique store. It was the kind of scope that used a mirror to reflect the sunlight through the condenser.

"I'm assuming your jungle will have plenty of sunlight," he teased her, while they posed for a graduation-day photograph, father and daughter, now both University of Pittsburgh med school alumni.

The distance from home was exciting at first, but now Kate just didn't know. Trying to balance being a mom, a wife, and a doctor was more challenging than she had expected. She wasn't ready to admit defeat, but it did get discouraging at times.

She shook off that thought and focused on her next patient, a Haitian woman with enlarged lymph nodes and severe weight loss—Yanick Monfils. Kate picked up her chart and entered the room. Standing at the window was a tall, attractive black woman in a brightly colored dress and black pumps. Her hair was done up in rows of tiny braids encircling her head.

"Good morning, Ms. Monfils?" Kate was unsure of her pronunciation and wondered why she was still in her street clothes. "My name is Dr. Rigando, and I'll be taking care of you while you're in the hospital." She crossed the room and reached out to shake her new patient's hand.

"*Bonjou,* Doctor. Oh, sorry, I mean good morning." Yanick smiled and accepted Kate's hand, but returned her gaze out the window.

"I'll need to ask you some questions and then examine you. Why don't I give you a few minutes to put on a gown and I'll be back?" Kate checked her watch. She would examine Yanick, see her third patient, and grab a cup of tea for her queasy stomach before morning report at nine.

"Thank you, Doctor. But I won't be staying. I'm feeling much better and there are other people who need this room more than I do."

"You are not leaving," Kerline, one of the nurses also from Haiti, said from the doorway.

"Doctor, did you know Kerline is my little sister? But today she thinks she's my mother." She picked up her purse and squeezed Kerline on the shoulder as she left the room. "Don't worry, I'll call you soon."

"What was that all about?" Kate asked. Yanick looked so thin that she might blow away with the late afternoon breeze off the San Francisco Bay. "Can you get her to come back?"

"Don't know. I'll explain later." Kerline rushed down the hall to catch her sister. "Oh. I forgot," she called back to Kate, who was about to enter the next room. "The patient you saw in the ER, Michael Rose, was transferred to ICU last night."

No one looked good in the intensive care unit and twenty-six-year-old Michael Rose was no exception. The intense bright lights made him look pale and fragile, and Kate wished again for a big picture window that would let in the natural sunlight.

She first met Michael two days earlier when his partner, George, brought him to the emergency room because he was having difficulty breathing while playing softball. The rest of his medical history, by Michael's account, was unremarkable; until recently, he had always been healthy. Exactly when his symptoms began and the specific details of those symptoms were shrouded in the typical cloak of denial that Kate had come to know with many of her AIDS patients. She suspected the fever, the night sweats, and the fatigue had been ongoing for more than the week he admitted to when she had first talked with him. She had asked about weight loss.

When Michael didn't reply, George had volunteered and confirmed Kate's suspicions, "None of your clothes fit anymore. You're down at least twenty pounds since summer."

George had also explained that Michael had been raised on a dairy farm in Ohio where his family still lived. After graduating from Ohio State a few years earlier, he had moved alone to San Francisco when he was offered a position with one of the city's largest accounting firms. He had joined the company's softball team to get to know the senior partners better, and to prove he was a team player on and off the field.

Kate thought he still had just enough of the rugged farm-boy charm and a touch of a Midwestern accent that didn't quite fit the big-city corporate image. She supposed he was just as out of place in Lees Creek, Ohio. From their conversation, she surmised that Michael's family had no idea their son was gay.

"Anything else we should know?" she had asked both men, hoping to gain a little more insight into Michael's social situation.

"Yeah, he loves baseball," George had replied. "You a fan doctor?"

"Not so much anymore," she had admitted. "I'm a soccer mom." She had thought of Danny and how much of his young life she was missing these past few months, with her long hours at the hospital.

That morning in the ICU, Michael looked as far from the baseball field as Kate could imagine. Sitting straight up in the bed with eyes closed, his breathing came in tight, frequent gasps.

"He's sleeping," Kate said quietly to Cara, her chief resident. "Let's round on him a little later." She knew how hard it was for patients to rest in the unit.

Michael's eyes fluttered open. "Hey, I've been waiting to talk to you." He managed a small smile. His nose twitched from the green plastic nasal cannula delivering oxygen from the bedside canister. "I think I'm feeling better today."

Kate scanned the numbers—the blood pressure, oxygen, and heart-rate monitors—before turning her full attention to Michael, hoping he would prove the machines wrong. "Well, good morning. Did you sleep well last night?" she asked.

"As good as can be expected with all the activity around here." He paused to catch his breath. Kate could see he was utilizing every muscle in his neck, chest, and abdomen. "But really, the nurses are great. Everyone has been so kind."

The note on his chart from the on-call intern stated Michael had had a difficult night. His oxygen level had dropped so low that twice the nurses had to administer an emergency breathing treatment.

She took the bell of her stethoscope and rubbed it between her hands before laying it on Michael's chest. As she suspected, the sounds from his lungs contradicted her patient's words. She closed up his gown and rested her hand on his shoulder.

"I'm doing better, don't you think?"

Michael was asking for the truth, but was he strong enough to handle it? She had no choice but to relay the bad news to him.

"Michael, you're on our two best antibiotics. Your chest x-ray, your labs, and your exam all indicate that you're getting worse." She paused to give him a chance to take in what she had just said.

He nodded in agreement but was waiting for her to continue, waiting for her to propose a new treatment. She hated to admit that she didn't have one.

"I think it's time to call your family." Kate thought about William. Michael would need all the support he could get.

"No." Michael stared straight ahead. "I don't want them to know yet. When I go home again, I'll explain."

"I understand that. But one week ago you were playing softball, now you're in the intensive care unit. If your oxygen level drops much more, I'll have to put you on a respirator." She paused, carefully considering the impact of her next words. "Michael, when patients with this type of infection go on a respirator, it can be difficult to get them off. Your family will need a few days to get here from Ohio. Please think about this carefully." Kate knew this might be his last chance to talk to them. "Just say the word. I can have one of the nurses bring you a phone."

Kate recognized a flash of fear before the resolve settled into his face and he turned to her. "Do whatever you have to do to me. I am going to get better and go home. That's when I will tell them— everything."

"Alright, Michael," she could see he was a fighter and sensed he needed to call the shots. She hoped he would indeed get that chance. "I'll stop by this evening to check on you and I'll be here all night if you need anything." She patted his hand resting on top of the bed covers and noted a small, purple patch above his wrist. She'd ask dermatology to look at that. If the lesion was what she thought, Michael was fighting much more than pneumonia.

Out in the hallway Kate pulled Cara into the nurses' lounge. She didn't want Michael to hear what she had to say. "I don't know what else we can do for him."

"I think you're right, Kate. We're out of options here," Cara shrugged her shoulders. "It's so sad, these patients."

"Out of options? This is 1984. There have to be options out there." Kate felt herself getting angry, but she wasn't sure to whom or what her anger was directed against. "We're losing almost all of them, Cara. And it's not just to the disease. We're losing them even before their bodies give out."

She thought about Kerline's sister Yanick, who left against medical advice and without any treatment. Who knew if they would see her again? She thought about William and his cold coffee. Michael still had the fight in him, but he was going to need more than his own sheer will to get through this infection and what was ahead of him.

"I know I'm pushing pretty hard about calling his parents. But I believe it's important for them to be here." To herself she admitted she wasn't sure for whom it was more important.

She thought about her son Danny, and how when he had the chicken pox last year, he had lain in bed clutching his soccer ball, like he always did when he was sick. His red hair that so closely matched her own only made him look paler. She had missed two exams and almost failed one class. But there was no way she would have left his bedside. No matter how old he was, she would want to be there. And she couldn't imagine loving him less for any decision he made, even if she didn't agree with it.

Yet that was only part of it. People had things they needed to say to each other. Kate recalled the circumstances surrounding her mother's death. She remembered the promise she made to herself the day they buried her. No patient of hers would die without the chance to say goodbye to his or her loved ones. But that promise was too complicated to explain to her chief resident on busy morning rounds.

"If Michael were my son, I would never forgive myself for not being here." At least Kate could be clear on that. "If we can just buy him a little more time."

"We don't have anything else to offer, Kate. I'm sorry." Cara signed off on Michael's progress note for the day.

"You know, I have a friend from undergrad. He's doing AIDS research at the CDC. Maybe he knows of some new treatment for *pneumocystis* pneumonia. I'm going to call him as soon as we finish rounds." She wasn't giving up on Michael or on her vow that he and his family would have their chance to talk before it was too late.

"Can't hurt to do some checking. But you know all the paperwork you're going to have to do, and we'll have to get approval from our infectious disease doctors. Got to follow protocol," Cara cautioned.

"All that red tape could be the bow on Michael's coffin." Kate was already plotting how she might shortcut the process.

Cara gave her a quick squeeze around her shoulders. "It's hard, I know. But it will get easier."

Easier for whom, Kate wanted to ask.

The 5:00 a.m. page interrupted her last and only hour of sleep for the on-call night. Kate took the stairs from the interns' lounge to the ICU two at a time. She paused outside the ICU room to catch her breath and quickly dressed in a yellow isolation gown with little doubt that she would need it. A wave of nausea gripped her as it had each morning for the last two weeks. She took a deep breath and held it for a few seconds; then she pulled the mask over her mouth and nose and entered Michael's room.

Even before her stethoscope touched the mottled skin of his chest, Kate could hear the rattle of fluid filling the airspaces in his lungs. Michael was coughing too much to talk, but tried to push her hand aside when she placed the mask to his face for a breathing treatment. The oxygen sensor argued with him as it flashed *80—*

LOW ALARM in bright red. She looked above his head where the heart monitor registered green blips at 160 times a minute, confirming the stress low levels of oxygen were having on his body. His lips were turning that ominous telltale shade of blue.

"Michael, we have to do this now. Your oxygen level is too low. Okay?" Kate heard the crack in her voice and hoped that Michael hadn't noticed. He nodded with resignation.

Kate pressed the red emergency call button on the wall. "Hang on, Michael. Stay with me."

Within minutes, a nurse arrived with the red metal cart containing the standard complement of emergency drugs, defibrillator, and an assortment of endotracheal tubes.

"Is anesthesia coming?" Kate asked the nurse. It was only her fourth month of internship. Sure she had intubated a few patients during her anesthesia rotation in medical school, but with a certified anesthesiologist by her side, and that was almost two years ago. She hadn't been cleared to do the procedure on her own yet.

"No one's on the unit and they haven't answered the pages. What are you going to do?" the nurse asked her.

Kate looked at the monitor; his heart rate was more erratic. His eyes rolled back in his head. He was fading fast. "I'm going ahead." She'd accept the consequences.

Quickly, she pulled two blue latex gloves from a box at his bedside and filled a syringe with precisely one cc of Valium. She eased the drug into Michael's IV and watched his breathing settle. Her hands began to tremble just slightly as she picked up the tube. When she noticed blood on her gloves, it felt like her heart leaped from her chest to her throat. Was it her blood? Had she nicked her glove with the needle? She pushed those thoughts out of her mind for the time being. She had only minutes to position his head and slide the tube past his teeth, down his throat, and into his lungs. She had only minutes to provide him with the oxygen his body could not.

Stay steady, Kate. She remembered what her dad told her once when she was fifteen and had watched him suture a cut over a young boy's eye. Her father had whistled a silly tune and his foot tapped in tempo, but his hands were as steady as stone. He had let her put the dressing on when he finished.

"It's okay to shake on the inside," he had reassured her when he noticed her hands trembling as she had struggled to apply the adhesive tape. "It's even a good thing, keeps a doctor from getting too cocky. But your patient doesn't need to see you nervous."

She could almost feel her dad's hand on her shoulder as she eased the tube into Michael's throat without resistance. Immediately his lungs began to rise and fall in a regular rhythm, his heart rate slowed and his color returned.

The on-call anesthesiology resident arrived with wet hair and an embarrassed look. "I'm sorry. I was in the shower." He checked the chart and Michael, and then he nodded. "Good job, Kate. I'll check the chest x-ray."

She stepped into the hallway and ripped off her mask. She needed some air. She checked her glove. There was a small hole and enough blood on the outside to be concerned about an exposure. She took her gloves off, and carefully inspected her skin. There were no cuts in her skin and no blood on her hands. Thank goodness. She would have to be especially careful in the months ahead.

A few drops of blood had also landed on her Nikes. She had bought the shoes when she started her internship, expecting to continue her five-mile morning jogs, if not every day, at least a few times a week. It had been weeks since she had run anywhere but up the steps to the ICU. Even more than a couple more hours of sleep, that's what her body craved right now—a good long run.

One of the ICU nurses handed her Michael's chart and a cup of coffee. "He's lucky you were on call tonight. Not too many interns would have been able to pull that off."

"Thanks." She gulped the coffee, no chance for a run or sleep anytime soon. She went back into her patient's room to write the procedure note on his chart.

After a while, Michael opened his eyes. He looked around, defeated by the machines, the tubes, and his body.

"I'm sorry, Michael. I know this isn't how you wanted it." Kate remembered her conversations with Cara yesterday morning and Brian at the CDC yesterday afternoon. They didn't have much to offer AIDS patients, but they had to keep trying. "You have to keep fighting. We're not giving up here." Kate handed him a clipboard with a sheet of blank paper and black marker. "Is there anything you need, anything I can do to make you more comfortable?"

He scribbled his answer: *Please call my father.*

"Of course, Michael." But before she made that call, she would wake up whomever she had to wake up at the CDC. If there was any chance the medicine her friend Brian told her about would work, she needed to get it there fast.

3

GISELLE LA FORTUNE

HAVANA, CUBA
OCTOBER 1984

Giselle flashed her Haitian passport, as she had practiced so many times, and quickly moved through Immigration and Customs in Havana with her valise and portfolio bag, eager to find Jean-Juste.

She noticed him immediately, smartly dressed in blue jeans and a button-down white shirt and standing a good three inches taller than the Cubans around him. His gold chain was visible with the top two buttons of his shirt opened. As they met, he gave her two brief kisses, first one on her left cheek and then the second on her right. She warmed at his touch and held tight to his waist. For once, she didn't need to hide her feelings for him.

This was her first trip abroad. But already she loved it. Everything from the way her heart quickened with the plane as it accelerated down the runway at Port au Prince airport to the way her stomach tumbled when they landed in Havana. Even if only for the week she would be attending the Caribbean Cooperative Art Conference in Cuba, Giselle had dreamed of this escape for most of her twenty-four years.

Somewhere around age eighteen, Giselle concluded there were three paths out of Haiti: she could marry a foreigner, preferably an American or a European; she could marry a Haitian politician— someone who was important enough to enjoy diplomatic privileges, but not so important as to be a target in one of the coups d'état that Haiti was so famous for in the international community; or she could take the chance her parents took.

When Giselle was sixteen, her mother and father took her to stay with an aunt and uncle in Petionville. Her parents sold all their possessions and, with the thousand dollars they made, booked passage on a wooden sailboat with ninety-eight other Haitians who prayed they would make it to asylum in the United States. The Haitians on that particular boat had a fifty-fifty chance. Exactly half of the men, women, and children on board made it to Florida—the survivors were rescued by a Coast Guard cruiser off the shores of Miami, and promptly returned to Port au Prince without so much as an American meal. The other fifty passengers on the leaky wooden boat, including Giselle's parents, met their fate at the bottom of the sea. Each day for two years after their death, Giselle would read the letter they wrote to her when it was imminent that the boat would not make it to shore.

May 13, 1976

Chère Giselle,

We have been at sea for seven days now. The first few were not so bad—except many people were sick from the waves. We helped each other to eat and drink a little when the water was calmer. We have gotten to know the other passengers quite well, as you would expect. We sleep side by side, taking turns because there is not enough room for everyone at the same time. We eat together standing. The sun has made us all a little darker. (You would not recognize your father.) We share our stories of why we are here on this boat and what we hope for when we leave it.

There is a young woman about your age. She is with her mother, who is unable to see. I don't know the cause for her blindness. The daughter reminds me of you. She is a dancer, too, and sings beautifully. Of course her mother can't see her dance, but she smiles such a proud smile when she sings like a bird her French songs from school.

We miss you, dear daughter. It was a difficult decision to leave you with Tante Carole and Oncle Joseph. We wanted to get to America first, get a little money together, and then we would bring you to your new home where we would all feel safe. But we have no regrets. We thank God now, for we know it was the right decision.

Yesterday, our little wooden boat started leaking. Some of the men tried to fix it with an old can of tar they found on board. It helped some, but we still have several more days before we reach land. Last night we ate and drank well; everyone shared what they had. Then we counted out enough food and water so we could each have a bite to eat for the next three days. The rest, along with everything else people had brought on board, we threw into the sea to lighten the boat. I am only holding this note and a plastic bag to keep it safe for you. I pray you will receive it.

The Captain told us this morning that there are not enough orange vests for everyone. We all agree that the children and the young woman with her blind mother should be the first. The rest of the group is still discussing who else will get one. Your father and I decided between us that we wouldn't ask for one. We swim a little and we will take our chances.

I know you want to be an artist someday and travel the

world. But darling daughter, don't forget that Haiti will
always be your country.
Avec Amour,

Mama et Papa

Even at sixteen, Giselle could imagine the effort it took for her mother to write the letter on the rocky seas. One of the surviving passengers, a woman about her mother's age, delivered the wrinkled and yellowed note, still in the plastic bag, to her aunt and uncle's house seven months after the tragedy. It took the woman that long to find their home in the mountains above Port au Prince and scrape together enough money for transportation. Haitians were good in that way—good at making and keeping promises to the dying.

Fortunately for Giselle, she was able to live with her aunt and uncle. Although it was not entirely safe for anyone in Haiti, her uncle was one of the few in a diminishing number of obstetricians remaining in the country, affording him some protection. He wanted her to become a nurse or even a doctor, but she didn't share his passion for medicine. Nor did she understand her parents' passion in joining the *bat teneb*—to *beat back the darkness* of oppression and poverty, as they said in Creole. What good were these protests by peasant women pounding pots and pans with cooking spoons? How could that noise do anything?

No, the way she saw it, one needed to be able to cultivate two things—a good education and respectable attractiveness. And then hope for a good dose of luck, which seemed to find her easily enough.

At nineteen, she was accepted to the University of Fine Arts and Literature in Port au Prince where she would spend the next four years painting and studying literature. At twenty she opted for marrying the Secretary to the Prime Minister, Max LaFortune, and soon after, took a lover from Paris. She didn't see any reason to tell the former about the latter. And well, the latter, Jean-Juste, didn't really give a damn.

Giselle first saw Jean-Juste one scorching Saturday afternoon at the Hotel Oloffson in Port au Prince, where she was having drinks with friends from the university. The ceiling paddle fans did little to appease either the mid-June heat or the group's intense discussion around one of their final exam essay topics: what should the international response be to the plight of the rural poor in Haiti?

She was facing the swimming pool when Jean-Juste lifted himself out of the water onto the deck. Taller than most of her friends, even the men, she sat straight up and stretched her neck to get a full view of him beyond the overgrown bougainvillea. She had never seen a man in such a swimsuit before. She later learned this royal blue, insubstantial thing was called a Speedo. It seemed a bit obscene at the time, hardly worth wearing for what it covered, and for what it emphasized—little was left to the imagination. From that first moment, Giselle thought that everything he accomplished seemed effortless, as if he owned the world, so unlike most of the Haitian men she knew who acted more like boys.

Jean-Juste listened in on their conversation, smiling while Giselle and her friends discussed the platitude, "Don't give a man a fish, teach him to fish." Her friends added their own corollaries, "What good is it to know how to fish if you don't own a fishing pole?" and "What good is it to have the pole if the fence around the lake is locked or someone else has already caught all the fish?"

On and on they chatted, fueled by three rounds of rose-colored rum punches. By sunset they deteriorated into a silliness that only the young, educated, and privileged of Haiti could enjoy.

Afterward, when the crowd broke up, Giselle introduced herself to Jean-Juste and apologized. "You must think we are awfully hard-hearted to laugh at the misery of our country."

"No," he replied. "I was thinking just the opposite. Before I came here, I knew that there was beautiful art and that there were many poor and hungry people with no food." He paused briefly. "But maybe Haiti is fortunate in other ways. Listening to you and your friends, I think that there are others, people like you, with enough food. Yet you are blessed with a hunger, too—a hunger to change the unjust ways of your country." As he spoke, Jean brushed a stray strand of hair from her forehead, damp from the late afternoon.

Her cheeks flushed hot. "I think I may have had too much to drink." Every inch of her body tingled from the top of her scalp scarcely protected under her American-style bobbed hair, to the tips of her brightly painted and pedicured toes, exposed in beige European sandals.

The next day, Jean sent a short note by way of one of the Haitian street boys saying how much he enjoyed meeting her and asked if she would be willing to show him around some of the art galleries in Petionville. She quickly agreed; Max was always working late, and she wasn't yet pregnant with Natali. She soon learned that Jean-Juste was pursuing his doctoral thesis at the Sorbonne. After serving as his Haitian cultural guide for the week, she became completely enamored not only with her new French friend, but also with the subject of his dissertation, Pablo Picasso. She and Jean spent hours browsing through the galleries, identifying the same nearly monochromatic blue colors and similar melancholy blind subjects that were depicted by some popular Haitian artists and mimicked Picasso's works from his Blue Period.

Inspired by what she saw and learned, Giselle painted a pair of blind women almost entirely in blue and green hues. One was a rural peasant woman sitting in a rocking chair under a banana tree. The only other color she permitted was the faint yellow of the banana fruit ripening in a wicker basket at the blind women's feet and a splash of bright yellow for a small bird singing in the tree. The second painting depicted a boat woman, like the one her mother had described, with her face turned to the sea. Again, a hint of yellow showed in the sun behind her.

Reluctantly, after three years, she finished the boat scene. It was like saying farewell to her parents again. When her paintings were accepted for showing at the conference in Cuba, she was delighted. The showing would be a tribute to her parents and she would meet up with Jean-Juste again.

"Come, my beautiful artist," Jean urged. "Let's hurry to the hotel."

For seven whole days she had her lover, her precious paintings, and this exciting adventure in Cuba. "I don't want to hurry, my darling," Giselle said. I want this week to last forever."

The next morning, Giselle and Jean sipped coffee from their demitasse at the Hotel Tejadillo in Havana's old town section.

"This place reminds me of the Oloffson—except the menus are in Spanish and English instead of French and English," Jean-Juste commented, setting down his cup.

"I was thinking the same thing—except there is no French man in a little blue bathing suit and I don't see any water in our pool here. Haiti has its problems, but at least for now, we have water in our hotel swimming pools."

As happy as she was on this adventure, she expected to be happy too when she arrived home next week and cooked dinner while her three-year-old daughter, Natali, danced around the kitchen. She and Jean-Juste had their special times together, and spent the rest of their mostly agreeable lives apart.

Despite her affair, Giselle loved her husband. Max was the sort of man with whom a woman would build a long comfortable life. He was kind, intelligent, and steady. But Jean, he inspired and challenged her, and she believed she did the same for him. The arrangement worked well for everyone—as long as Jean could make his trips to Haiti. As for that, Giselle was worried.

Things were changing rapidly in her country. She could see it from the downturned faces of people on the street. No one wanted to be recognized or accused of supporting any political position. And people were disappearing again—like they had when her parents fled. Last week two university students were found naked and beaten, their battered bodies dumped in an alley in Salinas—one of the more volatile slums in Port au Prince. The man was tortured—his genitals pierced with nails—allegedly because he spoke out against the government on a *Radio Soleil* talk show. He died a short time later. The woman was raped repeatedly. She was in hiding, fearful the *Tonton Macoutes*—the Haitian paramilitary police—would return to finish her off.

Max was oblivious or pretended to be. "It was a terrible tragedy," he admitted. "But these are isolated instances and there's always more to it than you hear on those foolish radio programs."

That was all Max would give her, dismissing her concerns as if she were a silly housewife.

Each day Giselle's husband went to the National Palace and listened to the president all day at work and then again on the nationally televised news he monopolized each evening.

This man they called "Baby Doc," evil and corrupt as any ruler in the history books, declared he would be "President for Life," just like his father, Papa Doc Francois Duvalier. *God help us.* Giselle prayed he would not live long.

She and Max disagreed frequently about the fate of Haiti. But more so each day, Giselle believed there was little they could do to influence what happened. She just hoped they could hang on long enough to get out before the situation got really bad.

She inhaled the salty Havana air and reached for Jean's hand. "It really is lovely here." She vowed to stop thinking about troubles at home, at least for a few days.

"*Bonjou! Buenos Dias*, Giselle!" An American couple dressed in shorts and T-shirts smiled at them. "We were hoping to see you again."

"Please sit down and join us for coffee." Giselle waved for the waiter while Jean-Juste pulled up two chairs.

"Liz and Jim, this is my friend and a fellow artist, Jean-Juste

Picard. Jean, this is Liz and Jim. I met them on the plane from Haiti yesterday. They're Americans interested in learning more about programs for reducing rural poverty. Did I say that right?"

"Yes," said Jim.

Jean-Juste posed the same questions that Giselle had wanted to ask since she met the American couple. "What brings you to Cuba? Is there a program here? It must be a risk for you to come to this country."

"You're right about that. The U.S. government makes it tough," Jim explained. "We could have applied for a special travel permit. But we decided to go through Haiti instead. It was no problem to get a visa from the Cuban Embassy in Port au Prince."

"Four years ago, we met a priest in Nicaragua," Liz added. "He invited us to come here and learn more about *educación popular.*"

"What is popular education? I don't know this term. Do you?" Jean looked to Giselle.

She shrugged.

"I don't know that I'm the best person to explain it. But I'll try." Jim paused. "It's a theory and practice of education that begins with the experiences of the people themselves, rather than what's in the books. The people decide what the issues are and how best to solve them. Have I confused you?"

"No, it sounds very interesting and makes sense, especially for people who are less educated or illiterate. So what do you do back in the States?" Jean asked as the waiter brought a basket of bread and a plate of fruit and cheese.

"I'm a nurse and Jim's in international finance. We met on the trip to Nicaragua. Jim was translating for our medical group. He spent two years in the Peace Corps."

"Actually, I make my living in international finance. But my real interest and passion is in microcredit, which involves lending small amounts of money at low interest rates to less-educated women," Jim explained.

"In Haiti, the peasant women have no choice but to borrow from moneylenders. They charge so much that the women can never repay the loans." Giselle remembered her mother had helped a few women who had gotten themselves into serious debt that way. "If this program is as successful as you say, it seems that it doesn't take very much to change a person's life."

"Exactly," Jim said. "But the sad thing is that for most women, even that little bit isn't there."

Liz checked her watch. "We need to get going, Jim."

"It was nice to meet you, Jean, and to see you again, Giselle." Jim shook hands with Jean-Juste, and both he and Liz exchanged a quick hug with Giselle.

"Interesting couple, aren't they?" Jean-Juste cut two thick wedges of white cheese, one for each of them, and handed the knife and a mango to Giselle.

"Yes." Giselle cradled the fruit in her hand and carefully made a slit through the tough skin exposing the orange flesh. She offered the first slice to Jean. "Someday, I'd like to know more about this popular education and microcredit." It sounded different from the usual missionary rhetoric that permeated Haiti. Believe in my god and you will be saved. If you give up your Vodou practices, you can have medicine from our clinic and send your children to our school.

Yet for now, all she wanted was to have an enchanting holiday with her exciting French lover and show off her paintings to other artists from around the world. She had no doubt this would bring her one step closer to escaping the gloom in Haiti.

"But today, *ma Chèrie*, I'd like to know more about *you*," she whispered as Jean accepted the mango directly from her fingers to his lips and kissed her palm. "Let's go back upstairs. We can see Cuba later."

4

KATE

SAN FRANCISCO
OCTOBER 1984

Kate was walking down Pier 47 on Fisherman's Wharf with Mark when she felt the bile rising in her throat. Unable to find a garbage can, she kneeled at the edge of the boardwalk and vomited her twenty-five-dollar lobster dinner from Grazzio's.

"Oh . . ." She groaned. "I did not feel that one coming. That had to be the most expensive puke of my life." She heaved again. "Ugh. All I could think about today was having a romantic dinner with you. Some romance, huh?"

Mark grinned and pulled a handkerchief from his back pocket. "Come on Katie, do you really think you need a pregnancy test?" He stooped beside her, lifted her damp red hair, and kissed the back of her neck.

"Thanks." She wiped her mouth and forehead and let Mark help her up.

He led her to a nearby bench, with a view of the final ferry streaming across the San Francisco Bay and back to the pier.

"No. I don't have any doubt that I'm pregnant, Mark. The

timing is not so great, though." Instinctively Kate rubbed her stomach. It was only six weeks, too early to feel the baby moving. She thought back to that night in August. It had been another rare evening when she and Mark were both off. Danny was staying at a friend's house for the night. They drank too much wine, fumbled with a condom, and laughed nervously when it came off prematurely.

"I guess you could say that I'm late, but ahead of schedule." Kate sucked on a peppermint; her nausea was already subsiding. Their plan was to get pregnant in two years after she finished her rotations abroad.

"It's going be tough, and not just for you, being up all night on call and tired and puking." Mark paused. "I feel so guilty even saying this. We're doctors, right? We're supposed to help sick people, aren't we?"

Kate had no clue where he was going with the conversation, but obviously he was worried about something. Maybe it was about money or the logistics of two kids and being away from family. "We'll work it out." Although she wasn't sure exactly how.

"I know it's what you want—tropical medicine, exotic diseases—but all the AIDS patients? Last week Tom, one of the surgery residents, was nicked with a scalpel during surgery. Turns out the patient has AIDS. Tom's freaking out and so are all the other residents."

Kate thought about her fear when she intubated Michael two days ago. "I'll be careful. I am careful." She promised herself again that she would be.

A sea bird squawked, flying low over their heads, and dropped sharply to fetch a fish from the water. Mark continued. "One of the OR nurses told me that there's a kind of unwritten rule that pregnant nurses don't scrub in if they think a patient may have AIDS." His voice rose. "Don't you think that we should insist on the same for our baby?"

"Mark, you're not suggesting I refuse to take care of AIDS patients?" Kate was confused, and her visions of Mark and her practicing medicine in a remote location blurred as she tried to rationalize his fear of this disease as different from those they might face.

"I don't think it's worth the risk. They're all going to die anyway." Her husband's words sounded much harsher than the look on his face indicated.

"You don't really mean that, Mark. I would never do anything to hurt this baby." She felt her eyes filling up. "You know that, don't you? Still, we can't let our fear paralyze us. Today it's AIDS, yesterday it was the bubonic plague, tomorrow, who knows?"

"I'm just saying maybe we should talk to someone about this—one of the infectious disease people? They might have more experience," Mark countered.

The ferry arrived at the pier and the disembarking tourists invaded their solitude. "Yeah, maybe you're right," Kate conceded, anticipating her next words might touch a nerve. "I talked with Brian a few days ago. You remember he's doing AIDS research at the CDC. Well, he's looking into getting a compassionate release for an investigational antibiotic for one of my patients who isn't doing well. Maybe he'll have some advice. I'll ask him about it tomorrow. He's supposed to call me back with the details."

"Yeah, good idea. When you talk to him, tell old Brian I said hi," Mark said, the sarcasm dripping from his voice. She and Brain had dated in college. Their relationship was brief but intense, as was most everything for premed students. When Brian announced he was accepted to Emory in Atlanta with a full scholarship for a combined MD/PhD program in infectious disease, they fell away and Mark stepped in; handsome, confident, and sure of what he wanted, which at that time was Kate.

"Mark, surely you're not still jealous over Brian. We've been married almost six years. We're having our second baby."

The streetlights came on as the last few moments of daylight faded across the bay.

"I guess you're right," Mark conceded. But Kate sensed the conversation was not really finished.

"Come on, let's go home. Danny will be in bed, and no need to use a condom now." She kissed him gently and rubbed his face with the back of her hand. Despite the fact that she was tired and pregnant and tomorrow was another long call day, she felt herself getting aroused.

He responded with more intensity. "I've missed you, Kate."

"Me too, Mark. It's been too long." And it had been, with a four-year-old, two crazy resident schedules, and the fatigue and nausea of this new pregnancy, they hadn't made love in weeks. He held her close as he rubbed her back, and she longed for him to continue. She spent much of her days touching other people. It felt so nice to have someone touch her. Then she felt his shirt pocket vibrate.

Mark checked his beeper quickly and then put it back in his pocket and looked around the wharf. "I have to answer this. I'm sorry. A patient, you know?"

Kate watched her husband walk over to a pay phone. She loved that he cared so much about their baby. She would do everything she could to protect their child and herself. But she wasn't going to abandon her patients. Mark would understand it wasn't an either-or situation; she could do both.

"Everything ok?" she asked when he came back, but she already sensed his mood had shifted.

"Looks like I have to go in."

"We could stop on the way home?" She was looking forward to the rest of their evening together.

"No, I'll take you home. I might be a while and you've got to be beat."

Odd, Mark didn't seem to share her disappointment. He was

walking so quickly back to their car that he didn't even notice she was crying. This was one night when Kate needed to be the one comforted.

"There's a call for you, Dr. Kate." Kerline passed the phone to her across the desk of the ICU nurses' station. "Long distance."

Kate made a few notes as Brian relayed the details about Michael's experimental treatment.

"This is his last chance. Thanks, Brian, you're the best. I owe you."

"What did he say?" Kerline was eager to know the details. "Does your friend at the CDC have something that will help Michael?"

"Yes. The drug will be here tomorrow." Kate was writing a note in Michael's medical chart as she spoke. "Brian had to pull some strings to get it for us. It hasn't been used much since Vietnam, I think. They gave it to some of the military personnel for parasite infections. It worked well enough. But there hasn't been much of a market for parasite drugs—at least not in countries that have money to buy them. It's an orphan drug—never even got a real name."

Kate finished her note. "Now with AIDS patients, a company here on the West Coast started manufacturing it again under provisional FDA approval. Michael needs to sign the consent form as soon as possible. Has his family arrived yet?"

Kerline nodded. "They're with him now. Did the ID attending give his blessing?"

"Got it covered," Kate replied, and walked away before Kerline could ask any more questions. Two days ago, she left a message on Dr. Dixon's answering machine. His secretary called back and relayed that he got the message, but wouldn't get back to her until he returned from a conference in Seattle later that week. Kate didn't like the deterioration in Michael's last chest x-ray. She was starting the medicine as soon as it arrived.

Kate presumed the woman sitting by Michael's bedside was his mother. She looked at least ten years older than the man standing beside her. He was dressed in black jeans and an Ohio State T-shirt, a more weathered version of Michael but with dark hair and a hint of gray at his temples. The woman's hair was completely gray and needed a trim. She wore no makeup. The black flannel jumper and white turtleneck did nothing to soften her face, which was serious, if not stern, as she read from the Bible resting open on her lap. His father held Michael's hand.

". . . the prayer of faith shall save him that is sick, and the Lord shall raise him up." His mother closed her eyes and waited.

"Amen," Michael's father responded.

Kate allowed a few seconds of silence. "Excuse me, I'm Dr. Rigando. Mr. and Mrs. Rose?" They both nodded. "As I told you on the phone, I've been taking care of Michael since he was admitted two weeks ago." She smiled at her patient. "Good morning, Michael. How are you doing today?"

Better, now that my parents are here, he wrote on the whiteboard. It was hard for him to smile with a tube in his throat, but Michael was giving it his best effort. *They have some questions.* He rolled his eyes, as if to say I told you so.

Kate gave him a tentative thumbs up. His eyes were bright but his blood gases were going in the wrong direction. Kate and Michael had agreed that they would not tell his parents that he had AIDS—at least not yet. Michael wanted to do that himself, but only after he was better and breathing on his own again.

It was going to be difficult navigating concerned parents while honoring Michael's wishes. Were they already suspicious that their son had AIDS? Not likely—the disease was pretty rare except in a few big cities. They may not have even heard of it.

Michael's mother started. "What's wrong with Michael?

Exactly what kind of infection does he have? Why is everybody wearing those gowns? Should we wear one too?" Her voice lowered to a whisper. "Is it okay to hold his hand?"

"Marian!" Mr. Rose glanced sharply at his wife but did not drop his son's hand. "The doctor will tell us everything. Just give her a minute. Please, Dr. Rigando." His eyes stayed on Michael's face as he spoke. "We're very worried about our son."

Kate was fully prepared to straddle the doctor-patient confidentiality fence as best she could. But she had hoped Michael would change his mind when his parents arrived and let her tell them everything.

"Michael?" Kate looked to her patient for a sign that he wanted to change direction.

His eyes were closed; he shook his head just enough for her to notice.

"Your son has what we call an atypical pneumonia—atypical because it's not caused by one of the usual bacteria." She paused briefly. "We have two pretty good antibiotics that we use in these cases. Unfortunately, Michael's infection hasn't responded to either, which is why we had to put him on the breathing machine. But, there's an experimental . . ."

"How did he get the infection? Is it contagious?" Mrs. Rose interrupted and backed her chair ever so slightly away from Michael's bedside.

His mother was as tough as Michael had warned. "I can't answer for sure how Michael got the infection, Mrs. Rose, possibly from the air or water. It isn't spread from person to person like a cold or the flu."

"You were about to tell us about an experimental treatment," Mr. Rose said.

"Yes. There is an experimental drug. Michael and I have already discussed the pros and cons. It's all outlined here in the disclosure packet and he's agreed to sign the consent form. We want to get started as soon as the medicine arrives tomorrow. Right, Michael?"

He nodded.

"I'm sorry, I know you just got here, but I do need to examine him now. Maybe you would like to get some lunch? The cafeteria is on the second floor. It was nice to meet you both. I'm sure we'll be talking more." Kate removed her stethoscope from her pocket. With all the questions his mother asked, she was afraid she might slip up and say something.

"We'll read this while we have lunch." His mother picked up the packet from the bedside table.

Kate was intently checking Michael's numbers on the clipboard—temperature, blood pressure, pulse rate, fluids in and out. "Sure. You can ask one of the nurses to page me if you have any questions."

"Did that go okay?" she asked as she helped him sit up to listen to his lungs.

You did great, Doc, he wrote on the whiteboard.

As Brian promised, a small Styrofoam container was waiting for Kate the next morning when she arrived for ICU rounds with Cara. Kerline guarded it as she reviewed patient charts for new orders.

"I'll call pharmacy to mix this up. Cara, why don't you meet Michael's parents?" Kate suggested. "Remember, they don't know his diagnosis."

"All set," she told Kerline when she hung up the phone. "Let's get it going as soon as possible. I'll be in his room."

Before Kate was halfway down the hall, she heard Mrs. Rose's voice but couldn't make out what she was saying. Mrs. Rose and Cara were standing in the corridor a few rooms down from Michael's. His mother was pacing back and forth, motioning to Michael's room,

Bible in hand. Her first thought was that Michael had taken a turn for the worse. Kate opened his closed door without knocking, but stopped on the threshold.

His father sat close to Michael's bed, his head bowed. He held one of his son's hands. Michael's other hand, partially restrained by an IV line, rested on his father's shoulder. The whiteboard was on the floor, blank, with no explanation.

"We'll get through this, son. I don't know how, but we will." His father's voice was muffled. "I wish we could have been here sooner . . . I can't imagine how hard it must have been for you . . . The only thing that matters now is that you get better . . . Your mother is just angry. She'll come around . . . You know we love you."

His somber monologue was answered only by the intermittent hissing of the ventilator and by his son's rhythmic massaging of his shoulder.

Kate backed out into the hall to join Cara and Mrs. Rose. Kate wondered what could have happened since yesterday?

"You had no right to keep this from us." Mrs. Rose delivered her accusations inches from Cara's face. "Do you think we're stupid— just some hicks from Ohio?"

Cara looked confused. "Mrs. Rose, please. You're obviously upset."

"What is it, Mrs. Rose?" Kate interrupted. "Come sit down so we can talk." She attempted to lead her to the family consultation room, but Michael's mother jerked her arm away.

"Yes. Now you want to talk. If I hadn't read that information about the experimental drug, I wouldn't have known. I had to call my doctor back home. Do you know how I felt when he explained it to me? I was mortified!"

Did the information from the CDC mention AIDS? Kate recalled the details of the material in her head. It was only in one place, but it did. Damn it!

"My son is dying from this . . . this disease of homosexuals.

When were you going to tell us? At his funeral?" Her tears unleashed.

"I'm sorry, Mrs. Rose." Kate could only offer the truth as her defense. "Michael wanted to tell you himself." Yet she realized how feeble her words must have sounded.

"No more secrets." Mr. Rose joined them and put his arm around his wife. "The aide is bathing him and after that, she said they'll start the new medication. We'll have time to talk later. Come on, Marian, let's get a cup of coffee and call home." He put his arm around his wife and they walked away.

"I need to go back and talk to Michael, Cara." Kate reminded herself she still had one more secret she hadn't shared. She started to tell Cara that the ID attending hadn't officially approved the experimental treatment. But she stopped herself. This could be Michael's last chance to have a conversation with his parents.

"You want me to come with you?" Cara asked.

"No. I need to do this alone." But the truth was, she would have preferred to do just about anything rather than walk back into Michael's room. Whatever else she was doing right for him, she had failed her patient in his last request to confront this disease on his own terms.

Michael was finished with his bath and stared at the TV. He clicked it off when Kate walked in.

"I'm so sorry. I wasn't thinking . . . I am so sorry, Michael." Over and over again in her head, the same accusation taunted her. How could she have been so stupid?

It's okay. No more secrets. Michael's message echoed his father's.

Unaware of the events of the last thirty minutes, Kerline arrived, smiling and holding a small plastic infusion bag with blue liquid. "Ready for your morning cocktail?"

Kate made her way to the ICU first thing Monday morning.

She had spent a quiet weekend at home with Danny and Mark. Even though they both agreed there would be no beepers, Kate had hidden hers in her purse on vibrate mode. She made Kerline swear to call her if Michael's condition worsened. If that happened, she'd have to fess up about shortcutting the protocol to get Michael started on the experimental drug. It had been less than a week, but he had already shown remarkable progress before she left on Friday. His fever was gone, his chest x-ray improved, and the respiratory tech had lowered the settings on his ventilator so that he was breathing on his own about 50 percent of the time.

"Hey Doc, where you been?" Michael's raspy greeting was accompanied by a crack-lipped smile that stretched from ear to ear. His partner, George, sat beside him with a matching grin.

"Well, look at you! I take a few days off and I miss all the excitement." Kate was delighted to see Michael off the ventilator, but shocked by how thin he had become. She hardly recognized him sitting in the chair by the window in his gray hospital gown. Without the pillows and bed sheets, there was nothing to soften the sharp angles of his face, arms, and legs. She couldn't think of a better description than the stereotypical analogy that her colleagues used—comparing the physical wasting of AIDS patients to concentration camp survivors. A survivor—yes, Michael was definitely a survivor. He had indeed survived like he had said he would, against the odds and despite her doubts.

"Yeah. We need to find him some new accessories." Kerline pointed to his stockinged feet and raised Michael's hand, unencumbered by an IV line for the first time in weeks.

George joined in the banter. "You're making Dr. K look bad, Michael. As soon as she's gone, you get some strange resident to pull the tube out. Kind of like the ninth-inning relief pitcher who gets all the credit for the win, when all the regular guy needed was a little rest because he already pitched such a great game."

"Well, as we soccer moms say, a win is a win," Kate teased back.

Kerline was busy tidying up the room. "Seriously, we do need the bed. As soon as you can clear him for transfer out of the unit, I'll get him a bed on the general medical ward."

"Okay. You heard the boss. Looks like you're moving to the cheap seats." Kate helped him lean forward and untied the drawstring at the top of his gown. "Let me listen to you and we'll get you out of here so someone who really needs this room can have it." There were several more of the violet patches on his back similar to the one she had seen on his hand a few weeks ago. Except these were larger and raised above the surrounding skin. One was oozing and left a pink stain on Michael's gown.

"Kerline, has dermatology been here yet? I haven't seen anything on the chart. It's been two weeks since I asked for the consult."

"Ah—well, sort of," Kerline said in a low voice, and then mouthed silently, "I'll tell you later."

"What's up with the derm consult?" Kate asked, back at the nurses' station. Kerline handed her the report. It was only one short paragraph.

"The dermatologist was here on Saturday. He barely went in Michael's room. I showed him the lesion on his hand; he said he didn't need to see any more." Kerline rolled her eyes.

Kate scanned the report and read the final recommendation: "AIDS patient with classic Kaposi's sarcoma. No need to biopsy. Recommend oncology consult."

"Oncology?" Kerline said. "Will they give him some sort of chemotherapy? I know it's cancer, but AIDS patients are already so compromised. It seems like that would be dangerous."

As Kate picked up the phone, she was so angry she could

barely punch in the beeper of the dermatologist. Her patients had to drink cold coffee because the cafeteria lady was afraid to bring the breakfast tray into the room of an AIDS patient. She had tiptoed around a mother whose shame kept her at arm's length from her critically ill son. She had to negotiate her position as a concerned doctor versus her role as a responsible mother with her worried husband. She had had more than enough of the fear and the guilt.

"After all my patient's been through, I am not going in there and telling him that he needs chemo, something that will almost certainly destroy what little immune system he has left, without a definitive diagnosis," Kate concluded to herself, after the doctor on the other end reluctantly agreed to do a biopsy.

"Kate." Cara interrupted her thoughts. She was with one of the senior attending physicians who Kate recognized from grand rounds. "I think you know Dr. Dixon, the chairperson of Infectious Disease. He wants to go over the protocol for the CDC's experimental drug so we can get our AIDS patient started."

They both looked at her, waiting for an explanation. The only strategy Kate had for this moment, which she knew would come eventually, was that in the absence of asking permission, she'd barter for forgiveness.

"Sorry, Cara." And she was, but only for the possibility that Cara might take the heat, too. "I guess I have some explaining to do."

5

ADELAIDE

PETIT (TI) MIREBELAIS HAITI
DECEMBER 1984

It was as if a heavy stone plunged to the bottom of her stomach—fast and hard until it had nowhere else to go. Adelaide heard the scream, but didn't realize that it had come from her own mouth until she felt the flood of warm liquid rush out from inside her and down between her legs. Darkness still owned the night in her sleepy rural village; only the moonlight disclosed the puddle of fluid seeping into the mud floor of their two-room house.

"Mama! Mama! Come!" she cried.

Her mother came quickly, as did the woman next door. Adelaide's mother reached her just as Madame Cereste pitched a bucket of water in the general direction of the hysteria. All three women joined in the wailing—Adelaide in gripping pain, her mother in sleepy confusion, and Madame Cereste in solidarity with what rural Haitian women are often known to do in a crisis—wail and hurl water.

The shocked surprise of the cold water in her face reminded Adelaide she was having a baby. She eased herself into a chair. The sudden pain in her belly was gone, but now she felt an insistent pulling and cramping stretching across her lower abdomen and into her back. It was similar to the discomfort she had with her monthly bleeding. It wasn't so bad. She could do this.

"*Gras a Dieu*—with the grace of God—it is time," her mother pronounced, and she gently lifted the drenched nightclothes over Adelaide's head and replaced them with a clean gown. It opened in the front but was incompletely fastened with safety pins. The buttons were long gone, traded to fasten a communion dress or christening gown or some other more ceremonious item of clothing.

Her mother dressed quickly in the clothes she usually wore to work in the market. She tied a clean blue apron around her waist. Its big pockets were designed to hold all the important tools of a peasant woman's life—scissors, rosaries, and a few goudes for luck. She took out a tiny box of wooden matches, struck one on the worn flint side of the box, and lit all the candles they had in the house. Adelaide's sisters were awake, watching from their bed and giggling.

"Cassandra, get me some water." Her mother handed her second-oldest daughter a large plastic bucket. "You help her, Myrland. Hurry now!" The woman knelt down and reached under the mattress, propped up on cement blocks, where Adelaide and her two sisters slept each night. She brought out a flat cardboard box and a roll of white paper. Wrinkled and stained, the paper held crude, hand-drawn diagrams depicting clean delivery practices and umbilical cord care with brief explanations in missionary Creole—a combination of simple English and bad Creole:

<u>CLEAN</u> HANDS

<u>CLEAN</u> PERINEUM

<u>CLEAN</u> DELIVERY AREA

<u>CLEAN</u> CORD-CUTTING INSTRUMENT

<u>CLEAN</u> CORD TIES AND CUTTING SURFACE

<u>NOTHING UNCLEAN</u> INTO VAGINA

One of the American volunteers had given this to Adelaide a few weeks earlier. The volunteer reviewed the steps with her and her mother. She also gave them a clean razor blade, two clean cloth ties sealed in a plastic bag, and a heavy plastic mat. Her mother could not read the words, but she hung the paper on the wall and studied the pictures for a moment before turning her attention to Adelaide.

Her mother took a plastic tablecloth with bright orange and yellow flowers and spread it on the bed. On top she laid the plastic mat from the box and a clean white sheet. "Do you want to lie down yet?" she asked.

"I don't think so. I'll sit for now."

The sun wouldn't be up for a few more hours, but the night sky was bright with the stars and moon. She preferred the distractions of the night, rather than staring at the walls. There was only one small window in the house. It captured the morning sun for light, but shunned the warmer afternoon brightness. Her sisters returned with the water and stared at Adelaide and their mother with timid curiosity.

"Go," their mother said. "Madame Cereste will see to you while this is done."

Her mother poured water into a black iron pot and went outside to the cooking area—a patch of dirt protected from the rain by a bent piece of tin suspended on four cut mahogany branches, secured in the dirt with small patches of cement. There were always a few chairs around, and spent bean casings littered the ground from the day before. Three families shared the space. They were related in the casual way that most families in the village were connected. Somebody's uncle was somebody's cousin was somebody's husband. It didn't matter all that much. They celebrated in good times, grieved in bad times, and in between they fought about most everything else.

Adelaide watched as her mother rearranged the partially

used charcoal into a pile under the pot, which she set on a small metal grate. She added a sliver of bamboo wood and dried orange peel to help speed the flames. Then her mother came inside and removed a teapot from the only shelf and set it on the table with a single metal cup.

Madame Cereste brought a small plastic bag of brown leaves. "I will make the tea," she whispered quietly. "The girls are with my mama."

Madame was the most respected of the community's traditional birth attendants, or *matrones*. She had no formal training in a hospital or nursing school, but she attended several sessions at the Red Cross the summer before. She could read and write a little, but not even as well as Adelaide's youngest sister, Cassandra, who was in third grade.

Nevertheless, Adelaide smiled at her *matrone*, grateful for her presence. Most women delivered their babies with only a friend or a relative at their side or, in some cases, no one at all.

Between contractions, Adelaide heard her younger sister Myrland ask their mother, "Mama, is Addie dying?" There was a lot of blood. She could feel the wetness between her legs and when she tried to wipe it away, her fingers were covered in the sticky red that came from inside her. She'd stayed on the mattress since the first morning, only standing when she had to pee in the metal bucket by the bed.

The pain had been so intense for the last few hours that she wished she would die or at least pass out. Then maybe a neighbor would run up the mountain and beg one of the *blan*—the white people from the U.S.—to drive their jeep down and take her to the hospital. They could cut the baby out of her while she was sleeping. One of her friends told her about that. She knew because her aunt lived in the United States. All the women had their babies that way;

there was no pain, just a few pills and a little needle in the arm. They woke up with a perfect little baby in their arms—all clean and warm and wrapped in pink or blue.

Adelaide had no idea how long her labor had lasted. She counted the hours by the sounds and smells of the daily routine of their lives. This both comforted and humbled her as she realized that all went on despite what was happening inside her expectant sixteen-year-old body. As Madame Cereste said, "All death begins with life. All life begins with pain."

Twice since the water left her, the market women chattered as they walked up the path outside her door in the late-night darkness. She imagined the fruits they carried on their heads—bananas and maybe some coconuts. Mangos and oranges were not in season yet. Her mouth moistened a little at the thought of the cool, sweet fruits of spring.

When the sun was up but not so hot, the children began teasing each other: "Wait for me" and "We're going to be late."

Most of them had only a piece of bread in their stomachs for the day and they were probably carrying their shoes—either too small or too large—as they ran down the path to the three-room school. There would be beatings if they were late, and if they had no shoes, they would be sent back home and more beatings would await them there.

Women pounded spices on stone. The garlic and the parsley roasted in the peak of the midday sun. The charcoal burned and the plantains fried. And as if her body knew that there was something more than the bitter tea she was permitted to prepare her body for childbirth, the next contraction seized her and she vomited onto the dirt floor.

Madame Cereste threw a cloth over the foul mess and massaged Adelaide's stomach and back with warm dark oil that smelled like clove and lime.

As the children returned from school a little girl cried, quietly at first, and then most insistently as little girls often do.

"Don't cry, little one," Adelaide said to no one in particular. "Women must be strong for our country." Her next contraction testified to the whispered advice.

Swish, swoosh, swish. The machetes cleared the brush that grew between planting seasons.

She imagined the men in the fields swinging their picks in unison as they cleared the rocks exposed by the fall storms. The spring planting and rains would not arrive for several months, but there was always work to do.

The choir practiced at the little Methodist church. It was a long walk away from their home, but the wind carried the tunes to her just when she thought she could endure no more. Listening to their songs in French, she smiled through her suffering because she had almost forgotten that it would be Christmas soon.

Later that evening, the drums echoed from the mountains, sending a message of their own, but Adelaide was too exhausted to understand. Her mother and Madame Cereste dozed in the darkness; even the most vigilant of *matrones* had to sleep a little. She was content as one could be in excruciating pain. She lost count of how many times her fingers had made the journey around her white plastic rosary beads.

In the stillest and quietest part of the night, the neighbors made love. It was the only time she thought about the father of her child. She had not seen him since the night they made the baby. Did he even know?

Early on the third day of her confinement, her mother argued with the moneylender from Mirebelais. "You're late with your payment again, Madame Delva," he said.

"Shhh. My daughter is having her baby. You'll get your money." Her mother spoke with the boldness of someone who had more important affairs to tend to. There was no further discussion.

Madame Cereste added red hibiscus flowers to the tea water. "You need your energy for this next part."

How many times had she and her friends plucked the flowers from the bushes along the path to school and put them behind their ears?

The roosters crowed. The dogs barked. It wouldn't be long before the rhythm of the day repeated its pattern. It wouldn't be long before her baby would come or she would die trying.

"I see the shoulder. I think it's stuck." Her mother's voice was low.

The pain made her want to not breathe.

Her mother raised her head. "Cassandra, Myrland, get in here! Do something useful. Pray for your sister."

Her sisters were keeping their own private vigil beneath the open window. Only the crackling of cellophane interrupted their giddy voices as they unwrapped *bonbons* that one of the neighbors sold.

At their mother's insistence, her sisters came quickly and claimed a spot in the corner of the room, as far away from the bed as possible. The sound of their young knees hitting the dirt must have made a special call to the angel who hears prayers from children. Something inside her moved with great purpose and the urge to push consumed and energized her.

Her mother lifted her back and neck as Adelaide grabbed her knees and pushed with each contraction. Despite the arduous and endless daily tasks of life in rural Haiti—carrying buckets of water or baskets of fruit up the long and rocky path, or clearing fields of brush and boulders—a person could never work so hard as a woman giving birth. This lesson Adelaide learned with each effort and vowed she would never forget.

"Rest between," the women encouraged.

She cried only twice—once with the last contraction when she pushed the baby out into the world and her body ripped apart with relief and agony. The second time was when her mama cut the connection between her and her new daughter. Yvonne's hands shook a little as she unwrapped the clean blade. As someone who had only known the misdirected sharp of a knife to her finger while chopping vegetables for soup, Adelaide expected to feel a horrible hurt when her mother sliced through the cord. But it wasn't pain Adelaide experienced; only an empty ache that she was certain would never quite disappear.

"Cassandra, read us the directions."

"Yes, Mama." She rose from her knees and hurried to the poster still hanging on the wall from three days earlier. "*Coupe ak pwòp gillette*—cut with a clean razor. *Kenbe e ak pwòp kòd*—hold and with clean string—tie . . . in . . . a . . ." She struggled and lingered over the last few words.

"Tie . . . een . . . a? Speak Creole, Cassandra." Their mother glanced at the diagram. Swiftly, with hands as steady as if she were tying ribbons in her daughter's hair for Sunday church, under Madame Cereste's guidance her mother tied the string around the ends of the gray opalescent cord.

When the afterbirth came, Madame Cereste carried it outside and placed it maternal side down to earth in a deep hole that had been prepared when labor started. It was covered with shovels of earth, tamped down to conceal the location. Adelaide, weary from labor, marked the spot in her memory.

"Have you chosen a name for your baby?" her mother asked.

Strangely, she had not. She thought it might be bad luck or maybe it just didn't seem real until now. With her first big decision as a mother, she looked at the wall and pronounced, "Tieina. That is her name."

Cassandra and Myrland giggled again. Her mother nodded with approval. And daylight relieved the night, entered the tiny window, and started a new chapter in the lives of three generations of women. The candles were extinguished, conserved for another vigil of life—or death. One could never know.

Her mother placed the baby on her stomach. It didn't take long for the little one to find her nipple and begin to nurse. With a perfect tiredness previously unknown to her, Adelaide slept. She dreamed the only dream her heart had room to hold—that of a better life for her daughter.

6

KATE

SAN FRANCISCO
DECEMBER 1984

"Mom, are you sad 'cause we're not going to Mars for Christmas this year?" Danny asked as Kate untangled strings of lights with Mark.

It sounded so silly, they both had to laugh.

"I think I'm a little sad," Kate answered. Her family had some good Christmases growing up, but some not-so-good ones too.

Mars was the small rural community where Kate's father lived, thirty miles north of Pittsburgh—a patchwork farm town with corn and cows, interrupted by a few small bars and restaurants, more than a handful of churches, a school, and a cemetery.

Kate grew up there until her sophomore year of college, when she moved to the city claiming she could study more and make the grades she needed to get into medical school. Only to herself did she admit the real reason she was moving out—her mother's drinking.

During Kate's freshman year in high school, her mother started up again after five years in AA. Kate had assumed much of the

69

responsibility for her sisters and for the housework. She cooked and did laundry for the family, cleaned up her mother's vomit, and once rode in the ambulance with her to the emergency room when she passed out and had a near lethal blood alcohol level—her father was away at a medical conference that day. One task at a time, mother retreated, and eldest daughter stepped up. Finally, when Kate could no longer watch her mother's self-destruction, she found every bottle of booze in the house, garage, and even the ones buried in the backyard. She dumped the vile liquids down the drain, all the time yelling at her mother that she was going to destroy herself and their family.

It was her father who insisted Kate move out. He had cried with her as they carried her boxes up two flights of stairs to her new apartment at the university. "For such a petite girl, Katie— you sure do have awfully broad shoulders—it's been a blessing for me that you've picked up so much of the slack with your mom being sick. But for you, I don't know. If you do become a doctor, and I hope you will, you're going to have to figure out a balance between caring for your patients and caring for yourself. The secret to success in medicine and in life is not to let yourself get used up."

Two years after she moved out, Kate was completely blindsided when she got the call that her mother was in the hospital and Kate needed to get there as soon as she could. She died that evening, never waking from a coma induced by an overdose of pills and alcohol. Kate never had the chance to say goodbye. She never had the chance to know her mother's last thoughts.

Kate unwrapped the handmade angel that had topped their Christmas tree each year when she was a child. Her mother made it the year Kate was born. One of its wings was broken and the once iridescent white robe was now yellow and torn.

"How about this? It's a present from Debbie." Mark handed her an elegant, five-pointed crystal star, a gift from one of Mark's fellow residents. "We could put this on top of the tree this year—start a new tradition of our own."

Kate hated to agree it was in better shape than her twenty-five-year-old heirloom.

"Danny's had so many changes. Let's keep our old traditions for this year, Mark." She couldn't help but add, "Why did Debbie buy you a Christmas gift anyhow?" She didn't know Debbie, although Mark mentioned her often enough.

"It's for us." But he didn't meet her eyes when he said it.

Kate fussed with the angel for an hour before she conceded. No matter how she tried, it either looked like a drunken cherub about to fall to its death or an unwilling sentinel painfully impaled by a six-foot Fraser fir tree up its gown.

"Okay, you win." She put the angel back in the box and sulked in silence, finishing the decorating alone while Mark went out shopping.

Everyone agreed Michael's going-home party that Christmas Eve morning was great and they would have another one soon. It really was more of a wish than a promise, given the fact that three out of four of the patients on the AIDS ward died before they were discharged to home or, as Kerline had said, "They were transferred to the Eternal Care Unit."

Kate pushed that thought out of her mind as she leaned over to check Michael's catheter securely positioned in a deep vein beneath his right collarbone. She brushed away a few crumbs from his cake. His lips and teeth were still stained green from the icing. He was bundled up in red plaid pajamas, black leather jacket, running shoes, and red ski hat. Suspended from his ears was a lopsided white beard made from cotton balls he had conned from the lab tech who took his blood each day. Beneath the hat all his hair was gone. It had fallen out in clumps at first. But after three weeks of chemotherapy, he was completely bald. Although he was hardly the plumpest of Santas, with the help of the Christmas cookies the nurses had baked for him, he had gained a few pounds. He was their favorite. Kate smiled—hers, too.

Michael scratched his faux beard. "Next Christmas, I'll grow myself a real beard and some hair to match." He managed a smile despite the tentative look that clouded his face when he touched one of the violet patches on his cheek, similar to the one on his hand, which turned out to be malignant as Kate had feared.

"Any questions about your discharge instructions, Santa?" Kate had no doubt the tumors were ravaging his internal organs, as well.

"I'll see you in two weeks, right?" Michael looked at her uncertainly.

"You're not getting rid of me," Kate assured him.

Michael was scheduled to receive a few more rounds of chemotherapy in the Oncology Clinic. The tumors were smaller in size, but more had appeared in the last few weeks. He would also come to Kate's resident outpatient clinic for his general medical care.

"Don't you cause Dr. K any trouble now." Kerline winked at Kate. "She's got that baby on the way."

No, Kate was hoping to stay out of trouble for the rest of her internship. She recalled Cara's response to her shortcutting the approval for Michael's experimental drug in October. Cara told her that if she weren't such a damn good doctor, she would have insisted they put her on probation. Apparently, Dr. Dixon also spoke up for her, reporting that six more patients had been treated with the experimental drug and five of them had made the same remarkable progress as Michael had.

However, Dr. Dixon was decidedly sterner when he called Kate a few days later.

"Don't try and be a hero again. The system isn't perfect, but it is designed to protect your patients and to protect you."

Kate was relieved about the program's decision, but at the same time didn't offer an apology for her actions—she wasn't sorry for what she did and she would do it again if she had to.

She shifted her focus back to the present. It was already three o'clock. She had five more patients to see, and every intention of getting home before Danny went to bed so they could put out the cookies and milk for Santa together.

"Okay. Okay. Time to go," George said, and tipped Michael's wheelchair back on two wheels and made a few tight figure eights in front of the nurses' station, as if he were showing off a brand-new Corvette to his high school friends.

Michael smiled like a man who had just received the most incredibly wonderful Christmas gift of his life. Only his tightly curled white knuckles gripping the arms of the wheelchair gave him away. "See y'all later. Ho! Ho! Ho!"

When Kate arrived home, all the lights in the apartment were off, yet the room glowed from the Christmas tree. Danny was in bed, Mark was asleep on the couch, and Santa had beaten her home. The gifts spilled from under the tree out into the middle of their small family room. She couldn't wait to see Danny's face when he opened his presents, a brand-new soccer ball and a set of goals for their tiny backyard.

She was so glad they had decided to splurge and get a real tree. Without snow and without family, the scent of pine was an especially precious reminder of Christmas. Her eyes scanned the almost perfectly symmetrical shape. The controversial star was gone, and in its place was her mother's lovingly crafted treasure looking simply and elegantly angelic.

She slipped Mark's present beside him on the couch. It was an oil painting she had purchased from Yanick, Kerline's sister. Kate would have it framed after the holidays. A Haitian artist, no one who was especially famous, had painted it. But something about it had touched Kate. She had paid fifty dollars more than the asking price, hoping to help the woman raise enough money to return to Haiti before she became too sick to travel. Where would Yanick and Michael be a year from now? And what about Mark and her, and Danny, and this baby growing inside of her?

Mark's beeper vibrated on the end table. Kate picked it up. It wasn't a hospital number. That was odd. Who was calling him at this time of night? She turned it off before it could wake him. They had agreed, no beepers, not even on vibrate mode.

The cookies and milk were in place on the coffee table. Kate took a big bite out of one of the sugar ones—a plump Santa with bright red icing. She gulped down the milk. Tomorrow morning, when Danny found what remained of Santa's snack, he would say the same thing he said the last two years: "See, Mom. Santa really was here!"

Her present was sitting next to the tree; on it a floppy red bow and a handwritten note from her husband: *Every mom should have a rocking chair to rock her babies. Merry Christmas, Katie! Love, Santa.*

Maybe it was foolish, but that Christmas Eve Kate believed anything and everything was possible.

CHAPTER

7

GISELLE

PORT AU PRINCE
FEBRUARY 1985

Giselle tapped the horn of her white Toyota Land Rover three times before the heavy, metal clinic gates parted to let her pass. She waved to the guard, Antoine, as he closed the gates behind her.

"*Bonswa*—good afternoon, Antoine. How are you?" Giselle offered the traditional Haitian greeting.

"*Pa pi mal*—not too bad," he answered.

Giselle eased her car into the shade of a large acacia tree to escape the heat of the afternoon and glanced at her watch. It was only noon, at least an hour before Uncle Joseph would return with the sisters. She could visit with the children in the courtyard like she had done the last two weeks or talk with Antoine, as she often did when the children returned to afternoon class. But instead she decided to stay in the car and read a little of her art history book, something that was difficult to do with a four-year-old at home.

"Damn flies." She rolled the window up except for a small sliver. After only a few pages, her eyes began to protest and she stopped fighting the sleep that begged to come.

Each Wednesday, Giselle made the forty-five-minute trip down the mountain from Petionville to the fringes of *Cite Soleil*. Her uncle volunteered one day a week at a clinic deep in the bowels of Haiti's most infamous slum. The Mother and Child Clinic, operated by the Daughters of Mother Theresa, was about a mile from their residence, along with a school the sisters had founded. Giselle had repeated this clandestine routine for several months now—ever since her uncle's Nissan sedan had broken down. She agreed to be his chauffeur, against her own best judgment and Auntie Carole's advice. Jean-Juste knew, but had long given up trying to tell her what to do; he was in France most of the time now anyhow. She couldn't tell Max where she was going. He would be angry with her. She was the wife of a public figure and had no business in the slums of Port au Prince.

Her uncle had only to get transportation to and from the school. The sisters got him the rest of the way to the medical clinic. It was a short but dangerous journey that these women, attired in their traditional blue vestments, were better able to negotiate without incident. The Daughters of Mother Theresa, an order of Catholic religious sisters from Belgium with three decades of mission work in Haiti, had a well-deserved reputation as the saints of the slums.

The Daughters' compound was a modest building with heavy metal doors that slid on rusty metal tracks. The doors were locked and guarded—although the security system was hardly intimidating to anyone but first-time international visitors. The guard, Antoine, was a sixty-five-year-old man dwarfed by ill-fitting clothes. Arie, a mixed-breed dog boasting a bark that promised more than her mangy frame could deliver, aided him.

"Madame Giselle." Sister Claudette, one of the novices, knocked on the half-open window of her car and interrupted her nap. "Is your uncle here? We have a mother with her baby. She is only a few days old. The baby is very sick."

Giselle checked her watch quickly and got out of her car. "He should be here now. But I don't see the van."

Like the sisters, the van gave the outward appearance of being not worth the effort to rob. "It's safer this way," Sister Jacquie, the sister in charge of the clinic, had explained to Giselle on her first visit. "We don't wish to call attention to ourselves."

But the battered exterior concealed a lion's heart of an engine. It had been completely rebuilt with new parts begged, stolen, and bartered from anyone and anywhere. The exterior parts, however, were more vulnerable to the hazards of the road.

"I hope they don't have another flat tire." Sister Claudette was more of a worrier than the older sisters. "I'm afraid the baby is going to die."

"Can I do anything?" Giselle said, though she didn't know what she might do.

"Come. Antoine, please when Dr. Joseph gets here, you must send him to the school—quickly. It's an emergency."

Giselle followed Sister Claudette. Inside the school, which was one big room with four partitions, the mother, Nadine, held something. If not for the sea of pink blankets, Giselle would have thought it was a large soapstone carving.

The mother thrust her rigid bundle at Giselle. "Please, please help me," she cried.

She first noticed the baby's face. Her mouth was locked tight and her expression was frozen in a helpless stunned grimace. Her head and spine were arched back with her arms curled in and her fists clenched like she held the most terrible of secrets inside her and couldn't get it to escape. She didn't cry, but every few seconds her little body trembled tightly.

"How long has she been this way?" Giselle tried to think what her uncle might ask.

Sister Claudette had already extracted some details from the mother. "The baby was born at home last week. She has been having episodes for two days. She hasn't taken any milk since yesterday morning. Is she having a seizure?"

"I don't know. It could be. Oh, where is my uncle?" Giselle rocked the baby like she had rocked her own, Natali, when she was fussy with colic. But this was so different. She felt utterly useless.

Finally, she heard a familiar voice. "We had a problem with the car. Let me have the child." Uncle Joseph took the infant from Giselle and placed her on the table.

"Oh, *mon Dieu*." The words escaped him. "Not again." He swatted the flies from his sweaty face and searched in his medical bag. He extracted a flashlight and passed the light over the baby's eyes. There was no response. "I need some valium, Sister. Do you have any in your pharmacy?"

"I'll check." Sister Jacquie hitched up her long blue skirt and ran like a thief intent on stealing a soul from death.

"Is it a seizure, Uncle?"

"No. It is much worse, I think." He turned to the mother, who had calmed down a little. "Madame, when your baby was born, what did they do to cut the cord—the connection from the baby to you?"

"I don't know. They put something on it. It smelled bad but I don't know. I was tired. It was a very difficult birth." She never looked up from her lap where her hands were knotted together.

Her uncle unswathed the baby. The residual stump of the umbilical cord, only a few inches long, was swollen and mottled, all purple and black.

"The baby has tetanus, Giselle." His voice was both angry and sad. "This doesn't happen where mothers are immunized and where people don't use animal crap during childbirth." He spat out the words.

"Can you help her?" She glanced at him hopefully. Her uncle had performed miracles before.

He shook his head. "Not this little one."

The baby's lips were turning blue and little bubbles of frothy saliva gurgled from her mouth. In a few more minutes, the kind of minutes that last a lifetime, the baby's tiny body relaxed. For just that instant, before the color left her cheeks and accepted the grayness, she returned again to the softness and pinkness of what a baby should be.

Sister Jacquie ran breathlessly into the room with a small glass vial, syringe, and alcohol. "Here it . . ." She stopped, with the medicine suspended from her outstretched arm.

It was too late.

Uncle closed the blanket back around the baby, placed her in her mother's lap, and walked outside.

Deep from her sisterly pockets, Sister Jacquie extracted a small bottle of holy water. She whispered something in the mother's ear. The mother nodded. Sister Jacquie touched the tip of her right thumb to the clear liquid. Her lips moved in silent affirmation as she traced a tiny cross on the baby's forehead. Then she kissed the crucifix on her rosary beads and made a larger sign of the cross, incorporating her own upper body. The four women said a few quick prayers in French, Creole, and Dutch.

Giselle and Sister Claudette led Nadine, with child cradled in her arms, into their simple private chapel and closed the door. Once again Giselle was reminded how tragic life was for uneducated women in her godforsaken country. The only consolation they could offer: at least this mother wouldn't have to grieve with flies in her face.

When it rained in Cite Soleil, the water spilled over into the streets and into the mud and brick shanties. Narrow streets outlined the haphazard maze of shacks and open sewers. Goats, pigs, and dogs wandered freely, feeding on the trash that filled the gutters. Even in a modest downpour like the one that morning, all things good and bad found their way to the lowest point in the slums without respect for sleep or children or the meager furnishings of the inhabitants. The nasty smelling, muddy mixture of human and animal waste and neglect embedded itself in tire treads and shoes.

"I'm going to have to get this car washed before I go home," Giselle complained to Sister Jacquie. "I'll probably have to pay one of those urchins an extra ten goudes to scrub the tires."

It had been exactly a week since the baby died from tetanus. The sisters' van had finally worn out its tires. Two more flat tires, in addition to the one from last week, left no spare to replace the spare, which replaced the repeatedly patched front tire.

Sister Jacquie begged Giselle when she arrived at her usual Wednesday time, "Please, dear. You must take me to the coffin-maker's shop. The baby's funeral is tomorrow morning. I promised the mother we would have the casket for her child."

The sisters were mostly focused on missions for the living. But in special cases, particularly with children, they made exceptions. Haitians did their best to reconcile a life of misery by arranging a proper mournful celebration at death.

"Alright, but I'm waiting in the car while you go in." Like her uncle, even in the best of times, it was impossible for Giselle to refuse to help the saintliest saint of the slums. But she wouldn't dare leave her vehicle unattended on the street. Hubcaps, tires, and accessories could disappear in minutes.

No one was brave enough to open a store or any kind of business in the feckless heart of the slum. But there were three legitimate businesses that thrived on the outskirts—medical clinics, lottery stands, and coffin-makers' shops. Only the latter two made any money. Haitians were willing to pay what they could for hope and death. The missionaries provided rudimentary healthcare with barometric support from the international community. In good times, the aid flowed like the swollen open sewers after the spring rains in April. In the most troubled times, it dried up like the waterless, garbage-ridden ravines isolating the streets of Port au Prince in July. Neither situation made for good health or healthy relationships. Like an abusive alcoholic parent, people loved the country with an overwhelming fierceness to compensate for the intervening times of hurt and neglect.

Giselle stopped in front of the coffin-maker's shop.

Sister Jacquie hopped out and said, "I won't be long. Just wait here."

She wasn't fooled by Sister Jacquie's Haitian time. "I won't be long" could be five minutes, but more likely an hour stretching into two. As her luck would have it, another vehicle pulled out from a place directly in front of the lottery stand. She moved the Toyota in quickly and smoothly ahead of another woman gaming for the same spot.

Giselle turned off the engine and prepared to wait. She pondered the brightly painted red-and-blue sign—*Borlette*—Lottery. She considered the odds. Lucky numbers didn't appear to her in visions or dreams like some Haitian players claimed. But after all, what did she have to lose? She put her keys and a twenty-goude bill, the smallest she had, in her pocket, zipped her purse, and stashed it under the front seat.

"One ticket please, number 808." She handed the toothless man behind the lopsided folding table her money, keeping an eye on her car. "Is your drawing based on New York?" It would be easy for her to check on the TV that evening if they had electricity.

"No, Santa Domingo." He quickly slid her money in a rusty metal lockbox.

"What about my change?" She noted the sign said fifteen goudes.

"Don't have change." He adjusted his New York Yankees cap and dismissed her for the next in a long line of customers.

Heat rose to her cheeks. She had fallen for an old market trick. Take the money and have no change. She should have known better, but it had been a long time since she bought anything on the street. She had forgotten the rules, which were there are no rules. No wonder Haiti was such a mess. Everyone was trying to hustle everyone else. All she wanted to do was buy a simple lottery ticket. For five goudes, though, she wasn't going to make a fuss, certainly not in Cite Soleil.

Giselle settled back in her front seat to wait for Sister Jacquie. Just as she slipped her newly purchased lottery ticket in her purse, the car door was wrenched open by a daunting figure with wide opaque sunglasses. A tightly secured red bandanna covered his nose and mouth. He was dressed in a denim jacket. The rest she didn't get a chance to notice. He grabbed her hair with one hand and held the edge of a knife to her neck with another.

"Move over. Give me your keys."

"Please—take my purse. There's money in it."

The kidnapper grabbed her purse, shoved her to the floor, and got into the driver's seat. He said nothing as they drove. Her thoughts raced. She would never see Natali or Max again, or Aunt Carole or Uncle Joseph. And then she made the kind of promise people make in desperate situations that demand impossible wagers: *Please God, if I get out of this, I'll do anything. I'll go to church. Be a better person, a better mother, a better wife. I'll end my affair with Jean-Juste.*

When the vehicle finally stopped, Giselle remained on the floor, curled in a ball under the dashboard. Her kidnapper locked the door and left her inside. In fear, she wet herself, and the smell of urine soured the airless car. She adjusted her position slightly so she could see outside. A sign read, ST. JOSEPH CEMETERY.

Another man, whose face was also covered, waited behind the high, metal-grated fence of the graveyard. He leaned on one of the colorful cement tombs that extended above the ground and looked like a miniature gingerbread house.

They went through her purse. The hijacker came back and shoved a piece of paper and pencil at her. "You need to write a letter for ransom to your family. We want money. Two thousand dollars U.S. by tomorrow or we'll kill you."

She briefly considered that she could write whatever she wanted as she was reasonably certain that neither of them could read. She could tell someone where she was. But then, whom else might they be working with? No, she would follow directions. But she wasn't going to give them Max's name. There was no telling how they would react if they knew she was the wife of a Haitian official. And there was her daughter, Natali. Her hand trembled as she wrote word for word what he told her.

> Uncle Joseph,
>
> I have been kidnapped in Cité Soleil. They will kill me tomorrow at noon unless you bring $2,000 U.S. to St. Joseph's Cemetery. Leave the money in a plastic bag under the tree.
>
> Giselle

"What is your uncle's name and where does he live?"

She hesitated for only a minute. "Joseph Pierre is my uncle. You can find him at the Daughters of Mother Theresa."

"Your uncle is Doctor Joseph?" Her original captor looked closely at her face. His dark glasses were impenetrable.

"Yes." She would say no more.

He motioned to the other man to step aside. They argued, but she couldn't make out everything they said except for the final words of the first kidnapper.

"No! We can't do it."

The other man returned to her.

"My friend is a fool. He's weak. Your uncle helped his nephew. Said he would have died if it hadn't been for him. You go." He waved her driver's license at her. "But I'm keeping this. If you say a word to anyone, I'll find you and kill you and your family." He threw her purse as far as he could in one direction and her keys in the other. He joined his friend and together they ran away.

Giselle could not stop shaking. She was certain her legs would never carry her to find her purse and keys. But they did and somehow she and the Toyota found their way back through the maze and to the coffin-maker's shop. She stopped a block before to straighten her hair and clothes and freshen up with some baby wipes she kept in her dash. It was less than two hours since she dropped Sister Jacquie off.

The nun was standing in the street with a small rectangular package wrapped in brown paper. "There you are. I thought you got lost."

She wanted more than anything to tell Sister Jacquie what had happened. But she didn't dare. And if Sister Jacquie noticed her hands still trembling as she gripped the steering wheel, her silence, or the vague smell of urine and baby wipes, she didn't let on. She just chattered away about how they loved to raise the price when they knew the sisters were paying.

When they arrived back at the compound, she gave her uncle an extra big hug and didn't even argue when he insisted on driving back to Petionville. She locked all the doors in the house and bolted the windows, despite the heat. Then she read Natali three bedtime stories and rubbed her back until she fell asleep. When Max got home from work, she didn't fuss about how late he was, again. She poured them both a drink and they watched TV—a Dominican channel. After Max went to bed, she saw the news. The winning lottery ticket was announced—8 . . . 0 . . . 8. She remembered her promise and finally the tears found her.

8

KATE

SAN FRANCISCO
MAY 1985

Michael's funeral took place in a small nondenominational chapel just outside the Haight-Ashbury District, three months before Kate's baby was due. It rained that morning, a respectable downpour, which reluctantly joined with the infamous fog that rolled in off San Francisco Bay. Cool and penetrating, the heavy mist defied umbrellas and raincoats and blanketed the city. Kate pulled her oversized cardigan around her for warmth, but it still gaped over her growing belly. She shivered as she walked the short block from the bus stop.

Inside the chapel there was no music, no singing, and no crying. Only the steady cadence of the raindrops tapped a gentle rhythm on two skylights, beneath which a simple pine casket was centered, its lid closed. A twisted wreath of lavender and cedar rested on top, along with a picture of Michael, tan, with full cheeks and a grin holding Tuffy, his Siamese cat. The photograph had been taken a year earlier, before Michael was diagnosed with AIDS and before he became Kate's patient. On either side were modest bouquets of wildflowers with daisies, jasmine, and yarrow. As Kate inhaled the sweet aroma that diffused into the dampness and filled the chapel, she was both sad and grateful to be there.

Only six people attended the service; just enough to fill the first two rows in the chapel. Kate knew each one of them and reminisced about the role they had played in the last nine months of her patient's life. She nodded to Michael's parents first. Edward, his father, moved closer to his wife, Marian, and made room for Kate between him and Michael's younger sister, Amy, who was seated next to his partner, George. With one giant arm encircling the girl's shoulders, Michael's sister rested her head against George's chest. Kate longed for the physical comfort of someone who shared this loss with her.

"Whoa!" Kate let out a cry when the baby kicked from behind her navel. That one was powerful. She looked around to see if anyone had noticed.

Sure enough, Edward leaned across Marian, winked, and whispered, "Do you think you have another soccer player in there?"

Kate shrugged and said, "Maybe!" She hoped for a girl this time. But she reminded herself that a healthy baby was all she really wanted. Her legs ached and remained swollen from morning to night to morning again these past few weeks.

Reverend Tom gathered his notes and Bible from his office behind the podium. Michael's mother, despite her son's initial protests, chose the Methodist minister. In his last months, Michael had practiced Taoism and would have preferred his own priest. But he had relented. His mother had requested little else of him in his last months.

On the other end of the aisle was Kerline. She had transferred to the outpatient AIDS clinic a few months earlier so she could spend the nights with her sister as she faced the final weeks with her disease. It was the same clinic where Michael had received his chemotherapy for Kaposi's sarcoma before he decided to stop all treatment the month before he died. For the past three months, Kerline had come to Michael and George's home twice a week to change his dressings. In the end, neither the poisons of modern medicine nor the mantras of ancient Chinese religion could halt the progression of the disfiguring violet tumors that marked his skin and throat.

A few weeks back, when Michael wasn't able to keep his clinic appointment with her, he had called Kate and invited her to stop by after work for a little party.

Michael had been on the couch, bundled in a blanket, and Edward and Marian sat at the kitchen table. Kerline was already there, ladling spoonfuls of lumpy orange soup from a big pot on the stove.

"Soup *jamou*," Kerline had explained. "It's pumpkin soup with potatoes, carrots, and onions. We serve it on New Year's Day in Haiti for good luck." Always the nurse, she added, "Lots of vitamins and calories."

It was delicious and everyone, including Michael, had asked for a second helping. In keeping with the spirit of the celebration, Michael had poured mugs of thick eggnog sprinkled with nutmeg. Then he led them all in a toast, ceremoniously and informally attired in bathrobe and slippers with the abandoned IV pole doubling as his microphone.

"Happy New Year, everybody!"

This small effort had left him coughing, and George rushed to his partner as he crumpled onto the couch.

The eggnog was a special request from Michael, a favorite tradition from his childhood. Edward had brought several quarts from his dairy farm in Ohio when they finally acknowledged that their son would not see another new year. Even Marian had accepted a drop of five-star Barbancourt. The premium Haitian rum was another of Kerline's contributions to their celebration.

That same night, Kerline confided to Kate. "I don't know

how much more I can take." The woman stared at the half-empty bottle of rum. Everything else had been scrubbed, washed, and put away in Kerline's usual efficient manner.

"I know, honey." Kate was tempted to take a drink herself. But with the baby on the way, she would never give in. Still she felt the same despair. AIDS was a brutal opponent. One minute she wanted to pick up her sword and slash through the virus and the devastating infections it caused, and even more, the shame and the guilt. The next minute she wanted to cower behind her shield and protect herself and everyone she cared about from the scourge of the disease.

After they had finished the eggnog and dishes, Kerline said her farewells, George went to the gym, and it was just Kate and Michael and his parents.

Kate requested something quite precious, something she never would have felt entitled to at the beginning of her residency. She asked, "Mr. and Mrs. Rose, can I have a few minutes alone with Michael?"

Marian started to protest, but Edward took his wife's hand and said, "I could use a walk. Please come with me, dear."

Kate wasn't exactly sure what she wanted to say during what she expected would be her last conversation with Michael. Turned out he took the lead.

"Guess we're in the bottom of the ninth and I'm about to strike out," he attempted a grin. "Always thought I'd go out swinging." He tried to mimic a batter's pose, but didn't even have the strength to lift his arms.

She just couldn't pick up the thread of his baseball analogy this time. "Michael, I think you have to be the most courageous person I know."

"Well, thanks, doc. That means a lot coming from you."

She met his eyes and held them, imagining they both needed each other to believe the significance of what had just been said.

"I don't think I've been afraid of dying. You guys are great with the pain meds." He gave her one of his thumbs up and smiled a small smile that contradicted the look in his eyes. "It's the being dead, the being gone. You know?"

It was hard to believe he was the same age as she was. He seemed so much wiser. She wondered if that was just Michael or if it was because he was facing death. It occurred to her that she hadn't known him when he wasn't facing death.

"Dad and George, they'll be okay. But I'm worried about her . . . my mom," he continued. "She carries that Bible around with her everywhere she goes. I swear she has it memorized from Genesis to Revelation." He looked off to some distant place. "But I think her God is as much a stranger to her as he is to me."

Kate just listened. What did she know about religion or God or faith?

"She'll stop blaming me when I'm gone—you know, for bringing the curse down upon myself because I'm gay."

She didn't argue; she had the same impression.

"There's going to be a lot of emptiness when that blame is gone." For the first time in their conversation, Kate thought Michael might start crying.

She reached out for his hands. They were so cold she wanted to hold them to her heart and warm them. "If that happens, Michael, maybe her God will find a way in." Perhaps that really was the way it happened.

Michael nodded. "My only other regret is I can't stay longer and help fight. Not just for people like me, but everyone—like Kerline's sister and that little boy on TV with hemophilia, Ryan White. The one they kicked out of school."

Kate felt ashamed of her own ambivalence the last few months. Michael must have sensed it.

"What about you? I hope you stay in the game. The team needs you," he said.

She hadn't told him that the doctor was worried about her blood pressure and had all but insisted she take the rest of her pregnancy off. Kate declined, explaining she just had to get through June so she could move on to a second-year position after the baby was born. But every day she felt more drained.

She thought about her plans to travel to far-off lands and be a jungle doctor. That her dream seemed so unreal to her now, made her feel sad and lost. Maybe it would never happen, or maybe her jungle really was in her own backyard.

"I'm going to do what I can, Michael." A vague promise, but one she could keep.

And now with Michael's passing, Kate was reminded that the stigma of AIDS didn't end with death; it just extended to those left behind. Edward called Kate the night Michael died, tears in his voice. "We can't find a funeral home that will accept Michael's body. I don't understand. We don't know what to do."

It wasn't the first time Kate had received a distressed call from one of her patients' family. She recommended a Chinese gentleman named Mr. Lee. He owned one of the few parlors in the city willing to embalm the bodies of AIDS patients. Edward had cried in gratitude when they finally found a place to take their son.

The morning of Michael's funeral, Mr. Lee respectfully stood at the back of the room. How many near-empty chapels had he surveyed in the last few years?

It was an unlikely assortment of individuals. Everyone dressed in black or gray. Such different faces, all wearing the same expression, pale and still with spent, red-rimmed eyes.

Kate was certain everything was just how Michael would have wanted it.

The Reverend stood at the podium. No microphone was necessary as he began. "Michael's mother asked that I read this in honor of her son: 'Let all bitterness and wrath and anger and clamor and slander be put away from you, along with all malice. Be kind to one another, tenderhearted, forgiving one another, as God in Christ forgave you. For God has not destined us for wrath, but to obtain salvation . . .'"

Michael's sister stood in the back of the chapel, handing a sprig of lavender and cedar to each guest as they exited. Edward approached Kate after the service.

"Thank you for coming." He grasped her hands with both of his. They were rough from his work on the farm, but imparted a familiar gentle strength, like his son. "We know how busy you are. Michael really appreciated your kindness—we all did."

His wife stood beside him nodding, but said nothing.

"That was a beautiful passage from the Bible, Mrs. Rose." She thought about her last conversation with Michael and hoped that his mother would find some peace beneath her grief.

"I'll never forget your son." Kate tried to hug Edward, but her stomach got in the way. They both backed off clumsily. She searched for the right words. But nowhere in her vast inventory of medical facts could she unearth a remedy to alleviate the pain of a mother and father who were about to bury their only son. "Take care. Call us if there's anything you need, anything else we can do." It was all she could find.

She had planned on taking a cab back to town, but when she stepped outside, she changed her mind. The sun was just beginning to break through the mist. She was a little tired, but a walk would feel good. She decided to collect Danny from daycare first. They would still have time to go to the park and feed the ducks, as she had promised that morning when she dropped him off. The daycare center was next to the hospital where Mark worked. His shift wouldn't be over until later that afternoon.

As she walked past the familiar sites—the coffeehouses, the street vendors, all the activity she had come to love about this city 2,500 miles from her home—she thought about the past year; what she had learned and how she had changed. She reflected on the clues she may have missed—clues about what her patients really needed from the medical system and from her, and clues about the increasing void in her relationship with Mark—the late-night emergencies, the phone hang-ups when she answered. She inhaled the sweet fragrance of the cedar and lavender. By the time she arrived at the daycare center, she felt better. Her path wasn't completely clear to her, but like that day's changeable San Francisco sky, the clouds were beginning to abate and she felt a renewed sense of what she needed to do.

Danny beamed when he saw her walk in. "Mom, are we going to feed the ducks? I saved part of my sandwich," he announced.

"Okay, Buddy. But just for a little while. Mommy's tired and hungry." She grabbed his jacket and knapsack. She looked for Mark's car in the parking lot, but it wasn't there. He was probably at home already. That would be great. She'd get her feet up and rest for a few hours like she promised her doctor.

After the park they stopped at the market to pick up items for dinner, and then walked uphill three blocks back to their apartment. She had to stop and catch her breath a minute before climbing the two flights of stairs to their unit. She peeled her shoes off her swollen feet, set the groceries and flowers on the kitchen counter, and put a tape in the VCR for Danny. Her husband was not home and there were no messages on the answering machine. She picked up the phone and tapped in Mark's beeper numbers.

She watched TV with Danny while she waited. Then she called the surgical residents' lounge. After ten rings, she gave up and paged Mark again.

"What's up?" He sounded annoyed when he finally returned her page.

There was laughter in the background and music.

"Hey Deb—get me another one will you?" a voice Kate couldn't identify called above the music.

Was that her imagination, too? Debbie always seemed to be right there when she talked to Mark.

"We just got home. Are you still at the hospital?" She was hoping for a credible explanation.

She felt an uneasiness, and her suspicions were confirmed when he answered, "Yep. I'm in the residents' lounge. We're uh . . . watching TV until we get some uh . . . lab results on one of the ICU patients."

She wasn't letting it slide this time. "I just called the lounge. No one answered."

"God, Katie. What's your problem?" He must have remembered where she had been then, because his voice softened. "How was it?"

"Sad. There weren't many people there. But still it was—I don't know exactly—nice."

Suddenly she didn't have the energy to offer any more details. Nor did she have the energy to confront him with what she suspected was another lie about being at the hospital when he was out for a beer with friends. There would be time for that later. "I thought I'd cook us a proper dinner. When do you think you'll be home?"

"Oh, I forgot to tell you. I'm picking up an extra shift moonlighting in the ER tonight. I'll be home after rounds tomorrow, hopefully by lunch."

"But Mark, we haven't had dinner together in over a month. I really wish you would just come home. Can't they get someone else to work?" This was the third time in a month this had happened, and she had the same sick feeling in her stomach this time, too. "Besides, I told you yesterday that I have to work tomorrow. You were supposed to be here with Danny."

"Ask Mrs. Cole if she can sit with him. We can use the money, Kate. You know that, with the baby coming." The irritation in his voice came through loud and clear. "Have you decided what you want to do after September when the baby comes? They're not going to hold your spot forever. It's a great opportunity for us to stay here and finish our programs."

"I know, I know," Kate conceded. "It's just that, well, it's been so hard, and with two kids . . . you're never here anymore." The last few months, as Mark was pushing more and more for them to stay in San Francisco, he was home less and less.

Just then she heard the insistent beep of his pager. "I have to go now. We can talk about it when I get home tomorrow?"

There was no point reminding him that she would be at the hospital all day and night Sunday. He had already hung up. Maybe she would just reheat macaroni and cheese for their dinner since it would only be her and Danny now.

She decided she needed to check in with someone. Someone who would be on her side of whatever decision she made. It would be evening news-time back home.

"Hello, Dad? It's me." She eased into the kitchen chair with the cordless phone and put her feet up on a stool. They were swollen to twice their normal size. "No, nothing's wrong. I'm okay. Just four more weeks, and I'll be done." She placed her hand on her stomach, reassured by the baby's eager movement within her. "No, the baby's okay, too." She closed her eyes and inhaled the lavender and cedar. If her conversation with Mark took the direction she expected, she would need someone strong and steady to help her navigate the next few months—a baby on the way, a four-year-old, and the uncertainty of where she belonged in medicine.

She looked at her sleeping red-haired soccer player and felt again the child growing within her. She knew that she would find her way back to where she belonged caring for her patients. But maybe like her dad had said years ago, she had to care for herself and her family first. Right now there was only one place she knew she could do that.

"Hey Dad . . . hmmm . . . yeah listen, Dad. Danny and I are coming home."

2

CROSSINGS
(1991–1993)

What the eye does not see,

the heart does not know.

—Haitian proverb

9

KATE

PORT AU PRINCE
SEPTEMBER 1991

Applause erupted throughout the A-300 Airbus as the front set of wheels bounced up then abruptly down again on the runway. The plane proceeded in a rumbling taxi toward the terminal at the Port au Prince airport. Kate looked up from her Creole-English medical dictionary. Gambling that the caramel-complexioned woman sitting next to her was Haitian-American and spoke English, she asked, "Is something wrong with the plane?"

"No, *Chèrie*." The woman's perfectly manicured hands were silently folded in her lap. "It happens every flight. No matter how difficult life is in our country, Haitians are always happy to come home. I'm sure you are, too, when you return to—the United States, isn't it?"

"Yes, I'm from Pennsylvania. But I've lived in Atlanta, Georgia, for the last two years." She extended her hand. "My name is Kate Rigando. This is my first trip to your country."

The woman raised an eyebrow but accepted her hand. "I'm Giselle." She nodded at the book in Kate's lap. "Are you a nurse?"

"A doctor, actually."

"Really? What is your specialty?"

"Family practice—mostly women and children immigrants and refugees, since we moved to Atlanta." For the time being, Kate was satisfied with her career shift. Her year of international health training in San Francisco and a three-year residency in family practice in Pittsburgh had prepared her well. "And you, what do you do?" she asked her seat partner.

"I'm from Port au Prince. I paint and teach at the University of Fine Arts and Literature." Giselle rubbed her right temple. "It seems that flying gives me such a headache these days."

"I have Tylenol. Would you like some?" Kate tugged at her overstuffed backpack wedged under the seat in front of her. As she leaned over, a photo she had been using as a bookmark fell from the dictionary.

"No, thank you. Medicine doesn't work very well. I think they're migraines." Giselle retrieved the photo. "Is this your family? Your children are beautiful. The boy has red hair like you. But your daughter, her hair is so dark. She must resemble her father."

Kate took the photo from Giselle's thinly tapered fingers. "Yes, Danny is eleven. He's my soccer player and definitely favors me. I'm mostly Irish—my maiden name was Murphy. Jen is only six and dark haired like her father. He's Italian." She stroked the photograph gently, like she was touching their little faces. "I hate to compare, but they have always been so different."

Kate thought back to the last few weeks of her pregnancy and the day Jen was born. She had started hemorrhaging one morning soon after Danny and she returned to Mars. They were staying with her dad, while Mark had remained in San Francisco, uncertain if he wanted to leave. Her OB was convinced she would lose the baby. But she didn't.

"I like to say Danny is my doer and Jenny's my thinker and my fighter." Two rocky months in the neonatal ICU testified to that.

"Yes, that is funny. Children can be so different. I have only one, a girl. She's ten, and she and I will be returning to the U.S. in a few weeks to join my husband in New York." The Haitian woman lowered her voice. "Your husband must be concerned about you traveling to Haiti. There's been some trouble, you know?"

"We heard a little about it." They had briefly discussed cancelling the trip, but their contact in Haiti had reassured them it was safe to come. "My husband is okay with me traveling. He's a doctor, too. He does research at the CDC in Atlanta. We moved there after we finished our residency training in Pittsburgh in 1989."

Kate thought about her dream to practice medicine in a third-world country. She had almost given up on it after she left San Francisco. Mark admitted his affair with one of the other residents in his program, and although they had agreed to separate, when Jen was born he rushed back East and gave up his residency in San Francisco for a position closer to them. When one of her colleagues in Atlanta called and said another doctor had to back out of the Haiti trip, Kate decided it was time to get back to her plan. Jen and Danny were old enough that she felt okay leaving them for two weeks with Mark and a lineup of sitters and friends who offered to pitch in.

She still couldn't believe it was happening—her first medical trip abroad.

In a low voice she said, "I've always wanted to help people in a poor country. This will be my first experience. I don't know what to expect."

"Ah. You want to be one of our medical missionaries then. Well, good luck." The cool tone in Giselle's voice terminated their conversation. She opened her paperback again and began reading. Their plane was waiting behind two others to enter the gate area.

Giselle was the first person Kate had spoken to, other than the flight attendant. Not usually so quiet on a plane, she was determined to memorize enough Creole medical phrases to be at least conversational by Monday, when they started the clinic. But her attention wandered frequently to the view from her window and the interaction of her fellow passengers. The tour books did not exaggerate. The extensively deforested and deeply eroded mountains arranged in parallel ribbons really did resemble spines of emaciated animals with their ribs protruding.

"*Tet fe mal*. Headache. *Stomak fe mal*. Stomachache," she repeated to herself, trying to remember the proper pronunciation from the Creole tapes she had purchased to prepare for the trip.

Kate waited while the other three people beside her got out, and about a hundred others cleared the aisle. Much of the plane was filled with Americans wearing an assortment of brightly colored T-shirts with hopeful messages such as "Save Haiti" or "Have a Heart for Haiti." After the Haitian woman's icy response, Kate was glad their team opted not to wear a slogan.

Stretching in her seat to get the attention of their team leader, Kate shouted, "Sue, I'll meet you guys as soon as I can." Her voice was lost in the commotion.

The medical team leader, Sue Gray, a pleasantly organized and enthusiastic woman, was on her third trip to the country. During their two pre-planning meetings she had been thorough when briefing them on the logistics and etiquette of international travel.

"You need only one small suitcase for yourself," she cautioned. "The rest of your luggage will be filled with medical supplies for the team."

Kate descended the aluminum steps from the plane, gingerly hanging onto the railing, and walked through the oppressive Haitian heat across the steamy asphalt tarmac to the terminal. In single file, their seven-member team lined up with the other Americans in the visitors' line at immigration.

"*Bonjou*. I mean, *Bonswa*," Kate greeted the man behind the glass shield.

He stamped her passport and handed it back to her without a word.

"*Mesi*," she said, wishing not to stand out as an American tourist.

Two guards with dark glasses dressed in tan uniforms, rifles slung over their shoulders, patrolled the baggage area. The luggage belt was replete with an assortment of boxes, picnic coolers, and suitcases. A red cooler leaked pink liquid onto the belt. One short woman, dressed in flowing, pale-blue religious attire, yanked it off, peeled away the shrink-wrap, and opened the lid. There were two frozen turkeys inside swimming in a pool of melting ice. She poked one of the turkeys.

"Damn it." The sister covered her mouth, looked around, and then quickly down, making the sign of the cross.

"Can I help you, Sister?" Kate smiled and thought back to her grade school days at St. Mary's in Mars.

"I don't suppose you have a refrigerator handy, do you?" She grabbed one handle. "I guess not. Well then, you could grab the other side and help me get this on the cart?"

"No problem." Kate lifted the other end and together they deposited the cooler onto a baggage cart. They both ignored the puddle that was rapidly forming on the floor.

Sister snapped the spout at the bottom of the cooler shut, threw a large duffel bag on top and waved away help from a young Haitian man dressed like a porter. "I guess we'll be having Thanksgiving in September this year. Thank you for your help." She turned and walked to customs.

All seven members of the medical team eventually emerged into the daylight, each dragging two bags. Outside, a crowd of taxi drivers, porters, and hundreds of other hands reached across a short metal fence, trying to grab anything they could.

"I help you. Five dollars."

One man said nothing but held out his hand and briefly

flashed up his gray T-shirt to show a bag filled with thick, brown-and-green liquid taped to his left lower abdomen.

"Was that a colostomy?" Kate asked Sue, who had just bumped into her, courtesy of another hurried traveler.

"No, I doubt it. He was here last year, too, and the bag was on the other side." Sue just smiled through it all.

Finally, they saw a bright-yellow sign floating above several rows of heads with the words, DIDI'S GUESTHOUSE, written in bold, black letters. They watched the sign move away from the pack and to a less-congested area where a smiling young Haitian man stretched up his arm with the placard.

Sue reached him first. "Thoma. *Bonswa! Bonswa!*"

"Hello, Miss Sue. How was your trip?" Thoma said, and took charge of the group. "You, you, and you," he said, and pointed to three eagerly waiting men and then grabbed a suitcase himself. "We're parked over there."

Kate and the rest of the team followed.

Didi's Nissan van was surprisingly comfortable and air-conditioned—more or less. Thoma insisted they roll up the windows. The air inside was cooler, but not exactly cool. The effect on Kate was pleasant enough after the closeness of the plane and the chaos of getting through immigration and customs. There was so much to see. Kate looked around.

"Look at that." Someone pointed to a brightly painted vehicle resembling a pickup truck with a cab on the back. Dozens of Haitians were crammed inside. Two goats were tied to the outside, upside down. Their bleating penetrated the windows of the van.

"It says *Mesi* Jesus. Thank you, Jesus—that must be a church group. Do you think they're going to a Vodou ceremony? Are they going to sacrifice the animals?" Kate asked.

"No," Sue answered. "It's a *tap-tap*—Haiti's cheapest and most popular form of public transportation. When someone wants off they '*tap-tap*' on the side to let the driver know. The goats belong to one of the passengers, probably bought at the market. Tap-taps always have religious messages on the side—'Thank you, Jesus,' 'Bless us God.'"

There were no traffic lights, and turn signals apparently weren't used. When the van needed to change lanes, Thoma gave two quick taps on the horn. At one complicated intersection that would have warranted four-way stop signs in the U.S., Thoma slowed the van. A wiry barefoot boy jumped on the front bumper and proceeded to wipe the windshield with a dusty rag. Thoma knocked on the windshield. "*Alle! Alle!*"

The boy stuck out his hand and rubbed his stomach. Despite his small size, his brown eyes pleaded through the smudged glass and tugged at Kate's heart. Her money pouch felt heavy around her neck. They had been forewarned not to give money to beggars. She didn't anticipate it would feel so contradictory, and she vowed to make a donation to the Red Cross as soon as she returned.

"*Alle! Alle!*" Thoma barely waited for him to step back before accelerating through the intersection.

For a few minutes, no one said anything. Finally, in a more somber mood, Kate broke the silence. "What time is it?"

"Five o'clock U.S., four o'clock Haiti," Sue answered.

It was almost four hours since they landed, and the pilot's predicted 50 percent chance of rain grew to a certainty. Some of the Haitians ducked in doorways. Others joined arms and walked under small sheets of plastic. A few had umbrellas. None looked fazed by the rapidly forming puddles and currents of gray water flowing down the streets carrying garbage. The cars didn't slow down either.

Suddenly it seemed like every street headed straight up.

Tires screeched. The smell of burning rubber and diesel fumes mixed with the rain.

Thoma turned and started up one of the more substantial hills Kate had seen so far. Within the first ten feet, the van was paralyzed, wheels spinning in vain. He carefully backed down, gunned the accelerator, and attempted to gain momentum. This time he made it a few feet farther but nearly knocked over a woman selling street meat. Kate backed away from the window when the woman shook her fist and shouted something in Creole.

Thoma shrugged at the woman and turned to them. "Sorry. I think you will have to walk from here. It's not far."

"OK. Everybody take your personal bag. Thoma will wait with the rest until some of the other guys can get here to help. Stay together," Sue instructed the team.

They inched up the hill on concrete glazed with rain.

"Bring sensible shoes," Sue had cautioned before they left the States.

Nikes were sensible, weren't they? Kate thought, just as her right foot slid beneath her and she landed on her right hip. Her water bottle fell from her hand and rolled down the street. Each time she tried to get up, she slipped like a kid on ice skates for the first time. She hollered, "Help!" and laughed at her own helplessness.

Sue was a few yards uphill. "Kate, are you okay? I'm coming to help you . . . oh . . . oh . . ." She began her own dance and barely stopped herself by grabbing onto a woman selling charcoal.

Insistent but gentle hands seized Kate's elbows and lifted her back to her feet and eased the backpack off her shoulders. Two Haitian men guided her up the hill. A little girl appeared with the runaway water bottle and skipped back to her mother, who waved in response to Kate's shout of "*mesi*."

With her escorts, Kate passed her team members and was the first to arrive at Didi's Guesthouse. One of the men rapped on a heavy metal gate. They deposited her with her backpack inside and continued up the hill.

"*Mesi*," she called behind them.

She walked up the short landing, found a wooden-and-rattan rocking chair on the front porch and waited. A group of barefoot boys kicked a deflated soccer ball around an empty field across the street. Partially surrounding the field was a huge cement wall with faded graffiti painted on it. In the corner of the field, a small tree held a yellow mango, ripe and ready to be picked. One of the boys kicked a ball at the trunk again and again. But the fruit held tight to its branch.

Just as the last of the team joined Kate on the guesthouse porch, an oversized Haitian woman who introduced herself as Didi welcomed them with warm hugs and cool drinks.

Thoma beeped the horn, gave a wave, and the gate opened yet again. Three young men sitting on the outside wall at Didi's began unloading the van. Kate and a few others got up and started toward the van to help.

"No, you all sit," Didi said and laughed. "They'll take care of your luggage."

After she finished her Coke, Kate took out her camera. "Okay, everyone—first group picture in Haiti."

She attempted to arrange the lot—Thoma and Didi as fresh as Sunday morning church and her seven teammates worn and ragged.

One of the young men who had unloaded the van stepped forward, pointing to the camera and then to himself, and said, "I take for you?"

"Yes, *mesi*." Kate gave him the camera and joined the rest. They linked arms and said, "Smile!"

Even though she had only met these folks a few hours ago, it already felt like they were old friends, and she was having fun—something she hadn't expected on this trip. So far nothing had been what she expected. In five hours her most-used Creole word had been *mesi* and the only person she had helped was a cursing nun trying to rescue a melting turkey.

CHAPTER

10

KATE

PORT AU PRINCE

After a quick breakfast of bread and peanut butter at Didi's, Kate, along with fourteen others—her medical team and translators— wedged into the nine-passenger van. They were on their way to the church, which would serve as their clinic for the next two weeks.

This was their third day in Port au Port, and personal hygiene, bad hair, and general cleanliness had been redefined by limited water for bathing and unlimited heat and dust. Kate's senses were acclimating to the earthy smells of the streets—burnt street meat cooking on charcoal, garbage rotting, and the gritty feel of the air. The seasoned members of the group scrambled for the window seats and quickly covered their faces with brightly colored handkerchiefs to ward off the dust and diesel fumes. The vehicle swerved around potholes, schoolchildren, animals, and market women, and stirred up dust on the rugged and rocky road as they jostled against each other, laughing and teasing. They looked more like a bunch of bandits than a medical team.

Kate didn't participate much in the constant chatter. She thought about their orientation session the evening before.

"Be flexible," Sue reminded them again. "We are here to serve." She had explained the schedule. For the first few days, women would have their Pap smears taken and, by the end of the second week, they would return for the results and a treatment plan if necessary. Children were also seen each day and, by mid-week, they would open up their services to the men, as well. Emergencies of all sorts could present at any time. Last year three babies were delivered during the two-week trip. Sue also relayed that there had been some talk about street demonstrations and if that happened, all their plans might change.

As they turned the corner, Kate had that knotty feeling in her stomach like she used to get in med school just before she would break the seal on one of their thick standardized test booklets. She never knew what would be on the next page and whether or not she would be up to the challenge.

The rest of the noisy group fell silent as well when they saw hundreds of women waiting for their arrival. Most of the women looked to be middle-aged. Some gathered in small groups and others were starting to line up at one end of the courtyard.

Kate was the first to comment. "My God, how can we possibly see all these people? We didn't bring nearly enough medicine or supplies for even one day of this."

"Don't worry. Madame La Belle will hand out numbers. She knows we can only see about eighty patients each day. The others will keep coming back. We'll do okay," Sue reassured her.

The last hundred yards of the road to the church, they traveled on foot, carrying the plastic crates of supplies. Kate and Sue were the last to descend the steep road. On the walk down, Kate noticed that within five minutes all the numbers had been distributed. A few women argued in protest. Most of the others walked away quietly or in small groups back toward the main road to Port au Prince.

The structure that looked neither like a church nor a clinic consisted of poorly aligned cement blocks with a battered tin roof, no door, and no glass in the windows. Nothing was square and nothing was plumb. The floor was simply the dirt of the ground, and true to their pre-trip briefing, there was no electricity or running water. Everything was covered with a thin layer of cement and road dust—ubiquitous and gray.

A man with a bullhorn stood outside and shouted directions to the crowd in Creole.

In one corner of the churchyard, Tim, one of the team members, was setting up for the educational sessions. The topics would include the importance of hand washing, clean water, and HIV/AIDS prevention and education. They brought small, hotel-sized hand soaps and little bottles of Clorox to distribute. Sue had typed printed instructions in Creole, along with a simple diagram on how to add precisely two drops of bleach per gallon of water.

One woman without a number sitting amongst the others captured Kate's eye for three reasons. First, she noticed the little girl sitting next to her with a protruding belly and ginger-colored hair, the marks of malnutrition. Second, the woman was pale with a complexion that reminded Kate of the gray and weathered driftwood they saw scattered on the beach during their drive along the coast the day before. But what prompted Kate to take the woman's hand and lead her inside ahead of the others was that every few minutes she grabbed her stomach, rocking back and forth on the wooden bench.

By the time Kate entered with the woman, the others had moved aside the wooden pews and had draped bed sheets over bungee cords, creating makeshift walls to allow a little privacy for the patients to undress and the doctors to make their examinations. There were three exam areas and a folding metal table brought by the team that would serve as a pharmacy and lab area.

The woman undressed behind a curtain and carried her

clothes, tattered but neatly folded, to the exam table. She wore one of the blue paper gowns that the team had brought with them. She eased herself onto the table. Kate noticed a pink stain growing on the exam sheet and although the woman tried to conceal it, there was no mistaking her bloody underwear. She handed Kate her intake form:

DELVA, ADELAIDE
AGE: 23

A quick glance at her chart told Kate that her blood pressure, pulse, and temperature were all normal. Her weight was listed at 40 kg. Kate did a quick calculation and realized the woman weighed only about 90 pounds.

Thoma, now serving as translator, stood between Adelaide and herself, and asked the usual opening question, "Madame, why are you here today?"

"The pain," the woman replied, her frail body collapsing in half.

"Your period?" Kate was skeptical; the woman seemed so distressed.

"I don't know. I bleed all the time now. So much my boyfriend left me for someone else." Adelaide's eyes were fixed on her lap and her voice was barely audible.

"Well, let's check you." Moving her hands clockwise over the thin abdomen, Kate sensed something. When she inserted her gloved hand for the internal exam, she found a mass extending deep into the vaginal canal. Nothing else would feel that way—rock hard and immobile. The woman had cervical cancer.

Kate pondered the dozen questions she might ask a patient in the U.S. She'd only seen this far-advanced cervical cancer a few times with her immigrant patients in Atlanta. It was a devastating diagnosis even with radiation and chemo. And this was Haiti. What could she offer this young woman? "When did you last see a doctor?" Kate kept her gaze steady; she didn't want to upset Adelaide until she knew all the facts.

Adelaide reported through Thoma that she came to this clinic a year ago. Kate searched through the medical records that traveled with the team. She located a manila file for Delva, Adelaide. *She had actually been seen twice before.* Kate scanned the next few pages until she found a lab report from 1989:

CERVICAL PAP SMEAR: SEVERE DYSPLASIA

The diagnosis was highlighted in yellow and initialed *SG 10/89.* That indicated the precancerous Pap smear result had been noted by Sue on an earlier trip, and recorded in the database created for the women's visiting health program. But what, if anything, had been done about it?

Flipping back to the front of the record she found a short note from September of the previous year:

9/29/90: PATIENT WITH WEIGHT LOSS AND RASH
ON BACK. PROBABLE HERPES INFECTION. SUSPECT
HIV/AIDS. REPEAT PAP DONE. PATIENT UNDERSTANDS
INSTRUCTIONS TO TAKE SMEAR TO LAB AND HAS SLIP FOR
HIV TEST. RETURN NEXT WEEK FOR FOLLOW UP.

Written next to the date a week later:

PATIENT DID NOT RETURN. MADAME LA BELLE
WILL CONTACT HER.

"I don't understand." Kate turned to Thoma. "What happened? Why didn't she come back to the clinic?" *And why didn't Madame La Belle or someone else find her?*

Adelaide picked at an invisible spot on her paper gown, quivering and tearful as she spoke in a low voice. Thoma translated to Kate. "They told her that she must take her exam to the lab in Pacot. The lab told her it cost 250 goudes for the blood work and the Pap smear reading and that she would have to return in one week for the results. That would mean two tap-taps each way and two days away from her market business. She didn't have the money."

Two hundred and fifty goudes was the equivalent of ten U.S. dollars, a bottle of cheap wine for her, Kate calculated. But in Haiti that was two weeks' profit from the market—if Adelaide was lucky.

Kate pulled out another document sheathed in plastic. She turned to the last page. There was a grant from the International Health Foundation and it included $5,000 for tests and treatment.

"Is that your daughter with you outside?" Kate asked Adelaide.

"Yes. I call her my little bird." Thoma translated for her, from *ti zwazo*.

"*Ti zwazo?*" echoed Kate.

"Because her daughter searches the ground for corn and peas after market is finished. Sometimes she finds enough for them to make some soup. It is difficult since she became sick. No one will buy her bananas and coffee."

"Oh." Kate recalled the stigma she encountered around HIV back in San Francisco and felt the anger and frustration return from her internship days. "Thoma, does this happen in Haiti?"

He nodded.

"Please explain, she needs a blood test, I'm giving her something for pain, and please, I want her and her daughter to come back in two weeks. I'll think of something by then. And this is for her." Kate reached in her pocket and pulled out 1,000 goudes. "What is her daughter's name? She must eat, they both must eat." To hell with what they were told about handing out money. This woman needed help now. Obviously the medical mission strategy had failed her. If Adelaide's abnormal Pap smear had been treated, she might have had a chance. HIV aside, cervical cancer was a horrible way to die, and her daughter was clearly starving. What chance would the girl have without her mother?

Thoma translated and responded, "Her daughter's name is Tieina. She's almost seven."

Adelaide took the money and the two slips of paper, one for the lab and the other for the medicine, and laid them on her clothes. As the woman stood down from the table for the first time, Kate faced her patient. Barefoot, a few inches shorter than herself, Adelaide grasped her hands.

In her only words of English that morning she said, "Thank you, doctor."

Adelaide gathered her clothes with one hand and with the other parted the curtain to re-dress, but stopped. Looking back over her shoulder with a small smile she said to Kate, "Your hair is very beautiful, you know. If you cut a little, my daughter could sell it in the market. She would get a good price for you."

"Thank you, Adelaide. Maybe I will." Kate touched her hair and realized Adelaide was simply paying her a compliment. But she thought if selling her hair really would help the child or her mother, she would shave it off at her scalp.

Kate nodded to Thoma to come outside with her as they left Adelaide to finish dressing. "I need to speak to Madame La Belle right away."

"She's not here yet, Doctor. But I can get her assistant, Miss Sylvie. Maybe she can answer your questions."

A few minutes later, Thoma returned with a lighter-complexioned Haitian woman wearing a crisp white blouse and blue skirt. "Yes." She peered over her black half spectacles. "You need something, Doctor? I will help you."

Kate was relieved that she spoke some English and briefly explained Adelaide's condition. "I think there must be a misunderstanding. There is money in the program to pay for lab tests and treatment."

Miss Sylvie answered to Thoma in Creole. Kate, listening intently and watching both of the Haitians, pulled out a few familiar words, *Bondye* and *puni*.

Thoma translated that there wasn't enough money for all the women to have lab testing; Miss Sylvie had to choose.

Kate began searching through her Creole dictionary. She remembered from last night's blessing at dinner that *Bondye* meant God. *Puni*? She didn't know. Turning to "P" in the dictionary, she found *puni* meant punish.

"Thoma, I need you to tell me *exactly* what she said." Kate looked directly at Miss Sylvie. Was this corruption, bad medicine, or the same stigma she encountered nearly a decade ago in the U.S.?

Thoma looked uncomfortable at being caught in the middle. "You see, Doctor, Adelaide has the Disease and since she is not married, she can only have gotten this from sinning." His voice became softer. "Miss Sylvie believes that her sickness comes from the hands of God and there is little she can do. She chooses to help the other women."

Beads of sweat formed on Kate's forehead. Miss Sylvie never moved her gaze from Kate's as she interrupted Thoma's translation and continued for herself. "You are only here for two weeks and then you go home, show your pictures, and tell your stories. You think you know how to fix everything in Haiti."

Kate recalled her conversation with the woman on the plane. Admittedly she didn't know much about this country. But she knew there was a young child soon to be motherless and perhaps that could have been prevented. She walked away from the Haitian woman without another word and returned to her exam area. There were so many others waiting to be seen.

11

ADELAIDE

PORT AU PRINCE
SEPTEMBER 29, 1991

Before the sun was completely up, Adelaide arrived at the church where the American doctors made their clinic. She wasn't going to be without a number today. She liked the red-haired doctor and for the first time in many years, she was hopeful. She told Tieina that morning when her daughter pouted about coming so early. "This woman doctor will do her best for us—with God willing."

It had been a good two weeks for them. With the money from the doctor, they had a hot meal each day and she made a deposit for Tieina to go back to school.

"But Mama, they won't let me go if we don't have all the money. And I'm still hungry."

"I'm going to ask the doctor for the rest of the tuition," she reassured Tieina. "She will get it for us—with God willing."

She must always remember to say that, even if God didn't ever seem to be willing to do much of anything to help her these days. Just when she found someone she could believe in, someone who might actually see her as a human being and not some animal, and that someone might be able to help her, the country was about to explode again. Haiti was never a stranger to trouble. It was always smoldering like a pot of porridge on charcoal. But now the evil men had turned up the heat in Port au Prince. That morning the radio reported rumors of manifestations. And the streets had been especially quiet, which was always a bad sign, like a snake that coiled silently before it struck. *Koulèv ki vle gwo rete nan trou-l.* The snake that wants to get big stays in its hole. She trembled at the thought.

When Madame La Belle appeared, Adelaide was watching Tieina as she practiced writing her letters. Madame wasn't as bad as Miss Sylvie, but she didn't have much to say to Adelaide; she never did, although she had taken a liking to Tieina.

"*Bonjou*, Tieina." Madame hugged her daughter, who gave her a kiss on the cheek. "Did you sleep well, little one?"

"*Oui*, Madame."

Like Adelaide, Tieina had learned to put on a good face. Most other Haitians didn't really care about their problems. She and Tieina hadn't slept in a proper bed in a month—not since they came to Port au Prince from Ti Mirebelais. They had a spot on the floor with Tieina's father's people. Tieina would curl up in a blanket, resting her head in Adelaide's lap. She had slept sitting up for several months now. It helped with the pain, which was always worse at night.

Women were setting up outside the clinic to sell food and artwork. One of the artisans showed her metal work. "Buy something as a gift for your American friends." Haitian women always took advantage of the opportunity to sell something— especially if Americans were around.

"I have no money." Adelaide said and looked away.

Another woman started a charcoal fire and was frying up plantains. Not the sweet kind, but the heavier ones that she used to love piled high with spicy *pikliz*. The pain in her stomach didn't take kindly to spicy food these days. But her heart still craved it and so many other things her body couldn't deliver—like her rendezvouses with Tieina's father. She missed him. They had so little time together. His wife was jealous, and then Adelaide got sick and he stopped coming around at all. His sister said he was sick, too.

The envelope with the results from her blood test was deep in the pocket of her skirt. She was certain Madame La Belle had seen right through her clothes and read the two little words that she prayed and prayed would be different this time—HIV: POSITIVE. Now, she could only wait and hope the doctor would come with something to help her.

Around the edges of the churchyard, a few stray dogs lapped at fading puddles of gray water, ribs jutting beneath their scabby coats. One black-haired dog growled, backed away from the others and the water, and claimed a rare grassy patch beneath a tree. Adelaide shivered, despite the heat. She pulled her daughter close.

A cloud of dust appeared on the road before Adelaide saw the van. Her heart quickened. The Americans would help her and her daughter. This time she knew it. God would be willing.

"*Bonjou*, Adelaide." The doctor remembered her name and what a nice smile she gave her. She looked smaller—like she had lost some weight and looked a little tired, too.

"*Bonjou*, Doctor."

"*Vini.*" The doctor motioned for her to come inside.

The man who translated last week told her she didn't need to undress this time. "The doctor just wants to talk to you for a minute. Do you have your lab result?"

Her heart stopped and her stomach dropped. She nodded and handed the folded envelope to the doctor. She saw no surprise in the doctor's face. She didn't step back from her like the person at the lab did when she got her results. No, she came closer, put her arm on her shoulder, and guided her to a chair before she said a word. Were those tears in her eyes? A person was in real trouble if her doctor cried.

"Adelaide, do you understand what this test is for? Do you understand about HIV?"

"Yes, I am going to die soon." Tears filled her own eyes.

"I'm sorry, Adelaide. HIV is a serious disease. But there is medicine that might help you. I'll talk with Madame La Belle about getting you into a treatment program." The doctor took both of her hands and held them—more like her mother would have done than any doctor Adelaide had known.

"But for today, I have a surgeon coming to see you for the tumor on your cervix, like we talked about the last time. Okay?" The doctor looked at her like she looked at her own daughter, Tieina, when she wanted something to be true, but wasn't quite sure it ever could be.

"*Mesi*, Doctor. I know you'll do your best for me." Adelaide felt certain of that, but as certain that even the doctor's best would matter very little.

"Wait here. I'll get Madame La Belle."

From the exam room window, Adelaide watched her daughter out of the corner of her eye. Tieina was sitting on the cement stoop just outside the clinic. Her head was lowered and she was intently drawing something on a piece of paper with the crayons the Americans had given her on the first day. Her daughter loved to draw and write. She made little poems for Adelaide on special occasions like her birthday, and when she was feeling especially sick. As hard as she tried to hide it from her, Adelaide knew it was only a matter of time. She had seen it before, the way people wasted away to nothing from this disease. Oh, what would become of her child if she died? Would everyone shun her, as well? She couldn't let anyone in Port au Prince know she had the disease. Surely Tieina would be left to die just as she would be.

Adelaide stared down at her test result and willed the words to go away. But of course they wouldn't. If she had any regrets about the past, she only had to think of Tieina. She made a promise, like the one she made at Saut d'Eau when she was pregnant. Trading all the dreams she had for herself for just one, she closed her eyes and whispered, "Keep my child safe." And when she looked out the window again, she saw him. The black stray dog that had frightened her earlier that morning was inching toward her daughter.

"No!" she cried. Her feet could not carry her fast enough to save her child.

12

KATE

PORT AU PRINCE
SEPTEMBER 29, 1991

The instant the mangy black dog sank its teeth into Kate's forearm, the clock started ticking in her head. Crumpled against the wall of the makeshift clinic, Tieina, the dog's intended target, covered her head and whimpered in a small voice, "Mama, Mama."

Kate was frozen in her position between the distressed child and the desperate animal. Froth outlined his mouth and partially obscured his teeth, bared and ready to strike again. But it was his eyes that captured Kate's attention—dazed and red, frightened and lost.

Even though she knew she shouldn't—she had nothing with which to defend herself or Tieina—she locked her gaze with the dog and stared into the madness, hoping for a glimmer of mercy, something she could appeal to. She found nothing. Slowly, Kate backed away toward the child, shielding her; fearful the dog might strike again and succeed in biting Tieina this time.

The *ti machann*—Haitian market women—who were squatting on the ground jumped up, knocking over their baskets of bananas and mangos.

118

"Alle! Alle!" Several men threw rocks at the dog. His attention diverted from Kate and Tieina, the dog yelped, backed away, and loped behind the building, disappearing down the street.

One small rock grazed Tieina on her forehead. She cried out, "Mama, Mama."

Kate reached out to console the frightened child and realized she was trembling almost as much as Kate was.

Adelaide burst through the doorway. She looked at the rocks on the ground and the blood on Tieina's forehead. She ran to her daughter, gathered her in her arms, and they were quickly gone. The child's drawing and the crayons were forgotten, scattered in the dirt.

With the animal nowhere in sight, a small crowd surrounded Kate. One of the men who had thrown the rocks appeared concerned and asked, *"Laraj?"*

Thoma whispered, "Rabies."

Sue came running. "Kate, what is it? What happened?" She hurried to her and reached for Kate's bloody arm.

Kate backed away. She covered her wound and the blood that was running down her arm. "No! Don't touch me." Even though she had spoken in English, her message was clear. It was only then that she acknowledged the pain throbbing and burning in her arm, momentarily distracting her from what Thoma had translated.

Kate insisted on cleaning and dressing the bite herself. Her voice was shaking, but her hands were steady. "Sue, I think that dog has rabies. Tieina is okay; she wasn't bitten. But . . ." She looked down at her wounded arm. "I was." She realized in that one instant, everything had changed.

"What do we need to do? There's a vaccine, right?" Sue asked. "We can go to one of the private hospitals. Surely Dr. Joseph will know someone."

"That's right," Kate said. "Madame La Belle said he would be here today." Kate brought her thoughts back to her patient,

Adelaide. The woman's cancer was too advanced for her to do anything, and Dr. Joseph was one of the few gynecologists still practicing in Haiti.

"Unfortunately, the doctor isn't coming," Madame La Belle said as she joined them. "He sent word with one of the street urchins. Car trouble again and he said it is too dangerous for his niece to drive him. Her husband works for the government. Or should I say *worked* for the government. The streets are getting crazy. Quickly, we must pack everything and go."

"We need to get Kate to a hospital," Sue said.

"I don't think that will be possible today." Madame hardly glanced at either of them before she began throwing patient charts and unused medicines in a box.

"Kate, how long do you have?" Sue asked.

"Ten days," she answered. She pulled a piece of first year medical school trivia from her brain and began to calculate. "I have ten days to get the rabies vaccine. We leave tomorrow. I'll call an old friend at the CDC and make arrangements when we get to Miami. That'll be three or four days at most." Her voice was calm now. "I think we should just go back to the guesthouse like we planned. I'll be okay." There was no need to panic. Tomorrow she'd be back in the U.S. with the best medical care in the world.

Fifteen minutes later they were packed and ready to leave.

"I've spoken to Miss Sylvie. We will do right by Adelaide if we can find her," Madame La Belle said, her voice softened as she looked from Kate's bandaged arm to the nearly empty streets around them.

Thoma picked up the paper from the ground with Tieina's drawing and handed it to Kate. She, Sue, and Tim climbed into the van. The rest of the team had departed for the U.S. early that morning. As they drove away, Kate stared at Tieina's picture of a red rose. Beneath it, in perfect Sunday-school penmanship, was written first in Creole, *Pa Bliye M*, and then in English, *Don't Forget Me*. Kate was already certain she never could; still, what a curious thing for a child to ask.

When the van descended the road to Didi's, Sue pointed to columns of dark-gray smoke rising from the zone where the National Palace was located. Even at this distance, the air was heavy with the pungent odor of rubber burning.

"Thoma, manifestations?" Sue asked.

"Yes," he answered, searching the radio for news.

He rolled the window down just enough to speak briefly with a young man on the street. They seemed to know each other.

"We have to go another way," he announced to the passengers.

Only a few hundred feet ahead of them were haphazard stacks of old tires forming an impassable barricade and dozens of Haitian men armed with rocks, sticks, and machetes. Thoma threw the car in reverse and accelerated, making a sharp right. He stopped so suddenly that all the boxes tumbled to the floor of the van, spilling bottles of medicine and supplies.

"*Oh Bondye. Non, necklacing.*" He shouted, "Get down on the floor! Don't get up!"

But Kate could not look away. Two men strayed from the crowd and began beating on the hood of the van with sticks. Not more than twenty feet from their car two other men, wearing bandannas and military helmets, dragged a boy not more than sixteen years old from the crowd into the middle of the street. One of the men tied his arms behind his back. The other dropped a tire over his head and doused it with liquid. He lit a match and ignited a rolled-up newspaper that had also been soaked in the same liquid. He held the flaming torch in front of the trapped man's face for just an instant, before he threw it onto the tire and ran away to escape the flames. The crowd scattered in chaos. Kate tried to open the door of the van. Sue grabbed her before she could unlock it.

"No! Are you crazy? Get down, Kate."

The flaming figure stumbled about and toppled to the street not five feet from Kate's window. For the second time that day, Kate found herself staring into eyes that were both terrified and doomed. She dropped to her knees between the rows of seats and covered her head, certain the image of the burning boy and the smell of his charred flesh would never leave her.

13

KATE

PORT AU PRINCE
OCTOBER 1, 1991

A swirl of pink surfaced in the sudsy water and threatened to stain the white bed sheet. Kate was up to her elbows in the soapy water, bent over the large metal *kivet*. She moved at the waist in the same rhythm as the two Haitian women who were doing the weekly laundry in Didi's courtyard.

A second *kivet* was filled with clear water and rested on the ground. So began the rinse cycle. This time, a towel cushioned her knees from the harsh concrete surface. For the final rinse, onto another *kivet*, she added a capful of lavender-scented liquid labeled Misteline—fabric freshener of choice in Haiti. Her arms and shoulders ached as she twisted and rolled the bed sheet with one of the other women, extracting as much water as possible before hanging it over the clothesline that was suspended between two trees in the courtyard. Kate's clothes, laundered earlier that morning, were well on their way to dryness, flapping in the tropical sun.

One of the Haitian women was gently turning little pieces of charcoal. Sparks jumped from the heavy metal grate and floated to the ground. Resting on the tabletop was a small, cloth-covered board and an iron. There was a little compartment for the hot charcoal.

The woman took one of Kate's shirts from the line and carefully pressed the stiffness from the fabric. Kate dried her hands on her skirt and walked over.

"Can I do this?" She accepted the iron. It was heavy and warm and full of purpose.

It felt good to do something, anything that had an end in sight, a task she could mark off on her to-do list. Laundry—check. Ironing—check.

It had been two days since the dog bite, two days since Haiti imploded when President Aristide was deposed just six months after his inauguration. Less than a year earlier the previously unknown, soft-spoken Catholic priest had appeared out of nowhere and beat twelve other candidates in a landslide victory. Now he was gone and Haiti was in turmoil, with all flights cancelled to and from Haiti. The horror from when Kate witnessed the man on fire had morphed into terror at the reality of being trapped in a strange and violent country. And this morning, after two sleepless nights, Kate had no clue when she would see her family again or what she could do about the rabid dog bite. She had eight more days to find the vaccine. She pressed down with the iron and refused to think about what would happen if she didn't.

Sue began, "I have some good news and bad news." She was drinking a beer on Didi's porch. Tim was napping.

"Bad news first," Kate countered. It was only two o'clock, the air was hot and still, her bangs stuck to her forehead, and her T-shirt clung to her back along with an assortment of insects.

"There are still no flights coming to or going from Haiti. I'm sorry, Kate. We have to sit tight for a few days."

"The good news?" Kate asked, and took a beer from the cooler. The ice was melted, but the water was still cool.

"The phone is working. You can make the first call."

Kate ran to the phone so anxious she nearly forgot her home number. Mark answered with, "It's so good to hear your voice, Kate. What's going on there? The news is showing all kinds of crazy things—riots, tires burning. When are you coming home?"

She tried to keep the tears out of her voice and decided not to mention the dog bite just yet. "We don't know for sure. But it should only be a day or two more. We're okay where we are staying. It's as safe as anywhere here. I'm going to let the others phone home now. I'll call again later. Please tell Jen and Danny I love them. I love you, too, Mark."

She quickly made a second call to her friend Brian at the CDC.

"Yes, Kate. You're right," he said. "You should start the vaccine as soon as possible, but definitely within ten days of the bite. Hold on just a minute."

There was so much static on the line, it was getting more difficult to hear. Kate grabbed a paper and pen to make some notes. She wished Brian would hurry.

He returned to the phone. "I don't know what's available in Haiti. I have my secretary checking with our international health division." A muffled conversation followed. "Are you sure? What about the military or the embassy? Kate, we don't know of any source in Haiti for the current rabies vaccine we use in the U.S. You may be able to get some of the older vaccine made from sheep brains. There's a veterinarian group working outside Port au Prince—the International Veterinary Corp. You've got to understand that there are more side effects and it's less effective. It's best if you get back to the U.S. Give me your number and I'll call you back when I get more information."

Before she could respond, the phone line went dead.

"What did he say, Kate?"

She took a long drink and handed Sue two notes: "Need vaccine in eight days," and "International Veterinary Corp."

Sue stared at the words. "What should we do?"

"I think I should try and find some of the older vaccine, and if we're stuck here and Brian can't find anything else, I'll start the shots and hope for the best. As soon as I get back to the U.S., I'll get the newer vaccine." Kate's beer was almost empty. "What else can I do?"

"Well, it sounds like a reasonable plan."

"Here's to a plan." She clinked beer bottles with Sue.

One more beer would be nice. What would it hurt? Kate watched the columns of smoke rising from the burning tires dissipate into the hazy sky. The patterns reminded her of the old inkblot tests from Psych 101. She had never been able to decipher the meaning in those either.

The nights crawled. There was too much time to think. After her conversation earlier that day with Brian, Kate finally conceded and joined Tim and Sue in their nightly ritual—journaling by flashlight. She found an empty spiral notebook in one of the clinic boxes and began designating day one as the day of the *coup d'état*—the day of the dog bite.

> Day Three: October 1, 1991: 8:00 p.m.
>
> Chaos—it's the best word I can come up with to describe my thoughts and feelings. One minute I'm sick with worry over Danny and Jen and Mark and what they must be thinking. The next minute, I'm terrified that someone will break into Didi's and kill us or that I'll die from rabies. Only 700 miles from Miami, less than a third of the distance from where I was born in Pennsylvania to where I did my internship in San Francisco. I'm that close to the medicine that can save my life. How can this be happening to me?

We were supposed to leave Haiti today, but all the flights were cancelled. We heard that on the radio. Didi has one that runs on batteries. She has to translate for us, since it's all in Creole. We only turn it on for a little while in the morning and afternoon. We have to conserve. There's no electricity.

Better save the flashlight batteries, too.

Kate switched her flashlight off and held her journal to her heart—afraid to close her eyes, for the horrible images that might return.

Jim and Liz were always the first ones up in the morning. The married couple became trapped at Didi's when they came to Port au Prince a few days earlier to stock up on supplies. They were long-term volunteers from a small village about an hour's drive from the city. In the group's post-coup routine, Liz became the maker of the coffee. Fortunately, Didi had an extra tank of propane, so it was easy enough to boil water on the gas range. Many things were in short supply in Haiti, but coffee and sugar weren't among them.

Liz poured a big scoop of ground coffee into an unfolded piece of gauze, courtesy of their medical supply bag.

"*Voila, voila,*" she announced the morning of day three. "We have coffee." She set the brightly painted lacquered tray down with three cups and a huge bowl of light brown sugar and poured the dark liquid into the mugs. They each added two generous spoons of sugar.

"Anything new?" Kate sipped her coffee. She had slept very little the night before.

"I'm sorry, Kate. The phones are down again this morning," Liz reported.

The streets were quiet this morning, as well. Too quiet—it

gave her too much space to think about what could happen and what she couldn't do about it. The sugar and caffeine fueled her fears and she felt like a wild animal caught in a trap and ready to bite her wounded limb off to escape. She must think of something else, she told herself.

"Do they play soccer in that field?" Kate asked. She pointed to the place across the street where the boys kicked around a ball the first day.

"They do. But it's only informal play—mostly barefoot kids who get hold of a donated soccer ball. They pound it hard until the air runs out—then kick it around a while longer, lose interest, and that's it until the next donated ball shows up." Jim shrugged.

"My son loves to play soccer. He's really good, too—made the all-state team as midfielder." She gulped down more coffee, hoping to keep the lump in her throat from expanding. "It's such a big piece of property. I'm surprised nobody has developed it."

"The field was donated to the church up the street by a doctor from Petionville. He stipulated that it remain as a community property. A soccer field was the cheapest way to do that. You see the walls on three sides?" Jim asked.

"Yes. They're covered with graffiti."

"Graffiti, no. It's a mural. The doctor's niece is one of the artists in the artisan's co-op who is painting it. There's a section for each of the thirty articles from the 1948 United Nations Declaration of Human Rights," Jim explained.

"We met the artist in Cuba back in '86, or was it '85?" Liz asked, and looked to Jim for confirmation.

"It was '84, the year before I left the investment firm," Jim said. "Her husband is with the government. He's one of the few who were reinstated when Aristide took office in February. We get together once in a while when we come to Port au Prince."

"I worry about them," Liz said. "With the coup, our friends Max and Giselle could be in real danger—a high-level politician with the deposed government, and an artist with liberal ideas, and lately she's not afraid to put them out there." Liz shook her head.

Kate said, "One thing has puzzled me since I got here. Haiti is only about the size of Maryland with a population of, what is it—seven million people?' Jim nodded at Kate's estimate. She continued, "There must be hundreds of U.S. NGOs working here."

"Thousands actually, if you count all the church groups, medical groups, and education groups. And it's not just U.S. organizations. There are groups from France, Holland, Canada, Great Britain, even China and Japan," Liz said.

"So why haven't things improved in Haiti?" Kate asked.

"You mean why are they getting worse?" Jim said. He looked discouraged. "I have my own thoughts on that. But this is your first visit. You'll have your own theories after you've been here a few more times."

Kate pondered the last comment as it hung in the air, along with the smell of the burning tires. The three of them sat in silence for a few minutes.

Then she had a sudden thought. "Would you know anything about a group called International Veterinary Corp?"

"The IVC? Sure, I know a little about them. They did a vaccination campaign for anthrax in the little community where we live. Are you looking for someone who works for them?" Jim asked.

"Not someone, *something*." Kate said, and proceeded to tell them her rabies dilemma.

"Well, it's a shame the phones aren't working this morning. We could call one of our friends and get word to IVC that way," Liz said.

"Wait a minute." Jim said, and stood up. "What about Dumond? He rode into Port au Prince with us last week. His family lives up the street. Maybe he can get a message out. He might even be willing to make the trip on foot. I'll ask Didi how we can get word to him."

Day Four: October 2, 1991: 3:00 p.m.

I can't stop thinking about all the people suffering in this country, like Adelaide, and the child who needed heart surgery, and all the others who depend on outside organizations to get them the medical care they need. Surely everyone is trying to get out of Haiti, just like us. Will there be anyone left to help them if and when the violence subsides?

I thought being a doctor meant I knew something about pain and suffering. Pain—yes. Pain is tangible—I can explain it, dissect out the anatomy, the chemistry, the physiology. Give me pain and I will conquer it!

But suffering? It is everywhere in this country and now I feel it too when I think about my own situation. There is no cure for suffering. It is only felt on the inside. It can't be treated with words or pills. Perhaps only by sharing it, can one find some comfort. Who can I share my suffering with?

The phones are dead. No planes in the sky.

Day Five: October 3, 1991: 8:00 p.m.

I'll never eat cornflakes again when I get home. Actually, the cornflakes aren't so bad. It's the milk that gets me. We make it from powder out of a big, yellow, metal can with a smiling mother and baby on the side. "Let de Vive"—Milk of Life—two heaping scoops to a quart of water, all the daily requirements of calcium, vitamin D, and fat.

I could be the mother on the can and the baby one of my babies. Smiling, that would be more like Danny—my good *little trouper. My dear serious Jen, I would love to see you laugh more.*

What kind of mother would I be in Haiti? How far would I go to help my children survive?

Tires are still burning. No planes, no phone, no word from Dumond. There are gunshots and they sound close. Didi says we need to put out the candles and turn off our flashlights.

In the darkness, Sue helped Kate move her bed to the farthest corner of the room, away from the window.

"Some of us are going to pray in the chapel. Do you want to join us?" Sue asked.

"Maybe later." Kate answered to be polite. She was pretty sure that if there was a God, he wasn't in any chapel, at least not in Haiti.

Day Six: October 4, 1991: 11:00 p.m.

What the hell is wrong with the U.S. government? Don't they have a clue what's going on here? There was an announcement on the radio this morning that all Americans should report to the corner of Rue Capois and Champs de Mars at 2:00 this afternoon. The U.S. Embassy was sending a bus to get all the Americans out of Haiti. An announcement on the radio, for crying out loud! We didn't find out until later. It was a good thing. The rebels showed up and several Americans were killed. I hope Mark doesn't hear about this.

And the Haitians, why can't people just get along? How can anyone help them if people in their own country are just plain crazy?

Kate threw her journal across the room and stared at it long enough to remember that it might be the only record of the last few days of her life. She went over and picked up the book and put it under her mattress. Then she buried her head in her pillow so no one could hear her sobbing.

Day Seven: October 5, 1991: 8:00 p.m.

Bad news: No phones. No planes. No word from Dumond.

Good news: No tires burning today. Plenty of beer in the cooler—but it's as hot as the day. We used the last of the water in the cooler to flush Tim's toilet.

Day Eight: October 6, 1991: 8:00 p.m.

Dumond arrived with two vials of the rabies vaccine. Expiration Date—March 1992. He's pretty sure it was refrigerated. So it's a go. I never met Dumond before. I gave him a big kiss.

Sue gave me the first shot today. I'm feeling pretty good so far.

I can hear them praying and singing in the chapel, Tim and Sue and the rest of them. The only prayer I can think of right now is the Hail Mary and I never cared for the ending. What if the vaccine doesn't work? I might have three weeks, four at the most. I may never see my children again. ". . . pray for us sinners, now and at the hour of our death. Amen."

Kate went down the stairs into the chapel, lit up with candles.

No worries about someone seeing in from the outside; the room had no windows. A Haitian woman, the same one who had helped her with her laundry that first day after the coup, looked up when Kate walked in. Everyone else was gone. Funny, she didn't look surprised to see her. Kate nodded and knelt beside her on the hard cement floor. The woman took her hand; neither one of them said anything, they just shared the silence.

Day Nine: October 7, 1991: Afternoon?

I'm very tired today. It rained last night so we have water to flush all the toilets again. I'll take a shower tomorrow if I'm feeling better. More later . . .

Kate didn't even have the strength to put her journal away or to move her bed from the window again when she heard the gunshots echo in the otherwise silent streets. Despite the heavy heat that locked her in, Kate curled up in her bed, covered her head with a sheet, and for the first time in a week she fell into a sleep so deep the nightmares couldn't get in.

CHAPTER

14

GISELLE

RURAL HAITI
OCTOBER 5, 1991

"Most people don't know that there are caves in Haiti." Giselle set her bag on the ground but held tight to her daughter's hand. She hadn't let go since they slipped away from their home in Petionville two days earlier, and she wouldn't let go until they were safe again—somewhere. "And almost no one knows the stories about them. Did I ever tell you the story about the Cave of Doko?"

Natali shook her head. Of course Giselle knew that she had not. Her own mother had told it to her, when she was about six years old, one night when she begged for a bedtime story.

She'd said, "Alright, Giselle. But tonight I won't read from a book. Not every story ends in *happily ever after* with princes kissing princesses."

Her mother was referring to Cinderella, Giselle's favorite bedtime story. Sometimes her mother would read it in French and sometimes in English. Giselle always preferred the French. The wicked words sounded so much more evil, and what was more beautiful to the ears than *amour* and *ma chèrie*?

Thoughts of Jean-Juste surfaced—strange how he came to her mind for the second time that week. After so many years, she had forgotten him—well, almost.

In her haste to pack a few items for Natali and herself, she grabbed her old portfolio bag. It was the one she carried to Cuba the first time she and Jean-Juste had travelled together. Deep inside one of the pockets was the unanswered letter he had written her when she ended their affair in 1985, as she had vowed during her kidnapping. All the other letters she had burned. But this one she kept, thinking she might just answer it one day. She also found the canvases with her two blue paintings rolled tight. She had sold a few copies before the showing, but hadn't even tried afterwards.

It was a lifetime ago, it seemed. And in many ways it was. Natali was ten now and she and Max were able to travel freely back and forth to the U.S. Thank goodness she had returned early from their latest trip. Otherwise, she would be stuck in New York with Max and beside herself with worry for Natali and her aunt and uncle. The air flights were cancelled beginning the day of the *coup d'état* and no one knew when it would be safe enough for them to resume again.

"Do you remember what you learned in school about the Taino Indians who lived in Haiti many, many years ago?" Giselle asked her daughter.

"Yes. They were a peaceful people. But when the Spanish came to Haiti, most of them died from diseases or because they were forced into slavery."

"Very good, Natali. Yes, they died from diseases that the Spaniards brought with them—diseases that had never been in Haiti before, like measles and smallpox. The Taino believed that caves were sacred because the first humans were born in them. They painted and carved pictures on the walls, and used them for gathering and religious ceremonies—and for burials.

"Well, one day, many years after all the Indians were gone, a little girl wandered into the Cave of Doko. She was playing with her friends, running up and down the mountains, when she got separated from them. Night was coming and she was very, very lost and hungry and thirsty and tired."

"Like us, Mama?"

"A little, I guess." She would have to be careful in telling this story. It wouldn't do any good to frighten her with ghost tales. There was plenty enough to fear. "Although there are caves everywhere in Haiti, the Cave of Doko is special for two reasons. On the one side is the Saut d'Eau. These are the waterfalls where Haitians come each year during the annual Vodou pilgrimage."

"Auntie Carole always tells me that Vodou is evil. I don't want to go to this cave," Natali said, and began to cry. "What will happen to Auntie Carole and Uncle Joseph? I'm afraid for them. Why couldn't they come with us?"

"I wish they had come with us too, my dear. But they decided to stay in their home and wait for peace to return. They'll be okay."

Of course those words were no more than a hopeful prayer. She wouldn't permit herself to speak aloud what she truly believed. Anyone who was known to have a connection to Aristide was in danger. A friend of hers from the artisan co-op was taken from her home that first night. She was raped and tortured and forced to eat one of the pro-Aristide posters that she had painted and put up around Port au Prince. She died the next day. Someone told her that her friend's intestines had perforated.

Her uncle had paced back and forth across the kitchen floor the night after the coup and said, "The journey will be difficult for Carole. Her knees are too bad. I won't leave her, despite what she tells me to do. This time, I make the decisions." He pounded his fist on the table. "But you and Natali must go tomorrow, early before the sun is up." He tore a piece of paper from his record book. It had his official letterhead. "Take this letter to my friend, Dr. Claude Phillipe. He lives near Croix de Bouquet. It is almost halfway to Petit Mirebelais. You can spend the night with him."

On the other side of the letter, he proceeded to draw a crude map of the route Giselle and Natali would take. "Stay away from the big buses. Someone may spot you and you wouldn't be able to get away quickly enough. Take a tap-tap from Port au Prince, but sit close to the back—not at the very end where you can be seen, but close enough that you can jump out and run if you have to. After you leave Claude's house, you'll have to walk over the mountains. He'll give you more food and water and he can tell you when it is safe to make the rest of the journey."

"You and Aunt Carole will meet us in Ti Mirebelais, won't you, Uncle?"

"Yes, I promise. We'll come as soon as it is safe. Don't worry, my dear niece. We have had bad times in Haiti before. We always come through them."

Giselle recalled the often-quoted Haitian proverb: "Beyond mountains, there are more mountains." For the past two days since they left Dr. Phillipe's house, their shoes had written the words of the proverb over mountain over mountain over mountain.

Giselle's right temple throbbed and she feared the veil of blackness would descend again. She rubbed the little place in the center of her palm—the place where the doctor in America showed her. Sometimes it helped, but not so much today.

"Is it your head again, Mama?"

"It is not too bad this time."

"Tell me more of the cave story."

"Yes. Well, most Haitians practice a little Vodou, but it's not an evil Vodou. It is more a way of honoring and respecting nature. Those that come to the pilgrimage each year are here to pray—to give thanks for what they have received and to pray for good things to come. It is only a very few Haitians who use Vodou for evil. Their power doesn't come from the evil spirits. But only from the fear they create in people's hearts and minds. Do you understand that, my darling?"

"Yes. What is the other reason the Doko Cave is special?"

"That is the story I'm going to tell you. But come on, Natali. We must keep going. The rain is coming."

Indeed, the sky behind them was veiled in mist that rolled down the mountain.

Giselle continued with the story as they quickened their pace. "Just before the night swallowed her, the little lost girl found the Cave of Doko. It seemed a safe enough place except it was so very, very dark—even darker than the night, because there are no stars in a cave.

"She found a big flat rock to sit on. It rested against the wall of the cave. She would be able to make a comfortable place to spend the night. In the morning she knew she would find her way back home and then she would have such an exciting story to tell her friends. Maybe they would want to come back with her to see the cave. She could charge them a goude or two for a little tour."

The mist was at their back now. The dampness penetrated her blouse and hugged her shoulders like a wet towel. Giselle pulled a scarf from her bag—bright blue and yellow—and covered Natali's head and shoulders with it. It was another item she might have left behind—a gift from Jean-Juste, brought from Paris when they first started seeing each other. It was even lovelier now, draped over her daughter. She looked older these last few days, more like a beautiful young woman than a ten-year-old girl.

"And the little girl began to plan all the things she would buy with the money she made. That may have been her first mistake. The spirits in the cave were not unfriendly, but they weren't happy to think that someone would profit from their beauty and mystery. It was a sacred cave, you know."

Natali nodded and pulled the scarf tighter around her chin.

"Her second mistake was that instead of sitting quietly or sleeping for the night, she decided to explore the cave. That way she would know more of its secrets and for a night tour, she thought, she could ask even more money. Then she could buy more things for herself."

"But it was dark. How could she see?"

"At first she couldn't. But after a little while her eyes adjusted to the darkness. And even though there were no stars, the clouds opened up a hole in the night sky and the moon was full and at just the right place to send a beam of light to brighten the tunnel that led from the entrance deep into the earth below.

"The little girl saw the primitive drawings made by her Taino ancestors on the walls of the cave. Mostly they were simple pictures, painted in white or black. There were day birds and night birds, frogs, and other animals and people dancing. But in some places there were vast panels of drawings that went on as long as the length of ten or even twenty people. The little girl's third mistake was not to respect the stories on the walls. Some told of the Taino culture; others gave warnings about the dangers of the cave. If she had stopped to notice, she might have seen the guardian with eyes not just in his head but in his hands, cautioning that one must see by touch in the dark and narrow passages. She might have stepped more cautiously had she noted the stick men climbing on ropes to descend the steep passages. Or she might have stayed right where she was, safe at the opening, until daylight found her, if she had recognized the pictographs of men, women, and children in boats, rowing down the dark passages. But she merely ran past all this and more, and stopped only at the crystals that jutted from the ceiling of the caves. They were beautiful, no doubt. The moonlight reflected off their multifaceted surfaces, illuminating the cave even more brightly. The little girl should have looked away, but she didn't.

"'These must be jewels. They are as bright as the stars. Only diamonds could be so splendid,' she proclaimed. 'I don't need to have silly tours or go to school or cook or wash or carry water anymore. I will have enough money to buy anything I want for the rest of my life.'

"It was then that a night creature—something like a bat—appeared. 'Little girl, what are you doing alone in a cave at night?' it asked.

"She had never met a bird that talked before, although she had heard there were some in a forest on the Dominican side of the island. There was no way she could know night birds were actually spirits and this one was charged with protecting the cave from ill-meaning intruders—even if they were only little girls.

"'I was lost and when night came, I found this cave for shelter,' she told the night creature. She wasn't intent to give too much detail to it. But he might have some useful information for her. She said, 'I'm only exploring a little before I take some rest. Can you tell me, where does the cave go?'

"'It goes for a very long way under the fields and the roads and the rivers and then it joins with another cave in the western part of the island. If you walk for many days you can travel under the vast sea. Although no one has ever made the journey, it is possible to arrive at the continent of North America.'

"'That's a nice story, but it doesn't concern me today.' The silly girl looked around, feigning disinterest in what the bird had said. But really her thoughts were skipping from jewels to America and visions of a very different kind of life than in her little rural village. She would have a big house with many fine things and all the servants she needed to do the cooking and cleaning and washing.

"The creature already sensed that the girl had other ideas and he was not going to leave her alone. 'The cave can be a very dangerous place. It can get very dark inside. I'll keep you company until daylight comes.'

"'Thank you. But I'll be fine.' She was already thinking that if he stayed, she would have to share the treasure or maybe she would get nothing at all. She skipped ahead of the creature, or so she thought. When she came to an especially bright and sharp crystal that grew from the roof of the cave, she took a handkerchief from her pocket and broke off a piece. It was about as long as her arm and heavy and sturdy enough that if she used it pointy side up, it made a grand and elegant walking stick.

"As she continued down the passageway, it became narrower, damper, and darker. She was not too concerned, as that was to be expected if what the creature had said was true. She would just go a little farther, she thought. Then she could return with a lamp and a bag tomorrow to get more of the diamonds and plan her trip to America.

"Well, the dampness of the cave grew into a rivulet beneath her feet and soon into a full-fledged underground river that reached above the little girl's knees.

"'I'll just go a little farther,' she said. 'With my sturdy walking stick, I can manage the water. Tomorrow I'll trade some of my treasure for a pair of new boots.'

"What the little girl didn't know was that the crystals weren't diamonds or jewels of any sort. They were something quite precious, but more practical and fleeting in nature. The crystals were salt. And as the force of the water grew, her walking stick quickly dissolved. Soon she was standing in the middle of a river with nothing to steady her.

"It is not entirely clear what happened after that. Some say she called for the night creature. He came to her rescue and she learned her lesson and only returned to the mouth of the cave to pray and bring gifts of food for the spirits who lived there. A few believe she still stands in the river bed, paralyzed by her greed and her fear, her body encased in a shell of crystalline salt that formed from the roof of the cave."

Giselle and Natali turned off the main path at the sign for Doko Cave and in a few minutes they came to the mouth of the cave. It was raining steadily now. Giselle kneeled at the opening with Natali at her side.

"We must say a prayer and do our best to be pure in heart

and thought before we enter," she whispered, as if someone might have heard her earlier thoughts of Jean-Juste that revealed that she never was and never would be pure.

In the cave they found shelter from the rain. But it was dark and damp. Tonight, there was no moon to light the way, and Giselle doubted that the sun ever found its place there either. It was nothing like what she had envisioned from her mother's tale. It was impossible to imagine the stories that might be painted on the walls with any sort of ending, good or bad. There was only total darkness.

She took a candle out of her bag and, after three attempts, the match held its flame long enough for her to light the wick. She placed the candle in a crevice within the wall of the cave and untied the scarf around Natali's head. She spread the scarf out on a flat rock and unpacked their dinner—a tin of sardines, a hunk of goat cheese, cassava bread, and a thermos of broth, which they passed back and forth. All things considered, it was a feast—meager, but a feast nonetheless.

"I hope the story hasn't frightened you, Natali. It is just a story, you know?"

"I know, Mama. I'm not frightened. I don't believe in spirits. But I was thinking. If I ever found all that treasure, I wouldn't keep it for myself. I would divide it into millions and millions of pieces and give a little to each of the poor people in Haiti. Then they could buy food or something they could sell in the market."

"You sound like your grandmother." Giselle smiled at the memory.

"I wish I had known her and Grandfather. If there really was a tunnel that went all the way to America, then they wouldn't have drowned on the boat and Papa could come to us here and we could live in the countryside with Uncle and Aunt."

"Yes, or we could all go to America. Wouldn't that be a nice story?"

"I don't think I want to go to America, Mama. Haiti is our country and I would miss my friends." With that her daughter stood and danced a little dance that she had been working on for her recital the next week.

"Bravo. Bravo." Giselle smiled and clapped with exaggerated merriment, recalling how her own mother had watched her dance when she was a child. Yes, Natali was a lot like her grandmother and a lot like a little girl, too.

Just then, something black and swift flew out from deep in the cave. The sentinel bat was followed by more black swiftness as hundreds and hundreds of bats rushed over and around them. The ground trembled and the candle flame extinguished. Absolute darkness returned to the cave once again.

"Oh, *Mon Dieu!*" Giselle shouted into the darkness. Her words echoed off the walls with her unanswered plea. She groped for her bag and found the matches inside it. Hastily she struck one after another, but the flint on the side of the box was damp and failed match after failed match snapped in her quivering fingers. She had forgotten how much she feared the darkness.

"Mama, I'm scared."

Her daughter's voice brought her back to her senses. She struck her final match slowly and when the light came forth, she heard a deep throaty sound from within the cave.

At first she thought a frog had been disturbed by the bats. But when she cast the light of the candle in the direction of what she had heard, she saw a woman huddled in the corner. Her knees were drawn to her chest; a large tear in her skirt exposed her thin legs. Her face was buried in a faded pink blanket that failed to muffle the spasms of cough that seized her frail body.

It seemed they were no longer alone in their journey.

CHAPTER

15

ADELAIDE

PORT AU PRINCE
FIVE DAYS EARLIER

Adelaide finally stopped to catch her breath a little ways from the house where she and Tieina stayed. As soon as they left the clinic, she realized something very terrible was happening in the streets of Port au Prince. Gangs of men carried sticks and yelled. Tires were stacked up everywhere, burning. Thick columns of black smoke rose from down by the National Palace. Momentarily, she forgot about the rocks and the crazy dog. It was a grave situation when the tires started burning. It wouldn't be long before the torture and murders followed. She must get inside with her daughter.

The radio announced, *"Coup d'état . . . Aristide is gone . . . coup d'état."*

She hated that they had to stay with his people. She didn't even know what to call them. They weren't really her family, only Tieina's. But that was so awkward to say—my daughter's father's family—like she and Tieina were from different families. So they just called them Madame and Monsieur Charles. People assumed they were kind relatives who had taken a sick woman and her daughter in until they could get back on their feet again. But the truth was they were anything but kind. She and Tieina worked from morning to night carrying water, washing clothes, and cooking meals. No one ever said thank you or offered them a bed to sleep in. They ate what was left when everyone else had their fill. Some days that was almost nothing. Adelaide wasn't sure how much longer they would let her stay. Unless the American doctor could help her, she wouldn't be of use to the Charleses for much longer—or to anyone for that matter.

Her legs were so heavy it felt like her feet were encased in cement. She was sweating and warm beyond what she should be for the weather.

"Tieina, you go inside first. I'll be there in a minute." She shoved her daughter through the door and doubled over in a coughing fit.

After a few minutes, she dabbed at her face with a damp handkerchief and straightened her blouse. Tieina was already setting the table for dinner when she entered the kitchen. There were eight instead of the usual four places. Perhaps with the craziness outside today, these people would be given to some kindness inside and she and Tieina would sit at the table and enjoy a proper meal. Her mouth watered with anticipation of the soup simmering on the stove.

"They want to talk to you, Mama." Her daughter didn't look up, intent on her task.

Adelaide's hopes for a proper meal sank to the pit of her empty stomach. When she walked into the small sitting room, in addition to the Madame and Monsieur and their two chubby little girls, there were four strangers, all plump and dressed like they were headed to church on Sunday. She caught a whiff of one woman's cologne as she got up and walked out without acknowledging Adelaide's presence. The other three strangers followed.

Madame was always the one to speak. "Adelaide, Aristide is gone and rebels have taken over the government offices. Our friends came to Port au Prince for a wedding this weekend and they cannot return to their hotel in Petionville. They'll be staying with us for a few days."

"Yes, ma'am. I'll help Tieina in the kitchen." She suppressed a cough, and feigned clearing her throat.

"Yes. Good. But our house is not big enough for ten people. Your health has not improved in the city. We think you would do better back in Ti Mirebelais with your mother to take care of you." She looked to Monsieur, who quickly nodded in agreement.

"But it is too dangerous for us to travel." As heartless as they were, she couldn't believe they would send the child out in these circumstances.

"Tieina can stay with us for now. She can sleep on the floor in the girls' room. Port au Prince is a better place for her."

Go away and leave Tieina. How could they suggest such a thing?

Madame continued, "The schools will open again soon. She's an intelligent girl and she should get an education. Oh, I almost forgot. Did the American doctor give you the rest of the money for Tieina's tuition?"

Adelaide grasped the thread of Madame's tale and wove a small tale of her own. "She told me to come back tomorrow. She'll bring the money then and medicine for me, too." It was only a wishful hope.

"Tomorrow? No one will be out on the streets tomorrow, except the rebels."

"The Americans will. They have been here before, many times. The doctor will be there and she'll bring the money. She promised." Sometimes one had to help hope along—believe in the possibility and meet it halfway.

"I suppose we can manage for another day. Do get to work on dinner. We'll have no electricity tonight and it'll be dark soon."

As bad as it had been the last year, Adelaide never had to beg—until that next day.

She returned to the church where the clinic had been. She

closed her eyes as she came down the final stretch of road, counting to ten for good luck. She wanted to believe as long as possible that the doctor would be there. If she had the money, she could buy a little more time to make a plan. She and Tieina would stay in Port au Prince. Her daughter could go to school and she would get well enough to sell things in the market.

But when she opened her eyes, there were only the empty benches in the empty courtyard. She peered into the window at the lopsided sheets abandoned in haste. The place where she had talked with the doctor was vacant—just a gloomy and dusty space again.

It was as if her heart had been squeezed by a giant angry hand so all the blood arrived in her head. Nothing was left to fuel the rest of her body. She sank to her knees, betrayed by broken promises and unmet hopes.

"No. No. No." She cried and pounded the ground with her fists, willing for the blood and the pain to come to remind her that she was still alive.

When nothing was left of her voice or her tears, she wiped her bloody fists on her dress and vowed that she would cry no more after this day.

She didn't give much thought to what would happen to her as she walked her way back through Port au Prince. She extended her hand to anyone she saw who didn't look like a rebel. She tried her best to mimic the mournful plea as she had seen so many times in the eyes of less-fortunate women. There were very few people on the street and those who were didn't even seem to notice her. She was invisible. For a while she considered that maybe she was already dead. But then she ran into one of the sisters, who placed five goudes into her upturned palm.

"God bless you, my child." The sister didn't look away like everyone else had done, and she cradled Adelaide's hands in her own much longer than she needed to.

The imaginary hand clenching Adelaide's heart loosened a little, and she continued through the nearly empty streets. She knocked at the side door of the National Cathedral where the Bishop lived. No one answered. She went to a little indoor market to buy something to eat. The door was chained and padlocked and the windows were boarded. Someone had broken them all anyway.

She was hours beyond thirsty. Her mouth was so dry that she couldn't get out her begging words. She was forced to buy two little plastic packets of water from a man in the street. His eyes burned through her blouse to the sagging skin and bones she wore beneath. For a moment, she thought he might want something else from her, something that could bring her more than a few goudes. She retrieved a smile from somewhere before.

But he snorted, spat on the ground, and said, "No change—go away old woman."

The imaginary hand gripped tight again.

An old woman—that was what she had become—at only twenty-three years. Perhaps he was right. If she didn't find some help, she was at the end of her life, and that made her an old woman. If only she knew where the doctor was staying. She would go there directly. She didn't care how dangerous it was.

She didn't know where the Americans were, but Madame La Belle lived just up the next street. She would go there now.

Adelaide saw the curtain behind the window part ever so slightly in response to her timid knock on the front door. She rapped harder a second time.

"Adelaide, what are you doing out in the streets?" Madame reached out and pulled her inside.

The door shut so quickly Adelaide's skirt was caught, tethering her in the small foyer.

"I need to find the American doctor. Can you tell me where they are staying?"

"My dear, I'm sure the Americans are gone home by now. You

need to go, too. Get back to your daughter. Give me your address and when things calm down, I'll find you."

"Please, Madame. I need money."

"Adelaide, I'm sorry I can't do anything for you now. Give me your address and go—carefully. It isn't safe to be out."

Madame scribbled the address Adelaide gave her on a piece of paper and pushed her out into the street again.

"We need you to write a letter saying we can make decisions for Tieina, and when the American sends money we will enroll her," Madame Charles demanded. She would not back down on her insistence that Adelaide would be better off back in Petit Mirebelais with her mother.

Adelaide had tried every argument to make her case that she should stay with her daughter in Port au Prince. But in the end a poor, sick, woman had nothing of value to offer.

"Tieina, come with me. I need your help to write a letter. It has to be perfect. You can do this better than I can. Bring your pen and a piece of paper. You have those, don't you?"

"Yes, Mama." Her daughter reached under the bed and pulled out a red-and-blue knapsack. It held all her personal possessions—a pen, a composition book, an extra skirt, a few blouses, and some underwear.

They found a private place in the little garden behind the house. Tieina sat on a rock and used her knapsack as a desk. Adelaide paced back and forth while the child wrote in her best Sunday-school cursive the words she dictated.

"I, Adelaide Delva, give my permission for Madame and Monsieur Charles to send my daughter, Tieina Delva, to school in Port au Prince. I have spoken with an American woman and she will send the money for the fees." It was not a lie exactly, but another whisper of hope yet to be heard.

Tieina handed the letter to her to sign.

Now another letter. Her plan might not work if Tieina's father were still alive. But good Lord willing, he wouldn't be. She wasn't a bit sorry for that thought. He had done nothing for either of them.

"In this next letter—for me to keep—I also want you to write if I, Adelaide Delva, die, Tieina's guardian will be her grandmother, Yvonne Delva. She lives in Petit Mirebelais."

"No, Mama." Tienia threw her pen to the ground. "I won't write that sentence. I won't do it."

"Don't be silly *ti zwazo m.*" Adelaide picked up the pen and handed it back to her daughter. "It is just a precaution. If writing something made it so, the world would be full of princesses and princes." She brushed the tears away from her daughter's face and swallowed her own before they could find a way out. As she vowed, there would be no more tears from her.

Early the next morning, Adelaide rose to leave. It would be best to make an early start. She had more energy and the road would be safer—not that she expected anyone to bother with a poor sick woman like her.

She leaned over and kissed Tieina, who was curled on the floor wrapped in a bed sheet. She didn't want to wake her. So she just stared at her sleeping child, trying to memorize every detail.

How could she leave her here? There had to be another way.

But when Adelaide stood back up, she felt the pain in her stomach. She ran outside, barely making it to the latrine before the diarrhea came. Squatting, her legs quivered, and she feared they would not hold her long enough. There was so much coming from inside her she worried the bucket would overflow, and then she would have an awful mess to clean up.

Her legs and the bucket held, yet it seemed like an hour before she could stand again and now she would have to bathe before she left. There was little water left in the container they used for their outdoor bucket showers. She pulled the curtain to the shower area closed, undressed, and splashed what was left on the most soiled parts. She re-dressed as quick as she could.

The houses and streets were stirring with the beginnings of the day. She grabbed the little sack that she had prepared the night before for her journey. His people gave her a tear of bread and fifty goudes for the journey. She added the thin pink blanket that had been Tieina's when she was a baby. She hurried out the door, determined to be gone before she had to greet anyone. Madame was already growling from her bed.

The last thing she heard as she passed down the street in front of the house was, "Tieina, get up. There's laundry to do and we need coffee for our guests. Go get the water and start making breakfast. Why are you crying, you silly girl? Get to work. Our guests will be hungry."

Adelaide stopped for a moment. What kind of a mother was she to leave her daughter in the hands of such cruel people? Her heart felt like it would split down the middle. She clasped the small handful of goudes and held the meager sachet of bread tight to her chest. If God were willing, could there be enough for two of them? Would he give her the strength to make the journey back home with her daughter? It would be worse for Tieina to be alone on the road. At least here she has a roof over her head and some food. Adelaide shivered and coughed. This time there was blood in her handkerchief. She covered it quickly and shoved it deep in her pocket.

Adelaide passed her time on the road imagining what Tieina would be like when she became a woman. She imagined her daughter would be smart like her and tough like her grandmother. She prayed she would be nothing like her father's people. By the time the second night approached, Adelaide was just hours from her village. She had almost missed the sign for Doko Cave, she was so exhausted. She remembered the cave from the time she made the Vodou pilgrimage with her mother when she was pregnant with Tieina. She planned to stay the night there before continuing on to Ti Mirebelais the next day.

She recalled little from her journey of the last two days. She found only clues that told her how difficult it had been—a rip in her skirt, a scratch on her face. The tiredness seeped from her bones like an old withered tree that had lost too many encounters with the charcoal-maker's axe.

She had passed a few other travelers on the way. They all wore worried, urgent looks. Sometimes they traded bits and pieces of their stories. Her journey had little to do with the violent collapse of her country. Her fears were her own and her dreams had succumbed to more practical matters. She was going home to die.

There were a few things that kept her going, despite the pain in her body and in her heart. She wanted to see her mother and sisters before her time came, and she wanted to die in the same bed where her daughter was born. But most importantly, she must give the letter to her mother. It was the only thing left that she could do for Tieina.

She entered the cave, noting the mist that rolled down the mountain. It was surely going to rain. She found a place not far from the opening where the floor was dry and there was dirt instead of rock. She ate her last piece of bread and folded her blanket up like a little pillow. She pulled her knees to her chest. The cough would be less that way. The burn of fever on her forehead fell onto the blanket. Tomorrow, she would complete her journey. And with that thought, her heart was finally free of the vise. She rested and waited for sleep.

16

KATE

PORT AU PRINCE
OCTOBER 1991

Day Eleven?

I have three angry welts on my stomach—at one o'clock,
two o'clock, and three o'clock. They are so painful I can only
lie on my back. My bones feel like they are breaking apart
at the joints. Only up for a few minutes to pee and choke
down some rice and rum. The rum helps the most. I think it
is all from the vaccine. It couldn't be rabies, could it? I can't
remember what the early symptoms are. I hope it's just the
vaccine. It has to be.

I won't journal at night anymore. My last pair of batteries
is fading fast.

Day Twelve: October 10, 1991: Afternoon

The U.S. military is supposed to arrive late today. A few

stores are open. Didi is going to ask Thoma to check things out tomorrow. We still have no phone and no electricity.

This is the first day the neighborhood children are playing outside in Didi's courtyard. Their mothers are watching them and braiding the older girls' hair. Everyone is laughing—the kind of deep belly laugh I've had when Danny pulled some crazy stunt on the soccer field.

I am so ashamed as I watch them.

Many emotions have come and gone these past few weeks—shock, anger, fear, pity, blame. All of these I experienced and all felt justified and shared with Tim and Sue and the Haitians around us. But the joy I see now with the little girls dancing, the boys playing dominoes, and the women teasing each other, it catches me off guard. I can't feel it with them and I can't feel it for them. It is so difficult for me to imagine joy in life here, and for that I am ashamed.

Kate closed her book and walked out to the courtyard. At first, she simply watched. And then she thought again about what kind of mom she would be if fate had given them life in Haiti instead of the U.S. Wouldn't she grab onto each moment of joy she could find for herself and her family? Wouldn't that wish for her children overwhelm the sadness and fear?

She was pretty sure they would say yes, and even though her Creole was good enough, she was shy to make her request.

"Will you teach me how to braid your daughter's hair?" Kate asked.

One of the Haitian women took Kate's hands and guided them through the steps until her fingers were familiar enough to continue on their own. And with that, Kate felt the beginnings of a smile cross her face.

Day Thirteen: October 11, 1991: 10 a.m.

The streets are calm, at least for now. Liz and Jim left early this morning. I cried like a baby. I didn't even care. We may be able to get home this week. But I don't want to count on it. I feel more tears coming on. Stop it, Kate.

I have five welts on my stomach. They aren't as angry today. I'm still aching though. But I think it may be from lying around too much. I AM going to walk around the soccer field later today and I don't care what Sue and Didi say about that.

Kate looked at the mirror for the first time in a week. Ponytail day. She gathered her unwashed hair into a rubber band, double-knotted her Nikes, and made her way across the street to the soccer field. Finally it was safe enough to leave Didi's compound. She felt like a little kid out of school for summer vacation.

It felt so wonderful to stretch her legs. But it was really the mural that she came to see.

UNITED NATIONS DECLARATION OF HUMAN RIGHTS
Adopted December 10, 1948

To ensure that all people are born free and equal in
dignity and rights and as a common standard of
achievement for all peoples and all nations.

Commissioned by the Haitian Artisans for the
People Co-op, August 1991

She walked the perimeter, unable to completely translate the Creole. She studied the pictures. How could she have thought this was senseless graffiti? The details were exquisite and the message, though simple, captured Kate's heart and planted a seed. She stopped at Article Four—*No Person Will Live in Slavery to Another.* A black man raised an axe above a rock, poised to break the chains that bound the hands of a larger black man. The slave's dark skin was stretched tight over high cheekbones, so characteristic of his mixed African and Indian ancestry.

Article Eighteen described freedom of religion. She recognized the National Cathedral from their sightseeing day almost three weeks ago now. Men, women, and children of all races and nationalities held hands and encircled the church.

Kate considered every declaration, but one in particular felt familiar to her. She returned a second time to Article Fourteen— *Right to Asylum.* This part of the mural hadn't been finished. There was a vast blue sea that all but swallowed a rickety wooden boat in a paler shade of blue. The outline of the sun had been drawn but not colored in. The boat was sinking but there weren't any passengers—neither in the boat nor in the water. Where were the people?

Kate finished her vigil at the mango tree and sat for a minute. It was the same tree the boys kicked with their soccer ball on her first day in Haiti. It seemed like a lifetime ago. The tree barely reached the top of the wall, about ten feet. The mango was gone. She wanted to take one more tour around the wall to study the mural more intently. But suddenly, she was inclined to run, just like she would every morning back home. And so she did.

Around and around the field she ran, each time a little swifter and with more purpose. Jim was right. She would need more time to understand this curious little country and all of the well-intentioned people who came here to help. If she were given the chance, if there were a God—a higher being out there—and if she lived through this ordeal, she vowed that she wouldn't just remember, she would do something.

The dinner dishes were done, the leftovers distributed to the neighbors, when the sweetest sound in the world broke the silence. The phone rang.

"Kate!" Didi called. "Hurry, it's Mark."

She practically skated down the cement steps and grabbed the phone from Didi. "Mark. I can't believe it. It is so good to hear your voice. I couldn't call you. The phones haven't been working."

"I know, Kate. We've been trying and trying to get through. Are you okay?" He didn't wait for her answer. "Listen, Senator Lawry got in touch with the U.S. Embassy in Haiti. They're sending a car with a military escort tomorrow morning to pick you guys up. You have to be ready by eight o'clock. A military flight will take you to Florida and they'll help you make arrangements home from there. You can only take one small bag each. I love you, Kate. See you . . ."

The line went dead again.

Kate grabbed Sue and Tim in a group hug and gave them the news, and her friends started babbling about what they would do when they got back to the U.S.

"Tomorrow at this time, I'll be taking a hot shower for at least an hour," Tim proclaimed. "After I flush the toilet a dozen times."

"I'm getting in the car and driving somewhere, maybe to my mom's with the windows down the whole way. Ahhh . . . fresh air," Sue said, and took a deep breath of the dusty, hot air and coughed.

"Eat ice cream and watch TV," Tim added.

Kate smiled but said nothing.

"Seriously guys, the re-entry after one of these trips can be a little rocky. With everything that happened this time, be careful with yourselves and stay in touch with me," Sue said. She reiterated her warning from their pre-trip orientation that some team members became dangerously depressed when they returned to their lives in the U.S.

"What about you, Kate? What will you do when you get back?"
Tim asked.

Kate couldn't wait to get her arms around Jen and Danny and for
Mark to get his arms around her—that she knew with every certainty.
But as crazy as the last two weeks had been, there were many things
about Haiti that had come to feel familiar and comforting. She would
miss the greetings each of the staff called and the routine of meals,
setting the table, the simple but overflowing bowls of beans and rice,
a little hot sauce for added flavor, singing, and even the praying. She
would miss their morning chats on the porch sipping the dark and
sweet coffee and the evening reflections shared between members
of their small group or privately recorded in her journal. She had
grown accustomed to the long tropical nights with no distractions of
electricity, and she loved the late evening and early morning sounds,
when the sleepy world prepared to rest and hope.

In addition to embracing her family, Kate was also thinking
about when it would be safe enough to come back to Haiti. But she
decided to keep that to herself for now. "I think all your ideas are
great and I'm definitely eating some serious ice cream, right after I
hug my kids and my husband."

The car arrived at 8 a.m. sharp, a light-blue sedan with a Haitian
driver and an African American who introduced himself as Sergeant
Dan Weber. He showed his official U.S. Embassy identification
badge but was dressed in jeans and a casual shirt.

"We don't want to call attention to ourselves," he explained.

Kate stumbled down the steps with her backpack.

"Are you okay, ma'am?" He caught Kate by the forearm.

"Just a little tired. And please, it's Kate, not ma'am." She didn't
feel right this morning. Her head was throbbing and she was having
trouble concentrating.

Her knapsack was stuffed like a college student off to class first day of freshman year, except it held only two books, the novel with the bookmark still in the midst of chapter one, and her journal more than half-filled with her almost daily musings. Also inside were the second of the two vials of vaccine, a nearly empty packet of birth control pills, one change of clothes, her camera, her photo of Danny and Jen, and Tieina's drawing. She even abandoned the Creole medical dictionary. She had pretty much memorized it in the last two weeks.

"I'll get that for you, ma'am—I mean Kate." Sergeant Dan lifted the knapsack off her shoulders.

With the final goodbyes, there were tears enough to fill the blue water container they used to flush the toilet. One last look around. Not even a parting photo. Their film was long spent on other moments. They promised to stay in touch.

They were in the car when a young boy ran up to the gate and called, "Miss Didi! Miss Didi! I have a message for you from Madame La Belle."

"It's for you, Kate," Didi said, and handed the envelope through the window as the car pulled out of the courtyard into the street. "Be safe everyone. Come back again."

It wasn't until she was seated on the military jet high above the azure Caribbean Sea that she pulled out the envelope and opened it. At first the words ran together and she had to close her eyes. It was the altitude and the stress and the fatigue, she decided, when the message finally came into focus.

Dear Dr. Kate,

I don't know if you will get this letter before you go home. I hope your arm is healing. I promised Adelaide, the young woman with AIDS, that I would send you a note about her situation. She has gone back to her village because she has no place to stay in Port au Prince. I don't think she will live long. Her daughter Tieina is still here with relatives. They will send her to school, but don't have money for tuition. I know you have already done so much, but if there is anything you can do to help the little girl, we would be grateful. Sue knows how to get in touch with me.

God bless you.

Marie La Belle

Kate felt like the seed that had been planted in her heart was starting to sprout. "I'll be back," she whispered to the mountains disappearing from her view as the plane gained altitude and turned toward her home.

CHAPTER

17

KATE

ATLANTA
OCTOBER 1991

"Mom!" Jen and Danny shouted as Kate emerged into the Atlanta Airport. They broke away from Mark and ran to meet her.

She wanted to gather them into her arms, but they were too big and she was too tired to do anything but let them hang onto her waist. Her children burrowed against her bruised stomach. She stroked their heads like when they were babies. Mark removed the backpack from her shoulders and surrounded their family with his embrace.

"I can't believe I'm home."

Jen and Danny chattered away the hour trip from the airport to their home outside Atlanta, in Roswell. It was hard to follow their intersecting and interrupting tales, competing in volume and urgency to catch her up on everything she had missed in the last five weeks.

Numb, Kate wandered from room to room of their house. The furniture, the knickknacks, all the carefully chosen details of their lives, seemed familiar. But it was as if she was on the set of a

TV series that she had watched each week for years. She knew the stories behind it all, but she didn't belong to them. She knew her time in Haiti had been a life-changing experience. But now that she was home, she realized it wasn't her life that changed, just her.

Mark said, "Mom's tired, guys. While she gets her shower, let's heat up some of that famous Rigando spaghetti and meatballs we made last night. She's not going back to work until Monday, so you guys can spend the next three days together."

"Thanks. I'm not very hungry. But I will take a hot shower—missed that a lot—but not as much as you guys." Kate squeezed his arm. "I'll just have a glass of wine."

She reminded herself that it was okay now to rinse her toothbrush under the faucet—something they were cautioned not to do in Haiti, even when there was tap water. And the flush of the toilet was like music to her ears. She stared as the bowl refilled and smiled when she recalled Tim's homecoming plan. Her seventh shot was due that day, but it could wait until after her shower.

The force of the water on her body was so unexpected that she retreated to the farthest corner of the shower stall to escape. The marble tile, the grout, everything was so white and clean it hurt her eyes. She lingered under the water until steam filled the room.

Finally she stepped out and wrapped herself in two fluffy white towels, one for her hair and one for her body.

Mark came into the bathroom with a glass of red wine. "Cabernet from Carmel, Kate—your favorite." He sipped first and handed the glass to her. "Welcome home." He kissed her and the familiar warmth of his lips lessened the numbness a little.

The first sip of wine tickled her tongue like a good Cabernet always did.

Mark undid the towel on her head and pulled her tangled hair through his fingers. She rested her head on his chest. His heart was strong and steady and just quick enough to let her know he really missed her. She felt so safe.

When he unwrapped the towel covering her body, he paused and gasped. "What the hell?" He stared at the five angry welts on her stomach arranged like some grotesque abstract painting.

She hadn't told him about the dog bite or the rabies shots. "Mark, there's something you need to know about my trip." She covered herself with the towel and took a generous gulp of the wine. "Maybe you'd better get the bottle."

"Why didn't you tell me?" There were tears in Mark's eyes after she related what had happened.

"I didn't want you to worry and we had so little time to talk with the phones not working."

"You always do that, Kate."

"Do what?"

"You leave me out of the important things."

"I leave *you* out? How can you say that?"

Mark looked away from her and then back again like he wanted to say something. But instead he took his wine, shook his head, and walked away.

"Mark, I didn't mean . . ."

He nearly collided with Danny and Jen on his way out of the bedroom as they rushed in with red cherry juice stains on their T-shirts and matching chocolate mustaches.

"Daddy made us banana splits. We had a race and I finished mine five minutes before Jen."

"So, you're a pig." Jen flashed a condescending glare at her brother, which quickly receded into a green-faced grimace. "Mommy, my tummy hurts."

"Come here, honey. Let me rub it. You, too, Danny, sit with me." They joined her on the bed. Within a few minutes both their heads were nodding off to sleep. She wanted to keep them with her for the night, Mark and her bookending their two children, like they did when Jen was a toddler. But they were too big for that now and she needed to talk with her husband.

"Okay, guys. Go wash up for bed and put on clean PJs. I'll be in for prayers." Kate knew she would never take any of this for granted again.

After she got the kids to bed and finished her second—or was it her third?—glass of wine, she brought a syringe and the vial to the bedroom. Mark was reading and didn't acknowledge her.

"Would you give me my shot? I could do it myself, but you know I'm afraid of needles," she teased.

"No problem." He opened her pajama top, and his eyes misted again when he looked at her stomach. "This looks like a good spot." He swabbed gently with the alcohol and penetrated her skin with the tiny needle.

Kate took a short, tight breath as the liquid burned when it entered. "It didn't hurt nearly so much this time."

Mark pressed tight with a dry cotton ball, rubbing the site in tiny circles to capture the diluted drops of blood that escaped.

She settled back on her pillow, not wishing to start up an argument again, but wanting to make sure Mark was on board with her plan for the next few days. "I have to call Brian tomorrow. I'm not sure what to do. Do I finish with the vaccine I got in Haiti or start over with the new one here? I think someone is going to get an interesting case study published out of this."

Mark nodded. "Probably. Don't worry. I'm sure Brian will know the right thing to do. He always was at the top of our class."

"I'm sorry I didn't tell you about the dog bite. I didn't want to worry you."

"I know. Whatever we have to do from here on, I'll be there. I'm just so glad you're home." He reached for her with an urgency she hadn't felt since before they were married. She had missed his touch, more than she realized. But for that night all she wanted was to be held; she still felt so distant. It was more than fatigue, more like a switch was turned to "off" in part of her brain. She thought about Sue's warning that re-entry back into life could be disorienting. Maybe that was the explanation.

"Me, too. I just need some time. I can't stop thinking about things—like one little girl. I think she is probably an orphan by now. She was so smart and beautiful. Her name is Tieina. Her mother has cervical cancer and AIDS. I got a letter right before I left. She needs me to help her daughter. It's an awful situation."

"We can send money. There are organizations that help families in these cases."

"That's what I thought, too. But I couldn't figure out who was helping whom."

"Does it really matter?" Mark rolled to his side of the bed and snapped off the light.

"I need to know if the people I am trusting are actually helping this girl. Or are they doing something else with the money?"

"You sound paranoid."

"You weren't there, Mark. I just can't send money. It's not enough."

"You're not going to go back again, are you?" Mark asked while he stared at the ceiling. "You have two children here. What about them? What about me?"

She longed to reach across the darkness to her husband and explain the rift that was forming inside her. She loved her family, but she couldn't forget what she saw and felt in Haiti. And the answer to his question about her returning to Haiti, she wasn't ready to share that just yet.

Brian entered the office with a warm smile and gave Kate a quick hug. "You look great. How long has it been?"

She was blushing, but Brian didn't seem to notice. "A few years, I guess." It was exactly eight years and four months; she had already calculated that while she was pondering what to wear. She had thought about calling him a few times after they moved to Atlanta, but it never seemed like a good idea, until the dog bite in Haiti.

As he had suggested, she brought what remained of the second vaccine vial with her. He studied the label. "I'll bet you have some nasty welts."

"Yeah, I think I freaked Mark out. My stomach looks like a drunken soldier took target practice and I was the target."

"Ouch." He leaned back in his leather chair. He had dark eyes and hair just unruly enough that he didn't seem arrogant and pompous. "But they will fade, Kate. Most wounds do, if we let them." He leaned forward again and locked eyes with her. "I see him once in a while at meetings, you know."

"Who?"

"Mark. I always ask about you. I don't suppose he tells you."

"He probably forgets." No point in opening that wound again. Brian was her first and Mark had been jealous of that.

She asked, "What do you recommend? Should I continue with the newer vaccine, or complete the whole series with what I started in Haiti?"

"There's not a whole lot of precedent for this. But I want you to start the new vaccine today and complete the series. That will be four more shots over two weeks. No more of the one from Haiti. I wish you hadn't had to start it. Are you having any symptoms—fever, tremors, headache?"

"Not really—maybe a headache or two. But it's been kind of crazy." She looked down at her hands. They looked steady enough. It was only on the inside that she was trembling. "Like I told Mark the other night, I guess I'm an interesting case."

Brian laughed. "No, we don't want you to be one of those. We'll take good care of you. My nurse will shoot you up and I'll see you again on Tuesday. You said you would be back at work, so how about five o'clock? You'll be our last patient. Maybe we can get a beer afterward and catch up."

"Sounds great." Kate was already looking forward to it. She was finally starting to feel like her old self again, and catching up with Brian would be a welcome diversion.

A single gunshot and the smell of burning tires broke through Kate's Saturday morning sleep. What day was this? It must be day fifteen by now. But something was different. It was the blanket, soft and warm against her skin. She wasn't sweating even with the blanket. Where did the blanket come from? Another gunshot? And the burning tires . . . no, it wasn't tires burning. It was . . .

"Mom, I made you a bagel. But the toaster burnt it." Jen set the tray on her bedside—a buttered whole-wheat bagel, cindery black on the edges, a cup of coffee, milk, and a jar of blackberry preserves.

Kate sat straight up in the bed and almost spilled her coffee when a thumping sound outside startled her.

"It's Danny's soccer ball," Jen explained. "He's warming up. He's making dents in the garage door. Dad's going to be mad." She shrugged. "Did it wake you up?"

"No, honey. Your dad should have gotten me up before he left." What was he thinking? They were only six and eleven. They shouldn't have been wandering around without a coherent adult. "What time is it?" She glanced at the clock. Nine o'clock. "Oh my gosh. I need to have your brother at the field for practice." She jumped out of bed and grabbed the coffee to take in the bathroom with her while she showered. "Thanks for breakfast, sweetie. I'll eat the bagel later."

Kate dressed in jogging pants, T-shirt, and tennis shoes. "Dan," she called out the kitchen window, "five minutes, in the car. We're leaving."

Danny connected with the soccer ball, shooting it between two lawn chairs he had set up as goals. Then he jumped in the air, tumbled to the ground, and back onto his feet emerging with an ear-to-ear grin on his face. Every time he scored a goal, he made that same move. He called it the Rigando flip.

"Careful, Dan." She watched him do that a hundred times. But never before did she feel like her heart stopped until he made it back on his feet again. Would she ever have a day unclouded by worry again? When she placed her coffee cup in the sink, she noticed the bagel was halfway down the garbage disposal.

"Mom, it's our day to bring the snack," Danny called from the front seat of her car.

Jen was in the back seat with her head down in a book.

"We'll stop for donuts." She made a vow not to eat one though. She should have made more of a fuss over the breakfast in bed.

"Do you buy all your patients a beer after their appointments?" Kate asked Brian. She took a long swallow, then another. At last, she was relaxed.

"No, only the ones who get rabies shots for trying to save kids in third-world countries. You are amazing, Kate." Brian's eyes were on her and she was glad it was dark so he couldn't see her blushing. "After all you went through. Now you're sitting here as pretty as can be. You look fantastic."

"And you were always the biggest charmer," she teased him back. "And thank you." She was pleasantly unsettled that the years hadn't dampened the chemistry between them.

It was just like they were in college again. Brian was such a good listener. He wanted to know everything about her trip to Haiti. She talked for hours, gleaning insights that she hadn't even known she had until she spoke them aloud to Brian, like his comment when she told him how detached she had felt from her family and friends since she returned.

"It sounds like what some of our military veterans describe when they return to the U.S. Post-traumatic stress can be pretty serious." He took the beer from her hand and looked into her eyes. "Kate, are you okay? *Really* okay?"

"I think so. I just need a little time." She forced the biggest smile she could find, but Brian's concern reminded her of Sue's warning. She would call her tomorrow just to check in and talk.

"When are you going back?" he asked.

"I don't know that I am. Mark is not too keen on the idea, and the kids don't want to let me out of their sight."

"You have to go back, Kate. I can hear it in your voice and see it in your eyes." His gaze was intent on her. "Wish I could go with you."

"Why not? You could. Although I haven't even asked—are you married?" Of course he wore no ring. But that didn't mean anything.

"Not yet. But we're talking about it. We've been together for five years. Lucy is a nurse in the ICU at Emory."

"That's convenient." Kate forced a smile.

"We have a great time together. But our schedules are crazy and honestly, I just can't see myself married."

"It does change things. But kids are great—makes it all worth it." She checked her watch. "Speaking of which, I should go. Mark's been single-parenting a lot lately. I promised I would be home for bedtime—stories and kisses. The best part of my day, I must admit."

"I'll walk you to your car. I'm parked in the garage, too."

The parking garage was dimly lit. Kate had her back to her locked car door and fumbled in her purse for her keys, hoping Brian wouldn't notice the hint of a tremor that continued to intermittently plague her the last few days. Why spoil the evening with medical talk? It was just nerves and stress, nothing to worry about.

"This was fun. We'll have to do it again sometime." She really didn't want to leave just yet.

"I'd like that." He inched closer to her. "You never answered my question—when are you going back to Haiti?"

"You don't think that would be crazy or irresponsible?"

"All I know is that we have to follow our hearts, Kate."

Was he still talking about Haiti? Brian was so close now she felt the warmth of his breath in his words. His eyes held a mixture of concern and admiration. Of all the people she had talked to about Haiti—her friends, her dad, even Mark, Brian seemed to be the only one to understand. She leaned forward and kissed him full on the lips, softly, then harder when he answered her with the same insistence. His touch, his kiss, the look in his eyes took Kate back to a time when the future was still everything she imagined it could be, a time when being a good mom and a good wife and following her dream weren't at odds with each other.

"We could go to my place. It's not far from here." Brian's face was buried in her hair and his chest expanded as he slowly inhaled her scent and kept it locked in his lungs until a long, low groan escaped as he exhaled.

"I'll follow you." Her lips lingered on his as he pressed against her.

Kate had a vague realization at the time that this was one of those forks in the road. If it had been a longer drive to Brian's place, maybe she would have come to her senses and changed her mind. If she had made that left turn onto the interstate and gone directly home and given Jen her happily-ever-after bedtime story, how different that night and so many things that followed might have been. But it was just a few blocks until she pulled beside him in front of his condo, and just a few more minutes until she was through the door, in his arms and his bed.

For the first fifteen minutes of the forty-five minute drive back to Roswell, she smiled and glowed with the memory. In the second fifteen minutes, panic set in and she chastised herself for being so stupid, for being such a cliché. It was nearly midnight. Mark would be worried, maybe jealous and angry. He had known she was going to be seeing Brian. And Brian—she didn't understand her feelings for him. She thought she'd put that all behind her years ago. Yet when she was leaving his condo, she wasn't so sure.

Apparently he hadn't let it go, either. "I've always loved you, Kate," he said. "You know that, don't you?"

She sat in her driveway for a long time before she opened the automatic garage door. Her headlights exposed the dents that Danny's soccer ball had made in the aluminum. She pulled her car into the garage and was immediately overwhelmed by fatigue. She'd just rest for a minute. Four beers in three hours, her head was spinning; she needed to collect her thoughts. Everyone would be asleep—she hoped. Her right hand began to shake again, but this time the trembling didn't stop there. For a brief instant, before she lost consciousness, the doctor in her knew what was happening. But that awareness was lost when her head fell onto the steering wheel. The sound of the horn echoed in the garage and she was back in Port au Prince on the day of the coup, staring helplessly at the man on fire before her. As with him, there was nothing she could do to stop the violent force from consuming her.

18

GISELLE

HAITI
OCTOBER 1991

"Is it a ghost?"

Giselle approached the figure, leading the way through the Doko Cave with a candle. "No, Natali. It's a woman, and I think she is sick." Not wanting to startle the stranger, she called out softly, "*Bonjou*, madame, are you okay?" The hollowness of the cave lent her words an unintended harshness.

The woman looked up but didn't or couldn't raise her head. Giselle stayed a safe distance, motioning Natali to keep behind her.

"Madame, are you okay? What is your name?"

She whispered, "Adelaide." Her eyes closed and she began to cough again.

Giselle took a step forward, instinctively wanting to help. But when she noticed the blood on the blanket, she retreated.

"Natali, go back to the entrance and wait for me there." She held the light until she could see that her daughter had made it to the moonlit opening of the cave. She turned again to the figure, crumpled on the ground and still, wondering for a moment if the woman might already be dead. "Adelaide, my name is Giselle." She placed her arm gently on the thin shoulder. When Adelaide didn't object, she felt her forehead. It was on fire. "You have a fever, a very high one. I'm going to get something to help you."

Exactly what that something would be, Giselle was not certain. She placed the candle in a crevice in the rock wall above Adelaide's head. She didn't want to leave the poor woman in darkness. The shadow of the dim light made the bent figure seem even frailer.

Giselle hurried back to the remnants of their dinner and returned with what was left of the broth and cassava bread. Carefully she encouraged Adelaide to sip. "Take a little broth. You'll feel better." She dipped a corner of the cassava bread in the amber liquid and brought it to Adelaide's mouth. "Now eat a little of this. Natali, can you bring me our water bottle and the scarf and my medicine?"

Natali held the scarf while Giselle poured water on it and blotted the woman's forehead.

"We have to get her fever down. Here." Giselle took a little white pill from the bottle that held her headache medicine, coaxed Adelaide's mouth open, and placed it on her tongue. "Now swallow," she persuaded her. "Good, now rest."

She and her daughter took turns sponging the woman's neck and head with cool water through the night until the bottle was empty. She spoke in brief phrases when the fever abated. Her name was Adelaide Delva and she was going home to Ti Mirebelais. She mumbled something about a letter and help for her daughter.

In the early morning, a shaft of light entered the cave and announced a brighter day. There was little else they could do for the woman if they stayed in Doko. But they couldn't leave her behind. Natali gathered their belongings. Giselle picked up Adelaide's bag and with a little encouragement, the sick woman was on her feet and walking, although still somewhat bent over from the pain.

When they emerged outside, Giselle was sorry she left her dark glasses back in Port au Prince. The sun was bright, brighter than it had been in days. It nearly blinded her after the dim of the cave. The first life they encountered was a black-and-white goat foraging in the brush, tied to a sapling. Glancing at them sideways, he continued on with his meal. With no houses in sight, the owner could be anywhere.

In fact, they walked for an hour before they met anyone else, and then it was just a woman and her daughter on their way to market. "*Bonjou.*" They smiled as if they knew Giselle, but of course they didn't.

This place was nothing like Port au Prince, which often felt like a rubber band stretched taut and ready to snap.

Giselle needed to get a firm hold on the woman, so she handed Adelaide's bag to Natali. Slowly, they made it back to the main road, but it was clear that Adelaide couldn't go the rest of the way on foot. She hadn't said a word since they left the cave. Her fever was back, but Giselle had no more food or water.

"We'll have to take our chances on the tap-tap." She covered her head with her scarf from Jean-Juste, the one that had already served so many purposes during their journey. She used her last twenty goudes to pay their fare, and with Natali and another passenger's help, they lifted Adelaide onto the small bus.

The woman, exhausted, rested her head on Giselle's shoulder and fell into a deep sleep.

They didn't have long to travel. When they got off the tap-tap, the first person they asked knew Adelaide's mother and offered to take them to her house. The man was about Max's age, but he was wiry and nimble. Barefoot, he wore a straw hat and carried a machete.

"My name is Jed," he said, and offered his forearm instead of a handshake because his hands were dirty, although Giselle thought he probably had bathed more recently than she had.

It was a pleasant walk down the mountain. They passed through a small market area with fruits and vegetables for sale. It was not too hot yet and Jed and Natali chatted away like school chums. Adelaide had perked up, as well. She smiled at the children who called her name, and shook her head when they asked her for candy.

For the first time in over a week, Giselle finally took a deep breath. People were laughing and trading small challenges back and forth across the road about whose prices were better and whose bananas were sweeter. It felt good to be among these people. Most of the men were out in the fields, turning over the damp earth for fall planting. The smell was fresh and vital. What had she and her daughter missed, living their lives only in Port au Prince, and why had it taken a *coup d'état* to bring them here?

She loosened the scarf and let it fall to her shoulders. Her body welcomed the warm sun. Natali turned around and smiled.

"You look beautiful, Mother."

For the first time in a long time, Giselle felt beautiful both inside and outside.

The weathered wooden floorboards of Adelaide's birth home groaned under Giselle's tired feet. She couldn't dismiss the feeling that she had been here before. The way the sunlight, chased by a rare afternoon cloud, traveled across the porch spoke to Giselle's artist's eyes. It was odd that of all the things she could have missed about her former life—a hot bath, a roasted chicken and all the accompaniments, or watching the evening news with Max—at that moment, what she longed for the most were the bare canvases and tiny jars of paint she had left behind in Port au Prince.

Just ahead of her, Jed had carried Adelaide over the last patch of rocky earth from the path to her mother's house. The woman who had been introduced as Yvonne, Adelaide's mother, motioned for him to lay her daughter gently on the bed. She paused only a minute to pour some water over her hands from a bucket on the porch. She had just come in from working in the fields.

Giselle deposited their bags, hers and Adelaide's, in the corner of the room where Adelaide was resting. She looked around for somewhere to sit. There was only one chair, which the mother had moved to her daughter's bedside. While Giselle eased down onto the floor with her back against the wall and waited for an appropriate time to introduce herself, one of the village girls was showing Natali the toilet.

A dozen women appeared in the doorway, three and four thick, whispering to each other. No one stepped across the threshold until the group parted in unison for a woman with the biggest breasts Giselle had ever seen. The new arrival's eyes went quickly from the younger woman on the bed to her mother.

"Yvonne, I am here to help you."

"Thank you, my friend. Her fever is high." Yvonne dabbed a wet cloth on her daughter's forehead as Giselle and Natali had done the night before. "Adelaide," she encouraged gently, "Madame Cereste is here."

Adelaide's eyes fluttered open and a small smile tugged briefly at her blistered lips before fading into a grimace and a low moan.

"Shall we try a little tea?" Madame made her way back through the crowd swelling at the door. "There is nothing to be afraid of here and it's no show, sisters. We need a fire and some fresh water. Surely one of you can do that much."

Giselle nodded off in a light sleep that was easily disturbed by the chaos around her. Nevertheless, she kept her eyes closed and a deeper slumber must have come, because a gentle tap on her shoulder awakened her. She had no clue how long she had slept. The big-breasted woman was offering her a cup of tea. "Jed told us that you helped Adelaide back home from Doko. Here, drink this— tea and honey."

"Thank you." She started to stand, but her legs, tired from the journey and stiff from the dirt floor, wouldn't cooperate. "Where is my daughter?"

"Oh, Natali? She has found a group of other girls outside playing dominoes. Curiosity has chased away her shyness. I think you have a champion out there. Shall I get her for you?"

"Yes, please."

The tea was warm and after a few mouthfuls the honey gave Giselle enough energy to stand. Only Giselle and the mother and daughter were in the tiny, two-room shack.

"Excuse me, my name is Giselle. My daughter and I were traveling from Port au Prince when we met your daughter." She looked from Adelaide to the rosary beads in her mother's calloused fingers. "I hope she will be okay."

"Thank you, Giselle. But there is not much we can do for her. There is not much anyone can do now, except God." Yvonne tucked a loose strand of her daughter's hair behind her ear as though she wanted to see as much of her face as possible while she still could.

"Is there a doctor in the village?" Giselle asked.

"No, only an occasional missionary, but they have all gone since the troubles in Port au Prince. You know she went there to see the American doctors. She had such hope that they would have medicine to help her." She looked around. "Do you know where my granddaughter is?"

"Adelaide was alone when we found her in the cave. But she said something about a letter. I'll check her bag."

It happened that quickly. Giselle turned for a moment and walked to Adelaide's bag. While she searched through the woman's few possessions, Adelaide gasped and released a small whimper.

The mother's eyes were fixed on her daughter's quiet and still body. Only her bottom lip quivered as she sat poised in her chair. There was no sense of surprise on her face, only a solemn acceptance as if it were not the most unnatural of events, a mother outliving her daughter.

Giselle whispered a silent prayer for the woman who had just departed and for the one who was left behind. She retrieved the envelope and after a few minutes of silence, handed it to Adelaide's mother, who opened it and stared at the letter.

"Please, can you read it to me? I don't see well enough," Yvonne said, and sighed. "Oh, sister—why do I pretend to you at a time like this? I don't read or write at all, not even a little bit of Creole. My Adelaide is—was—so smart. She could have been a great teacher or maybe a nurse. But it was difficult after Tieina was born. She never finished primary, never learned French, only Creole and a little English from the Americans who came through." She paused and gathered a deep breath and released it with great effort. "Please, read it now before the others come."

"'I, Adelaide Delva,'" Giselle said, with a pause at the mention of this stranger who had just passed, "'give my permission for Madame and Monsieur Charles to send my daughter, Tieina Delva, to school in Port au Prince. I have spoken with an American doctor and she will send the money for the fees.' The next part says, 'If I die, Tieina's guardian will be her grandmother, Yvonne Delva. She lives in Petit Mirebelais.' It is signed by your daughter and dated a week ago. There is a birth certificate for your granddaughter, as well."

Giselle paused for a moment. "There is more." The next words, scribed in English, spoke to her in a different voice, although the handwriting was unchanged. "'Please, help me. These are not good people. I am hungry and they beat me. I know my mother is too sick to take me with her. But I am going to run away.' It is signed 'Tieina.'" She folded the note and pushed it back into the envelope and placed it on the bedside table.

"Oh my poor little Tieina, my poor Addie." Yvonne shook her head from side to side. "Yes, there was a day when we had dreams for her, too, my granddaughter, when she was born." Yvonne stared at her hands folded in her lap and lifted them palms up as if they were heavy with a great burden. She slapped the back of one hand to the palm of the other, alternating left on right, a gesture of helplessness repeated by Haitians for generations and generations. "How do we stop this? We Haitian women struggle to give our children a better life. But we always end up doing the same thing—washing our hands and drying them in dirt." She repeated the Haitian proverb.

"We must do something, Yvonne," Giselle said, and grabbed the woman's hands to stop the senseless motion.

"Yes, we must." She looked at Giselle for the first time since her daughter died. "In a few days I will bury my daughter and after that, I'll think of something. But today I go to see the man who will lend me money for a coffin and I will borrow a little more so I can offer my neighbors something to eat—if they will come. He owns most of me anyhow. If I live to a hundred years, I couldn't pay him back. What is a few more goudes?"

Giselle wished she had something to offer. No money, not even a proper dress to wear to the funeral. "Natali and I can help prepare the food."

"Oh. You know how to cook on charcoal?"

Giselle had to admit that she did not.

"It doesn't matter. There are other things you can do. We will teach you what you need to know in time." Yvonne's face brightened ever so slightly. "Now, I will give my daughter her final bath. Please, will you help me?"

That evening, after Adelaide's body had been washed and perfumed and her hair was braided with tiny beads that sparkled like jewels, the *dernier priye*—days of final prayer—began. Instead of the customary seven, Adelaide's soul would have only three days to prepare for passage to the next world. Yvonne announced that would be sufficient time; there would be no one coming from outside the village. Although earlier, Yvonne had confided the real reason to Giselle and Madame Cereste. Yvonne could not afford to be away from her fields for any longer.

"What about her daughter?" Natali asked her mother. "Won't they wait for her to arrive? I would be sad not to say goodbye to you."

"It may be too dangerous to travel," Giselle whispered, offering a simple explanation the child could understand. She had heard the whispers of the Curse and the Disease and had surmised Adelaide had died from AIDS. The family would likely be shunned by their neighbors until the body was buried, perhaps even longer.

Each of the three nights, only a handful of women arrived with offerings of food—delicate pastries filled with spicy lentil pate and sweet flour with honey and sugar. Each brought a chair and a candle. They sat in a half-circle with Yvonne and her other two daughters, Myrland and Cassandra, in the center, and they kept a vigil around the bedside from dusk to dawn. Periods of silence filled the space between tearful prayers and shared memories of the young woman, relating important events from her birth to the birth of her daughter. Little was mentioned about her life after that. Songs were sung and at least a few times each night, one of the village women erupted in a fit of wailing and prostrated herself on the dirt floor in front of Yvonne. The mother never joined her friends in the hysteria. It did not seem to be her way. She sat quietly and thanked her friends for coming to be with her.

Giselle shared a lopsided rattan chair with Natali. Each time she nodded off, the chair rocked and brought her back to startled consciousness. And each time, she swallowed her sadness for her own situation so that she could share in the pain around her. It was odd how this tragedy brought her close to strangers she hadn't even known a week ago and how the tragedy she had known a week ago was like a stranger.

Nevertheless, Giselle was grateful they did not continue for the full seven nights. Her headache returned with a fierce vengeance and she longed for her soft pillow and the quiet of her bedroom in Petionville. There was no word yet from her aunt and uncle. From time to time, worry crossed her mind, but not too much. News from Port au Prince traveled to the provinces by word of mouth, and bad news was always swifter than good.

In the mornings, Madame Cereste prepared coffee and they spread thick layers of peanut butter on sliced bananas. On the day of the *prise de deuil*—funeral—someone brought a basket of hard-boiled eggs, and another brought a packet of warm and dense bread.

Adelaide's funeral was sparsely attended. The meager procession ascended the same path they had descended when they brought the dying woman home. Everyone was dressed in black and white. Jed and another neighbor carried the coffin, modestly fashioned by the village coffin-maker in paper-mâché from used cardboard boxes. Many of the villagers stopped to watch as they passed. The rhythmic swing of their machetes and hoes were temporarily suspended. A Catholic priest who traveled among the villages gave a short eulogy, and they placed the coffin in the care of the cemetery owner, who would put it in a cement tomb once the family had the money to build one.

After the guests left, Giselle approached Yvonne and Madame Cereste. "I know this is a difficult time for you and I am sorry to add to your troubles. But my daughter and I need a place to stay until the rest of our family arrives. My uncle has friends up in the mountains." She nodded in a general direction although she had no knowledge of where exactly the people lived. "But for now, I come to you *ak de men vid*—with two hands empty." She extended her hands palms up.

After an awkward moment of silence, Yvonne spoke. Her words were slow, as if carefully chosen and extracted from a deep pit of gloom. They were not the expected words, words entitled to a mother who was grieving the death of her oldest daughter, a grandmother who was angry and worried about her granddaughter. They were not the words of a woman who had lived the last few weeks in fear as her country collapsed. Instead, she spoke words of gratitude. "All of our hands are empty these days. But yours are not. You brought me my daughter. For that, my heart is full for you and Natali."

"Yes," Madame Cereste agreed, "you and your daughter can stay in the room off the clinic. We could use someone to teach our children until it is safe for the school to reopen. You can start Monday with English and French for the secondary. Perhaps we can find some paper and paints for the younger children. Natali tells me you are an artist."

Giselle nodded in agreement, although she had never imagined she would be teaching peasant children to read and write. For now it seemed that would be their best chance of surviving until she and Natali could finally get out of Haiti and safely to the U.S.

CHAPTER

19

KATE

ATLANTA

OCTOBER 1991

Kate could hear conversations, but the words drifted in and out of focus. If she could just open her eyes or move her hand, maybe she could answer all their questions. She knew what they wanted to know. They were the same questions she would have asked if she were standing there instead of lying in the bed.

"No. She's never had a seizure before. No. She doesn't use drugs." Mark sounded annoyed. "Alcohol? Well, before Haiti not much, an occasional glass of wine. But since she came back, it's been four days and she's had three bottles that I know about. I took the recycling out yesterday."

He was lying. She couldn't have drank that much.

"Fever? She didn't say. But Kate is pretty tough. She might not tell me or even notice herself."

Why was he making her sound stupid?

"That high—103.5! No, I'm sure I would know about that." Mark sounded worried.

Oh my God. What was wrong with her?

Why was everyone wearing those yellow isolation gowns? Her eyelids were so heavy. She could only open them a tiny bit before they closed again.

"Malaria, parasite, alcohol withdrawal?" Brian ticked off the possibilities.

No! She needed to explain.

"I think we should continue with the vaccine and finish the series," Brian said, though he didn't sound so certain. "We'll rule out everything else. Anything we can treat. You know, Mark, if it is rabies . . ."

Why was someone holding her knees to her chest? Ouch! Did someone stick a needle in her back?

"I need to call her father. I'll be back as soon as I can." Mark's voice drifted off.

Someone was moving her left leg up and down from the waist and bending it at the knee, like a marionette. Her back and leg muscles ached with stiffness.

"It hurts," she struggled to say, not certain she had actually spoken aloud.

"Oh my goodness. You're awake." The young woman in blue scrubs pressed the call light for the nurse, who appeared promptly, looking alarmed and then relieved.

"How long?" Kate asked.

"You've been here for two weeks. You're at Emory in the intensive care unit."

"Rabies?" She hoped she could find her way back in one-word questions for now.

"No. You've been quite the mystery patient for the doctors— even my boyfriend, Dr.—Brian, was stumped. He told me you all went to college together. " The nurse was taking her pulse and temperature.

Kate was trying to remember something about Brian, something important. What was it?

"You had encephalitis. That's an inflammation of the brain. Oh, I'm sorry. I forgot you're a doctor, too. The vaccine you got in Haiti caused the encephalitis. Not uncommon from what Brian said. The old vaccine is made in sheep brain cells. You would understand better than I would. And don't worry, the doctors have explained all this to your husband."

Mark and Brian had been talking? Now she was even more concerned. Each time the nurse said Brian's name, she felt uneasy. Still, she couldn't quite remember why.

"Can I get you anything?"

"My children—have they been here?"

"Not yet, but maybe soon. Rest now, Kate. You'll have lots of time to catch up."

Just over three weeks after she had the seizure in the garage, her medical team declared that she had made a full recovery. Her lab tests were normal. The pinpricks felt like pinpricks. She could feel them everywhere they touched her and nowhere they didn't. Her legs kicked just high enough and not too fast when they tapped her knee. She could do the finger-to-nose drill, the stand-on-one-foot-and-jump drill, and all the other drills that tested her muscle and nerve functions. The CT scan reported the swelling was gone, and the electrical spikes were back to the smooth regular pulsations of a normally functioning brain. She was required to pass an extensive battery of mental status tests before she could return to her medical practice. She did well, counting in serial sevens, remembering five objects after three minutes, interpreting abstract analogies, and everything else they threw at her. As always, she batted a thousand.

Her memory came back too, like an elaborate jigsaw puzzle.

The pieces, fuzzy at first, gradually came into sharper focus and one by one she put them in place. Then came the last piece—the memory of the night she had the seizure and was admitted to the hospital. At first she wasn't sure. Was it a memory or a dream? Was it only her imagination that Brian's eyes never met hers or Mark's?

But on the day of her discharge, she knew she hadn't imagined that night.

"The neurologist will follow Kate's progress after she goes home. He'll keep me posted, and if there is a need for an infectious disease person, my partner will see her in our office." Brian tore off a page from his prescription pad with the name, date, and time of her appointment with the neurologist and shook hands with Mark.

"What about this?" Kate indicated the IV line under her collarbone.

"Oh, of course. Lucy reminded me that I would need to remove that." Brian still didn't look at her. His gloved hands shook as he removed the tape and gauze, and then extracted the needle. It stung a little when he put the ointment on and covered the wound with fresh gauze.

I will always love you, Kate. Hadn't Brian said that? Or was that her imagination, too?

She hadn't had her period since she came back from Haiti. She assumed it was because she was sick. Then a few weeks later, the nausea started with the fatigue, and her breasts were tender—just like when she was . . .

Pregnant.

Was it possible?

With her headphones in her ears, she took one of the Waterford crystal wine glasses from the dining room china closet and poured a generous glass from the bottle of Welch's grape juice. No more drinking. She'd done enough damage.

She had intended to go for a long run that morning. Still working only three days a week since her discharge from the hospital, she vowed to devote some of her extra time and energy to getting back in shape by Thanksgiving, which was only a little over a week away.

It seemed overly ambitious now. She really didn't have any energy to spare and she certainly hadn't counted on failing her self-administered test that morning. After all, she had passed the rest with flying colors. Not this one, though. Fifteen minutes after she peed into the little white cassette, the little blue dot lined up with the POSITIVE on the pregnancy test. She repeated it a second and third time to be sure. If anything the blue dot only got bigger and bluer with each attempt, mocking her.

She took her juice out to the patio. The fall day was warm in the sun. But in the shade, she shivered, and it was hard to deny that winter wouldn't find its way before too long. She chose the sun, closed her eyes, turned up the volume on her Walkman, listened to one of her favorite jogging songs—Jackson Browne's "Running on Empty"—and waited for a plan to surface.

Someone removed the earphones from her ears. She must have fallen asleep for a few minutes. It was Mark. What was he doing home so early and what was he holding in his hand?

"My computer has my article on it. It's due to the publisher today," he explained. Then she realized he had one of the pregnancy tests in his hand. The dot had faded to a pale blue, but it was still accusingly positive. "Are you pregnant, Kate?" he asked. His gaze moved to her Waterford glass, still half-filled with the purple liquid.

"It's only grape juice."

"I thought you were on the pill, and I thought we agreed to talk about this before."

"I was taking the pill until I went into the hospital."

A perplexed look crossed his face, like he was searching for an answer to a really complex exam question. She braced herself.

"But we haven't had sex since before you went to Haiti. How . . . what else happened while you were there? Was it that Tim guy on your team? Oh my God, one of the Haitians?"

"Tim is gay. It wasn't anyone from Haiti." She just couldn't find the words to tell him.

"Well then. I know it isn't me. Who is it?"

She looked at him and she knew that he knew—like he expected it to happen for years.

"That bastard! He was supposed to be your doctor. I should have his license taken away. I should report him to the medical board and sue his ass."

"Mark, I'm sorry." Kate knew those were the right words to say. But the truth was, she felt more numb than anything else.

"Congratulations, Kate. You finally did it."

"What?"

"You got your revenge. Bravo! We're even and then some."

"It wasn't like that." The tears welled in her eyes. The hurt from Mark's affair in San Francisco was nowhere near as buried away in the past as she thought, apparently not for either one of them.

"No, Kate? Well, if it wasn't revenge—then tell me what it was." He turned and walked back into the house.

She waited to hear the front door slam. But instead she heard him on the telephone.

"I won't be back into the office today. My wife is not feeling well."

They kept to their own corners of the house for the next few hours. More than anything she wanted Mark to hold her and tell her he loved her. But she had no right to expect that. Three times she went to the refrigerator, opened it, and looked at the half-empty bottle of wine sitting on the shelf.

She decided to go for a walk, and expected her husband

to be gone when she got back. But his car was still there in the driveway, and he had tuna salad sandwiches and vegetable soup ready for her when she returned. They sat in the kitchen, neither of them eating much and neither of them looking at the other. The silence was worse than yelling would have been.

"I don't think I can do it—raise another man's child—especially *his*." He spoke as if he was talking about someone else, ticking off options for an acquaintance and not his wife. "An abortion is out of the question. Neither of us could live with that. Maybe adoption."

"I don't know if I can, Mark. It's my baby, too." She longed to reach across the table for his hand. "Are you saying you want to stay together?" A part of Kate wanted him to say no. She still loved her husband, but they had grown so far apart, and she didn't think she could find the energy to fight her way back to him.

"I just never thought that you would be the one. You've always been so . . . perfect." As if he was searching for a better word. "The perfect daughter, perfect mother, doctor, wife—I guess I figured I would be the one to screw things up—again."

"I'm not perfect, Mark. Maybe I've learned better than most how to keep people at just the right distance so they can't see the flaws." At that moment Kate couldn't think of a person in her life she could confide in. Work, family, even with her few girlfriends, she kept them all at a distance.

"Should we go back to the marriage counselor?" he asked.

"If you want to," Kate responded.

"Doesn't sound like your heart's in it, Kate."

She put her hand to her chest and thought how strange it was to feel the beat beneath her palm. She was beginning to believe her heart wasn't anywhere anymore.

20

KATE

ATLANTA
MARCH 1992

For the longest time, Kate couldn't separate her sadness from the shame. One was so vast that she couldn't keep it to herself; the other so deep that she couldn't let it out.

Her affair with Brian only lasted a night; her pregnancy with his child lasted less than two months. She never even told him. Mark and she wanted to have some time to sort things out—decide where their marriage stood. A week before Christmas the cramping started; then the bleeding, and following one night in the emergency room, it was gone. Everyone naturally assumed it was Mark's baby and they found no good reason to say anything different.

She dragged herself through her days at the clinic, put some food on the table for the kids, and after that all she could do was rock in the rocking chair that Mark had given her for Christmas when she was pregnant with Jen. She sipped wine—just a glass at first, then two, and then empty bottles taunted her morning after morning for two dreary winter months.

Mark was still living there. But his work hours had grown,

by necessity or design, it hardly mattered. They seldom saw each other. They quit arguing, they quit their sessions with the marriage counselor, and soon after, they quit talking completely. They agreed to stay together for the usual reason, the kids. Funny thing—how husbands and wives could keep secrets from each other and how those secrets could destroy a relationship. But for her and Mark, it turned out to be the secret they shared that finally unmoored their marriage.

The kids had a sleepover at a friend's house and Kate couldn't think of a thing she wanted to do. It was too early for a nap and besides, that stubborn bird was chirping away outside her window again. It was hard to ignore, even with the windows shut.

Kate finally opened a card from Sue Gray. It was a photo card. Inside was a picture of their team in Haiti. It must have been one of their arrival shots. They were all smiles.

> Kate,
>
> Hope you are feeling better. I had a phone call from Haiti. Madame La Belle was asking about you. She said that Adelaide, the woman with AIDS, died. Her daughter is living in Port au Prince with relatives, but it is not a good situation. It sounds quite awful for her actually. So sad—isn't it? The violence has subsided, but the country is still unstable. Don't know if we'll be able to make the trip this year. Would you consider going again if we do? I know it's a lot to ask after what happened. But, it was great to have you on the team.
>
> Kenbe fèm,
>
> Sue

Kenbe fèm—endure. She closed her eyes and rocked. In another time, she would have relished the silence. But it had been too quiet for too long. Even the little bird agreed and refused to leave her alone any longer with her sad thoughts.

Her little bird.

The three words tugged at her memory. After a few more minutes it came to her. She searched through a drawer and found her journal from Haiti. She had made no entries since she returned last October. She rocked a while longer, reading what she had written in Port au Prince. So much of it seemed unreal, like reading a novel. She was incredibly lucky to be alive. How could she have forgotten that?

Between two of the pages, she found the little girl's drawing. Tieina was her name. *Don't forget me* was her message. Yet Kate had forgotten. What might have happened to the girl—her mother's little bird? Hadn't she promised to help them both?

"Okay little bird. I hear you." Kate welcomed her song as she gathered up the dirty clothes first, and then the wine bottles. She realized she was well on her way to becoming an alcoholic, like her mother. But unlike her mother, she was determined to fight her mounting addiction.

She turned on the shower, shaved her legs, washed her hair, and put on fresh clothes—real clothes, not scrubs. After that, she called the airlines and booked a flight to Haiti for the following month, and then she called the Alcoholics Anonymous hotline and marked Monday night at 7 p.m. in her calendar for the next six months.

When Mark came home with the kids a few hours later, a pot roast with all the fixings was in the oven, the house was dusted and vacuumed, and her long red hair had been traded for a more manageable style. She saved twelve inches of hair in a sheet of white tissue paper for Tieina, remembering her first conversation with Adelaide.

Four weeks later, going on her own to Haiti, Kate had no plan. But she put that out of her mind, as she did all the other unknowns of the past few weeks since she had decided to make the journey. All she knew and all she had to remember was that she was going to find Tieina. And if what Madame La Belle said was true, she wouldn't leave until Tieina was safe.

She was on her third cup of mediocre Miami airport coffee. Her original noon flight was cancelled. There were few passengers in the waiting area. She saw none of the smiling groups in their slogan T-shirts. Apparently, Haiti was not a popular place these days, not even for missionaries. She tossed the cup in the trash. She would have preferred a beer to coffee, but she vowed not to drink again until she had her head on straight. The remnants of her last conversation with Mark echoed as she waited to board the plane in Miami. She had anticipated every reason he would throw at her why she shouldn't go back to Haiti:

"It's too dangerous."

"The kids need you."

"I can't do it all alone."

"What if you get sick again?"

For each one, she had a reasonable and logical answer, except for the last. "I'm leaving if you go. I mean it. Your choice." Stated calmly, as if it were that simple. As if one action, one decision, dissolved over a dozen years of marriage.

His final threat almost stopped her. But in many ways, the most important ones, he was already gone. Well, if this trip gave him his last bit of courage to cut the cord, then she saw that as more of a reason to go than not. She thought of a caveat from their med school surgery rotation. "Don't cut what you can untie. But if you have to cut it, cut it clean." If only it were possible to cut the marriage clean.

Still, she would have liked to have heard Mark's voice one more time before she left the country. But she resisted the urge to call his office and dialed the house instead. It was four o'clock and the kids would just be getting home from school. The babysitter put Danny on the phone first.

"Are you in Haiti now? Did you find the little girl? Is she okay?"

"Just in the Miami airport, Danny. I'll be in Haiti in about two hours." Kate dabbed her eyes. "Are you ready for your game?"

"Sure, Mom. If we win, Dad promised we'd go out for pizza after. But I know we'll have pizza even if we lose," he whispered. "Don't forget to give the kids the soccer ball. I hope someday I can play with them. I could teach them my famous Rigando flip."

"I'll bet you could, honey."

Her son had used his own money to buy a soccer ball and a ball pump for her to take to Haiti.

"Let me talk to your sister now. Love you."

"Hi, Mom," Jen said, followed by silence.

"How was school today, honey?" Kate coaxed her daughter, who had grown more sullen, almost angry the last few months—not unlike Kate's reaction to her own mother's drinking when she was a child.

"Okay."

"Do you have a lot of homework?"

"I guess." Jen wasn't giving an inch.

"Be a good girl for Daddy. I'll see you in a week. When I get back, you and I will do something special, just the two of us." Between getting stuck in Haiti, the encephalitis, and Kate's depression and drinking binge after the miscarriage, Kate felt a distance growing between them. It frightened her mostly because it reminded her of how she had felt when she was Jen's age.

Kate didn't want to hang up the phone, but it was time to board the plane. She closed her eyes and wished the words could ease the strain between them.

"Maybe we can go to the Carnegie Science Center?" Jen offered.

Kate heard a trace of excitement in Jen's voice and smiled. How many six-year-olds would choose the science center for a special day with their mom?

Well at least there was one thing Mark and Kate agreed on. Their daughter was extremely bright and focused.

"That would be wonderful, honey. I need to get on my plane now. I love you, Jen." Kate waited until her daughter hung up before she placed the receiver back in its cradle, and for a brief second regretted her decision to return to Haiti. Maybe Mark was right. Her children needed her. Why did she feel so compelled to help someone else's little girl?

Five hours later than she had anticipated, they were in the air and she was on her way to Port au Prince. She didn't have much of a plan for the week ahead, but she had even less of one for her return to Atlanta.

21

GISELLE

PETIT (TI) MIREBELAIS, HAITI
APRIL 1992

If she rocked with just the right rhythm, Giselle hardly noticed the throbbing in her head. The pain was buried deep in her skull between her eyes and came almost every day now, worse at night. So mornings became her favorite time, especially when there was no market. It was quiet, except for the roosters and the dogs, and she could sit in the old rocking chair sipping her coffee. It was the only empty space in her day where she could try to make some sense out of her situation—what remained between her fading dreams and the uncertain reality. There wasn't a minute that she didn't grieve over her aunt and uncle. She received the news of their brutal murders just a few weeks before Christmas. She couldn't even go to claim their bodies and arrange a proper burial. No doubt, one of the crazed members of the deposed military would have gotten her, too. That was the way it was in Haiti. People disappeared.

Yvonne was distraught, as well. "I'm going to Port au Prince, even if I have to crawl on my hands and knees," she threatened at least once a week.

"I promise I'll go with you as soon as it's safe." No one could guess when that might be. But Giselle knew that, even in less violent times, the trip would have been a challenge for the peasant woman who, other than a pilgrimage to the Saut d'Eau, had never been more than a few miles from her birth home.

Giselle stood up and stretched in the early morning light. Others were up and on their way to market or their fields. Settling into the routine of life in rural Haiti was easier than Giselle had anticipated. Much of the day was occupied by the tasks of daily life—carrying water, preparing food, and washing clothes. She had taken so much for granted in Port au Prince. Here everything revolved around the daylight—there was no electricity—and the weather.

Their survival depended on nature sending enough sun so the crops could be planted, and enough rain so they would grow. But not so much rain that the seeds and tender plants would be washed away from the steeply sloped fields. As for water, except in the short rainy season, every drop was precious. It was an hour walk to the only captured source for the community, so they traveled in small groups for companionship and safety, the empty buckets swinging from their arms as they made the journey up and down the rocky path. The women and the girls walked carefully, balancing the large plastic buckets of water on their heads with only a small rolled towel between the load and their scalps. They went in the mornings and again in the afternoons after lessons were finished.

The clinic was close to Yvonne's. She and Natali stayed in one of the little rooms that had been the exam area. Madame Cereste helped them find a bed, a dresser, and a chair. Giselle placed her painting on the wall. It was more than most anyone in the village had. Yet it was hard not to compare with what they had lost.

"I miss Port au Prince. I don't even have my own room here," Natali reminded her on a daily basis.

"I miss our home, too." She reminisced about her old kitchen that was as large as their entire living space now. Propane tanks fueled the heavy stove, and the refrigerator always filled with food from the Caribbean Market in Petionville. Maybe the electricity was not always reliable in the city, but they always enjoyed a hot breakfast and evening meal together.

In Ti Mirebelais, they ate their one main meal a day with Yvonne or Madame Cereste's families. They bought a small charcoal stove in the market so they could make coffee in the morning and sometimes a little soup. In return for the room and food, Giselle taught French and English to the children in the village. For the first two months, the schools everywhere in Haiti were closed by national decree and none of the regular teachers came. It was so everywhere in Haiti. For anyone to challenge this was dangerous. Such actions could be construed as anti-patriotism against the new regime. Even in this remote village, pictures of Aristide were removed from view. Many families burned them; a few kept them carefully hidden away in hopes that their president would return one day.

Now that the schools were open again, Giselle held classes for the adults who wished to learn to read and write. Soon she would teach drawing and painting for the children. Madame Cereste assured her she would be able to get the art supplies when the Americans returned.

But today she was on her way to Saint Marc. This was her second trip in the last three months. She needed to find a working telephone to get word to Max. Saint Marc was a much longer trip, but not as risky as Port au Prince. Nobody would know her there, and Madame Cereste had a friend with whom she could stay. Max was still in the United States and she and Natali had no money. When she last spoke to him in February, he promised to wire her some and reassured her that he would try to get them visas to come to the U.S.

"It's going to take time, *Ma Chérie*. There are many people asking and the U.S. government is not very sympathetic. We have a better chance than most because I can make a good case for political asylum. Still, they are estimating six months."

"Six months?" she pleaded into the phone. "We can't wait that long." It had already been six months since they arrived in Petit Mirebelais. But the urgency she felt to escape lessened each week as her friendships grew with the other women.

For the day-to-day expenses she received enough from teaching, but there were so many other things they had done without for the past six months—clothes, proper schooling for Natali, and a doctor to prescribe her some medicine for her head. There were more days when she could not lift her head from the pillow and more frequent times when she felt like she was walking in a dark tunnel and she could only see the world that was straight ahead of her. She planned to stay three or four days in Saint Marc, allowing enough time, she hoped, to get the wire transfer and see a doctor.

"I want to go with you," Natali whined. "There is nothing to do here. I'm sick of carrying water and sitting around all day talking about nothing."

Giselle was about to scold her for her attitude when Yvonne came down the path with a notebook and pen.

"Do you have time to look at my homework?" the woman asked shyly.

She was the first woman to sign up for the adult education classes. Yvonne was an eager student. Giselle caught her studying late at night by candlelight and lent her a flashlight. The batteries only lasted a week, and then she was bent over her notebook in the candlelight again.

"Of course." Giselle took the notebook from her friend. Yvonne volunteered to write a summary of the covenants for their newly formed women's group. Her printing was quite neat and precise. There were just a few mistakes. "Would you like to read it to me?"

Yvonne began timidly:

"April 4, 1992

"**A.** Purpose: The purpose for the Ti Mirebelais Women's Group is for peasant women in our village to organize in solidarity with each other so we can advance our businesses and education for ourselves and for our children.

"**B.** Meetings: We will meet two times a month on Wednesday at three o'clock in the afternoon at the clinic building. Each woman must attend at least one time a month or she cannot participate in voting.

"**C.** Officers: We will have elections for officers (President, Secretary, and Treasurer). Every woman has one vote and the person who gets the most votes wins the office for one year."

"Will you run for president, Giselle? I know everyone will vote for you."

"I don't think so, Yvonne. I have only been here a few months and we may not be staying. There are many other women who could do a better job." It was flattering to think of the possibility. "Please, continue."

Yvonne's voice grew stronger.

"**D.** Activities:

1. Start a co-op so we don't have to borrow money from moneylenders.

2. Start small business activities such as needlework, crafting, and roasting coffee.

"**E.** Finances: Each woman will contribute twenty-five goudes a month. When the total sum is 2,000 goudes, one woman will receive 1,000 goudes and the rest of the money will stay in the co-op common fund. A woman may trade her turn with another woman, but only one time. Any money from business activities that the group organizes will go into the common fund. The group will vote on how that money is spent, but it will be for education and health programs in the community."

Together she and Yvonne worked through the math. She was surprised that the peasant woman had such a good head for numbers, too.

"Has he been back, the moneylender?" Giselle worried about her friend and the debt she had incurred for her daughter's funeral.

"Yes. Each week he torments me. I hope we can start the co-op immediately." Yvonne had asked to be first to receive the 1,000 goudes. "He frightens me. He has the smile of a snake wanting to swallow me up." She quivered at the mention of him.

Giselle agreed and hoped that she could help her friend if Max sent the money.

"I think the group will be pleased when you meet this afternoon. You have done a good job writing the covenants, Yvonne. You are the best student."

"No, it is you who is the best teacher. Did I ever tell you my Adelaide wanted to be a teacher, just like you?"

"No, I—" Giselle stopped. She wanted to say she was not a teacher. She was an artist. But instead she concluded, "No, I didn't know that. I think she would have been a very good teacher."

They hadn't talked much about Adelaide. She would have liked to share a cup of coffee and some memories with her friend. But she was getting anxious to get on the road. She waved for Natali to come over.

"Thank you again for looking after Natali while I'm away."

"It is no problem, sister. But do go with good speed before the day is gone."

"Natali, please be a help to Yvonne." She kissed her daughter on the cheek. "We can go to early church on Sunday. I'll be back before dark on Saturday." She already felt her own darkness descend into the outskirts of her vision. She gathered a small bag of clothes and a bottle of water. On the way out of their little room she reached for her scarf, the one Jean-Juste had given her years ago. The blue was faded almost to gray now. But it would keep the dust out of her face on her journey. The rainy season was still two months away. Like the rest of the peasants in her new village, she prayed it would come early this year.

CHAPTER

22

KATE

HAITI
APRIL 1992

Kate's driver pulled up in front of the address she had been given for Tieina's relatives in one of the middle-class neighborhoods of Port au Prince. As Kate stepped out of the car, a rock the size of a baseball flew past her head and hit the already cracked windshield. She instinctively covered her head and looked around for a place to hide. The driver, not as easily intimidated, jumped out of the car and ran into the courtyard from where the rock had come. A small girl came darting out and threw another rock, just missing the driver and ran straight into Kate. She wrapped her arms around the child, who reciprocated by pounding her chest with her fists and yelling, "Leave me alone. Help! Help!" The girl struggled to get away.

"Tieina? Is that you? I'm not going to hurt you." Kate thought she recognized the girl from her ginger-colored hair. She was even thinner than she had been nine months ago, and her dress was gray from wear and dirt, barely covering her backside. She had one tennis shoe with no laces. There was a wildness about her that frightened Kate.

Tieina grabbed a fistful of Kate's cropped hair and stared silently as if she was trying to remember something. At the mention of her name, the girl stopped her assault on Kate and showed a glimmer of recognition.

"Mama, Mama. I want my mama," she cried in a small voice.

"It's okay, Tieina. I've got you now." She took the child to the car. "Can you get her something to eat and drink, please?" She handed the driver fifty goudes.

He returned with a Styrofoam container of fried chicken, rice, and sweet plantains. Tieina devoured the meal with her fingers and drank down two bottles of orange Tampico.

"Slow down, Tieina." The girl probably hadn't eaten that much in weeks.

Sure enough, a few minutes later, she burped twice and retched on the seat.

"Mama, Mama," she cried between hiccups.

With a packet of hand wipes, Kate cleaned up Tieina and the seat. "Please, keep her in the car," she told the driver.

Kate knocked on the door of the house. There was no answer. She walked around and looked in the windows, but she did not see anyone. She returned to the entrance and tried the door. It was locked. A basket of potatoes, half peeled, sat on the ground next to a large *kivet* overflowing with wet laundry. A few articles of clothing had been hung on the line to dry. It reminded Kate of a scene from Cinderella. How long until the evil stepsisters and their mother returned?

She got back in the car. "Let's go. Back to Didi's. Now."

Didi prepared a bath of hot water in one of her largest laundry *kivets*. Kate scrubbed Tieina's hair, touching her as gently as she could, and fought the urge to vomit. The strands were riddled with lice, and her scalp was covered with crusty scales of ringworm outlining scattered bald patches. She used an extra toothbrush she had brought to gently scrub the black dirt caked under the girl's fingernails. On her back, purple welts crisscrossed in the shape of a belt. And Kate didn't even want to think how she got the bruises on the inside of her upper thighs. The girl whimpered as Kate gently washed away the dirt that covered her wounds. She tried her best to keep the anger brewing inside her under control.

She managed a smile. "Tieina, you look so pretty. Let's find something special for you to wear. Okay, honey?"

The child was silent.

Tieina's clothes weren't worth salvaging, so Kate dressed the child in one of her own T-shirts. She gave her clean socks and a pair of panties that she pinned at the waistband. It took an hour to get a comb through the tangles in her hair. She would have cut it short to her scalp so the infection might clear, but it seemed too much trauma for this evening.

After she was sure Tieina could keep a small bowl of chicken broth and rice in her stomach, Kate laid her in one of the twin beds in her room and covered her with a light sheet. She sat beside Tieina on the bed, and searched for a place on her that wasn't bruised and abused. She rubbed one of her thin upper arms, the only part of the tiny body that wasn't wasted to skin and bones. What cruel labor had this little girl been made to do these last months to have such muscles in her arms despite the wasting of her body everywhere else?

After Tieina was asleep, Kate joined Didi on the veranda. She wanted a drink more than she could remember ever wanting one before. Didi couldn't have known about her drinking problem, yet she appeared with a tray of tea and a plate of crackers and Cheez Whiz.

"We are lucky this evening. The government has given us some electricity to make tea." Didi nodded up the hill to where there were several of the nicer homes in the zone. "There must be a party at one of our government official's houses."

Kate had missed lunch and dinner, but she couldn't think

of putting solid food into her stomach. The warm tea with sugar soothed her craving for alcohol. Just holding the warm mug in her hands was comforting. She looked out over the soccer field. One lone spotlight that hadn't been knocked out cast an eerie glow over the dirt play yard. Actual graffiti now covered the mural depicting the United Nations Declaration of Human Rights, and a heavy chain blocked the entrance.

Didi was looking in the same direction. "The doctor who sponsored the field and his wife were found murdered in their Petionville home just weeks after the coup. His niece and her daughter are missing. The niece's husband received political asylum in the U.S.—one of the few to get out." She paused to sip her tea. "The neighborhood children have been told to stay away. Their parents fear that there will be retaliation if they play there. Anything that Aristide had done to promote human rights is seen as a threat to the current regime." Didi walked over to the gate guarding her compound and checked the lock for the second time since they sat down. "The little girl, Tieina, is a *restavek*, you know."

"*Restavek?*" Kate repeated. "I don't know the word."

"*Restavek* is, how would you say in English—a euphemism? In French it means literally to stay with. In Haiti, it means a child who is given to someone, often a relative who promises to provide a home and food and send the child to school. The parents are usually very poor—maybe there is only a mother and many other children. Everyone knows what usually happens. The children become household servants at best, but many times they are physically and even sexually abused. Very few ever go to school."

"But what about the police? This must be illegal. Can't they stop it?" Kate wondered how many more secrets were hidden in the troubled country.

"Police? Where are they? Whose side are they on? Even the human rights organizations can't find all these children. There are tens of thousands of them, and where would they go? The street is even worse."

"I can't send her back to those people. We have to do something."

"There are no easy answers."

"But there are options—yes? I can fight if I have to. I have a daughter at home, a year younger than Tieina. I can't walk away from this. I won't."

Didi nodded and checked the lock on the gate for the third time. The neighborhood lights flickered briefly and then there was total blackness. Kate sat in silence with her friend, waiting for her eyes to adjust.

After a few moments, up and down the street one, then two, then many candles appeared in the neighbors' windows. The individual flames ignited in solidarity and challenged the darkness.

"I don't want to make trouble for you and your staff. That's why we are leaving." Kate held tight to Tieina with one hand and picked up her duffle bag with the other. She tried to pass Didi, but the Haitian woman blocked her way with a considerably more ample body. "Please, just let me use one of the drivers for the day. I'll pay whatever you ask."

"It's not the money and I'm not afraid for myself. You just can't take a child from her family—even if they are evil." Didi lowered her voice with the last phrase and simultaneously clasped her hands over Tieina's ears. "It's still kidnapping, and Haitian prisons are terrible places. Americans have no special rights."

"I have to do something." As strange as it seemed, Kate knew she couldn't return home and make things right with her own daughter if she abandoned this child.

"You must find her legal guardian. It depends on the birth certificate and if the mother signed papers. If her father is alive, it may well be him. I don't know. The answer may be in Petit Mirebelais. Leave the child with me. I'll return her to the family. I'll think of some explanation. My driver will take you to her grandmother. The roads are not too bad for most of the way. Thoma can go with you to translate."

"How can we be sure Tieina will be safe?"

"I know some people in that neighborhood. I'll have them keep their eyes open, ask a few questions. If they know somebody's watching, they'll treat the child better. You don't want to make enemies of her family. You may need their permission for what you are trying to do."

"But I haven't said what I'm trying to do." Kate looked at her friend confused.

"You are trying to adopt her, of course."

Kate started to protest. Adopting Tieina had not occurred to her. She was barely managing with the two children she had, especially Jen, and now she was going to be a single parent. But the sureness in her friend's voice made her pause.

"Could I actually do that?" she asked the question more of herself than her friend.

Thoma had refused to roll down the windows more than a crack. "It's not safe," he had said.

Despite the commotion outside and the sudden stops and starts of the vehicle, Kate nodded off in the stale air of the backseat. Sometime later, a warm breeze woke her. The car was moving faster now that they were away from the city, and Thoma had opened his window. The smell of damp earth was refreshing after the acrid intensity of garbage and diesel fumes. Kate stretched and studied the sights.

Burgundy stalks of knotty sugar cane defined the road for miles and miles. They rose straight up from the ground ten to fifteen feet high. Wide-brimmed hats obscured the faces of the peasants who labored between the plants. But the strain of their toils was evident from the sweat on their backs and the harsh outline of their ropey muscles. In one hand, the men wielded machetes that cut the cane. In the other, they drew metal hooks from holsters around their waists. The hooks were used to strip the leaves from the stalks.

Every so often there was a church or schoolhouse or a group of women selling fruit and vegetables on the side of the road. Peasants walked along the road singly or in small groups and occasionally with a donkey loaded with items that must have been purchased at market. The chaos and tension of Port au Prince was gone. Even the driver and Thoma were more relaxed. He turned up the radio and they sang along. And the colorful *Lotto* booths, similar to Port au Prince, were everywhere. They unwrapped and ate the cheese sandwiches that Didi had made for them. Thoma bargained with a market woman for three lukewarm bottles of Coke.

After a few gulps she was ready to tackle anything and anyone that stood in the way of Tieina's safety. As they turned off the main route they nearly ran over a woman getting off a tap-tap. She was tall and beautiful and wore a faded blue scarf.

Thoma hit the horn. With a startled look, the woman jumped out of the way just in time. "Crazy woman!"

"No. I don't think she even saw us." Kate recognized the vacant look on the stranger's face. It was the same expression that had looked back at her from the mirror the last few months.

It was well into the afternoon when they came to a little wooden sign with block letters: PETIT MIREBELAIS. Thoma asked for directions to Adelaide's mother's home and she learned her name was Yvonne.

They made brief introductions and explained the reason for their visit.

"You are the American that was going to send money for my granddaughter's school?" The woman regarded her with a suspicious look.

Thoma translated for her.

"Yes, but I got sick and I was only able to return last week. Your granddaughter's situation in Port au Prince is not good."

"Yes, I have been afraid of that. My friend is going to go with me. But we didn't think it was safe yet. Please, take me back with you."

Kate glanced at Thoma. Perhaps Didi was wrong and the child belonged here with her grandmother. "Can we do that?" she asked him. He looked skeptical.

"We can talk more about that later," she answered Yvonne. "A woman in Port au Prince told me that the birth certificate is most important if we are to get Tieina someplace safe. Do you have her birth papers?" Whether Tieina ended up in the U.S. or Mirebelais, the papers were critical.

"Yes." Yvonne went to a small dresser and pulled an envelope out from under a pile of clothes.

She and Thoma looked at it. "Mother—Delva, Adelaide. Father—Charles, Ramon."

"I begged her not to give his name. But she was a silly young girl. She thought it would make him come back and love her if he knew that they had a child together." Yvonne spat on the floor. "All he did was give her that disease that killed her. The father is dead, too. His aunt lives here. She went to the funeral months ago. I am Tieina's guardian. I have a letter from my daughter. See? I will decide what is a safe place for my granddaughter."

Kate nodded and silently scolded herself for charging in on her white horse to save the little girl from this woman who clearly loved her.

It was good to be out of Port au Prince and walking in the fresh country air. Kate took long hikes up and down the mountain road, pausing to take photos of the fields and the children. Despite their tattered clothes and thin bodies, they were incredibly photogenic. The older ones preferred to be photographed in somber poses. Their eyes, penetrating and wise, captivated her heart. Was it poverty that gave them that look? The younger ones would ham it up, linking arms with each other or showing off their little biceps in a feigned muscle-man pose. They were all giggles and smiles. Except for the children being shoeless, they could be a group of Danny's friends just finishing a pickup soccer match.

"Will you come back again?" one young boy asked. "Will you bring my picture and can I have one of you, too?"

What was it about the people she encountered here that tugged her heart so fiercely? It wasn't guilt or curiosity, or at least not entirely. It was as if they awakened something in her heart that had always belonged to them.

Kate initially regretted her concession to attend church on Sunday morning. Drums and chanting from a Vodou ceremony had kept her awake until well past midnight. She had a lot on her mind, too, and wanted to write in her journal, which she had started keeping again. But Yvonne seemed so happy she had agreed to accompany her, she couldn't back out now. So off she went a little after seven in the morning. They stopped at Natali's house, where she and her mother would join them.

But when they arrived at the abandoned clinic, Natali informed them, "Mother is not well after her trip from Saint Marc. She asked me to tell you that she won't be at church today. But she wants us to pray for her."

The church was larger and better furnished than the one where they held clinic last fall in Port au Prince, but it was simple nonetheless. The altar rose above the congregation several feet and was beautifully carved from dark mahogany and covered with a hand-embroidered cloth. A large leather-bound Bible lay open on the cloth-covered surface. The church was full. It was hard to imagine that these were the same farmers she had seen toiling in the fields or the same women she had passed in the market or the same barefoot children that ran up and down the road each day. Everyone was scrubbed clean with pressed clothes and shined shoes. The church smelled like soap and the incense that floated from a metal urn on the altar. In contrast, Kate felt frumpy with her dusty sport sandals and wrinkled skirt. Ripples of sweat ran down her face, neck, and back.

A small group of young men beat on drums at the front of the church. One played a keyboard. A generator hummed in the background, barely audible above the music and singing. Everyone participated, from youngest to oldest, male and female, their voices blended in a perfect rhythm and harmony that ebbed and flowed like the sadness and hope of their lives. It was the loveliest music Kate had ever heard.

The service started with a procession of peasant girls from shortest to tallest, dressed in white, dancing up the aisles. The older ones carried baskets of colorful fresh fruit and vegetables on their heads. The younger ones stopped every few feet and made deep sweeping bows to the ground. The baskets were deposited on the altar and, with a nod from the priest, the girls took their seats next to the drummers.

Even though it was a Catholic mass, Kate had trouble following the progression. Years had passed since she had been to a formal church service and it had to be a hundred degrees inside. Now she understood why Yvonne had chosen this spot and why all the Haitians moved in to let her sit on the end of the wooden pew.

There were two fans in the church. One was on the altar to give air to the priest and the other just above her head. Nevertheless, after two hours in the crowded building with only a small cup of coffee in her stomach, she was ready to pass out.

"Excuse me," she whispered to Yvonne as the last of the congregation returned to their seats after communion. She made as discreet an exit as she could to the outside, being that she was the only white person amongst hundreds of Haitians. Yet she had felt less apart from the people surrounding her than she ever had when she attended church back home.

Thoma followed her with a concerned look. "Are you okay? Do you need some water?"

"Thanks, I just needed some air. But I do have a question. Thoma, during communion, the women behind me, I couldn't understand what they were saying. But it was the same few words they repeated over and over. I wanted to join them, but all I know are my Catholic prayers from when I was a little girl, and English seemed so inappropriate. What was the prayer?" Indeed with so much misery and poverty and violence, what did one pray for in Haiti?

"It's not a Catholic prayer or Protestant. It is just a very simple request. They ask only that God will see them again."

The prayer, the young boy she photographed a day earlier, and Tieina's message on the day of the coup—the plea was the same. Don't forget us. So many things seemed impossible to her. But forgetting these people, Kate couldn't imagine it.

It took considerable effort on Thoma's part to convince Yvonne that it was not a good idea for her to accompany them back to Port au Prince that afternoon. In the end he persuaded her by suggesting, "You have crops to tend to so you will have money to help your granddaughter and food to give her."

Kate was shocked speechless when Yvonne pulled her aside as they were leaving. "I want you to take my granddaughter back to the United States. Her mother is gone. Too soon her voice was silent. But Tieina can have a chance." There were tears in the woman's eyes. The kind of tortured tears Kate could only recognize being a mother too. She continued with the words, "I'll sign the papers."

Kate nodded and promised, "I will bring Tieina to you before she comes to the U.S." She then hugged Yvonne, wondering if she would have enough courage and love to stand in for Tieina's grandmother.

"Thank you. Now I know I am making the right choice." The grandmother looked as if she had found a friend rather than lost a granddaughter.

It was a mostly silent walk back up the mountain in the early afternoon sun. The road was so steep she had to lean forward to balance her backpack. The dust clung to the sweat that covered her skin and soaked her clothes. Even her mouth tasted like dust and sweat as she panted with exertion trying to keep up with Thoma. Kate focused on the rocky ground beneath her feet to keep from stumbling. She wondered if the enormous boulders that jutted out of the earth were bedrock exposed by generations of soil erosion. Would there be enough soil to hold the fragile shoots from the early crops? Would the rain they begged for arrive in time to nourish their roots? Would there be enough to feed one more generation of Haitians?

Didi reported that Tieina was doing okay. Her cousin, who was a neighbor, stopped by each day and showed casual interest in the girl, inquiring about schooling and commenting about how thin she looked. They offered to have a doctor friend examine her for worms.

"Such a problem in these peasants, you know." Didi mimicked her cousin's inquiry. In just the last few days, she reported Tieina was looking better. Her clothes were clean and she was getting at least one meal a day.

"Good. But I fear this is just a temporary fix. As soon as we let our guard down, Tieina will be in the same situation again."

Didi nodded in affirmation.

"I wish I could stay longer to get the paperwork started. But I have to be back to work Tuesday and I miss my kids and . . ." She almost said "my husband." Then she remembered her marriage was over and the sadness that she had submerged for her failed marriage came to the surface with an intensity that threatened to overwhelm her to tears. "How do you do it, Didi—stay here with everything that goes on? You could get out, come to the U.S.?" Kate knew she had family in Miami. "Don't you get angry or discouraged? It seems so impossible and complicated."

Didi nodded sympathetically. "There is a widely quoted Haitian proverb—*Dye mon gen mon.* 'Beyond the mountains are more mountains.' I have my moments of anger and despair along the way. But at some point, you don't see the endless mountains. You see the person beside you. So you do what you can for that one person."

"Like Tieina," Kate concluded. As uncertain as she was about how this adoption would affect her life and her children's lives, she was certain it was what she was meant to do.

23

GISELLE

PETIT (TI) MIREBELAIS
SEPTEMBER 1992

An artist surely knew when she was losing touch with her colors. The blues became gray and the yellows a pale, lemony vanilla. Giselle studied the dollops of paint on her palette. They were organized the way she had always arranged them, the way she had been taught in university. She dipped the tip of her brush into the blue mound, planning to paint a clear, crisp sky full of promise. Instead she stroked a stormy gray across the canvas that wanted for even paler and more somber clouds. It became the kind of day not for a bright yellow bird to sing her bold song, but for a cautious creature, one that hid in the broad leaves of the banana tree. The textures were wrong, too; everything was flat and one-dimensional. What kind of song would this insipid yellow creature make? Would she have a song at all?

That was the way it had been for the last few months. Max had wired the money as he had promised, but he had made little progress in getting her and Natali their travel visas to the United States. She used most of the money to see a doctor while she was in Saint Marc in April. Trained in France, he was supposed to be a specialist in his field of neurology. But still, he could offer her nothing for her headaches and her fading vision. A brain tumor, he had said, or more precisely, a tumor just beneath her brain in someplace called the pituitary gland.

"I've seen similar cases, when I was in Paris. The tumor is benign; it's not cancer and it's quite curable. But it's a very delicate operation. No one can do it in Haiti." He shook his head and then gestured toward his diploma hanging on the wall like it was the Mona Lisa. "Of course in France or the United States, the procedures are commonplace, done every day." Then he had showed her a pictograph from one of his fat books.

She stared at a human brain cut in half right down the middle. The right side of the brain totally split from the left. The man's face was still on the skull and she could see in profile that his eyes were blue. She wondered how someone could have his brain split and still have his eyes open?

"Right here." He touched the pictograph.

She shuddered like he had touched her deep between her eyes where the pain resided.

"I suspect your tumor might be pressing on the large nerve that connects your eyes to your brain." His look bored through her forehead and settled to her eyes as if she was a specimen under his microscope.

She looked at the diagram, so lifelike it could have been a photograph, but no, it was a drawing.

"A medical artist named Frank Netter," Dr. Neurology from France told her. "He has made a whole series of detailed diagrams of human anatomy. Isn't it amazing?"

She had to agree. If she had the surgery and her vision returned to normal, she would like to make illustrations like that—pictures of the human body that could be used to explain disease and good health, too. Diagrams to teach the women of her country how they could take care of themselves—like when they were pregnant.

"If you can get to the United States," he had said, "maybe surgery will save your eyesight. Otherwise . . ."

Otherwise, he didn't know. She could stay the same or she could get worse. There was no talk of getting better. He gave her a bottle of little orange pills.

"These are stronger than what you are taking now. Acetaminophen won't help you much longer."

She had taken the pills and studied them, hoping for a clue. How would she tell them apart—these powerful orange ones from the feeble white ones—if the colors faded much more?

Giselle sighed, regretting her decision to take her canvas and paints out again. It was the first time in nearly four months. It should have been a good day to paint. There was a breeze just cool enough to speed the paint drying and just eager enough to keep the sweat from dripping onto her palette. September was always an unpredictable month in Ti Mirebelais, more so this year than others. It was still hurricane season.

There was little hope that she and Natali would join Max in the U.S. anytime soon. Since Aristide had left and Cedras had assumed power, almost nothing and no one was getting in or out of Haiti. The embargo, meant to stop the craziness, only made it harder on those who already had so little. The misery and fear continued. Men were building boats as fast as they could get the wood down off the mountains.

"Just wait," Max had urged when she spoke with him by telephone last week. "There is going to be a new president in the U.S. in January. He will be different. He is going to be a friend to Haiti. He has made firm promises. Just a few more months, I will get you and Natali to New York, where you'll be safe with me."

Promises from politicians, she thought. Haitian or

American, they all speak the same language. "Well, everyone here is waiting for Aristide to return. They're convinced only he can make things better."

"I don't know. They say Aristide is different. It is hard not to change when you are in the U.S. for a year."

As hard as it was not to change living with rural peasants for a year? she wanted to say. "Natali misses you terribly. I do, too." He seemed like a stranger. Even his voice sounded different and the words he used—bits and pieces of English infiltrated their usual Creole conversation. What did he know about her days and what did she know about his? If it weren't for Natali, their connection to each other would have been cut months ago.

She hadn't told him all the details of what the doctor had said. Even if she got to the United States in time, where would they find the money for an operation? She kept the true weight of the secret to herself. Her friends in Ti Mirebelais knew about the headaches, but she had not told anyone except the doctor in Saint Marc about her fading vision. Not even Natali.

She could have confided in Yvonne. But her friend hardly noticed anything these days. She was worried sick about her granddaughter, Tieina. It was impossible to get to Port au Prince. They tried one time in July. But they didn't even make it as far as Carrefour before they had to turn back. A manifestation blocked all the roads.

When her friend Yvonne wasn't worrying over Tieina, she was all caught up in the women's group. The energy from the group was palpable some days. Once they established the co-op, the discussions moved on to how they would change their community, their department, and then all of Haiti. Some days Giselle believed they really could. Other sessions they became mired like an old cow with its feet stuck in the mud.

This rural solidarity was something new to Giselle. Even though she was elected as the first president of the women's group and they looked to her for guidance with many decisions, she was learning a lot from her peasant neighbors. She remembered the passionate discussions she and her university friends had years ago, sipping rum punches on the porch at the Hotel Oloffson. She looked at her hands now; they were slightly calloused and her nails were short and unpainted. Not the hands of an artist, not quite the hands of a peasant.

She took out a fresh canvas and picked up her paintbrush again. The last of the summer mangos were ripe and ready to fall to the ground, and the bananas were sweet and yellow. Today a cool breeze and gray and vanilla suited her just fine. She must continue to paint as long as she was able. The little bird must not hide any longer. Pale or not, she had a bold song to share.

For the next few weeks, Giselle painted furiously from sunrise to sunset. She worked in muted shades, each day more of what she remembered and less of what she had hoped for. And she walked about memorizing the details of her world in case the time came when she had only her dreams and her memories to brighten the darkness. When she finished her work, she rolled up the canvases and sealed them in a plastic bin left by one of the missionary groups when they abandoned Haiti during the coup. Her works of art were not the sophisticated masterpieces she envisioned back when she was in university and when Jean-Juste was in her life. Yet in their own ways, they were beautiful and meaningful and full of a richer purpose.

24

KATE

UNITED STATES
SEPTEMBER 1992

"I won't accept that explanation, Tom. It has been almost six months since Tieina's grandmother agreed. Why is this taking so long?" Kate folded warm towels out of the dryer and set the timer for fifteen minutes—a reminder that she was on the clock with the lawyer and a reminder that Mark would be coming for Danny and Jen. It was his weekend with the kids. Although she missed them, she was looking forward to having a block of time to move forward with the new non-profit organization she was starting for the work she hoped to do in Haiti.

"I'm doing my best, Kate," Tom replied. "But the embargo against Haiti is making everything more difficult."

"I know. I know. I just don't get it. Is there an embargo against getting abused children out of Haiti?" A beep on the line alerted her that she had a call waiting.

"I'll keep pushing. Do you have a name for your organization yet?" Tom was also working on the articles of incorporation for her non-profit.

"No, not yet. But something will come to me." A second beep interrupted. "Tom, I've got to go. I have another call. Thanks again. I mean it. I do appreciate how difficult this has been."

Kate pushed the button to switch to the other call. "Hello," her father's voice said.

"How is everything?" he asked.

"It's taken longer than I expected to get the organization up and running—and more money. With the divorce and all, I want to spend more time with the kids—they need that. I need that. And I'm just frustrated with all the obstacles to getting Tieina here."

"Whoa, girl. Take it easy. Just remember everything that's happened in the last year. Last year at this time, we all thought we were going to lose you." His voice cracked.

"I know, Dad. Thanks. If I could just get Tieina to the U.S., I could be patient with the rest. But thinking of her in that awful place in Port au Prince . . ."

"That's the priority then. What's the holdup?"

"Partly it's her family—not the grandmother, but her father's people in Port au Prince. They keep asking for more money. More money for the Haitian lawyer, more money for Tienia's medical release forms, money for shoes and a uniform so she can go to school. I'm happy to pay for that, of course. And then with the embargo, it is nearly impossible to get anything into the country or anyone out."

"Have you tried the media? TV or newspapers? I have a lady friend who works with the Pittsburgh paper. It seems like people would be interested in a story like yours. You never know whom you might connect with. I could have her call you."

"Okay. I guess it couldn't hurt." The timer reminded her it was time to get the kids together. "I'm going to have to run. Thanks, Dad."

"I'd love to do more. Any chance you and the kids could

move back this way? Sure could use a good lady doctor for the women here in Mars. I could help out with the kids."

"I'll think about it." Maybe her dad had a point. Moving back to Pennsylvania sounded like a good idea right now. Mars was a pretty small town. But Pittsburgh was only a short drive away on the new interstate. She just had to convince Mark of that.

One month later, with the Sunday *Pittsburgh Times* folded under her arm, Kate took her coffee out to her father's patio and settled down to read the article that her dad's lady friend had written about her plight with Tieina's adoption. "Western Pennsylvania Doctor Attempts to Save Haitian AIDS Orphan." It was a good article. She would have to thank Anne. Not too much about her but enough about the non-profit she was establishing. Mostly the story focused on the plight of AIDS orphans in countries like Haiti.

Her dad showed up with the coffee carafe. "Refill?"

"Thanks." She handed him the newspaper. She was so glad that she and the kids were spending a few days with her dad.

He shook his head as he read. Then he beamed. "What a wonderful story. Anne is an amazing writer!"

His happiness was infectious. "You really like her, don't you?"

"She's quite a gal."

"I can't wait to meet her." She had never seen her dad so happy before. "I'm already a big fan."

"I'm sure glad you're moving back. It's been fun having you these last few days."

Kate had held her breath when she brought the move up with Mark. But it turned out that he was in complete agreement, since he was offered a position at the University in Pittsburgh working under a CDC grant. So once again, the surest path to her dream was leading her back home.

After a few hours of raking leaves and a few minutes of watching Jen and Danny jumping in the pile, Kate left the kids asleep on the couch with her dad while he watched Sunday football. She didn't tell him she was going to the cemetery. It might upset him.

With a water bottle and journal in her backpack, she walked the mile to the cemetery. She couldn't recall the last time she had visited her mother's grave. She took her journal and pen out of her pack and sat on a small wooden bench. She didn't write every day, but enough to keep a record of what was going on and what she was thinking. It helped her keep her thoughts organized.

The old oak tree was still standing. Most of the leaves were still on its gnarled, twisted limbs, but the surrounding maples had given theirs up to the ground. Nothing in Atlanta compared to crisp country air and fallen autumn leaves. She took a deep breath. There was a sweet odor, too. She looked around. It was an apple tree. Kate picked a fruit from a low-hanging branch, inspected it for signs of bugs, and rubbed it clean on her sweater. The tart, sweet flavor of the Granny Smith made her pucker. She picked as many more as she could carry in her pack. Wouldn't it be fun to make an apple pie with Jen? She and her mother had done that on occasion.

Truth was, she was more comfortable cutting an appendix than a loaf of nut bread, more comfortable sewing a scalp laceration than a hem. In the last couple of years, she had sometimes envisioned herself as a country doc like her dad. But lately, even that didn't fit. She closed her journal and walked back to the house.

When she entered the front door, her father said, "Kate, the phone is for you."

"I'm looking for Dr. Kate Rigando."

The Midwestern accent on the other end of the line was vaguely familiar.

"That's me," she answered.

"I don't know if you will remember me. It's Edward Rose. You took care of my son when he was in the hospital in San Francisco. He died of AIDS in 1985."

Michael Rose! There were some patients a doctor never forgot. "Of course, Mr. Rose, I remember Michael. How are you? How is your wife?"

"Marian died about six months ago. Her heart gave out. That's why I'm calling—well, sort of. Michael had a life insurance policy and we collected on it a few years back. You remember Marian and Michael had their differences?"

"Yes, I remember." The old sourpuss, God bless her soul. "I am sorry about your wife." She unloaded the apples into a big glass bowl as she talked.

"I appreciate that. The insurance policy was pretty substantial. We had to use some of it for Marian, toward the end. But before all that we had agreed the money should be used for something Michael would have cared about. I saw an article in our local paper this morning about your work with the AIDS orphans in Haiti."

The syndicate must have picked it up. Her heart began to pound. "Right now it's just one little girl that I'm trying to adopt. But I know I can do more."

"When I read the story, I remembered how hard you fought to help Michael. You never gave up until he was ready to. It just feels right. I would like to donate the money to this cause."

"I don't know what to say. Are you sure?"

"The way I see it, Michael's death put a thorn in my heart seven years ago—his mother's, too. Sometimes thorns will fester and destroy a person. I think that's what happened with Marian. But I won't let that happen with me. Something beautiful should come from his death and our pain."

"Thank you, Mr. Rose. I promise to honor your son and you and your wife's dreams."

"Let's make it Edward, and if it's okay with you—Kate?

"Absolutely."

They chatted a little longer and she learned that he had $200,000 he wanted to contribute over the next three years. When the paperwork was complete, they would arrange a meeting and set up the transfer of funds. His dairy farm was only a two-hour drive from Mars.

"Would you consider joining the Board of Directors?" she asked when she learned he was so close.

"But I don't know much about Haiti and I'm not medical." His words belied the excitement in his voice.

"You know what it is like to lose someone to AIDS and, if I recall, you're a successful businessman. I know medicine, but I don't have any financial background. You would be a great asset to our board. Please."

"Well, I wasn't expecting this when I sat down with my coffee to read the paper this morning. Thank you, Kate, I accept."

After she hung up the phone, she planted a big wet kiss on her father's forehead.

"What was that for?" Jen and Danny were nestled in the crooks of his arms—one on the left and the other on the right. She couldn't imagine a safer spot for her two babies.

"Just for being you and for being supportive of your crazy daughter."

"Does that mean that my crazy daughter is going to bake a couple of apple pies for dinner tonight?"

She had forgotten about the apples and that tonight she would meet Anne for the first time.

"Yes, Dad. I sure hope I remember how to make a pie. It's been so long. But first, I have to make a phone call. Are you good with the kids there?"

"Never better."

She dialed the lawyer's number. "Tom, I'm sorry to bother you on Sunday. I'm going to set the organization up in Pennsylvania, rather than in Georgia, and I think I've found my first two board members." If Anne was as good as she sounded on the phone and in print, Kate planned to ask her later this evening. "How about this for the name—Roses for Haiti? And our mission will be to help women and children affected by HIV/AIDS."

All the details were falling into place—except for the most important one. When would she get Tieina out of that awful situation?

25

KATE

PETIT (TI) MIREBELAIS
JUNE 1993

Kate sat at the desk in the dim light of the three-room clinic and contemplated her reasons for being in Petit Mirebelais. Most importantly, she had promised Tieina's grandmother that she would bring the girl to visit her before they went to the United States. Just shy of a year after beginning the process, Tieina was hers and she couldn't wait to get her safely back to Mars to meet Jen and Danny. The kids were excited, too, mostly Danny, but Jen would come around. The newspaper article last September had caught the eye of a Pennsylvania state senator who had the ear of someone in the Clinton administration. She was in Haiti before the ink dried on the adoption papers and before the flashes from the TV reporters faded. It was a photo-op moment for the new president and Roses for Haiti.

The second reason for her visit was to see patients at the clinic. The third reason was to follow up their first grant to the Ti Mirebelais Women's Group. Last December they had requested funds to expand the clinic for sicker patients who needed a place to stay for a few days. They also asked for a dozen solar panels and a diesel generator to provide power for the clinic, including a refrigerator to store much-needed vaccines for immunizing children in the community. For now, it was just the blind woman and her daughter who stayed there.

For the first few months since provisional approval as a non-profit, their small board had struggled over establishing a process to make grants to Haiti. There were only five regular board members—herself, Edward, Anne, Bridget, the lawyer that filed the articles of incorporation, and Ron, an energetic forty-year-old who recently worked as development director for a Pittsburgh-based organization that had built and run a large clinic in rural Haiti since the 1970s.

The board discussions got pretty heated sometimes.

Ron was adamant. "We just can't hand out money without some kind of application process; there's no accountability. It doesn't work with donors, either. They may give a hundred dollars once out of guilt or compassion, but they won't give the thousand a year that we can count on to keep things going."

In the end, Kate was satisfied with the system they developed. The application form was simple. The process required there be a local champion from Haiti and a board member champion who was responsible for ensuring financial accountability and overall reporting, as well as promoting the project to potential donors. Madame Cereste was the local champion for the Ti Mirebelais clinic initiative, and Kate was the board champion.

Kate identified the various items scattered about the clinic that were listed in the grant application last December—a file cabinet, refrigerator, exam table, desk, and chairs. The small, dorm-sized refrigerator was strangely quiet. Kate opened it expecting to find vials of vaccine, maintained in the required cold chain to ensure their potency. But there were only two bottles of warm beer and a Styrofoam container with moldy food. The refrigerator was plugged in, but apparently the outlet was not working. She checked the thermometer inside. It read sixty degrees Fahrenheit, not nearly cold enough for safe vaccine storage.

As Kate walked from room to room, the only evidence she found of working electricity was the overhead light in the room where the blind woman and her daughter stayed. She rapped softly on the half-opened door. "Excuse me, can I borrow your light bulb to use in the exam room?"

"Of course," the blind woman, Giselle, answered.

Her daughter Natali was sitting next to her reading the Bible. The odor of stale food, urine, and sweat hung heavy in the air.

The cause for her blindness was unclear, but several months of violent headaches preceded her loss of vision. A doctor in Saint Marc offered his opinion—a brain tumor. A visiting medical team suggested a rare autoimmune disease. The peasants in Petit Mirebelais whispered Vodou curse and all the while Madame Cereste and Yvonne prepared a place for her to rest, to eat, and to pray. It was those two women, not Giselle, who had requested a consult from her. Giselle would be her first patient of the week.

Kate flipped off the light switch. "Natali, can you help your mother to the room with the exam table?" Kate pulled a chair over to unscrew the light bulb from the ceiling socket. "I'll put this back after we finish."

The girl led her mother from one crowded room to the next, moving boxes of unpacked medical supplies and equipment out of the way as they went. They were both tall and beautiful, although the older woman appeared ill-kempt. Her hair was uncombed and there were food stains on her rumpled dress. She walked hunched over in slow, short steps as if she had the weight of the world on her shoulders.

"Thank you, Natali. I'll talk with your mother for a few minutes and after I examine her, I can help her back to your room. Or would you like to go outside and sit for a bit, Giselle?" Her Creole was good enough now that she seldom needed a translator. She had practiced relentlessly in anticipation of Tieina coming to the U.S.

The woman shook her head and a look of fear further clouded her sightless eyes.

"Okay. I'll help you back to your room then when we're done." She gently touched the blind woman's shoulder.

Reluctantly, the daughter let go of her mother's hand. Natali walked backwards out the door.

"Don't worry, Natali. I'll call you if we need anything." Kate looked from mother to daughter and wasn't sure which of the two was more frightened. She searched for a sheet to cover the brown vinyl exam table but found none. She also could not find any patient charts in the three-drawer file cabinet, although two of the drawers were overflowing with half-used packets of gauze and alcohol wipes.

Kate shook her head. Chaos. She had come to accept the chaos she encountered nearly everywhere she had been in Haiti.

She moved a chair to the center of the room and gingerly stepped on the rattan seat. She carefully screwed in the light bulb that she had borrowed from Giselle and Natali's room. But when she flipped the switch, there was no light. She would have to talk with Madame Cereste about the electricity later.

"You'll find the current has been redirected." It was the first time that Giselle had spoken to her.

"I don't understand." It had not been easy to get the money to Haiti—all the phone calls, the negotiating, and paying more than she knew she should to get each item. They had been so concerned about corruption and someone stealing items from customs. Now she would have to explain to her board of directors that everything had arrived, but it was not working or being used as specified in the grant.

"The World Cup of football is on. They found a TV somewhere. That's where you'll find your current. It's been nearly twenty years since Haiti even qualified and Haitians are passionate about football." She attempted to smooth her wrinkled dress. "I don't think you care so much in the United States."

"Actually, that's true for most. But my twelve-year-old son is crazy for the sport, too. We call it soccer there. He'd use his ball for a pillow if I'd let him."

Giselle had a lovely smile. "He would fit in well in Haiti, then. Like you, I think. But for different reasons."

"Thank you, Giselle. Have we met before? You seem familiar?" Kate asked.

"Perhaps. Paths cross all the time in Haiti," the blind woman answered.

"I'm finding that is very true." Kate thought about Liz and Jim and their contact at International Veterinary Corp. "I guess I can worry about the electricity later. The sunlight is enough for us now. May I examine you? Your friends thought that I might be able to help."

The blind woman's smile faded, but she nodded in agreement and lifted her head ever so slightly. Her sightless eyes seemed to focus on something unseen outside the tiny window.

Kate wondered what it would be like to live in darkness, dependent on others for her every need.

CHAPTER

26

GISELLE

PETIT (TI) MIREBELAIS
JUNE 1993

"Natali! Where are you? I have to go to the bathroom. I need your help!" Giselle called.

"Yes, Mother. I'm coming."

The truth was, she probably could have made it to the pot beside her bed. But she didn't want to. She had heard Natali and her friends laughing outside her window—always they were talking about boys. She had no one else to depend on and Natali needed to be there for her as long as possible. Six months ago, she was the one everyone came to for advice. She was the one who had the most education, the most knowledge. Now, she was a helpless blind woman—Vodou cursed. She couldn't paint and she missed that as she would have missed her right arm if it had been cut off. She couldn't read; she couldn't even carry water. She was as useless as an old barren goat. And she felt betrayed by all she had believed in—her body, her husband, doctors, and any God out there she had ever heard about. For the first three months after her vision left, she prayed all the time. In the mornings she prayed to the

Christian God—Father, Son, and Holy Ghost, and to the Mother, too, especially to the Mother. At night, when the drums played, she prayed to the *lwa*. Something she had never done before.

It didn't matter, though. The darkness was unrelenting. She had awakened one morning after Christmas, and there was nothing. Inevitable as her blindness was, it was her last vision that haunted her. As hard as she tried, she couldn't even remember the last thing she had seen. Was it her face, her daughter's face, or something as inconsequential as the ceiling above the bed?

"What is it, Mother? Are you hungry, thirsty? Do you have to go to the bathroom again?" Breathless, her daughter spoke to her like she was an inconsolable infant.

"Just sit with me. It is the headaches again."

"What did the doctor say? Can she do anything? She's nice, don't you think?"

"Yes, she is. But there is nothing anyone can do for me." So many patients came to see the American doctor in the clinic that day that she hadn't been able to rest. It was strange how her hearing had sharpened since she lost her sight. From the surrounding shacks, she could identify each sound and each person to whom it belonged.

Madame Beauvais couldn't sleep. It was probably because her *boz*—common-law husband—was staying with his other woman and she had four of his children to feed and only the little money she made at market. The doctor gave her some pills to help her sleep at night, but what could she do about the reality of her days? And then there was Lucia, one of the younger members of their group. She complained that her stomach hurt. She was pregnant, the doctor discovered. Giselle heard her pee into the small plastic cup and then she heard her crying softly outside her window after the doctor gave her the results of her pregnancy test. She got vitamins and antacids, but what she really needed was food. Lucia's family was one of the poorest in the community. Their roof was thatch, not tin like Yvonne's, and they didn't even have a baby goat to graze. On and on they came and she listened to their stories and the *blan* doctor gave them medicines. But there was no cure for them . . . or for her.

"Stay with me. I'm not hungry. I just want to rest." Funny, in her dreams she wasn't blind and she was always painting and with bright and vivid colors again. But then she woke up and the dark, which should have stayed with the night, remained.

"We can pray?"

"I don't think so. Not tonight."

"Please, mother. I've been thinking about when I was younger and you taught me my prayers."

True, Giselle had given up on prayers and dreams for herself, but she couldn't give up the hope for her daughter.

"You are right, Natali. I would love to hear your prayers. Come sit beside me on the bed." Giselle rested her head on the pillow and listened as her daughter's voice brought the slightest bit of brightness to the dark.

27

KATE

PETIT (TI) MIREBELAIS
JUNE 1993

Kate still couldn't believe the little girl was hers, and Tieina wouldn't let Kate out of her sight. She chatted about what it was going to be like to fly back to the U.S. in a few days while she kept her eyes on the child's battered pink Cinderella flip-flops beneath the outhouse door as she sat and peed. They were filthy and faded and the straps on the right one were patched with silver duct tape. The stickiness only served to attract more dust. The image of beautiful Cinderella with her long, blonde hair in her fairy godmother-contrived ballgown was faded, barely visible. Tieina's heels hung over the back by an inch. Hardly the enchanted slippers one should expect from a fairy godmother. Kate berated herself for not bringing new shoes. The Cinderella sandals never moved, patiently waiting for her to finish. She opened the outhouse door and grabbed a breath of fresh air.

"Let's go, honey. Why don't you draw some pictures? I need to talk to your grandmother and Auntie Cereste for a minute."

She found the two women shelling peas at Yvonne's.

"Can I talk to the two of you about the clinic grant?" She

carefully chose those words so as not to incriminate Giselle. "I noticed the electricity wasn't working for the refrigerator and for several of the lights."

"The electricity works. We switch the current when we have no patients."

"But the WHO requires that we have a refrigerator that is only for vaccines and the refrigerator must be between two and eight degrees centigrade. I think that was explained to you. If we can't show documentation when the health inspector comes, we won't keep our license, and we won't get free vaccines anymore." Until she said it, she had forgotten that she had not found any vaccines. She looked from one woman to the other. Neither was looking at her. "Where are the vaccines?"

"Doctor Kate," Madame Cereste spoke first. "We are grateful to your organization for the grant. We thank God every day for you and pray your goodness will continue. But patients don't come."

"Thirty patients came today."

"Because you are here. Other days we don't have a doctor or a nurse. It is just me and Giselle, before she got sick."

"We never got the vaccines," Yvonne confessed. "One of the women in the group went to Saint Marc to talk with the health ministry. They said they would add us to the list, but first they had to do an inspection. We still wait."

"But that's my point. We need to show them that the clinic is operating well." Her head was throbbing from the heat and the frustration. "It sounds like you need a doctor or a nurse."

"We have no money for that. It is difficult to get a nurse, more difficult to get a doctor to come this far. Many doctors and nurses left the country after the coup. Even with the troubles in Port au Prince, no one wants to live *en deyo*—in the country—with the peasants and the cows."

"Then why did you ask for the money for the clinic? Why not something else?" They could have used a school.

"Because that is what we thought you wanted to give us money for."

"What?" Kate asked louder than she intended. She struggled to keep her first reaction—something between anger and frustration—in check. Funds had not been misused; no one was dishonest, and it sounded like Madame Cereste and Yvonne had done their best to follow through with what they had talked about. Yet she was disappointed with herself for not understanding all the details about the clinic project, and she was hurt and confused. Why hadn't they trusted her enough to be honest about what they really needed?

She thought carefully about her next words. "As much as I love this work, I will always be an outsider. It's true; many obstacles can be removed with money, ideas, and persistence. But you, Yvonne, Giselle, and Madame, you are the eyes and the heart of this community. I need your help as much as you need mine."

We are not animals
You can kick us
But we won't stay down
You think we don't see
But we know
Together our voice is heard
We will sing
We will dance
In solidarity we are strong.

Kate listened to the song as it was sung three times. It was accompanied by the sound of metal on metal. She smiled at the now familiar but always noisy expression of passion by Haitian women.

"Where is Tieina?" she asked Yvonne's daughter, Cassandra, who was pounding spices for dinner.

"I think she's with Natali." She tilted her head toward the clinic where a group of women sat on benches in the only patch of shade. It had not rained in the six days that Kate had been in Ti Mirebelais and apparently not for many weeks before. The water barrels were empty, the streams were dust, the crops were wilting, and all her clothes were on round three of wear without being washed.

She found Tieina with Natali standing behind a hibiscus bush. Both girls were watching the meeting intently. Every woman had a pot and metal spoon. They struck them in unison as an accompaniment to their song. She stayed back to observe the girls. There was no space between them. Each sucked on a bright red hibiscus flower. Natali had her arm around Tieina, who was more than a head shorter. They turned to each other, whispered, and giggled. They could have been sisters. Should Kate really be taking this girl from her country, from her people? But she looked at the orange hair, her protruding belly, and her two-sizes-too-small, duct-taped sandals. She remembered that this was her grandmother's wish and her mother's dream for Tieina to have a better life. She didn't know how she could do that in Haiti, but she could do that in the United States. The child would have enough to eat, the best medical care and education in the world. She would never have to be afraid again of being abused. Whatever bumps in the road there were in the United States, they would be nothing compared to how her life would be Haiti. Yvonne believed that and she believed her daughter Adelaide would have agreed. Kate needed to believe it, too.

"Natali. Come here. I need water. I'm thirsty." Giselle's voice broke the girls' camaraderie. She didn't sound like the helpless frightened woman Kate had met last week.

Kate walked up behind the girls and tapped Natali on the

shoulder. "I'll go to your mother." She walked into the room. The smell of urine and sweat was overwhelming and her eyes burned.

"Natali, what took you so long? I had to go to the bathroom. Now you have to wash my sheets again." Giselle was sitting on the bed, looking as unwashed and rumpled as the stained bed sheet.

"It's not Natali, Giselle. It's Kate. The girls are outside."

"I need my daughter."

"I'll help you. You know the toilet is right next to your bed. Why don't we walk it a few times so you'll feel more confident and then you can go to the bathroom yourself."

"I'll fall."

"Not if we practice. Sightless people in the U.S. do it all the time. They do lots of things, with practice and a little help."

"This is not the United States. Surely you noticed that." Giselle stood up and faced her.

"I'm sorry. You're right." She looked around the room for a clue as to something else they could talk about. Her eyes settled on a painting. She hadn't noticed it before. The same painting hung in Mark's office in Atlanta. "The painting on your wall, the one with the woman on the boat, I bought that for my ex-husband when we lived in San Francisco. I love that painting. Do you know the artist?" She stepped closer and saw that the same person had signed it, G. LaFortune. She turned to face Giselle. "It's you? You are the artist?"

"Yes." Giselle sat back down on the bed. The mattress heaved a sigh. "I *was* the artist. I can't paint now."

"No, of course not." What could she possibly do for this sad woman who had lost so much, but stood to lose even more if she didn't stop taking her anger out on her daughter? "You're a very talented artist."

"Thank you. You are very kind. But that was another lifetime."

"Yes." Kate thought about San Francisco. "It was."

As soon as they arrived at Didi's for their last night in Port au Prince, Tieina grasped her hand and didn't let go. Only her appetite was unaffected. She ate everything on her plate and stared at the big bowl of rice and beans in the center of the table until she was offered seconds, then thirds. Her head just inches from the plate, she shoveled the food in so fast that Kate was afraid she would get sick. But she didn't.

"Let's take a walk," Kate suggested to Tieina after the dishes were finished.

The long evening stretched in front of them with only a few moments left of the daylight.

"We'll just go across the street."

The guard at Didi's would keep an eye on them.

The chain link blocking the entrance to the soccer field was more symbolic than threatening. She easily stepped over it and Tieina ducked under. The ground was dry and dusty like most things in Haiti. She would have liked to have run and stretched her legs. Three weeks was a long time not to exercise. But she didn't want to let go of the girl's hand until Tieina was ready for her to let go. They walked the perimeter of the field and studied the faded mural. Several of the articles of declaration had been marred by graffiti. In turn the graffiti was smudged as if someone had tried to remove it.

"'Article Four. No Person Will Live in Slavery to Another.'" Tieina stared thoughtfully at the words and then read them to her in English and Creole. Her voice soft and tentative at first, then strong and steady.

Kate nodded and put her arm around the girl. "I hope you'll like school in the U.S." Kate knew it would be tough at first, but she knew that she and the kids would love Tieina enough to get her through it.

Kate imagined Tieina and Jen sitting at the kitchen table in Mars years from now. Maybe a fire in the hearth, sipping hot chocolate and doing their homework together, laughing at the things teenage girls laugh at when they think no one else is around. Or would they fight over clothes and boys and her attention, like she and her sisters had done? Probably both, and that would be just perfect.

"My mother told me I was very intelligent." Tieina stuck her chin out, as if she dared Kate to argue. She was speaking in English most of the time now.

"I think your mother was right." Kate wanted to ask her how she was feeling about Adelaide. But Tieina must have felt a sense of happier and safer days ahead, because she dropped her hand and ventured over closer to a small group of children who kicked a partially deflated soccer ball at the far end of the field. They looked at her and continued with their play. Kate turned slightly toward Tieina and pretended to read the message on the wall. She felt an ache for the little girl, soon to be officially her daughter, like she would feel if Jen or Dan were ignored by kids playing in the park back home.

The soccer ball flew past her face, hit the wall, and landed dead at Kate's feet. Before she could bend to pick it up, Tieina's foot landed on the deflated object and she gave a hefty sideways kick, which aimed the ball smack into the makeshift goal. The girl smiled at her and ran down the field. Not bad for a girl with duct-taped Cinderella flip-flops. She smiled again. Yes, Tieina and Danny would get along just great, too.

28

GISELLE

PETIT (TI) MIREBELAIS
JUNE 1993

Giselle walked gingerly through her small room, holding onto the bed and then the chair, counting her steps like they had practiced. She missed the American doctor, who had left two weeks earlier. She had challenged her, the first person to do that since she lost her sight. Everyone else avoided her or pitied her except Natali, who was devoted and afraid. That was the hardest of all, realizing her daughter's fear and knowing there was nothing she could do about it except pretend to be angry so the girl wouldn't know how scared she was herself.

There were small things she accomplished—getting to the toilet herself, making her bed each morning. Every day she made it a little farther to the door on her own. She hadn't told Natali what she was doing. She practiced when her daughter was at school and the women were at market, like now. That way no one heard her banging into things or knocking things to the ground. She reached down to rub the raised spot on her shin. The bruise happened two days ago when she banged into the table. It was a little smaller today but still tender.

Distracted, she miscounted her steps and collided with the portable toilet. Urine splashed on her dress and legs. She wanted to sink to the floor and cry. But there was likely a mess there, too, and she and her daughter had lived with that wretched smell for too long. She took three steps and found the table. She continued counting, only five more steps to the door. Her hand moved along the wall until she reached the opening to the porch. There should have been a bucket of water beside the door. It was the first time she was venturing outside on her own. She kneeled on the wooden floorboards and felt her way to the tall plastic bucket that held water for her and her daughter. She had only her damp dress to cushion her bony knees.

She would take the bucket inside and clean up the floor, wash herself, and change her dress. She could do that.

She reached inside the bucket, deeper and deeper until her fingers scraped the plastic bottom. There was no water. She grabbed the edges of the bucket and lowered her head. The tears she had denied for so long came and fell into the empty bucket. Her sobs resonated in the plastic vessel. After a few minutes, something cold and wet touched the back of her neck. One drop, then two, then many—it was raining. She sat back on her legs and turned her face to the sky and let the tears from the clouds wash away the tears from her eyes.

"I am not an animal. You can kick me," she began to softly sing, "but I won't stay down." She lifted herself up off the ground. Carefully she stepped off the porch. The rain was steady now and it penetrated through her soiled clothes, through to her soiled and bruised skin. "You think I don't see. But I know." She found an empty metal pot and a metal spoon. She brought them together time and again to *bat teneb*—beat back the darkness—as an accompaniment to her voice. The rain poured down and she sang as boldly as she could. She laughed and she danced. "Together our voice is heard. We will sing. We will dance. In solidarity, we are strong. In solidarity, we are strong."

3

Bat Teneb
(To Beat Back the Darkness)
(1994–2008)

If you have come here to help me, you are

wasting your time . . .

but if you have come here because your

liberation is bound up in mine, then let us

work together.

—Lilla Watson,
Australian Aboriginal Woman

29

KATE

MARS, PENNSYLVANIA
APRIL 1994

"Moooom! There are ants in our room!" Jen announced.

With a coffee cup in hand and her damp hair in a towel, Kate entered the bedroom that Tieina and Jen shared.

"What the . . ."

Kate discovered a mound of tiny brown ants formed in the corner behind Tieina's bed. She lifted the mattress and found their final destination—a peanut butter sandwich bleeding strawberry jam onto the white protective cover of the box springs.

"Tieina!" Kate called.

The girl came running.

"Why do you have a sandwich under your mattress?"

Her new daughter studied the carpet.

"You should punish her. You'd punish *me* if I did that." Jen inhaled deeply and stood with hands on her hips staring at Kate.

It was a suggestion she made frequently about her adopted sister the last few months.

"Tieina." She paused briefly to be sure she had the girl's

attention. "If you're hungry, I'll make you something to eat. I've told you that before."

"What if all the food is gone?"

"That's stupid." Jen exhaled, picked up her book, and stormed out of the room.

"Jen, go get the vacuum—*please*," Kate called after her. She sat down on the bed and pulled Tieina onto her lap.

The child's pudgy stomach rolled ever so slightly over the waistband of her jogging suit—the same pants that Kate had pinned three months ago to keep them from falling down.

"Honey, this isn't Haiti. I promise you we will always have enough food to eat." She ran her fingers through her daughter's hair.

It was warm brown, like dark chocolate, with just a hint of cherry. She had her first American haircut last week. It had taken eight months for the ginger-colored strands of malnutrition to grow out, the last visible scar of the abuse she had endured. But the scars on the inside, the ones she couldn't see or cut away, would they ever fade?

At first, the nightmares came so frequently that Tieina refused to sleep anywhere but in Kate's bed. The darkness transformed the otherwise confident and active child into a frightened, silent one whom Kate couldn't reach with any words of reason; only hold until the daylight brought her back. Most nights the child just whimpered and curled herself up in a ball. But sometimes she would fight back.

"No. I won't do it. I hate you," she would scream in Creole, thrashing about.

Kate was exhausted from the lack of sleep and took Tieina to the pediatrician, who found nothing physically wrong and recommended counseling. It helped some, but Tieina was reluctant to talk with a stranger, and the more Kate tried to encourage Tieina to open up, the more she withdrew. Then she reemerged as a completely Americanized little girl who refused to eat rice or beans, and who never mentioned Haiti or her grandmother.

Instinctively, Kate knew not to push her. It would take time for Tieina to get over the shock of what had happened to her, not all of which Kate understood herself. With no road map to guide her, she decided she could only love her daughter through it.

Over the next few months, Kate moved Tieina from her bed to a cot of her own at the foot of her bed, and then into Jen's room. Most nights now, Tieina slept in her own bed, but still insisted on a nightlight.

It wasn't entirely fair to Jen, sharing a room. But Kate hoped it would also bring the two girls closer together. Danny and Tieina hit it off immediately. She responded to Danny's easy sense of humor and teasing with giggles and comebacks, and of course, they connected on the soccer field, as well.

But Jen and Tieina argued about everything from clothes to chores to food.

Kate vacuumed up the ants, threw the sandwich in the trash, and gathered up the bedding to be washed. *"Ti zwazo m, ede mama ou*—my little bird, help your mother?" she prompted in Creole.

Her daughter stared at her with a puzzled look.

"Tieina, don't you remember any of your Creole?"

She was such a bright girl. Her teachers claimed she picked up English like a sponge. Only in her nightmares would her native tongue surface.

When Kate remade the bed, she nearly knocked over Tieina's soccer team picture. There wasn't a smile missing from the fifteen girls huddled together in their bright gold-and-blue soccer uniforms. Tieina stood in the front row, her soccer shorts billowed over her spindly legs. It was hard to imagine that she wouldn't be swept away by a strong wind. Yet it was her performance as a midfielder that helped the Mars Rockets seize the division championship. Her teammates insisted she hold the trophy for the photograph. Tieina was a head shorter than most of them, despite the fact that she was almost a year older. The pediatrician cautioned Kate that she might never catch up in height. But the weight would come much easier, as Kate could affirm seeing how her cheeks had filled out since the photo had been taken.

"Tieina, you haven't answered me. Don't you remember any of your Creole?"

The girl shook her head forcefully, picked up the garbage can and started downstairs. "I don't remember anything," she said.

She followed her daughter with the dirty sheets. "You do remember we promised your grandmother that you would write a letter to her for Christmas and that you would read it to her on a cassette tape?" She paused, waiting for an answer that didn't come. "It's four months past Christmas now. Do you think you can do the letter today?"

She shrugged. "Not today. Maybe I'll try tomorrow. I'm hungry now. Can we have pancakes for breakfast?"

"Blueberries?" Kate asked her daughters, hoping for a consensus.

Tieina nodded eagerly and licked her lips.

"No." Jen made a face like she had just been asked to eat raw worms.

"Sit up straight, Jen."

Her shoulders were always rounded and her head down, as if she was already studying some disease under the microscope.

"Okay. No problem. We'll do both." Kate stirred the thick yellow batter with a wooden spoon. It was good to have the girls in the kitchen with her. They so seldom ate a meal together between her schedule and theirs. Round and round she stirred. The rhythm consumed her attention and calmed her. She sprinkled a little cinnamon and nutmeg in the batter, poured a dozen neat little circles onto the hot griddle, and sprinkled a handful of blueberries onto half of them.

"Bring your plates, girls."

"Can I get mine first?" Jen asked, not usually so anxious for breakfast. "Dad's coming to pick me up."

"What? I was hoping we could spend the day together." Tieina had occupied most of so much of Kate's time and attention since she came to the United States.

"I told you last week. We're going to the Carnegie Science Center in Pittsburgh. There's a high school science fair. I want to get some ideas for my project this year. Besides, you'll be at soccer all day." She lowered her voice. "Just like every Saturday."

"You could come and help me cheer."

"Mom, you know I don't like watching sports. Besides, I'm going to be famous some day when I find a cure for cancer," she announced.

"That's stupid. By the time you finish school, somebody else will already have done that," Tieina said between bites. She flashed a purple smile at Kate.

"Now, Tieina. Jen, I think you can do anything you want if you work hard enough."

"That's why I'm starting now." She grabbed the syrup from Tieinia. "Your teeth are blue. Freak. And what do you know kicking a dumb soccer ball around all day? Are you going to do that for the rest of your life?"

Tieina looked intently at her plate, studying the swirls of purple syrup like tea leaves at a fortune-teller. After a minute, she looked up from her plate.

"I'm going to be famous, too," she announced. "I'll write stories that everyone in the world will want to read." She settled back into eating her pancakes.

"Hmph. Well that will be pretty impossible if all you do is run up and down a soccer field all day," said Jen.

"They're going to invent a special award just for me because my stories will be so important."

"Well I'm going to win the prize for science." Jen looked

doubtful for just an instant. "That's a lot harder than winning a prize for writing."

"Can the two of you just eat your pancakes? I'm sure you'll both change your mind a hundred times before you grow up." Kate gave each of them a kiss on the forehead.

"Not me." Jen took a precisely cut piece of pancake and dabbed it in the syrup.

"Me neither," Tieina mumbled after shoveling half a pancake in her mouth.

Kate smiled. A Nobel Prize-winning scientist and a Pulitzer Prize-winning journalist—she hoped they would prove each other wrong someday.

Jen reminded Kate so much of her at that age, focused and stubborn and afraid of change. Kate vowed to make some extra time just for her as soon as she got through the next board meeting and her next trip to Haiti.

Their board meeting agenda was short this time—fundraising. Money was tight for just about anything but HIV/AIDS programs, and even then there were restrictions. Haiti was low on the list, or not on the list at all, of countries that foundations and even individual donors were willing to donate to.

"Pictures might help," Ron offered. "Donors always love to see what organizations are doing."

"Okay, I can do that." Kate really needed to get back down to Haiti. It had been several months. But she was reluctant to leave the kids with her ex-husband. Tieina was just getting adjusted to life in the United States and Mark had a second family now.

"Great, and any numbers you can get would be helpful for grant applications. Like how many women listen to the education sessions on the radio program—what's it called?"

"*Sante fanm*—Women's Health," Kate answered.

"I'll work on the newsletter and the grants," Anne said. "Your dad and I can stay with the kids while you're gone."

"Thanks, Anne." Kate reached across the conference table and squeezed her hand. She really had no one else in her life she could count on but her dad and Anne. Sometimes she felt so vulnerable.

Edward had been relatively silent for most of the meeting. "Our operating account is getting low. I don't think it's enough to pay for your plane ticket, Kate."

She waved off the comment. "I'll take care of it. I just wish we had more to support the programs." It had been three months since she had received her small director's salary. Thank goodness for the three days she worked at the Mars Clinic.

"I don't know if anything will come of this," Edward said. "My pastor has been asking about our work and wants me to talk at the services next Sunday." He looked tentatively at her. "That's really not my thing. But Kate, if you could do it . . . we're not a wealthy congregation. But there are a few with deep pockets. We might just be able to reach inside their hearts and pull out some cash."

"Of course I'll do it," Kate agreed. She'd shake any tree she could to find the money to keep the programs running in Haiti.

Kate's stomach churned as she got up in front of the congregation at Edward's church. It had been a few years since she had done any public speaking. The church was small. Still, she felt a little like a shy high school girl making her first speech as she stood beside Reverend Mosseso, a bulky man with a booming voice who had no need for a microphone. He easily captured the attention of his congregation, even before he spoke.

"Today, Dr. Kate Rigando, Executive Director for Roses for Haiti, is going to share some of her experiences helping our poor brothers and sisters in Haiti." He smiled at his flock.

They smiled back.

"Many of you know Edward Rose is on the board and he has been a big supporter of the mission. After the service this morning, we'll have a reception downstairs with donuts and coffee. I hope everyone will stay so they can hear more about the good doctor's missionary work."

A missionary? There was that word again.

"Thank you, Reverend, for your kind introduction and for the opportunity to speak to your congregation today. We do appreciate your support and I'm happy to be here." Kate began.

At the reception after Kate's presentation, she overheard a woman loading her plate with bagels and donuts comment, "I don't know how else to say this—but don't you think we should help people in this country before we go gallivanting around the world? After all, we got people here with no jobs and losing their homes. They can't pay for medicine either."

Another woman replied, "Yes, I feel bad for those people in Haiti, too. But I agree. There are people right here in Lees Creek that are really bad off. You know that family down by the bend in the creek . . ."

"I hear the South Americans are running drugs through Haiti and the Cubans are trying to overthrow the government," someone interjected.

"What about AIDS? Isn't that where it started?" someone else asked.

She was about to say no, that myth of AIDS had been disproven years ago, and no, the Cubans were only trying to improve the rural agricultural production, and yes, drug running was a problem—another example of others taking advantage of the poverty and corruption in Haiti. But before she could answer, a man came up and shook her hand.

"I sure enjoyed your talk. God bless you." He smiled and looked deeply into her eyes. "But when you say they go to church, what church do they attend? Is it a temple? I hear they practice Vodou in Haiti. Is that true? Do they really sacrifice animals?"

Kate took out one of her business cards and wrote the name of a book, *Vodou and Haiti*. "I've heard this is a good reference about that topic. I don't know much myself. I think most people practice a little Vodou, but it's not what we typically think it to be. It's more like superstition or rituals, like we might say 'don't walk under a ladder or you'll have bad luck.'"

He looked skeptical, but took her card.

Another woman with salt-and-pepper hair, designer suit, and perfectly manicured nails handed Kate a fresh cup of coffee. Kate wondered if she was one of the ones with deep pockets.

"How do we know people in Haiti will ever get the money we send them? Isn't there a lot of corruption in that country? Don't get me wrong. I pray every day for the poor people everywhere," she assured Kate.

"Thank you very much for your prayers. They are always appreciated. I understand your concerns." Kate gave her usual answer in as thoughtful a voice as she could muster, reminding herself this was an opportunity not just to get money, but to educate people about what organizations like hers were trying to do, and were doing, in Haiti. "We receive monthly financial reports and I make site visits at least twice a year." Kate felt compelled to give the basic fundraising spiel. But she quickly realized that she was losing the woman's attention as fast as the donuts were disappearing. More importantly, she was boring herself.

"Look, Ms. Curry," she read the woman's nametag. "I can't deny that Haiti is a challenging place to work. Yes, there is corruption, but children are starving and dying from diseases that could be cured for less than what this cup of coffee costs." Kate took a much-needed breath to put it out there, the million-dollar question for this crowd. "And yes, people practice Vodou, but most of the same people also practice Christianity."

Ms. Curry took a step back at her last comment as if in disbelief.

"Despite the corruption, the Vodou, nobody," she said, "*nobody* deserves to get a disease like AIDS. And I've never felt more spiritual, more close to God than when I'm in Haiti." Kate paused, surprising herself with her last comment and the sudden realization of its truth.

"I've come to know and work with a remarkable group of women. These women struggle to survive and do whatever they can to make sure their children survive. That's why I'm here." She watched the doubt on the woman's face subside just a bit as she nodded and walked away and then out the door.

Kate listened to the buzz of conversations amongst the parishioners, talking about what they were having for dinner, talking about who was hosting the next Bible study, and she recalled her conversations that morning, not unlike conversations at other fundraising events. "What a shame about those poor people in Haiti, but . . ."

It always came down to the same fears: Vodou, AIDS, corruption. As if those three things were rational excuses for eight million people to live without basic human rights.

The phone rang early the next morning. It was Edward.

"Well, you did it. You got through to at least one person. After you left, I stayed to help clean up. Pam Curry, she owns the local real estate office, handed me a check for ten thousand dollars. She's not usually one to open her checkbook either. The only thing she asked for is that we hang a plaque with her sister's name on it somewhere in the village. She passed away from cancer last year. I hope it's okay. I told her we would do it."

Kate agreed. "I can't believe it. I didn't think anyone was really listening."

30

GISELLE

PETIT (TI) MIREBELAIS
MAY 1994

Giselle grabbed the arms of the oversized chair and eased herself down into the seat. She felt the table in front of her for the microphone. On her left was a set of headphones. She put them on and moved her chair in so she was directly in front of the mic.

"Okay, Erold. I'm ready." The rumblings from the generator warming up vibrated her chair and the floor beneath her. The rhythm of the motor energized her and her voice rose from somewhere inside, a place where she now knew the darkness could never reach. She really was like one of Picasso's blind finches. In spite of, or because of her blindness, she had finally found her voice.

"Three, two . . ." Erold tapped her on the shoulder to signal that the broadcast was going live.

"*Bonsoir, mes amis nan Ti Mirebelais*—Good evening, my friends in Ti Mirebelais." Her voice grew stronger. "*Se Giselle pou nou ak Sante Fanm*—it's Giselle for you with Women's Health."

The radio program had been Giselle's idea. Most of the rural peasants had radios and batteries, and with a $2,000 grant from Roses for Haiti, they purchased a generator, transmitter, and her precious sound system. Twice a week she did her program on women's health topics, *Sante Fanm*. She was confident her messages were reaching far out into the community, to those who couldn't or wouldn't come to the clinic. They would stop by to see her on their way to market.

"Giselle, I heard your program yesterday. It is like you know my heart."

"I never thought about my body that way. What will you talk about next week?"

It was this encouragement that gave birth to *Nou ti pale*—"We Talk a Little"—the interactive segment of *Sante Fanm*. More than anything, Haitian women wanted to be heard. They flocked to the radio station each week and sat in a circle passing around a little cassette player. Tape after tape they filled with their hopes, their dreams, and their ideas for creating a better way. After minor editing, Giselle would play excerpts on the radio the following week. Recently, she decided to have them speak live on the air. Their messages were more effective that way.

She never let the women give their real names. They used radio names like *Gwo ti machann*—big little market lady—and the *fanm chante dous*—sweet singing woman. Giselle recognized that voice as the one woman she knew who could not sing a note in pitch.

Erold, who had set up the system, showed her how to disguise their voices by slowing down the speed just a little on the recorder. He called it a scrambler. Even though they were *en deyo*, it could still be dangerous for them.

Giselle shook off that thought like an especially troublesome fly and continued with her broadcast.

"Today is May first. It is Mother's Day—a day we celebrate the women who have given us life." Giselle thought of her mother and her courage and kindness. "It is also a day where men and women celebrate their love for each other." She smiled at the memory of Max bringing her flowers one year. "Love is a good thing—yes, sisters?" She paused for her radio audience to visit their own memories. "Of course it is. But love can lead to things that change a woman's future. So today we are going to talk about planning our futures—and one way we do that is by planning our families."

Dr. Kate had cautioned her about bringing up this subject. Apparently some of the U.S. donors for her organization were opposed to talking about birth control.

But today, she needed to speak out and there was no Dr. Kate to give approval and no wealthy American donors to silence her. It was just her, Giselle. Her and the thousands of other peasant women who might hear her voice and believe that just perhaps, there were other choices out there for them and their daughters. How could they improve their health and escape the chains of poverty if their bodies were always big with babies?

She pulled the microphone closer to her lips and lowered her voice, like she had a big secret to share. "Today we will begin our talk about birth control."

Her message was short and consistent. "There are options for us. But we must educate our daughters and ourselves. Education is power. Power to control our bodies and control our lives!"

As was often the case in Haiti, not all the women were in agreement with Giselle. She found an empty spot on the bench and prepared to defend her position at the women's group meeting the next week. Their discourses on the best methods of birth control and strategies for improving their economic opportunities were under discussion again.

"I want children and grandchildren. Who will take care of me when I get old?" chimed in one woman whose daughter was pregnant.

"Have you thought about that, Yvonne? Who will take care of you? One of your daughters is dead and your granddaughter is gone to the U.S. forever. And Giselle, you are blind. What will you do if Natali goes off to university?" Those questions came from the group member who often raised the tough issues.

There was a great silence with the last comment. Giselle could only wonder what Yvonne was thinking and waited for her friend to say something. When she didn't, Giselle shared the sadness that had come to live in her heart these past few months.

"This is something I have thought about many times." For once she was glad Natali was not at the meeting. "It is my second greatest fear that my daughter will move away and I won't have her with me each day. But . . ." She paused and turned her head so that every woman in the circle could see her face, even if she couldn't see theirs. ". . . my greatest fear is that my daughter will stay because of me or because she is afraid to take a chance."

Another moment of silence followed when Giselle was certain she had gained some ground with the dissenters among the group.

"Instead of putting big ideas in our daughters' heads to be important business people or doctors or lawyers, we should make more opportunities for them here in our village. We could start a cooking school or a sewing school," argued one of the older women in the group.

"Yes, these are good skills for a woman to have. Our daughters can be good wives and get a little money selling what they make," said another woman who had two daughters and four sons.

"But aren't we fighting for real independence," Yvonne responded, "not just a few goudes here and there to buy some soap or a dress now and then? But enough money that a woman can support her family, without depending on a man who only comes around when he wants something."

Giselle heard some, but not all, of the women murmur in agreement.

"So we need enough money to send *all* our children to school and not just a year or two. Our daughters must go to university so they can be the ones to make the decisions and the laws that will govern our country in the future." Her friend's voice was filled with the passion of dreams that could still happen even if time was shorter for her than many of the women in the group.

After another silence, Giselle spoke. "Perhaps we can do both. Make opportunities for our daughters here—like a sewing or cooking school, and for those who are inclined, encourage them to go elsewhere for university."

It was a temporary resolution. In the end, it would all come down to money. They had so little of their own and they were almost completely dependent on aid from charitable organizations like Dr. Kate's. There were always strings attached, and if they planned their futures around money from the outside, they would be as vulnerable as they were now to their fickle government—a different person in charge every few months with different strings attached. Sometimes the women of Haiti were like puppets tangled in the strings of naïve and feuding puppeteers. Giselle was encouraged that these women were claiming their voice. If only they would stop using their voices to argue.

The group settled on three things they might be able to do: educate women about their bodies, give them information about birth control as Giselle was doing, encourage each girl to finish their *rheto* and *philo* courses, pass the national exams, and choose university or trade school. They would find the money for at least three girls each year to get this type of education. She would talk with Dr. Kate about that when she came for the HIV/AIDS program in July.

For the second half of their meeting, nurse Mandy was making a presentation and all the women in the village were invited to participate.

Was it only a year ago when the American Dr. Kate had seen her female anatomy posters and asked, "Have you painted anything since you came to Ti Mirebelais?"

"Nothing much," Giselle had answered. At Kate's insistence to see what she had done, Giselle had groped under her bed, opened up the plastic bin and unrolled the drawings she could no longer see. She spread them out on her bed and couldn't have felt more exposed to the doctor if she had been completely naked. No one else had seen them until that day.

"These are wonderful, Giselle." Dr. Kate had sounded sincere. "I haven't seen any better illustrations of a woman's reproductive system in my anatomy books, and yours are so different, so unique."

After Giselle's trip to Saint Marc, when the Haitian doctor told her she would likely lose her vision, she returned to Ti Mirebelais and found an anatomy book in one of the boxes at the clinic. She sketched in pencil and then began to fill in the details with watercolors, working relentlessly to make the drawings come alive.

And certainly they were unique when compared to the pictographs in the book. Giselle's depicted dark-skinned women, and their bodies were like Haitian women's bodies really looked. She didn't use the same perfectly pale skin tones she found in the American book. Those women had stomachs that were flat or pertly plump with pregnancy, and their breasts were peach-colored like ripe mangos ready to be plucked from the tree. What Haitian woman could relate to those? Maybe that's the way women looked in the United States, where they had artificial milk in bottles and husbands who stayed with them and would help feed their babies and change diapers. Mothers could sleep all night and could say no to sex without fear of losing their man and being alone or being beaten. Yes, one of her illustrations showed that, as well. Bruises inflicted by an angry man crazy with rum. It happened even if no one talked about it.

No, few women in her country over the age of twenty-five had firm breasts. She sketched breasts like she had seen on her neighbors when they came to the clinic. They resembled more the wrinkled brown mangos that fell to the ground and had managed to escape the children's ravenous appetites and the animals' foraging. And Haitian women, their bellies were only briefly flat, passing through on their way from swollen with hunger to swollen with baby after baby.

She spent weeks working on the eyes, even though they had nothing to do with the reproductive organs. She made them dark and somber and wise, and in doing so, she came to understand the true strength of her Haitian sisters. Yes, their bodies would eventually fail them, just as hers had done. But oh, the spirit of the Haitian women! Now that was something no one could extinguish.

Dr. Kate's organization had given her the money to have the illustrations copied and laminated, and Mandy was using Giselle's illustrations that day to explain the female anatomy and physiology. Then the nurse told about a method of natural birth control called the rhythm method. Mandy worked for a Catholic organization and arrived in Ti Mirebelais with a bag full of beads. Cycle beads they were called.

"There are thirty-two colored beads that represent each day in your menstrual cycle, and a rubber ring that can be placed around the individual beads to help remind you where you are in your cycle. You can wear them like a necklace," Mandy explained.

The women laughed.

Mandy passed the beads around and Giselle held them, trying to visualize in her mind what the other women were seeing. The beads reminded her of the rosary beads so many of the peasants carried and used to pray.

"You see the beads are red, brown, and white," Mandy began. "The red bead is for the day you start bleeding. On that day, you move the rubber ring to the red bead. Each day, after that you move the ring to the next bead. The brown beads represent the days during your cycle when if you have sex, you *probably won't* get pregnant. The white beads represent your fertile days. If you have sex on these days, you *probably will* get pregnant."

Giselle heard the "probably" loud and clear but doubted the other women in the group paid much attention.

Mandy added, "And, in case it's night and you forget and wonder—should I or shouldn't I have sex—the white beads glow in the dark." Mandy sounded so pleased with her beads. "Any questions?" she repeated three times, until the giggles from the group subsided.

"What if he doesn't respect the beads?" one of the younger women asked in a low voice.

"Good question," Mandy said. She was prepared. "There are two other . . ." she paused as if searching for the right word, ". . . techniques you can use. The first is called the withdrawal method. You ask your partner to withdraw before he ejaculates."

There were no giggles, only silence.

"You ask him to pull his penis out before he comes inside your vagina," Mandy explained further. She said the words so fast, like she needed to get them out without them actually touching her lips.

After that abrupt explanation, it took five minutes before the whispers, the jokes, and the teasing subsided.

Mandy was persistent in getting her message out. "The second technique is to take a piece of a sponge—a *clean* one. Soak the sponge in two tablespoons of vinegar or lemon juice or salt boiled in *clean* water."

There was a pause and Giselle could tell that she was showing the group something.

"Push the sponge into the vagina one hour before and leave it in six hours after. And you can reuse the sponge many times. But boil it again in the solution, of course."

Giselle listened to the women chiding each other.

"I don't know about you, sister. But my man is too big to share me with a sponge."

"I sure hope I don't forget and use my sponge to wash the dishes."

"When do I get an hour notice that he's going to want it? I might just run the other way if I knew that far ahead of time."

A few whispered their questions privately to Mandy. Giselle, sitting beside her, couldn't help but overhear.

"What if we have relations," the woman said, lowering her voice shyly, "with someone who is not our husband? Can we get pregnant?"

"Sometimes I try to say no. But then he gets mad and so I say yes," one woman offered.

And if you don't say yes, he'll go to someone else or beat you or both. Again Giselle sighed in frustration.

"We have other options." Giselle decided that they had to do something more than move a rubber ring around a strand of beads or soak a sponge in vinegar.

She knew there were medicines—pills a woman could take each day. She had taken the little peach-colored ones after Natali was born. But they were so expensive, as much as a peasant woman would make in market for the whole month. Recently, she had also learned that some international organizations were giving shots to women to prevent them from getting pregnant.

"If some of you would like to participate, I'll get the information. You could go together by tap-tap." Giselle believed this made more sense than the other options they had heard that day.

But one woman, whose voice Giselle did not recognize, spoke up.

"I went to one of those clinics. They gave me a shot in my leg and told me to come back in three months. I was bleeding so heavy I couldn't get on the tap-tap. When I went there two weeks later, they wouldn't give me another shot. You can't see me, Giselle. But I'm pregnant." The woman didn't give her name.

Giselle pondered the situation as the others consoled the woman.

No injections, no glow-in-the-dark beads, not even expensive pills would save the women of Haiti. Giselle was more convinced than ever that solidarity was the key. They could not win the fight alone. One drop of rain cannot put out a fire or quench the thirst of a parched mouth or provide for crops to grow. But many drops of rain can become a glass of water, then a bucket of water, then a stream, and then a river. That was what they must become. Like the *lavalas*—the flood—they must become a force that would rise and wash away the ignorance and fear.

"Courage," Giselle reminded the group. "We must have courage. And if fear starts to creep in like the mosquitoes that wiggle through the holes in your screens, then we stand together and strike them down before they wound us."

"Yes. Yes." A few of the women, including her friend Yvonne, agreed.

But Giselle heard many more thank Mandy as they took their cycle beads home. She checked her frustration and stayed silent and reminded herself that in Haiti, the fastest way to change was often two steps forward, one step back.

The early July heat was so intense that Giselle considered canceling her *Nou ti pale* session that morning. But she needed to continue to reinforce her Mother's Day broadcast message on birth control. She dressed in her lightest cotton outfit and promised herself a nap later in the afternoon.

"Can I speak on your show today?" a woman asked when Giselle arrived at the radio station.

Giselle recognized the voice of the pregnant woman who spoke at their last group meeting.

"You can call me *Mal Bet*—sick animal." The woman explained that she delivered her baby two weeks earlier.

Giselle reminded Erold to put the voice scrambler on when the woman talked.

"I don't want any more children—God forgive me for this. I can't do it again." She was only twenty-one and had already had four children.

"I know." Giselle reached out and touched the woman's arm. It trembled. When Giselle tried to hold her hand, her fists were clenched. And she had an odor that told Giselle she hadn't bathed in many days.

The woman explained that she had a problem—the baby had been too big and wouldn't come out. Her mother found a man with a truck and they went to the hospital for a Cesarean section.

"It took all the money I had and my mother's and sisters', too. They cut the baby out. I begged the doctor before he started. Please cut my tubes. I can't do this again. My other babies are starving and I am too weak to work."

The woman told her that she herself thought she had the Disease a few months ago. The doctor who was about to do the C-section thought so, too, because she was pale and thin.

"But I had to tell him the truth," she confided to Giselle. "My test was negative. I think he would have done it—sterilized me—if I had been positive. But no, he refused. 'I need the father's permission,' he told me, and I said to him, 'But he is not my husband. He gives me almost nothing for the children.' The doctor just shrugged . . ." Her voice trailed off and she paused briefly before continuing. "'We need the father's permission. Is he here? No, then I cannot.'" She cried softly as she recounted her tale. Oddly, the scrambler made her voice sound like a contented cat purring rather than a desperate woman.

"Too many babies."

Her tears fell like drops of warm spring rain on Giselle's hands that were still wrapped around the woman's clenched fists.

"I can't take any more. I'm like an old goat tied to a tree in last year's field. There's no more grass. I'm forced to eat dirt and rock because I'm too weak to break the cord around my neck and no one will cut it for me."

Giselle made an appeal to her listeners. "If there are others out there, you must speak out about your experiences, too. We will keep talking until we find some answers." She turned off the mic and said to the woman, "Please leave me your name and how I can find you. We will get food for you and your children now, and I promise, we will keep trying. Do not despair."

Giselle turned on the microphone again and held it out in the air for the next woman.

"It's your turn." She felt the long thin fingers wrap around hers as she let go.

These hands she knew well. They bathed her when she first lost her vision and they cleaned her soiled body when she didn't care enough to do it herself. Even though she was blind now, she could see these hands in her mind—copying lessons from the blackboard at school, playing dominoes with her friends, making graceful movements in the air as she danced ballet as a young child.

"Natali?" She turned off the microphone and whispered, fearful that her daughter's voice would be recognized on the radio, despite the scrambler. "Are you sure?"

Her daughter took the microphone from her and she heard her click the switch back on.

"My name is *fanm nan fanm nan fòs*—woman from courageous woman. Each week our mothers speak out. They are very brave women. For the young women out there, open your ears and listen. We are not children any longer. It is time for our voices to join theirs. The future belongs to us, as well."

Giselle's heart swelled with pride. Perhaps Natali would succeed where she herself had failed. Perhaps her daughter would make it safely out of Haiti *and* find a way to help the women she would leave behind.

KATE

HAITI
AUGUST 1994

Kate was both oddly comforted and mildly amused by the Coast Guard boats lingering in the bay and American Marines peppered about the airport and streets of Port au Prince. The camouflaged tanks that crawled down the congested streets amidst the goats and *ti machann* reminded her of a Salvador Dali painting. The Haitians seemed oblivious to their new peacekeepers.

"Life in Haiti is as back to normal as it can be," Didi claimed.

Kate had no clue what normal would ever be for Haiti. Her trip had been delayed by two weeks as Operation Uphold Democracy was implemented by the U.S. and United Nations joint efforts. Thank goodness a full-force military intervention did not happen. She might not have made it back in the country for another six months. It was hard to make a case with funders for programs in Haiti under the best of situations. But when travel was cut off, it was impossible. If it weren't for their loyal individual donors, like Edward and a few members of his congregation, they would not have been able to continue.

August was not her favorite time to be in Haiti. It was hotter and dustier than usual. But it was critical that they get the community HIV prevention and education program started this trip. It had been almost a year since she received the money and she needed to make a report before September. She planned to spend only two nights in Port au Prince—one coming and one going. That would be enough to catch up with Didi. As always, she visited the old soccer field where the UN Declaration of Rights was faded beyond recognition. She reread the short entry in her journal she had written earlier that day. It was spotted with drops of sweat.

> August 20, 1994
>
> Agenda for trip: HIV/AIDS Program, pictures and financial accounting for Sante Fanm and family planning—how can we support this initiative, without breaking the agreement with our donor??
>
> Port au Prince is definitely calmer. It only took us 20 minutes to get to Didi's from the airport. The streets are far from clean but I don't think it's my imagination that the garbage piles are smaller. I even saw some trashcans and it seems like everyone is painting their homes and businesses. Didi says they're putting "a spit and shine" on the place in anticipation of Aristide's return. For the first time in three years, I feel hopeful that we can really move forward with the programs.

She placed her journal back in the Ziplock bag, laced up her old Nikes, and took her customary ten-lap jog around the soccer field. Her legs were a little tired today. At first it felt like her running shoes had lead instead of rubber soles. But after a few laps she loosened up and her thoughts wandered back and forth in time.

The afternoon before the HIV/AIDS program, Kate sat around the fire in Mirebelais to make final plans for the program with Yvonne and Giselle while the dinner soup cooked. Natali joined them after adding the vegetables to the pot. Kate couldn't get over the transformation in Natali. She was only thirteen, just three years older than Jen, yet she had the maturity and grace of a young woman. She was so much like her mother. Although Giselle had lost some weight, it only accentuated her high cheekbones. Silver had crept into her dark hair. Nevertheless, she had such energy and passion that Kate hadn't appreciated before. And when her daughter was near her, it was electrifying. She moved around so easily that Kate forgot she was blind.

"For many months before and after my sight left me," Giselle confided, "I believed I was cursed." She gave a little laugh. "An artist who loses her vision—what other explanation could there be?"

Natali took her mother's hands and held them to her cheek.

"But then like my friend Picasso said—losing my vision helped me to find my voice. The radio program, Dr. Kate, it saved me. And I think it is saving others, too. Women from all over share their messages with each other on the radio. We are talking about our bodies and taking control of them. It's a good thing. We thank you for this." Giselle pulled her chair closer. "But we have more to ask."

Kate leaned forward and listened as Giselle and Yvonne outlined a plan for sponsoring three young girls from the community at university. They had done quite a lot of homework and they made a good case. Not only that, but what pleased Kate most was that the idea had come from the community and not from her. She thought back to their first undertaking with the clinic and the failed immunization program. They had come far in building the kind of trust and openness that Kate knew was essential to success of the programs.

"With room and board and books for three of our young women to attend a university in Port au Prince, we need $3,000 U.S. . . . each year," Yvonne reported, and handed her a proposal.

Kate scanned the document. It was short but had all the financial information neatly outlined in a table. Nevertheless, she could hear the arguments from her board members. That amount of money could send well over thirty children to primary school for a year.

"I can't promise anything today. I'll take it to the board and let you know in a few weeks."

When they finished their tea, Natali left to find her friends. Kate hesitated to bring up the next item on her agenda. But she had seen the boxes of condoms with the other items for the seminar tomorrow. The box was in the clinic exam room, directly below the plaque with the major donor's name from Michael's church. The wooden plaque read: IN MEMORY OF MAGGIE CURRY, IN SUPPORT OF WOMEN'S HEALTH IN HAITI. Besides the plaque, the other stipulation for receiving the funds, and possibly more money, was that there would be no promotion of birth control. Not a requirement unlike some major donor organizations. Kate conceded only because she had no other options at the time.

"We need to talk about how you are presenting birth control during your program, Giselle."

Her friend nodded but volunteered nothing. This was not going to be easy—direct was best.

"I saw the condoms. Are you planning to give them out tomorrow?"

"Yes, they were donated by another organization."

"I understand that. But the grant money we received from the Currys for the conference specifically states that it is only to be used for HIV prevention and education through abstinence and being faithful in relationships, not for promoting birth control." It sounded hollow even to her.

"You mean the ABCs of HIV prevention without the 'C'? Dr. Kate, you know Haiti. Will that work?"

"Some studies have shown it will." Actually, only one of the dozens of studies Kate had read reported that finding. Even that study was heavily biased and funded by a Christian-based organization with major funding from Washington.

Giselle leaned closer to her. "All we want is to give the women of Haiti a fighting chance. Abstinence is a good message for the young single ones. I preach it every day to Natali. For a Haitian woman, being faithful in marriage without using protection doesn't *decrease* the chance of HIV. I would argue that it *increases* the risk. It gives her a false sense of security. How do you think women are getting the disease? Most of the cases we see now are women who are married and have only one partner—their husband." She paused. "Asking a Haitian man to be faithful—well you may as well ask a ripe mango to stay on the tree."

"I just want to be sure we don't jeopardize the funding for future programs." Kate hated feeling like her hands were tied on this issue. But until she could find other funds, she had to respect the agreement she had signed with the Currys.

"And why shouldn't we have access to birth control? You only have two children—not counting Tieina." This was one of the rare times that she had ever heard Giselle raise her voice. "Didn't *you* use something to limit your family size? I know I did."

"Giselle, you know I'm in a tough situation with family planning." Kate checked her feelings at her friend's anger. She would forgive her for touching a wound she couldn't know was there. She had never mentioned her miscarriage. "As a woman and as a doctor, I agree with you. But as the executive director of the organization that received the grant, I have to respect the funder's stipulations."

"What do you want us to do tomorrow?" Giselle's voice had softened but still held such resolve that Kate knew her friend might postpone, but would not abandon, her cause. Giselle's passion was as exasperating as it was inspiring at times.

Kate thought about her daughters and what she would want for them if they lived in this country, in this village. "This is the way we'll do it. None of the grant money can be used to purchase condoms or any other method of birth control. That is not negotiable." She carefully chose her next words. "I have some business farther down in the village and will have to leave the seminar a little early tomorrow. That might be a good time for your discussion."

"I understand," Giselle replied cautiously.

"Someone who knows how to use them will do a demonstration? Or would you like me to go over that with you tonight?" No sense handing out condoms if they were going to sit in a drawer somewhere or be used as balloons by the children.

"No, thank you. We have that covered. Natali is bringing some bananas." Giselle smiled. "It's the best we could come up with."

Kate smiled back. "Bananas should work quite nicely." The condom issue settled, Kate took the opportunity to quietly query her friend, "Giselle are you really doing as well as you say? Please, don't pretend for my sake. I want to know. Are you really okay?"

Giselle never spoke of leaving Haiti or Ti Mirebelais anymore. She never mentioned her husband either. But Kate knew from Yvonne that he was out of the picture for good. He had set up a business somewhere in New York. Six months ago he stopped talking about Natali and Giselle coming to the U.S. and he still thought it was unsafe for him to come back.

Yvonne had repeated what Max had told Natali when she called him to tell him her mother had gone blind: "Claimed he wouldn't make it out of the Port au Prince airport alive."

"Yes, I am okay," Giselle replied. "I have just one regret. That I cannot see with my own eyes the beautiful woman my daughter has become. She is beautiful, isn't she? I can sense the beauty inside, the strength and the compassion. She reminds me of her grandmother—she wanted to save the world, too. At her age, all I thought about was art and boys and boys and art."

"Yes, Giselle. Natali is lovely inside and out." Kate held her friend's hands and they smiled. "I believe she reminds me of her mother."

There were at least 300 in attendance at the seminar, twice the number Kate expected. She took in the faces around her. Women more than twice her age, who she knew couldn't sign their names with more than X, were there because they had watched this disease take their sons, their daughters, their husbands from them for over a decade. Women half her age, starting families and facing the greatest risks. Young girls the same ages as Tieina and Jen, just coming to terms with the changes in their bodies. Most arrived before the sun came up, eager to get a seat in front. Yvonne made the introductions using Giselle's sound system from the radio station.

"Good morning and welcome to Ti Mirebelais and our first annual community program on HIV."

The crowd became quiet.

"This is our day to talk about a disease that no one wants to talk about." Yvonne paused. "HIV is our enemy and the enemy of our children and our children's children. But the bigger enemies are silence and fear." She paused again.

Kate looked around to see many of the women nodding in agreement.

"Today we will not be silent and we will face our fears together." Yvonne's eyes seemed to find and lock on each and every person in the group. "I would like to introduce a few people before we begin." She motioned for Madame Cereste and Kate to join her.

After the introductions, the entire group stood and sang a song. Kate found it difficult to get the words past the lump in her throat.

She was so touched by the passion and dedication, grateful to be part of it. It was a rare moment when peace of mind and sense of purpose came together, and she was reminded of her dream years ago, to help bring medical care to people in a country like Haiti. What she hadn't dreamed, what she couldn't have known back in her idealistic twenties, was how rich her life would become being part of these other women's dreams.

Kate's only role, other than supplying the funding, was to present a short program on the facts and figures of HIV/AIDS in Haiti. They weren't good, and most of the experts expected them to get worse. Haiti was the perfect storm for an epidemic, some cautioned. Poverty, corruption, desperation, and lack of education—these were all the forces that could create a disaster. Of course, her message was simple and designed to give hope. She explained the ways they could get the disease and the ways they couldn't. She encouraged people to get tested and encouraged them to respect each other's privacy and stand together with those who were infected.

"With the information you get today," she concluded, "you and your community and your children can conquer this disease." Again, she reinforced the idea that fear and ignorance were the real enemies, not the virus.

All listened intently and a few asked questions: "What is it like in your country?" and "Will there ever be a cure?"

Following lunch—fried chicken, rice, and beans—they had the women break into smaller groups to work on skits. This was Giselle's idea.

"It will be a fun way to reinforce what they have learned. We might also find some lingering myths about HIV that we can dispel—or at least try to dispel."

She was right on both counts. They really did have fun performing the skits and listening to one another. There were a few poignant moments that let her know that they had listened and understood. Like the second group's performance, where a young woman learned she had HIV after she received the results of her blood test. The nurse at the clinic lived in the same village and told everyone. Now no one would buy from her in the market and her friends didn't invite her for coffee anymore. The poor woman, who was not yet sick with the disease, was alone and depressed and contemplating suicide. The skit ended there.

Yvonne was the first to speak up. "What could we do for this woman?"

That started a long discussion on the risks of getting HIV from casual contact.

"What if your boyfriend wants to—you know? And you want to do it too . . . ?" was the next question, innocently asked by one of the younger women.

This offered a segue to the next discussion. Kate took her cue to pursue her other business, just as Yvonne lifted the box of bananas and condoms to the demonstration table.

That evening after dinner dishes were finished, they talked over a cup of tea, rehashing the day's events and planning for another program in six months, this time aimed at a younger crowd.

Kate also gave Yvonne a report on her granddaughter and showed her pictures. Tieina's hair was straight now, short and dark, and she had continued to put on weight a little more each month it seemed. Kate had to buy her new jeans at least four times that year because the waist and hips were too tight. But always they had to be hemmed; she was not catching up in height as quickly. Kate gave the pictures to Yvonne in a small album along with the letter Tieina had written and recorded on the cassette. Even though it was in English, Kate wanted her to have it so she could see how beautiful Tieina's handwriting was. As Yvonne looked through the album and turned the pages of the letter, her eyes moistened.

"She looks so healthy now her hair is all black and her cheeks are full."

"Yes, she is beautiful," she said, and then paused. "She still won't speak in Creole."

"Never mind. I am so happy to hear her voice. Giselle, can you translate for me now?"

"Of course."

Kate placed Giselle's hand on the cassette player and moved her fingers to show her the "play" and "pause" buttons. Yvonne studied her letter as Giselle translated Tieina's recorded words.

Dear Grandmother,

I am sorry for not writing sooner. Mama Kate encouraged me to do so every day. But I wanted to wait until the happy words found me and now they have. I hope you will come to the United States someday, too. I could teach you to speak English and read and you could walk me to school.

At first I was hungry and afraid all the time. I worried that a stranger would come and take me from my new home and I would never find my new family or my old family. My new mother told me this would never happen and there would always be enough to eat. Still, I had to wait until I could know it myself.

Sometimes Jen and I fight. Well, actually, we fight a lot. She is so smart and I am jealous of that. She has big dreams to do important things when she grows up. She wants to find a cure for cancer—like my first mother had. Sometimes she fixes my hair and we talk about clothes and she always helps me with my math homework. It's hard for me—the numbers. They don't make sense. But I love using the words. English is like a song that sings in my head and my heart. There are so many ways to arrange the words; it is hard to choose sometimes. One small word, like a bit of sugar, makes the story sweet, or another word, like a drop of vinegar, makes it bitter. Words are very powerful in that way.

My new brother, Danny, he has red hair like our mother. We play soccer together, but not on a team. They have different teams for boys and girls here. He helps me practice and tells me I'm not too bad for a girl. I don't mind when he says that, because he's really smart about soccer.

I do miss you, Grandmother. But I can't think about my life before. Sometimes, I'm still frightened. But I'm too old to cry and run to my mother. So I just lie awake until the daylight comes. Danny tells me I am tough and brave, but I don't always feel that way. Jen gave me her flashlight and her Beanie Baby—it is a little brown bear with tiny beans inside.

I know it is hard for you to write me. But I hope you will send me a picture of you. I will try to write again someday.

Your granddaughter,

Tieina Delva Rigando

Yes, Tieina had a good and safe life with her in the United States. Yet each time Kate came to Haiti, she felt the love and support of Yvonne and Giselle surround her like a warm blanket. How could she keep her daughter from all of this?

"Yvonne, I am going to bring Tieina back for a visit." It might take some time, but she would make it happen.

"Oh, please, when it's safe. Will you really? Bring her to me?" Yvonne's face brightened with the possibility.

"I promise," Kate answered, and she knew in her heart they would be reunited one day.

Kate sat with her two dear friends in comfortable silence as the tape continued to the end with just a rhythmic whisper of static as an accompaniment to their thoughts. Fighting HIV and helping women become educated was her passion. But without friends and family, her passion was like a beautiful song with no breath to sing it.

Between the Miami and Pittsburgh flight connection, Kate had just enough time to call home. Her dad and Anne were staying with the kids this trip. It was ten o'clock but her dad would still be up. He never missed the late-night news.

When final boarding for her Pittsburgh flight was announced over the loudspeaker and after ten rings with no answer, she had to run before the attendant closed the Jetway door. A dozen explanations traveled through her mind over the three-hour flight. The phone was out; they went somewhere; her father was in the shower and everyone else was sleeping. Still, her worry persisted until she landed in Pittsburgh and tried again from another pay phone. It was 2 a.m. After decades of taking night calls from patients, she knew her dad would never not answer the phone. Something was definitely wrong.

The note was on the kitchen counter. A huge bowl of spaghetti and meatballs, a basket of bread, and a salad surrounded by four clean place settings were patiently waiting on the table. Only the overturned chair seemed out of place. Kate didn't even take the time to set it upright before running back to the car and on to the hospital.

During the ten-minute drive, she resurrected any prayer she could remember, each ending with, *please let him be okay.*

She recognized the look in the ICU nurse's eyes when she asked her where her dad was. The "I'm so sorry you're not in time look"

Kate had mastered so well herself back when she was a resident in San Francisco. Kate didn't wait for the words. She saw the crash cart in the hallway outside one of the intensive care modules. The curtains were drawn shut so she couldn't see inside the glass enclosure. A tired-looking young man in blue scrubs, probably a resident, exited while snapping off his gloves.

"Hey, you can't go in there." He tried to stop Kate as she pushed past him and rushed in.

Anne was sitting on the edge of her father's bed, holding his hand. The haphazard and bloody discards of a failed Code Blue taunted her. Kate felt her heart twist backwards in her chest when she realized she was too late.

"He didn't want to tell you until you got back from Haiti. He knew this trip was important. We thought there was more time." Anne looked up and patted the bed next to her for Kate to sit.

"Last month, the doctors found a mass in his pancreas, inoperable. He was going to start radiation next week when you got back.

"We were getting ready to have dinner and then go to soccer and he grabbed his chest and passed out. We got him here, but he never woke up, and then his heart stopped." Anne had to be in shock; her voice was so calm. "They said it was probably a blood clot to his lung. That this sort of thing is common with pancreatic cancer."

Kate nodded, not caring why her father was gone, only that he was and she hadn't been there to say goodbye, again like with her mother.

"I'll leave you alone for a minute. I need to make a phone call. The kids are in the waiting room, just through the double doors. They'll be okay for a few more minutes."

And as Anne left, she said, "Don't feel bad for not being here, honey. Your dad was so proud of you and what you're doing in Haiti."

Kate tried to take some comfort from Anne's words. She remembered all the times her dad had been there for her—when her marriage fell apart, when Jen was born and spent two months in the neonatal ICU, when she needed help with the kids so she could pursue her dream to work in a country like Haiti. He was her role model, her mentor, her friend, and her father, and now he was gone. Silent tears streamed down her face and she took his hand, still warm, and kissed it. "Goodbye, Daddy. I love you."

Kate splashed cold water on her eyes, took a couple of deep breaths, and found Danny and Tieina in the waiting room. Someone had put a couple of chairs together for each of them and turned off the lights. They were snuggled in blankets, sleeping in their soccer uniforms.

Nothing would ease the mounting grief that threatened to overtake her. But gathering the sleeping children in her arms was the best she could imagine.

"Is Grandpa okay, Mom?"

"No, honey," she answered softly. "He's gone." Her son looked at her, confused at first, like maybe Grandpa had simply gone to the store for milk. Then he began to cry with the kind of sobs Kate knew were still locked inside of her.

"I didn't even get to say goodbye." He looked at her like he wanted to ask a question but didn't know how.

Tieina sat quietly staring at the floor. Perhaps, Kate thought, she was remembering her mother. She tried to pull her closer but the little girl stayed rooted where she sat, apart from Kate and Danny.

"Where's Jen?" Kate asked.

"At her dad's," Tieina answered, still tearless. "She's been there all week."

Kate decided the details of that could wait.

"Let's find Anne and go home. I'll get your sister in the morning."

Despite her exhaustion, Kate had only slept an hour when her eyes popped open. It took a minute before she remembered what had happened. She called upon one of the neighbors to stay with Danny and Tieina and set off on the forty-five minute drive to retrieve her daughter. It was only eight; she didn't want to tell Jen over the phone and she couldn't stand not having all her children with her right at that moment.

Mark's wife answered the doorbell with their three-month-old on her hip. "Kate, is something wrong?"

"I'm here for Jen. Can you please get her?" She wanted to break the news to her daughter before anyone else. Jen was close to her grandfather, even closer than Danny. Like Kate, they shared a love of science and spent hours exploring the woods and looking at books together.

Kate was ushered into the kitchen and given a cup of coffee, despite her protests. Mark appeared in his bathrobe.

"Kate, I was going to call you today and explain," he started.

"Where's Jen?" she interrupted.

"Jen's upstairs, still sleeping. She asked me to come and get her. She wants to live with us and go to the Montessori School."

"Mark, I don't have time for this right now."

"That's Jen's point, Kate. Between your trips to Haiti and your clinic work here and Tieina's problems, you don't have time for Jen."

"You work as much I do, Mark." Kate was now fully armed for the conversation she was having, which was so different than the one she was anticipating.

"But there are two parents here," Mark countered with another surprise dagger.

This time Kate had no quick response. Since the divorce, she had a date or two with a friend of a friend, but never a third. True, she didn't have time for men; she didn't have time for close friendships, unless they were related to Haiti. But how dare he accuse her of not having time for her own daughter? She stood up and closed the gap between her and her ex-husband.

"You don't know what you're talking about." She felt her face burning and surprised herself by how much anger she could muster, despite the fatigue she felt, despite the grief she felt for her father that threatened to surface any second.

"He's right, Mom." Her sleepy-eyed daughter appeared. Without her glasses, she looked so much like her grandfather it startled Kate. "Since Tieina came, even when you're home, you never have time for me." Jen stood there, not aligning with either her or her father.

"Jen." Kate rushed to her daughter. "I love you so much. I'm sorry. I didn't know you felt that way." How could she explain to a nine-year-old, as precocious as she was in some ways, a mother's heart wasn't like a pie divided into smaller pieces with each additional child. A mother's heart could only expand with more love with each child.

"Honey." They would have to sort this out later. "I didn't come here about where you are going to live. Honey, your Grandpa died last night. I need you to come home with me."

Mark murmured his condolences and left them. Kate held Jen in her lap, like she had when she was a baby and for the first time that Kate could remember, she couldn't make it all better, so she rocked back and forth and cried with her daughter.

While Jen was getting her things together, Kate waited alone, mourning not only the death of her father, but also her mother's death. The grief from over fifteen years ago, renewed by her present loss, did not seem less to her at the moment. At least she had known her dad, really known him—his habits, his strengths, his foibles. She knew what he cared about and how he showed his incredible love for his family. Her mother, though, had been a relative stranger, someone she loved, someone who loved her, but a person she had never really understood.

And now her daughter was pulling away from her. Had she been as distant with Jen as her own mother had been with her? Only instead of a bottle of vodka standing between them, there were noble causes.

32

KATE

MARS
SEPTEMBER 1998

"First place, Mom. I won first place! My article will be published next week." Tieina slammed her lime-green creative writing folder on the counter and danced around the kitchen singing, "You said I couldn't do it. But I did! You said I couldn't do it. But I did! Watch out, Jen. Here comes that Pulitzer Prize!"

Kate smiled at Tieina's victory dance and considered joining her. But she was cooking Danny's favorite dinner for his birthday—fried chicken, mashed potatoes, peas, and German chocolate cake. Kate pulled out the mixer and the flour and poured her daughter a glass of milk. She started to make her a sandwich. The fine tremor she sometimes noticed in her right hand made it difficult for Kate to spread the peanut butter on the bread.

"That's great, honey. I know how hard you worked on it." Out of the corner of her eye, she saw her daughter take a page out of the folder and fold it into her jacket pocket.

"Only the school newspaper. But it's a start."

"Here's a sandwich. Dinner is going to be late. Jen is coming."

"I'm not hungry," Tieina said and pushed away the plate. "I'm going to go for a run before soccer practice."

"Running *and* soccer?" Kate asked. "Don't you think you should eat something? After all, you're still growing."

Tieina took Kate's shoulders and looked up into her eyes. "Mom, get real. I'm never going to be tall like Jen." She patted her stomach that had become flat this past year. "The only way I'm going to grow is out *and* I eat plenty. Besides, I like being short like you." She flashed that smile that none of the Rigandos could match or refuse. "Then when I get my boobs, I can borrow *your* clothes. They're more my style anyway." She shoved her feet into her running shoes without unlacing them. "Jen dresses like an old lady."

With that she started back into her dance and sang, "You said it couldn't be done. Watch out, Jen! Here I come."

"Get out of here before I start calling you *Sanba*," said Kate, smiling at the old rivalry between her two daughters. It was more good-natured now that they were a few years older and living apart.

"*Sanba*, what's that? Italian or something?"

"No," she replied. "It's Creole. A *Sanba* is like a troubadour—a person who writes poetry or songs that tell stories or are used to motivate people. The *Sanba* chants a phrase and the people answer back in a chorus."

"Oh, I didn't know about that." Tieina looked at her and opened her mouth as if she wanted to say something but stopped, gave her a kiss instead, threw her jacket on the kitchen table, and ran out the door. "See you in an hour."

"Hang up your jacket and don't forget the birthday dinner is at seven." But she doubted Tieina had heard, as she was already out the door. As she picked her daughter's jacket up off the table, she felt the paper in her pocket. Maybe she shouldn't read it. If Tieina had wanted her to see it, she would have left it out. Well, that's what mothers did, wasn't it? Check up on their teenage daughters. She unfolded the paper and found a short verse in Tieina's handwriting.

One voice from many . . .
a child learns to speak.
But if the many shout in anger—
will her voice become an echo of their fear?
Or will the chorus silence her sweet song,
And leave the memories forgotten,
and the dreams untouched?

Kate stood with the crumpled poem in her hand, staring at the words and trying to decipher the message between the lines. Did Tieina remember more of Haiti than Kate could get her to talk about? Her thoughts were interrupted when Danny slammed his car door. He was home from school. She tore a piece of paper off the notepad she used for making the grocery list, scribbled down Tieina's poem to keep for herself, and replaced the original in her daughter's jacket.

"Happy Birthday, Dan!" she greeted her son.

"Mom, you're home early. Anything wrong?" He kissed her cheek and grabbed the sandwich and milk his sister had refused.

"No, there's nothing wrong. Just took off a little early to bake a cake for my favorite son."

"I like that idea. What's this?" He picked up his sister's green folder and read the article inside. "Wow, she really is good. I can't believe she's only thirteen." He stared at his unfinished sandwich, his usual smile missing.

"You okay, Dan?" Her son usually inhaled his food.

"I'm really proud of Tieina and Jen. They're both so smart, and they seem to know exactly what they want to do, and then they just go after it."

"Like you do with soccer," she chimed in.

"Soccer is just a game, Mom." He closed the folder. "What am I going to do with my life?" There were tears in his eyes. "I'm eighteen today. One year away from college and I can't do anything except play a game."

"I thought you were okay with liberal arts for the first year or two?" Again, her seemingly uncomplicated child had slipped beneath her radar. "So what do you see yourself doing in five or ten years, as they like to ask on the essay questions?"

"That's the problem, Mom. I don't see myself doing much of anything."

"Nothing?"

"Actually, I couldn't be a doctor or a medical person, but I like what you do—traveling and helping out in poor countries. I could get into that. Maybe I could work with kids somewhere and help organize soccer teams, kind of like a boys club?" His smile returned.

"I think that's a great idea. But college first, right?"

"Yeah." He gave a second look to the green folder. "I think I'll get little sister Number Two to write my application essay."

"We'll get started on those when I get back from Haiti at the end of the month. Okay?"

"Hey, why don't I go with you? I'm sure I could get excused from my classes for a week."

"I'd like that, but let's talk about it for the next time. I'm counting on you to run Tieina back and forth to practice. Speaking of, would you mind picking up little sister Number One? I've got a birthday cake to decorate."

Peeling potatoes for dinner in front of the kitchen window, Kate watched Danny open the door for his sister. No one else could get Jen laughing like her brother could. He was only a few inches taller than her. Both wearing sunglasses, except for Dan's red hair, it was easy to see them as brother and sister. But that didn't last long—as soon as Jen switched to her regular glasses, on came her serious face. She heaved her backpack over first her left, then her right shoulder. No wonder she was always slouched; the lumpy bag didn't look like it could hold a pencil more.

"Hi, Mom. Something smells good."

"Probably the fried chicken and biscuits." She kissed her daughter. "They're warming in the oven. You know I can never get everything done at the same time."

"Dan told me Tieina is getting her first article published. Can I see it?"

"Right there." Kate nodded to the green folder and set the pot on the stove to boil after she sprinkled salt in the water.

Jen sat on a stool and read. "Wow. This is really good stuff. How does she know all that?"

"The Internet—just like you." She marveled at both her daughters' breadth of knowledge. "Just like Bob Dylan said, 'The times they are a-changin'.'"

"Oh yeah, everyone always says stuff like that." Jen unloaded her backpack onto the chair. "Do I have time to look something up before dinner? I've got a paper due tomorrow and I want to check a reference."

"The potatoes will take another half hour. But can't you visit with me for a while? I hardly see you and you're always studying when you're here." Kate was stirring the gravy.

"I'm sorry, Mom. It's just that I want to get out of high school in three years. My guidance counselor thinks I can do it."

"Jen, there's more to high school, and college for that matter, than academics." They'd had this discussion before.

"I know, Mom. I think about that, too." Jen answered without any bristle, like they were two friends discussing a movie they had just seen. "Let me finish the gravy and I'll do the Internet when I go home."

Home? She wanted to say this is your home and you should be here, with me, every day for every dinner. No doubt her daughter was growing up, but she was determined not to push her away.

Kate looked up to see Jen staring at her right hand, which was shaking again.

"Mom, are you okay?" Jen asked with the slightest alarm in her voice. "Let me do that for you."

"Thanks, honey. You make the best gravy." Kate felt less certain her tremor was simple fatigue. But there was no use in worrying the kids for now.

Instead she smiled as her daughter stirred the bubbly mixture with her own precise and perfect rhythm that Kate was finally beginning to understand.

33

GISELLE

PETIT (TI) MIREBELAIS
SEPTEMBER 1998

A drum sounded, and a single voice called out . . .

Men anpil—**When the hands are many** . . .

Two hoes clanked together; after all, one cannot make music alone.

Then many voices joined in response like a well-rehearsed chorus . . . *Chay pa lou*—**The burden is light.**

The *Sanba* continued . . .

Yon sel nou feb—**Alone we are weak** . . .

In response . . . *Ansanm nou fo*—**Together we are strong.** *Ansanm, ansanm nou se lavalas*—**Together, together we are an avalanche.**

And then everyone together, *Chef*—**chief,** *Sanba,* **cook, and farmer** . . .

Yon ede lot . . . **One helping another.**

Giselle sat in the *lakou*—yard—with her face uplifted to the early morning sun and listened to the rhythm of the hoes breaking the rough ground for fall planting. She recalled from her sighted memory the peasants standing shoulder to shoulder, raising their hoes and machetes in unison and striking the earth with such force that even the rockiest and driest fields yielded under their collective efforts.

The week before, the labor seemed as endless as the hot summer sun under which they toiled. The swoosh of machetes thrashing down the cornstalks and the grunts of her neighbors ripping out the old and stubborn vines filled the space from dawn to dusk. There was little reward for the efforts that went into clearing the land. Giselle had helped by squeezing a few citrons into the water bucket and adding a generous dose of sugar. Natali offered to carry the water out to the grateful workers in the field. A cup or two of water was all that they expected, and it was all they got until they went to their own homes in the evening.

But today, for the final preparation of the land and the planting, it was different. Even as the sun barely peeked over the valley, the smell of coffee and scorched pig already touched her nostrils. Those women who didn't work in the fields gladly prepared the food. Onions, potatoes, carrots, parsley—whatever they could find that was left from the spring harvest—went into the pot for the soup they would serve at midday meal. The *Chef Konbit*—the owner of the land being planted—had a good year, so they would roast a pig for the evening meal.

Yvonne was somewhere out there among the peasants. Although approaching sixty, she was one of the most productive workers in the village. The *Chef* always invited her to join the *gwoup peyizans*. When Giselle first arrived in Ti Mirebelais, she thought this an insult, being asked to work like a slave on someone else's land. But after living in the village, she came to understand that being part of the *konbit* was a sign of mutual respect. Her friend's labor in a neighbor's field today was exchanged for his labor in her field tomorrow or next year or the year after when, and if, they were prosperous enough to host the group. Though most of the peasants' plots would always remain too small to collectively farm, like Yvonne's. She had only a small plot a long walk away from her house. That was all she could afford with her money from the co-op.

Natali told her, "It is so steep, she has to tie herself to a tree so she won't fall down into the ravine like Boz Lionel did."

While trying to coax a stubborn weed out of the ground during last spring's planting, Boz Lionel had lost his footing and rolled down the rocky crevice into the ravine below. It was two days before a young village boy heard his cries for help. His ribs were broken and one leg crushed. They had to amputate it below the knee.

The members of the women's group marveled at Yvonne's ability to feed her family from her meager land. And she always had a little extra for those who weren't as lucky. They jokingly accused her of using magic—or in this case fertilizers or pesticides—to increase her crop yields.

"No," she assured them. "It is less, rather than more, that I ask of the land."

Yvonne squeezed her hand as she spoke. For it was Giselle who had shared the little she had learned about sustainable agriculture from the American couple she met in Cuba, Liz and Jim. They still lived nearby and visited occasionally. Giselle did not keep the information to herself and Yvonne; it was just that the others refused to try new techniques. Two bean seeds instead of five went into each hole and each hole was twelve, not six, inches apart. This year she would plant beans and cassava, but next year corn and sweet potatoes. Liz and Jim had given Yvonne a few small clumps of grass called *vetiver*. Giselle had felt the thick clumps in her hand. They were substantial but compact and quite unlike any other plants she had touched.

"Plant these at the highest and steepest parts of your fields," they advised her friend. "The roots grow deep but don't spread widely. They keep the soil in place and will protect the crops below them even if the rainfall is heavy."

Yvonne tried these few techniques and she harvested twice as much as the year before.

Of course, there were still rituals that must be followed to ensure good favor from the spirits who influenced the rains, the sun, and the winds. So after the land was cleared, the ground prepared, and the seeds safely placed in their beds, Yvonne would ask Giselle to join her in making an offering. She would make the trip up and down the rocky road with her friend, each carrying a basket of fruits and vegetables and a small bag of grains, usually rice and millet. They would kneel on the ground at the far edge of the field where Yvonne placed a small statue of Saint Isidore and a cross woven from straw likened to the one Saint Brigid from Ireland carried. Liz and Jim were Irish but also respectful of the Cuban influence. And as not to leave anything to chance, a picture of Azaka, the Vodou *Iwa* of harvest, was included. The two women scattered the grain over the fields and prayed. The fruit was left along with the icons until the first sun after the first rain, when the icons were brought safely home for the next season. Nothing brought out the humble spirituality of her simple peasant neighbors more than planting, as if turning over the earth was an opportunity to turn over their souls and plant the seeds of goodness again.

Today's *Chef Konbit* had one of the larger plots of land in the village and the means to gather the labor to plant the crops, which meant in one way or another everyone had more opportunity for food. *Yon sel dwet, pa manj*—one finger cannot stir the stew, and *yon ede lot*—one helping another. Good principles, but sometimes words fell short in practice. Giselle thought back to when Yvonne's daughter, Adelaide, was sick and died, and when she had lost her vision. *Yon ede lot* was a powerful force in rural Haiti, but not immune to corruption by fear and greed. It was good to remember that.

"I'm leaving, Mother," Natali called from inside. "Can I get you anything before I go?"

"Just a kiss."

"I'll see you in three weeks." Her daughter kissed her lightly on the forehead.

"Do you have enough money for the tap-tap and food?"

"Yes, Mother. I have money and some bread and fruit."

"Please send my greetings to your cousins. And good luck on your exams, *Chérie*."

"I will. I love you." Natali's voice faded and the sound of her steps quickened as if her feet couldn't carry her up the path fast enough.

A tiny bit of sadness came into Giselle's heart like a lone cloud in an otherwise clear and sunny sky. A mother never stopped missing her child. Even if it meant she would have the best chance possible to graduate from school and go to university next year.

"Giselle, do you have time to help us shell the peas for those in the fields?"

She recognized Madame Cereste's voice. The woman was too large to work in the fields but of perfectly generous proportions and spirit to coordinate the days of meal planning and preparation.

"Of course." She pushed away her gloomy thoughts, hitched up her skirt, and carefully slid from the chair down to the ground. Already the women were gossiping as they began the task at hand.

"Who will guard the fire this year?" one woman asked.

"You mean from the evil spirits or from the lazy men who aren't working and plot to steal the rum?"

"Yes, if we don't have something for them to eat, we'll listen to cries of hunger instead of their boasting."

"I remember one year *Chef Konbit* fed them only soup with vegetables. We had no meat to prepare. Man after man they complained as they filled their bellies with the soup. 'We are worse than animals. We get no meat for our work. It is like we are drinking Clorox.'"

The group erupted in laughter that bounced off the tin shacks.

Giselle inched her fingers along to the center of the mat and found the pile of waxy pods that must have been three feet high. She retrieved several generous handfuls and placed them on the mat in front of her. Someone handed her a cool metal bowl, which she placed between her thighs as she sat cross-legged on the ground. She joined in the conversation, her hands moving rhythmically. With her thumb she raked the tiny peas from their cradle and listened as they fell into the metal bowl. Even with the laughter and conversation, the sound of each pea as it struck the vessel was clear to her sensitive ears. She scooped up her first handful and held it for a second. It felt so significant and so vital.

"It is going to be a good harvest this year," she proclaimed.

"Yes," they all agreed. "The signs are there. The moon had just a touch of orange to it last night, and the toads have been especially active the past few weeks. It certainly will be a good year."

After what seemed like hours, the pile had vanished and Giselle emptied the contents of her bowl back onto the mat with the others so the peas could dry in the sun for a few hours.

It was time for her to get dressed and prepare for her radio program. She grabbed the railing and carefully felt her way up the two steps onto the porch and then into the house. After she washed up in the *kivet* of clean water that Natali had drawn for her she settled at the table to drink her coffee and eat a piece of bread. The dirty wash water was discarded into the garden and she set her dishes in the *kivet* to be washed later that evening. She chose a hanger from the short rod that held five sets of her clothes, skirt and top, matched by Natali when she did the wash each week. Yvonne would help her while her daughter was gone. But as she buttoned her blouse, she was reminded again how much she depended on her daughter or someone else for her day-to-day needs.

Always, she was cognizant of the fact that her daughter would likely leave their village someday. She wanted that dream to come true for both of them. If she passed her national exams this month, she would be one of the first three recipients of the Roses for Haiti university scholarship. By the end of October, Natali could be enrolled at the university in Port au Prince, studying business management.

She smiled at the thought. *One, two, three, step down . . . one, two, three, four, five, take a left.* She counted the paces to herself as she made her way to the radio station and tapped her cane from left to right in a steady rhythm to ward off unexpected obstacles and identify the familiar landmarks that outlined her way.

Once again the drums sounded from the fields and the lone voice called out . . .

Men anpil

In response, the tired voices answered . . .

Chay pa lou.

Nou lapriye pou soley—**We pray for sun . . .**

Men pa two gwo—**But not too much.**

Nou lapriye pou lapli tonbe—**We pray for rain . . .**

Men pa two gwo—**But not too much.**

Nou lapriye pou manje—**We pray for food . . .**

Se pa ase—**There is never enough.**

Giselle joined in . . .

Yon ede lot.

Like a naughty child who waited in fear as her father raised his switch, Giselle felt the empty space suck the air from her and she waited for the thunderous blow to fill it.

Since the storm began mid-morning, she had lain on her bed and counted the seconds between the bolts of thunder that rattled her bones and shook her mattress. She prayed the roof would hold. Yvonne had told her about one of the neighbors whose tin roof had been blown off like a piece of tissue paper only to slice open a village girl's scalp like a sharply honed machete.

"There was blood everywhere." Yvonne's voice shook as she recounted the hours it had taken her and Cereste to stitch the girl back together.

"How are the fields? Has anyone else been hurt?" She knew so little of what was happening in the village, unable to navigate in the wind and rain. All her landmarks were gone.

"The fields are not so good. No other serious injuries that we know about so far," Yvonne reported. "But it is always after the storm that it is the worst—the mud, the mosquitoes, the bad water, and the disease."

Giselle wouldn't think about that now. It was only Natali's safe return that mattered. Please let her be safe.

"Surely Natali will have the sense not to start out in a storm." Yvonne must have anticipated her worry.

"Yes, but this time the *siklon* came on so suddenly. She may have already been on her way."

Hurricane George, they called it. Wasn't it Saint George who had slain the dragon? Well then, she would pray to Saint George for Natali's safe return. And she would pray to Saint Isadore and Saint Brigid and whatever *lwa* was listening to spare the crops only three weeks in the ground.

For hours she moved from her mattress to the rocking chair and back again, thinking of the tender shoots that would have just begun to poke through the earth. It was the first rain since the planting. They always celebrated the first rain. But this storm was not something to celebrate. How would they survive if the floods washed it all away? Oh, how would she survive if anything happened to Natali?

For hours more, she twisted her hands and moved from rocking chair to mattress and back again. She prayed over and over again that Natali would be safe. She wrapped herself in a blanket and rocked in her darkness that seemed darker from the storm.

When the door burst open and slammed against the outside of the house, a rush of wind and rain entered and nearly knocked her over in the chair.

"Mama, Mama." Her daughter's voice trembled in the darkness. "Where are you?"

The hair on her skin raised and tingled from the back of her neck to the tip of her spine.

"Mama!" Natali must have seen her in the flash of lightning.

The thunder answered almost immediately.

"Natali! Are you okay? Come to me." She stretched out her arms in the direction of her daughter's voice.

"The rain started after I left. All the roads are washed out. I've been walking for hours. I thought I would die," Natali cried. "My books are ruined. I tried to keep them dry." With the next round of thunder her daughter was in her arms.

"No matter about the books." She stripped the wet clothes off the girl's quivering body and enveloped her in the dry blanket. "You are safe now." She encircled her daughter with her own warmth to take the chill upon herself in a way she hadn't since Natali was a baby. "You are safe now," she repeated over and over again and silently thanked the dragon slayer. "Nothing else matters."

Like the beat of a drum, the thunder called out once again. The wind sang out in response and a chorus of rain answered. All three came together in an unending symphony which lasted throughout the night, and so far into the next day that not even the roosters knew when to start crowing.

34

KATE

HAITI
SEPTEMBER 1998

Kate tied back her hair and let the young Haitian man place his helmet on her head. There was no point in arguing; he wasn't going to let her on the motorcycle without it even though she argued that it meant he would only have a baseball cap to protect him. In the end, he had the *moto*, and she needed the ride to Ti Mirebelais.

It was getting dark and she still had three miles to go. Didi told her that much of the road had washed away from the thirty-nine inches of rain dumped by Hurricane George the week before. The sections of road that had survived were covered with mud. Didi's usual driver had reluctantly handed her off to the young man on the motorcycle with the Yankees cap.

"You'll need to take a *moto*, ma'am, once we get past the main road," the driver had cautioned before they left Didi's. "You should wait a few days. They'll dig the road out and I can get you through then."

Although it was tempting to linger in Port au Prince, the bulk of the work she needed to do was in Mirebelais. "No, I'll pack light. A *moto* will be fine."

Indeed, most of Port au Prince had been spared heavy devastation from the storm, except the lowest lying areas like Cite Soleil. In that neighborhood, the slightest rain encouraged sewage to fill the shallow ditches between dwellings and seep into areas where local residents slept.

Instead of the usual three-hour drive from Didi's to the turn in the road to Ti Mirebelais, it was six, and another hour by *moto* to go the last two miles.

Now the final mile confronted her. She had no idea how bad the situation might be at the clinic, the radio station, and Yvonne and Giselle's tiny homes; although not much, it was all they had. Her heart reached out in anticipation of the devastation she expected to find.

"Sorry, ma'am." The *moto* driver cut the engine but left the dim headlight illuminating the remainder of the road that was rutted with mud and pools of water. "You'll have to walk the rest of the way."

A group of Haitian boys, teenagers she guessed, were sitting on an upturned tree trunk sharing a stalk of sugar cane. The sun was fading fast and there weren't many options if she was to make it the rest of the way to Giselle and Yvonne. It was a twenty-minute walk in the best of circumstances. Tonight, who knew?

Kate removed her socks and shoes and tied them onto the outside of her knapsack—easier to wash her feet than her Nikes. The *moto* driver had a short conversation with one of the boys who jumped up and ran off.

The boy returned a few minutes later. He had fetched a stick from somewhere. It was a relatively straight branch about shoulder height for Kate. He smiled and stood before her, barefoot as well.

"I am Milo." The boy placed the walking stick in her right

hand. "I'll take you down, ma'am." He took the backpack from her shoulders.

"Thank you, Milo." Once again she was touched by Haitian kindness that was always extended to the person in greatest need.

They walked in silence for a while. She had to focus on each step. With only a tiny sliver of a moon and residual clouds from the storm, it was impossible to see more than two feet in any direction.

"Ohhh." She nearly lost her footing and almost ended up with a mud bath.

"Don't worry, Mrs. Kate," the young guide reassured her, grabbing her elbow tight. "I will get you there, no problem."

At one point the mud was so thick she got stuck and could not take a step forward. Milo called for someone from the village to help them. Two wiry, tall Haitian men came forward and extracted her from the mud and carried her on a seat they made with their hands the rest of the way down the mountain. She held the walking stick in front of her like a queen with her staff on her throne.

For once, she was glad it was dark.

An hour later, they trudged up the steps to Yvonne's house.

"Wait here, ma'am," Milo instructed.

A few minutes later he returned with a bucket of water and began washing her feet. Yvonne soon appeared, the bottom of her dress and her bare feet also mud-caked. Her hair was hidden under a bandanna. Despite the fatigue that clouded her eyes, her smile was warm and she laughed when she saw Kate's feet entombed to mid-calf in thick layers of Haitian mud.

"Thank you, Milo. You can go home now. Tell your mother I'll call on her tomorrow." Yvonne began washing Kate's feet as Milo ran off into the darkness. "We were worried about you. I'm sorry I couldn't get word to you in Port au Prince not to make the journey. Was it very bad?"

"I've had better." And worse. "But Milo was very helpful and sweet."

"Yes, he's a good boy. Their family lost everything in the storm—their house, the crops—like most of us. But they were really unlucky. Their two goats were trapped under a mudslide and died. They didn't find them for two days. It was too late to save the meat." Yvonne shook her head from side to side. "Praise be to God no one was killed."

"Yvonne, please, I can wash my own feet. Sit down and rest."

"Rest? What is that? For the past five days it has been wind and water and now the mud is everywhere. We just finished our fall planting three weeks before the storm. Now everything is gone—the potatoes, the cassava, even the mango trees this time." She took a chair next to Kate. "The hardest part is the animals. You know a goat sends a child to school for a year. A pig can be sold to pay for a funeral. We have no savings accounts in Haiti. We only have our crops and animals. It is all gone now."

"I am so sorry." Kate stood and put her hand on her friend's shoulder. "You know I'll do whatever I can to help."

"Thank you. We have some patients for you to see tomorrow, Dr. Kate." The older woman smoothed her soiled skirt. "We'll start over again. We always do." She eased herself out of the chair, unfolding her hips, then knees, and then her back and neck. "I saved some soup for you. It's on the fire. The first time in three days we could make one. Then we must get some sleep. You will see what I mean in the morning."

While she made a few notes in her journal, Kate listened to Yvonne's humming and traditional greeting as people came and went on the path.

"*Onè*—Honor," the Haitian woman called out.

"*Respè*—Respect," her neighbors answered before entering the *lakou* to discuss the day's news.

Stiff, more than she expected, from her travels the day before, Kate wandered gingerly outside in her bare feet. Her shoes were on the porch, clean and drying in the sun. Yvonne was fixing a basket of food—a bag of coffee, a *mamit* of dried beans, a small plastic bag of oil, a bunch of bananas, and a generous load of charcoal that she wrapped in a piece of newspaper.

"Good morning, Yvonne. Can I help with something?" She was handed a cup of coffee in response.

"I am fixing this for Milo's family. It isn't much but it'll get them through another day."

"Please, I'd like to contribute, too." She reached in her fanny pack knowing cash would always be welcome. But she had left most of her money at Didi's and after paying the drivers of the car and *moto*, she had only about five dollars U.S. "I'm afraid I have only a little to offer."

"*Bay piti pa chich*—to give little is not cheap. Sometimes it is all we can do and that, my friend, can be enough."

Kate nodded and handed over the money.

"Your shoes should be almost dry. Come walk with me and I'll show you what has happened to our village. Your patients will be here after lunch. At least today we have been blessed with *yon Soley Laviktura*—a Victory Sun. Everybody will be cleaning up this morning."

"Should I bring my camera?"

Yvonne nodded. "We will need your help to rebuild, and the photos will be good for your friends in the United States."

Many of the houses were roofless. Mattresses had been pulled out into the sun, and muddy shoes were lined up on every porch. Before heading up the mountain to Milo's, they stopped at Giselle's. She and Natali were dragging their furniture out into the sun to dry. Yvonne and Kate stopped to help and have another cup of coffee.

"The radio station is gone," Giselle said calmly, but there were tears in her eyes. "We were able to save some of the equipment, but the transmitter and the generator were crushed.

Natali was thinner than Kate remembered. "Are you okay, honey?" she asked her when she got the younger woman alone for a minute. "Is your mother okay?"

"I'm supposed to start at the university in a few weeks. I think I did well on the exam. But how can I go now? There is so much to be done here."

"What does your mother say?" Kate knew the answer even before Natali confirmed it.

"She says I am going, no matter what. But I don't want to leave her now." She bit her lip as if to keep the tears from spilling out of her eyes.

"I know. It will be hard. But it's important to your mother that you go and you worked so hard to win the scholarship." She stroked the girl's hair like she would have comforted Tieina or Jen. "And she has good friends, Natali. They'll watch over her."

"For once those with thatch fared better," Yvonne explained as she pointed to a bent piece of tin that had been someone's roof. "Be careful. It's sharp," she cautioned as Kate took a picture.

As they continued walking, Kate saw several families shoveling three feet or more of mud from inside their houses. Barefoot peasant women were elbow-deep in muddy laundry. Some were stringing clotheslines between the remaining trees to hang sheets and towels.

Milo's house had crashed down the hillside. He and his family escaped with only what they had on their bodies at the time and what they could grab with their hands. For Milo it was a radio.

Kate and Yvonne found him sitting on the same rock where he had been the night before. The small black box held to his ear, he turned the knob through static before he found a little music. He grinned.

"Good morning, Mrs. Kate. Did you pass a good night?"

"I did. Thank you again for your help." She pointed to her camera and then to him.

He nodded and smiled with his radio for the camera. Kate snapped quickly, and then ruffled the boy's hair.

"Is your mother here?" Yvonne asked.

"We are staying with my cousins." He motioned to a wooden shack, not more than two rooms, but still standing.

They stopped to talk a minute and had a piece of sweet bread. Kate politely refused a cup of water for fear that it might not be safe to drink. When Milo's mother found the five-dollar bill in the basket of food, the woman grasped her hands.

"*Mesi. Mesi.* God bless you for your kindness."

"I promise we'll do more to help you and your neighbors rebuild your homes and begin again in the fields," Kate vowed, and excused herself to take more pictures while Yvonne offered to help the women prepare something for lunch with what she had brought to them.

The lump in Kate's throat grew as she walked. The quietness surprised her, until she realized that there were no goats bleating, no pigs rutting, no roosters crowing. Most had been swallowed in the mud or had run off to higher ground.

"What will people do for food? How will they survive?" Kate asked her friend.

"It is still early enough in the season. Those who can afford to buy more seed will replant. That will start in the next few days." Yvonne folded her hands together in prayer and looked up to the sun, near midday high in the sky. "But for many, it will be a most difficult time. As you know, we are farmers and traders here." She opened her arms wide to include every family in their little village. "The *siklon* has taken much from us. But we will survive. We always do."

"*Yon ede lot?*" Kate asked as she took a photo of another fallen house.

"Ah, you really are becoming a Haitian." Yvonne said and smiled. "But there are a few of us who fared better than the others. Come, I'll show you."

They detoured off the main path and climbed up and down a ravine so narrow that, at one point, Kate had to crawl on her hands and knees. It was almost an hour before they arrived at a little plot of land lush with tiny crops on as steep a hillside as any she had seen that day.

"This is my land. I bought it a few years ago with a loan from the co-op." Yvonne beamed with pride.

"But I don't understand. Didn't the storm come here, too?" The plot was nearly vertical, and she estimated it to be an acre. She noticed a tiny cross woven of thatch, a statue of the Virgin Mary, and two faded paintings that she couldn't identify. A shriveled orange rested on the ground amongst the icons.

"This grass . . ." Yvonne stooped and stroked a clod of thick, green grass that grew in small mounds throughout the field at regular intervals where the grade was steepest. "Your American couple gave me this. It helped to stop the rains from washing out the crops. They showed me how to make these little grooves to keep the water close to the roots of the beans and potatoes." She picked up a handful of dirt. It was dark and rich, looking like what Kate would buy in bags back home. "Giselle and I, we mix the remains from our coffee, and the fruits and vegetables we eat and add it to the soil."

"Composting," Kate said.

"Yes, that's the word."

Kate looked around and took more pictures. The contrast to what she had photographed earlier made her giddy with possibility. "Why don't the others use these techniques? Have you told them? We must show them."

"Of course. This is not magic or my secret. Although it is always good to ask for help." Yvonne touched the faded paintings. "These are ways that the American couple learned in Cuba. I have told my neighbors. They did not want to change. But perhaps they will listen now."

Despite all the loss Kate had witnessed that day—homes, crops, and animals—she marveled at the resilience in her friend's voice, and the resolve in her face as Yvonne stood straight on the steep slope of her field, only slightly swaying in the breeze like a bamboo tree. Kate was moved to capture the moment for the rest of the world to know, as well. She seized a final photo of Yvonne with her icons. A mango tree behind her was heavy with promise of fruit.

It was well after noon when they returned to Yvonne's home, and there was a long line of people waiting outside the clinic. At least that building had survived. Her organization had paid for its renovation a few years earlier. Some members of the board had objected to the cost, but Kate stood firm that whatever they did in this community, they would give it their best. Her persistence clearly paid off. Yvonne pulled one young girl and her mother out of the line and brought her inside ahead of the others.

"This is the one I was telling you about." Yvonne gently unwound the roll of thick white bandage that encircled the girl's head.

The child's hair had been shaved and a ragged incision ran from the top of her right eyebrow back to behind her left ear. A series of perfectly neat and spaced stitches had brought the flesh together. It was pink and healing nicely. Not even a wince from the patient as Kate poked and prodded for tenderness or other signs of infection.

"You and Cereste did this?" Kate replaced the girl's turban with a smaller piece of gauze.

Yvonne grinned from ear to ear.

"She'll need a tetanus shot," Kate said.

"Already done."

"Antibiotics?"

"Penicillin for ten days."

"Yvonne, are you trying to put me out of business?"

"No, Dr. Kate. We still need you. You are our teacher."

Even though her feet were swollen and achy from her trek up and down the rocky terrain, she felt like she was walking on a cloud when she gave Yvonne, the best student she ever had, a hug and a kiss.

It was nearly dark when they closed up the clinic and sat down to a meager evening meal of rice and potatoes.

Kate said, "Diarrhea and malaria will be the big challenges for the next few months. When the driver comes tomorrow, we can go to town and buy more Clorox and mosquito nets—at least for the children and the pregnant women."

"We will stay vigilant," Yvonne promised. "Do you think you can help rebuild the radio station? It is a good way to get our messages out."

"I can make a good case for that and I hope for your model farm, too. If you are willing?"

"I have always been willing. But change is hard for Haitians. There is so little we can count on in our lives."

She sat with her friend in silence and pondered how change was thrust upon them time and again. "You said the replanting would start again soon."

"Yes, I think tomorrow we will begin over there." She pointed to one of the larger fields in the village.

"I know it is not really my place. But I would really like to help before the driver comes in the morning. Is that possible?"

"I think we can arrange that. You may get some stares. We are not used to white people toiling beside us in the dirt. It is hard work, too. But I know you are no stranger to that."

Before the sun was up, Kate was awake and dressed. She tucked her pant legs inside her socks and slid her feet into a borrowed pair of high rubber boots that some of the peasants wore in the fields. She decided on a *koulin* instead of the traditional machete. The handle was longer and the blade narrower. It wouldn't be good to wound one of her co-workers or herself.

Yvonne grinned and leaned on her hoe. They waited for the signal to begin.

"Today, there are no drums. We have heard enough of such noise from the storm," Yvonne explained.

Just as the sun peeked over the mountain, an airy hollow tone carried over the field. She looked toward the sunrise where a peasant stood in silhouette against yet another *yon Soley Laviktura.* Head tilted back, he held a massive conch shell to his lips and the sound echoed on the naked mountains and wrapped around the many hands that shared the burden of replanting and rebuilding.

A single voice called out . . .

Nou lapriye pou manje—**We pray for food . . .**

They answered in one voice . . .

Se pa ase—**There is never enough.**

The *Sanba* returned . . .

Mon nou pi laj—**Our mountains grow old . . .**

Many hoes struck the ground . . .

Mare senti nou—**We tighten our belts . . .**

Kate joined in, her sweat mingled with the earth, and the *koulin* resonated in her hands as she dislodged a small rock in preparation for new seed . . . *Yon ede lot. Yon ede lot . . .*

35

KATE

NEW YORK
SEPTEMBER 9, 2001

Alberto's, a little Italian bistro in Brooklyn, was four times as long as it was wide. It was filled with a hungry crowd and the aroma of garlic and tomato sauce. Even with the tables arranged flush against the walls, the waiters had to walk sideways, balancing the carafes of Chianti and overflowing bowls of pasta and marinara sauce. This was Kate's third trip to New York with Danny since he started at NYU a year earlier.

"Cheers!" She tapped mason jars with Danny, her water to his Chianti. It was their tradition to have dinner here their last night in the city.

Kate picked up the menu. "What shall we order? Remember, it's going to be rice and beans for the next week."

They were headed to Port au Prince tomorrow after they attended the microcredit conference in Manhattan where Natali was speaking about the program she directed in Haiti. Roses for Haiti had given her and Giselle seed money to start the project three years earlier. Finding funding for microcredit was easy compared to HIV/AIDS treatment. Empowering women was the new millennium cause to support, and microcredit was the golden tool to accomplish that goal.

"Lasagna," Danny declared and snapped his menu shut. "If that's okay with you?"

"My favorite."

The last course, as always, was tiramisu. They split an order.

But tonight, the tiramisu tasted flat, as had the lasagna. Only the garlic and salt stood out and impressed her palate with their usual intensity.

"I must be getting a cold. The tiramisu wasn't as good tonight. Did you think?"

"No, Mom. It's perfect like always." Her son pulled her chair out for her. "And thanks for agreeing to spend the extra day in the city. I submitted a proposal to do my junior essay on microfinance. I hope I can make some contacts at the seminar tomorrow." Her son pulled her chair out for her.

"I can't wait to hear Natali speak tomorrow and for you to meet her. We'll have to run after the conference though. Our plane leaves JFK at two." Kate felt suddenly tired and was glad it was only a few blocks back to the hotel. It took a moment to get up out of the chair—her legs didn't seem to want to cooperate with her mind. "I wish your sisters were coming to Haiti with us, too."

The girls were coming to New York the next day to look at colleges.

"Mom, you know Jen. She has her mind set on certain things and there's no distracting her. And Tieina, I think she'll go back someday. After all, she wants a career in international journalism." As usual, he always defended his sisters.

"No, you're right. I'm really proud of both of them. Wouldn't that be great if you all ended up here in New York for school? More excuses to eat at Alberto's."

"I'm for that." He helped her with her jacket. "Will we see them at all tomorrow?"

Kate checked her itinerary for the next day, September 10th. "No. They don't get into New York until tomorrow evening. Your dad arranged for the hotel somewhere toward lower Manhattan."

The cool, late-summer air sent a chill through her light jacket.

Back arched, her head high, Natali ascended the steps to the stage with the gentle grace of her Haitian ancestors. Like her mother, she was stunning. She nodded in appreciation until the applause dissolved.

She smiled. *"Bonjour*—Good morning. I am very happy to be here with you today."

"I wish her mother could be here for this. Isn't she beautiful?" Kate whispered to Danny.

His eyes were fixed on the woman on stage. His only response was to squeeze her hand.

The rest of the attendees, less than a hundred, were equally captivated as Natali began to paint a picture for them of how microcredit had changed the lives of women in her village.

"This is what Haitians see when they talk about women having strong heads and strong shoulders." Natali showed a split-screen slide. The picture on the left depicted two men lifting a thatch basket with a fifty-pound bag of rice on a woman's shoulders as she squatted before them. On the right, the same woman was shown in silhouette, the load balanced on her head as she began the long journey up a mountain.

"The rice you see this woman carry, she'll try to sell it in the market for a little profit. It was bought on *eskonte*—credit—from the moneylenders. They charge 50 percent interest on the loan. But no one can pay the sixty goudes for a bag of rice. Three months ago it was half that. She must either lower the price or she doesn't sell." She shrugged her shoulders. "But she must sell to pay the moneylender. So the more she sells the more she loses.

"These baskets and the loads we carry wear away the hair in the middle of a woman's head." She bowed from the waist and showed the top of her head with a circular bald patch in the middle. "On Saturday, if we sell enough during the week, we buy hair in the market and take turns weaving some stranger's hair into each other's heads so no one will know how poor we are.

"The loads we carry also compress the bones in our necks." She showed another picture of a forty-year-old woman bent at a forty-five-degree angle. "It is true that Haitian women are strong, like bamboo many say. They don't break under great force, but they do bend."

The room was silent.

"When you ask what a Haitian peasant woman dreams for her daughter, she will answer, 'I don't want my child to sign her name with an X.'"

She moved from behind the podium and closer to the audience. "Peasant women will tell you, 'I don't work.' Yet we are up before daylight carrying water, preparing food, and sweeping the dust out of our two-room shacks. In the afternoon we wash clothes and we prepare meals. Our door must always be open to a neighbor in need and our legs to a man who will beat us if we refuse.

"Is it possible to change the future for our daughters and granddaughters?" She paused and seemed to search out each individual in the audience, challenging them. "There is a way to move from the misery of poverty to respect with dignity."

Even though Kate knew what was to come, she sat on the edge of her seat.

"With microcredit," Natali continued, "we have redefined what it means for a Haitian woman to have a strong head and strong shoulders."

In the next slide, a group of women sat shoulder to shoulder on a bench, heads together learning to read and write. The third slide showed the same women three months later head to head going over their business ledger—a simple spiral notebook and a cheap solar-powered calculator.

"I know most of you have far more experience with microcredit programs than I do." She acknowledged the other speakers sitting in the front row. "But I want to explain how our program works and share with you some of our success stories."

"Like this little boutique." She showed a woman in a brightly patterned dress measuring out rice and beans into plastic bags for a customer. Then another woman spooning *picklez*—spicy pickled relish—onto a plantain just lifted out of the fryer by a third woman.

The rationale for lending to groups of women, instead of individuals, was simple.

"If one woman becomes sick or has a problem so she can't open her business for a day or two, or longer, the others are there to continue. *Tet ansanm, Yon ede lot*—heads together, one helping another," Natali explained.

In the next slide, all three women were repaying the loan and smiling with money left over.

"When the women repay the initial small loan, it goes into a revolving fund so others may borrow. The solidarity group becomes eligible for larger loans, or a woman can apply for an individual loan of up to $1,000 U.S. We believe that rural Haitian women can climb out of misery, can climb out of poverty. It is our goal to accompany them on this journey."

Everyone in the audience nodded in agreement.

"Three years ago, a hurricane destroyed all of the crops in our village. Many animals were killed in the mudslides that followed, and one-third of our village was left homeless. One peasant woman's small farm survived." Natali looked at Kate and smiled as she showed a picture of Yvonne and her crops. "This woman received a larger loan to educate others in sustainable agriculture practices she learned from Cuban agronomists."

Kate heard a woman behind her murmur something about the Cubans plotting to overthrow Haiti and attack the U.S. She turned around to argue but decided Natali's message was more important.

"And there is more." Natali flashed a slide with large block letters written on a blackboard. "*Analfabet pa bet*—the illiterate are not stupid. Yet, when over 50 percent of rural Haitian women cannot read or write, they are at a great disadvantage."

Again, there were many nods from the audience.

"After the first loan, the women are encouraged to participate in literacy and small-business skills training sessions, and their children are eligible for scholarships at the local elementary school." She brought her fist to the podium and spoke more slowly. "We must break the intergenerational cycle of poverty."

Next, Natali switched to showing the statistics.

"I can't believe she is only a year older than me. I could never do this, never," Danny whispered in Kate's ear. He was clapping so hard his seat was shaking.

The moderator took the stage as the entire audience came to their feet with applause. Indeed, Natali had gleaned much from her two years at Quisqueya University in Port au Prince.

During the presentation, Kate noticed a man sitting alone. His navy-blue suit blended with the others. But he looked Haitian and he seemed especially moved by Natali's testimonial of Giselle's role in the program. Quietly he removed a handkerchief from his pocket and dabbed at his eyes.

Danny could not stop talking about Natali as they waited in line to meet her during the break after two more speakers.

"When she talked, everyone listened like she was telling a story and not giving a lecture to a roomful of strangers." It had been a long time since Kate heard such excitement in her son's voice.

They were last in line except for the Haitian man. He kept his eyes down, studying the program. There was something vaguely familiar about him.

"You were wonderful, Natali!" Kate exchanged a warm hug with the young woman and introduced her to Danny.

"How are you finding your first visit to New York?" Danny asked.

"I love it. I am so lucky to stay here at the Marriott. We're going to get a tour of Wall Street and the World Trade Center tomorrow. I am really excited for that," Natali answered.

"You'll have to come back so I can show you the real New York sometime. I go to one of the universities here."

"Yes, I know. Your mother has told us." She smiled at Kate.

"Dan, we have to get to the airport." Kate had to peel her son away from Natali. "You and Natali can catch up later this week when she gets back to Haiti."

"Your mother is right." The young woman kissed them both on the cheek. "We'll have lots of time to talk and get to know each other."

As they turned to leave, the tall Haitian man stepped in their place. "Natali, I'm so proud of you."

Kate looked back as they retrieved their coats from their seats in the auditorium. Natali was standing stiff as a soapstone statue with her arms glued to her sides. The man, who had been weeping, enveloped her in his arms in an unanswered embrace.

Danny noticed, too. "Is she okay? Who is that guy? Should we go back?"

"Let me see the program." She scanned the list of attendees and stopped at a name halfway down the second column. Max. The bastard! He has a lot of nerve coming here. "She's okay, Danny. We need to catch our plane."

CHAPTER

36

KATE

HAITI

Only when the plane descended into the Port au Prince Airport did the smile fade from Danny's face. As she watched her son stare out the window, already dirty from the dust and smog, Kate saw Haiti again for the first time.

"I had no idea how bad it was." He was so intent on the view as they landed that his breath fogged up the window. "The mountains are completely bare. What happened to the trees? And their homes—I guess that's what they are—stacked on top of each other, like houses of cards that could topple at the slightest tremor."

Kate reminisced about her dream to practice jungle medicine and smiled to herself at the irony. The "jungle" that had found her was, as her son described, almost completely deforested. Life was certainly full of twists and turns and innumerable surprises. That thought caused her to shudder, so she reached over and grabbed her son's hand. Sharing this experience with him was a gift beyond anything she had ever imagined.

"I'm so glad you're here with me, Danny." She followed his

gaze to where he was staring out the window to the world below, the deeply troubled yet remarkably resilient country of Haiti. The struggles and joy of which never ceased to touch her heart.

Didi was waiting with a smile and drinks in hand. "A Coke for you, Dr. Kate. And what about this young man—Danny, the soccer player?" She set the tray on the table and gave him a big welcome hug. "The boys are waiting for you. I don't think they'll let you leave in the morning without a short match. The first drink is on the house. What can I get you?"

"I'll take a beer, please. If it's not too much trouble."

"No trouble. Okay, Mom?" She winked at Kate and whispered, "Yes, he is your son."

Just as they finished their beverages, the bell for dinner rang. In the center of the dining room, there was an enormous mahogany table with brightly painted scenes of rural life overlaying the lacquered black finish. She commented to Didi on this new addition to the guesthouse.

"We don't even need to cover it for meals," Didi responded. "That finish is indestructible."

Internet was also available, although it was as slow and unreliable as the electricity. Didi had bought a small generator and a few solar panels for the frequent power outages, but diesel was expensive and even the generator was out today. No chance to e-mail the girls to see if they had made it safely to New York.

Kate sipped her morning coffee and watched in awe as Danny and two young Haitian boys batted the soccer ball back and forth across the dusty field—the same field where she had watched Tieina join in a pickup game. Was it really ten years since her first visit? This was going to be an unforgettable week, having Danny with her.

"Hey, Dan," she shouted from the veranda at Didi's. "It's

nearly nine. The driver will be here to take us to Mirebelais soon. Are you packed up?"

"Sure enough, Mom." He kicked the ball back to one of the boys who smashed it in between the two piles of sticks and stones they had designated as the goal lines. "Bravo!" He ran over and high-fived the Haitian boy. Then he waved away his offer to return the ball to him. "No, man, it's yours. *Pita*—later."

He ran the short distance to where Kate was standing, and just before he reached the porch, he did the Rigando flip, and as always, her heart did its own little flip.

"That move will be the death of you—or me." She laughed as he landed back on his feet unharmed. "Let's go."

"Hey, did you know these soccer balls are made in Pakistan? Isn't that something?"

"Yes, it is pretty amazing how things can travel around the world. And with all this new technology, I keep thinking how much good we can do for people in countries like Haiti. When it works, that is." Kate thought about her failed attempt to send an e-mail to Jen and Tieina this morning.

On their second morning in Haiti, Kate lay in bed in Mirebelais lazily thinking about what she needed to accomplish during this trip when Yvonne called out.

"Dr. Kate, come quick!"

Kate pushed her feet into her Nikes and got dressed.

"What is it?"

Four men were running down the mountain, a dark rectangular piece of wood with something on it she couldn't make out. "Is that a door? What are they carrying on top of it?" she asked Yvonne.

"Not just a door." Yvonne was already moving toward the clinic. "Come, Cereste. I think we have another baby on the way."

As the group moved closer, Kate could see a small woman on top of the intricately carved mahogany door. Her belly was large. But she wasn't moving like a woman in labor should move. She was completely still. Her face was the color of charcoal ash except for a patchwork of raised white scars that divided her face. Kate and Yvonne alternated in firing off a series of questions and instructions.

"Get her inside the clinic, on the table."

"How long has she been unconscious?"

"I don't know."

"What is her name?"

"Fatra."

"Fatra?"

"When is the baby due?"

"In one month, I think."

"Are you the father?"

"He's in Port au Prince on business. We sent word to him this morning."

"Did she have a seizure?" Kate suspected eclampsia, a common complication of pregnancy in Haiti.

Yvonne clenched her hands into fists and set her body to trembling, mimicking a seizure. "Convulsions," she explained to one of the young men who had brought Fatra to them.

"Yes. Yes," they answered, looking as if they wanted to be anywhere but staring at an unconscious pregnant woman on a detached door.

Far from a well-orchestrated trauma team, the four men and three women moved the woman from the door to a table in the clinic that Yvonne had quickly covered with several sheets. By the time Kate had a first blood pressure reading, their patient started moving from side to side. Not quite coherent, but intermittently groaning each time her belly tightened with a contraction.

"Her pressure is very high—180/110. Has she been here before?" asked Kate.

"I'll get her dossier," Yvonne said.

"Is this her first baby?" When no one answered, Kate repeated, "Is this her first baby?" She snapped on a pair of gloves.

"She was pregnant one time before."

She inserted her hand into the woman and checked her cervix and the baby's position.

"It looks like this one is coming fast. We're going to have to deliver her here," she proclaimed to the other two women who already wore a knowing look.

Yvonne went outside to boil water and Cereste attempted to put an IV into the woman's arm. Kate tried again to find a heartbeat for the baby. She clenched the stethoscope to block out all the other noise around her.

"It's there. It's faint, but it's there." She tapped her foot with each beat as she watched the second hand of the clock on the clinic wall advance. "Not too bad—120 a minute. That's good." Her own pulse was probably close to that at the moment.

Yvonne took position at the woman's head. "Rest between the pain," she said in a gentle voice.

Cereste stood behind Kate, who sat on a wooden stool at the opposite end. With each contraction the three older women encouraged the younger one, "Push! Push! Push!"

Kate gently eased out the head, dark hair matted with waxy varnish from the birth canal. Left shoulder, then right quickly followed and the rest of the baby landed in her lap and announced herself to the world with a loud cry. Thank God! Kate hadn't delivered a baby in over ten years. She immediately counted the fingers and toes like she did when her two children were born. As if the perfect ten of each ensured everything else was there, as well.

The mom looked a little bit better than when she arrived. Her face had more color now that she was past the seizure and into her second bag of IV fluids. After the placenta came, Kate packed her vagina with gauze as best she could.

"She needs a transfusion." She looked around at the blood-soaked gauze on the floor and estimated that the woman had lost two units of blood, maybe more. "We need to get them to a hospital. The baby might need antibiotics and an incubator."

Yvonne and Cereste exchanged a look.

"What?" Kate felt left out.

"We sent someone to get a car. There's only one vehicle that works in the village," Yvonne answered.

"It's a two-hour drive to the nearest hospital," Cereste said. "And she has no money to pay for the hospital or blood."

"I have $200 U.S. cash. Is that enough? I can get more when I get back to Port au Prince." Kate was not going to let this woman or this baby die.

"That'll be enough for a day or two and the blood. But a hospital in Haiti is no place for a new baby with a sick mother," Cereste said, with her hands firmly set on her hips.

"I agree." Yvonne stepped beside her Haitian friend. "We'll feed the baby and take care of her here. We've done it before."

Overruled, Kate went over to the mom and explained as best she could what was happening. Then she asked, "Fatra, will you give us a name for your daughter?"

The young woman looked more frightened than she had looked all day. Yvonne came to her side with the baby cleaned and bundled and placed her beside her mother on the table.

"You have a beautiful baby now, a husband that loves you, and a new life ahead for all of you. What will you call your daughter, *Chérie?*"

"*Espere*—Hope," she whispered. "I'll call her Hope."

"Hope." They all smiled.

Kate started a new dossier for the baby.

> Date of birth, September 12, 2001, ten o'clock
> in the morning.

She and the other two women busied themselves cleaning up

the clinic and Fatra for her trip to the hospital. Cereste prepared a metal tin stack of food—beans, rice, and vegetable sauce for the day's meals. She gathered clean sheets, a towel, soap, and several hospital gowns from the clinic. The hospital would provide none of these essential items.

The unmistakable grumble and the stench of diesel alerted them that the truck had arrived to transport Fatra to the hospital.

"Where's Dan?" Kate hadn't seen him all day. "We could use his help. I guess our ambulance crew went home."

"I think he's with Giselle at the radio station." Cereste coaxed the young woman to hand her the baby and move from the table to the door. "I'll go with her." She had packed herself a small bag, as well.

"Don't worry. We'll take care of Hope until you come back." Yvonne picked up the swaddled infant who was already rooting for her mother's milk.

Kate shared a towel with Yvonne after they had washed their hands in what remained of the hot water. Despite the gloves they had worn during the delivery, their forearms and clothes were splattered with blood.

"Fatra is an unusual name," Kate remarked. "I haven't known anyone by that name before. Doesn't *fatra* mean . . ."

"Garbage? Yes. She changed her name when she was fifteen."

"I wanted to ask you about the scars on the woman's face. Was she in an accident?" Kate had been thinking maybe she hit the windshield of a tap-tap. It didn't look like a machete accident.

"No accident, those are cuts from a razor."

"Who would have done that to her?"

"She did it to herself. She came to our village a few years ago. You remember when things were really bad? She was raped in Carrefour on her way home from work one night. They left her in the street. Someone had the courage to bring her here. After a few months, she started vomiting and found out she was pregnant.

That's when she changed her name to Fatra, after she did something to herself so she lost the baby. She has never left the village since, until today, that is."

"But why did she cut herself?" Kate struggled to connect the pieces of the woman's story in her mind, the horrible tragedy of her past to the miracle of her and the baby's survival that day.

"She did it so no one would recognize her. She was scared and ashamed. She believed she was cursed for all time."

"Will she be safe at the hospital?" Kate doubted it, given her limited knowledge of the broken healthcare system in Haiti.

"Yes, Cereste will stay with her until her husband comes. He's a good man, an artisan. He goes to Port au Prince on the weekends to sell what he makes. Sometimes he takes crafts from others in the village, too, and sells them on consignment."

Kate looked around. "Now, where is Danny? I want to show him around before something else happens."

37

GISELLE

PETIT (TI) MIREBELAIS
SEPTEMBER 12, 2001

Giselle listened with amused interest as Erold gave Danny a tour of the radio station. Although he claimed to know little about radio broadcast and recording, his questions were insightful and he was exceedingly polite. As if that wasn't enough to warm her heart toward him, he complimented Natali's presentation in New York and related in great detail how she had captivated the audience.

"Your microcredit program sounds incredible and it's such a simple concept. It could help so many women. I can't wait to learn more." Danny spoke with the energy she'd felt at that age.

"It's true. Microcredit is an important tool that can help women escape poverty. But like most tools, it can also be used to harm."

"What do you mean? Natali was so positive in everything she talked about and the numbers were awesome."

"Natali was speaking to a room of colleagues and, we hope, potential donors. The numbers are important but there is always more than the numbers." She did not want to discourage his enthusiasm on the first day of his visit. But some women participated in more than one loan program and had trouble paying back all the money. Some programs kept increasing interest rates so that they were almost as high as the traditional moneylenders. And as was often the case, men took advantage of the women who were eligible by taking part of the loan money for their own needs. Yes, it was important to have safeguards in place, as she and Natali and Kate had discussed many times.

She turned the receiver knob hoping to tune into the ten o'clock news from Port au Prince. "Since your mom helped us get the new equipment after the hurricane three years ago, we usually have good luck during the morning—but not always. Yesterday, we had no reception all day." She fiddled a little longer with the knob.

"Good morning, Haiti."

Finally, she was able to find the channel she wanted. "That's the host, Dominique Jean. We can only get the broadcast in Creole," she told Danny as Erold tied the news program into her broadcast system for those in her listening area to enjoy.

"That's okay. I'll just look through your music a little longer."

"Choose something you like. I'll play it after the news. Maybe you would like to go on the air for a few minutes?"

"Really? That would be great!"

The plastic CD cases clicked together more quickly. A baby cried out in the background. Giselle knew the sound of a delivery at the clinic. She couldn't wait to hear the details later. She always announced births on her program.

"We have more news from the United States after yesterday's tragedy," said the radio voice.

Giselle motioned to Erold to turn up the volume on the receiver in the broadcast room.

"It is still unknown how many are trapped or dead after two hijacked planes crashed into the skyscrapers known as the Twin Towers in downtown New York."

"Oh my God. Natali!" Giselle gripped the arms of her chair and her heart dropped to her stomach. Natali was staying in a hotel in Manhattan. Fearing she would vomit, she reached for a trashcan beside her station desk.

"All air travel to and from the United States has been cancelled indefinitely."

"Giselle, what is it?" Danny's hand was on her shoulder.

The radio announcer continued. "A third hijacked plane damaged the Pentagon. The fourth plane crashed in a remote area in Pennsylvania. The number of trapped and dead beneath the rubble in New York and Washington is still unknown, but feared to be in the thousands. United States officials have confirmed that these are acts of terrorism."

She vomited into the can and the last thing she remembered was Danny's fading voice asking, "Giselle, are you okay? What are they saying on the radio, Erold? What happened?"

CHAPTER

38

GISELLE

PETITI (TI) MIREBELAIS
LATER THAT DAY

When Giselle woke up, she was in Yvonne's house. She could tell by the pattern on the quilt. Her fingers traced the interlocking circles that reminded her of wedding bands. Round and round she traced them; not knowing where one ended and the other began. The rhythm of the pattern calmed her and somehow she knew Natali was alive. She was safe.

"Isn't there another vehicle that can take us to Port au Prince?" From the way Kate's voice moved about the room, Giselle knew she was pacing the floor.

"No," Yvonne answered.

"I'll take a tap-tap. I'll walk. I'll crawl. I need to get somewhere where I can make a phone call or use the Internet." Each vowed attempt to describe her getaway was interrupted by sobs.

"The driver will be back tomorrow. It is too late to get a tap-tap and too dangerous and far to walk."

A baby cried.

"Whose baby is that?" Giselle spoke up.

330

Kate picked up her hand. "Are you feeling okay? You passed out in the radio station. Erold carried you down."

Giselle said, "Did you hear anything else about New York? I don't know if Natali was staying near where the planes hit." The room was silent except for the baby's cry and the sound of a soccer ball being kicked somewhere outside.

"Kate, you saw Natali before you came. Was her hotel near the skyscrapers?"

"Giselle, I'm sorry. She was staying in the Marriott at the World Trade Center. But that doesn't mean that . . ."

"No. It doesn't. Natali is safe. I know that," Giselle said with more resolution in her voice than she had ever heard herself use before. "And Jen and Tieina too." She added this a little more slowly because she was less certain of it.

Again a baby cried, more insistently this time. "Who is that baby?"

"Hope," Yvonne and Kate answered together.

"Yes, Hope. We must keep talking about them, all of them—Natali, Tieina, and Jen. It brings good luck and will keep them safe from harm."

The baby's insistent cry became unrelenting and filled the room.

"Now, can we get Hope something to eat?" Their daughters were alive; she just knew it.

39

KATE

PETIT (TI) MIREBELAIS
LATE THAT NIGHT AND NEXT DAY

In less than twenty-four hours, old age had appeared on Yvonne's face. The tiny crow's feet that previously only visited her eyes when she was especially tired deepened in a way that Kate knew would never leave. Her shoulders and head turned inward and down toward the ground except when she looked up at the sky and folded her hands trembling high above her head in prayer. She muttered in Creole words that Kate, engulfed in her own fear, could not understand. Although she suspected they offered the same helpless bargains and questions of anyone who was separated from loved ones during this tragedy. Why did this happen? Of course, there would never be a good enough answer to that question.

After they determined they were stuck in Ti Mirebelais for the night, Danny had kicked the soccer ball around with some of the village boys until all the air was gone. Then he rocked Hope until she finally drifted to sleep in his arms. Kate guided the pair to a back room where they would not be disturbed. None of the rest of them could sleep that night. Kate was packed and ready to go as soon as the driver returned in the morning. She stared at her bag and Danny's knapsack waiting on the dirt floor by the door at Yvonne's. Giselle's faded blue scarf was knotted in her hands and they each had a mound of Kleenex in their laps. The box Kate had brought with her was emptied hours ago. The three of them sat together in considerable silence that only seemed to suspend time.

"Until today." Only Yvonne's lips had enough energy to move. "I never regretted letting her go. I thought she would be safe in the United States—have a better life."

Kate had never seen her friend so immobilized.

"But I always believed she would come back, someday. And now this?"

"Giselle is right." Kate reached out and grabbed one of each of her friends' hands. "We must keep talking about them, our daughters. It will bring good luck and keep them safe."

"But the things I need to say, I need to say them to my granddaughter. And there are things I want to give her that are her part of her past that she does not even know about." Yvonne stood slowly, went to her bed and took a box from underneath it.

"I can take them to the U.S. for you." Kate helped her to lift the box to the table.

"No. I need to see my granddaughter and explain."

"Let's go through them together," Giselle suggested. She set aside her scarf. "Do you still write in that journal of yours, Kate?"

"Yes. I've filled quite a few since I first came to Haiti." She understood where Giselle was going with her question. Kate retrieved a pen and her latest brown leather journal from her backpack.

She and Yvonne dragged the table over to where they sat, and Kate moved their chairs so close together their knees touched beneath the table. She sat back in her seat and opened to the next blank page. *September 12-13, 2001, midnight.* She began to write as Yvonne removed each of the keepsakes from the box.

There was a tiny pair of knitted baby booties that were just right for Hope. Yvonne told them the story of Adelaide's pregnancy and Tieina's birth.

"What's this?" Kate lifted out a poster that had been rolled and tied with a ribbon. There were pictures showing how to deliver a baby and written instructions in English. She noticed it right away. "Tie in a knot." The first three words were crowded on the edge of one line. "Tieina! Is that how she got her name?"

"I think you'll recognize this." Yvonne pulled out a yellowed envelope that held a long lock of red hair. "Tieina gave it to me to sell before you took her back to the U.S. She was worried that I would need money. She said you gave it to her, Kate, when you came after our Adelaide died." Yvonne's voice broke for an instant, yet she continued with the next item. "This is her mother's school uniform, and these are her report cards from school. I kept every one of them. She never finished high school. Her marks were so high; she could have been something. All her teachers said that."

Kate turned page after page recording what Yvonne said between tears and laughter until she had filled nearly half of the book. In a pocket at the back, she found a scrap of paper with the poem that Tieina had written a few years ago. Kate quickly copied it onto a page in her journal and handed the original to Yvonne. "Tieina wrote this when she was thirteen. She doesn't know that I found it. Please, keep it for her with the other things and give it to her when she comes."

Yvonne looked at it and held it to her heart before gently placing it among the other items in the box. She didn't even ask what it said.

Giselle picked up the frayed scarf again. Her eyes seem to gaze into the barely perceptible pattern that once would have been as stunning as the memories the fabric held.

"Did Max give that to you?" Kate asked. She still had not mentioned that she recognized her husband as the man who talked to Natali at the microcredit conference in New York.

"Not Max." Giselle touched her lips as if she couldn't decide whether or not to let the words out.

"Go on." Yvonne covered Giselle's hand with hers. "Maybe it's time for all of us to share our secrets."

Kate closed the journal to listen.

"No. I want you to write my story in your book, too. Yvonne is right. Someday Natali will need to know this, too. I'd like to think my choices, good and not so good, have made me who I am." She began with a deep breath. "I was young and rather foolish at the time . . ."

Her hand already cramped and stiff from writing, Kate filled all but her last two pages with Giselle's story—her parents drowning while attempting to escape, the story behind her paintings, her kidnapping years ago back in Cite Soleil when she vowed to give up her lover from France, her gradual vision loss, and her dashed dreams to escape Haiti with Natali. And Kate realized that even as the darkness had threatened to engulf her friend, she had beaten it back and transformed her fear and grief into a passion that could never be silenced.

Hope let out a small cry and Kate went to get her before she could wake up Danny. She quietly closed the door to his room and gave the baby a few ounces of the milk that they had made for her earlier. After she burped, they all laughed, and Kate used a towel to make a small bed for her on the table between them.

"So, Dr. Kate, what about you? We've always wondered if there was another man in your life. Such a pretty woman, surely there must have been some interest?" Yvonne queried.

Kate set her book on the table. "It has been a kind of therapy for me over the years. My story has already been written down on the pages of diary after diary." With only a slight hesitation she continued. "But I've never shared it with anyone before. At least, not all of it."

She talked and her friends listened in silence until dawn came and Hope's persistent cry refused to let them linger in the past any longer.

The news of the terrorist attack had infiltrated the informal communications network in their village. Kate was known to nearly anyone who had been to Petit Mirebelais in the last ten years. And of course, everyone knew that Natali was in New York, too.

"We are so sorry for you and your families and your country. How could such a thing happen? We will pray for you."

Kate nodded with numb gratitude as the peasants conveyed their sympathy.

Despite the sleepless night, they all still had so much energy. Yvonne was cooking anything she could find for anybody who would eat. Kate paced, anxiously awaiting the driver's return.

"I'll go through the Dominican Republic this time. I will get home."

"Mom, it's not getting out of Haiti that's the problem. It's getting into the U.S. So unless we can swim, we're going to have to sit tight."

"I'll try every phone and computer in Port au Prince to get through to your dad. He'll know something."

Giselle announced, "I'm going to the station. I'll check for more news from the United States."

"I'm going with you," Kate announced. News, any news was the best she could try for until they could get back to Port au Prince.

Giselle tuned into the news from Port au Prince. Kate's fear grew as her hope faded when she learned that all air flights to and from the U.S. were still cancelled. Giselle turned off the radio receiver and began to transmit her own message.

"Good morning, Haiti," she began. "Many of you know about the terrible tragedy that has occurred in the United States. Some of us have known and worked with Americans who have friends and family members who are missing or dead. Some of us in Haiti have family and friends who may be missing or dead, too." Her voice cracked with the mention of death for the second time. She took a sip of water. "I ask all my listeners to give one minute of silence in solidarity with our brothers and sisters in the United States."

Kate counted the seconds off silently and as the minute drew to a close, the rumble and odor of a diesel truck reached her. The vehicle had returned and now she and Danny would be leaving the village and one step closer to knowing if her daughters were safe.

"Giselle! Mom! Come quick!" Danny shouted.

The engine stopped and voices erupted, but she could not make out who they were or what they were saying. Yvonne's hand touched Giselle's shoulder. "Natali is here, Giselle. She's here. The driver picked her up on his way back. She was walking from Port au Prince to get to you."

Kate helped her friend outside. But Giselle quickly took off without her assistance in the direction of the voices. Kate stood motionless and watched. Even in her deepest darkness, her friend found her daughter and they fell into each other's arms. She watched Natali comfort her mother, who lifted the hem of her dress to dry tears of gratitude that overflowed from her heart like a cup of tea onto a saucer.

Kate struggled to push aside the fear for what might await her in the United States as she shared in the joyful reunion.

Natali explained that her father convinced her to stay with him at his condo in Brooklyn for the night so they could catch up.

"I wondered if he would come," Giselle said.

"You knew Max might be there?" Kate asked.

"I sent word to him before she left for New York," Giselle

answered. "There are a lot of opportunities for Natali there. He could help her make contacts, finish her education, and find a job."

"He saved my life." Natali said. "The hotel was destroyed."

"How did you get here to Haiti?" Kate asked. "We heard all the flights were cancelled."

"My father helped me get across to Canada. He knows a lot of people." She sounded proud. "We booked a flight to Haiti from Toronto. He wants me to come back to the U.S. and finish university and then go to graduate school," Natali said.

Giselle stayed silent.

"At first I said no. But then we talked a while and had dinner. He took me to the restaurant where the planes crashed, Windows on the World. We looked out over the city. There was so much to offer. I told him I would consider it. He made a good case that I could do more for Haiti with an education. But now . . ."

"The world has changed now," Kate interjected quietly.

No one offered a contradiction.

The driver had returned not just with Natali, but also with Fatra and her husband. Kate was pleased to see how well the mother looked, and how happy she appeared with her husband. Their parental smiles so broad, Kate no longer noticed the scars on the woman's face. There was no good news about the situation in New York, according to Fatra's husband. There were very few survivors from the World Trade Center collapse.

"*Bon voyage!*" Kate kissed the baby's forehead and held the tiny bundle close to her. The heartbeat of Hope echoed in her chest and she allowed herself to believe in the possibility again. If Giselle were right about Natali, then maybe she would be right about Tieina and Jen. Maybe they were safe, too.

The ride back to Port au Prince seemed interminably long. The car was hot, the road dusty, and they had little conversation to keep her mind off her daughters. When they reached the guesthouse, Didi came running to meet their car, portable phone in her hand.

"Dr. Kate, someone named Edward is on the phone for you. He says it's an emergency!"

For just an instant, her arms froze by her side. As long as she didn't take the phone, it couldn't be bad news. Didi yanked the car door open and shoved the phone in her face.

"Edward?"

"Kate, Kate—is that you?" The connection was infiltrated with static.

"It's Kate, Edward. What is it?"

"We've had a terrible tragedy in the U.S. Oh God, it's been awful."

"I know, Edward. We heard on the radio. I need you to call Mark. Tieina and Jen were in New York."

"I know. Mark called me." The low battery alarm sounded. "He didn't know what else to do. He said you didn't answer your e-mails."

She ran up the steps, hoping the battery would not die right now. "We didn't have Internet. Has he heard from Jen or Tieina?"

She reached the landline phone just as Edward answered, "Tieina and Jen are . . ."

The line went dead.

She threw the portable phone on the table and pressed the other phone to her ear. Her hand shook so much that Danny covered it with his to steady it. "Are you there, Edward? I didn't hear what you said. What about Tieina and Jen?"

Danny was beside her and had his arm around her.

"They were just a few blocks away when the first plane hit. It was awful, Mark said. But they're safe, Kate. They're safe."

"They're safe," she echoed the words to Danny and collapsed in his arms; the dread that had settled in her heart for the last few days lifted so quickly that she thought she might be transported straight into the arms of her daughters.

40

KATE

MARS
SEPTEMBER 2005

Kate's cell phone rang as she walked down the stairs to her family room. She could either stop and answer it or wait until she reached the bottom step. No longer could she perform both activities at the same time. She paused and fumbled in her pocket for the flip phone. It taunted her with six rings before she could negotiate opening it. For the second time in three months she had extended the number of rings before it went to voice mail. That was how long it took her to answer the phone—six rings now instead of three, instead of two.

"Hello, Hello."

No one answered. She walked the rest of the way down the steps and pressed the callback function.

She recognized his number on the caller ID. "Dan, did you call? I'm sorry. I was in the shower." A little fib for now, no sense causing worry.

"Mom, I can't hear you? Are you okay?"

She cleared her throat, as she often had to do these days to be heard. "Yes, I'm okay." Although she feared more each day for the past two years that she was not.

"I know doctors are supposed to have bad handwriting. But Geez, Mom. I need a magnifying glass and my old secret decoder ring to make out what's on this grocery list!"

"It's the computer." Another little fib—she didn't want to say what she suspected until after she saw the neurologist the following week. "I've forgotten how to write." She forced a laugh. The tremor had become more pronounced and affected her left hand now, too. Some days it was hard to eat. Peas quivered off her spoon and cutting meat was impossible. Food landed on the table, the floor, her lap, anywhere but in her mouth. And those bad days were becoming more frequent.

She initially passed off the stiffness as from too much running in the past, and a few extra years. But she seldom ran anymore and the stiffness got worse. After she got moving she felt like one of those little wind-up toys she played with as a child. She just kept going faster and faster until she stumbled or she grabbed onto something. She was propelled by the momentum of starting, but had no way to stop. And the tiredness, it never completely left her and many days it engulfed her so that all she could think about was one nap to the next.

"Mom? Are you still there? Natali is supposed to call in a few minutes. You know how hard it is to get a connection from Haiti. Look, I'm sorry, but can you tell me what's on the list?"

She eased herself onto the bottom step and repeated to Danny in the loudest voice she could muster what she could remember from the grocery list she had made earlier that morning.

"Does anyone else in the family have neurological problems?" the doctor asked.

Kate sat, partially clad in a paper gown, goosebumps covering her failing legs. The doctor was thorough in her exam. Kate remembered enough of her medical school neurology to know that.

"No." She pretended to study her chipped, red-painted toenails and pretended it wasn't really her sitting there on the exam table about to hear the awful news she had been denying for the past year.

"Are you experiencing any other symptoms?"

"At first, I didn't think much about it. But for the past five years or so, my taste has been off." Her palate could only discern a hint of the strongest flavors like sour, sweet, salt, and garlic. "And my voice," she made an extra effort to speak louder. "It's very weak some days."

"These are some things patients will report." Dr. Owens made a note on her chart. "The medicine may help your voice and we can have you see a speech therapist too. The loss of taste, unfortunately, there isn't much we can do for that."

"I see."

The doctor put down the clipboard. "You're relatively young. But the physical signs are fairly conclusive—the stiffness, the tremor, your gait."

So the doctor *had* noticed when she walked down the hall to the exam room.

"I'm going to order a few tests." The doctor paused. "Kate, I believe you have Parkinson's disease."

She had suspected this diagnosis, but somehow suspended out there unspoken, it belonged to another patient and not her. Now the pendulum was in motion. It struck her full force with the realization that her life was irrevocably altered.

"I'm only forty-six." She bargained with the statistics, but she reasoned with the facts of her increasing physical limitations.

Then the question she had been asked so many times over the years by others in her position.

"How much time do I have left? Good time, I mean. There are things I need to do." Although right then there was nothing that seemed to matter. And of course, the doctor wouldn't give her a number, just as she never did when asked. She didn't have to—it was always the same unspoken answer—never long enough.

"This is a lot for you to take in today. Let's get the MRI and the EEG just to make sure there isn't something else going on. After that we'll see how you do with the medication. I am only going to start with a small dose for now."

"Doesn't the medicine stop working after a while?"

"Yes, but that can be many years. Do you have someone in your life you can talk to—a boyfriend or family? You'll need support through this."

"No boyfriend. My sisters and I were never close." The loss that she felt when her dad passed away flooded back. Who else was there but the three people she least wanted to burden? "I have three children."

Dr. Owens nodded. "The disease may have been brought on by the encephalitis you had fifteen years ago. It's unusual, but it has been reported. I would still recommend genetic testing. There are some studies that show, particularly in early onset of Parkinson's, that there is an inherited tendency."

"I've read a little about that." Actually she had read quite a lot. "But not yet. I'll think about it."

"There are some promising results with a newer technique called deep brain stimulation. But we can talk more about that later, if necessary."

Between scans and doctor's appointments, Kate spent the next few weeks in what the self-help books called a "life review." She took long walks—the medicine was helping with that. She made her bucket list. She wanted to go to Ireland, where her family roots started. And she wanted to spend more time with her children. She hardly saw the girls; they were young women now. Tieina was in San Francisco writing for an international non-profit organization. She had to get her to Haiti. She promised Yvonne. She added that wish to her bucket list in capital letters.

Jen, on the other hand, seldom ventured beyond the research lab. She had found her place early in life and was already publishing papers on molecular genetics and cancer. She was well on her way to getting her MD/PhD before she was twenty-six.

Danny had become a huge help to her with the programmatic aspects of Roses for Haiti. He taught economics and coached soccer at the local high school. He seemed drawn to the international work and had made several trips to Haiti on his own in the last year. They were planning to go there together in a few weeks. Would it be her last trip to Haiti?

And everything was so much more difficult since 9/11—from getting through the airport with the increased security and travel restrictions to raising money for the programs. The U.S. government and so many Americans were suspicious that any country, even Haiti, with all its problems, was harboring terrorists. Added to the fear was the lingering effect of the post-9/11 economic collapse. Endowments built by many foundations as the basis for their grants had disappeared in just a few weeks and individual donor money was tighter than ever. Revenue was so meager that Kate hadn't received her salary in three years.

But Kate couldn't give up. She just had to keep trying, trying harder as long as she could. She couldn't abandon Yvonne or Giselle or the other people she had come to know and love. She needed a succession plan. Edward came immediately to her mind. He was such a good man—such a good friend. Oddly, over the years, despite their age difference, he had become one of her closest confidants.

Edward was the one she called two weeks ago once the news settled in that the diagnosis of Parkinson's disease was confirmed. He came over and sat with her while she made plans and cried with her when she acknowledged what little time she might have left. He agreed to keep her secret for now. She wanted no one else to know.

41

GISELLE

PETIT (TI) MIREBELAIS
MARCH 2007

Once, years ago, Giselle heard about a blind painter who continued to paint after he lost his sight. He claimed he could feel the different textures in the colors of paint. Blues were cool and bubbly. Reds were warm and grainy. White was calm and felt like air with just a touch of dew. She hadn't believed it until she became blind and learned to smell, hear, and feel the phases of the moon and how the earth and her body reacted differently as it waxed and waned and disappeared completely. Moon spells, moon smells, was her name for the new gift.

She felt the cool earth beneath her feet. It was alive with earthworms tunneling through the dirt. The tiny plants lifted their heads to touch the night sun. She could hear them growing. Even at this time of year, well after the harvest and before the crops shared food. The hungry months they were called. It was when more babies died, more prayers were said, and more women defaulted on their microcredit loans.

It happened each year since they began the program ten years ago. Natali gave special warnings to the solidarity groups that they must plan and save for the months when there was little to buy or sell in the market. More listened now than they used to—experience was the best teacher. But still some ignored her advice, and this year was especially difficult with three tropical storms passing through Haiti and the terrorist attack on the United States. Kate had to cut back on the money her organization was able to send. Giselle wondered if those crazy men hijacking the planes had any idea how their actions would hurt countries like Haiti. Fear was contagious and heartless.

She walked into the night, and voices came to her in the darkness. She stopped to listen before they could hear her footsteps.

"Do you think we should tell them now?" Natali whispered.

"Yes. We'll have them both together when my mom gets here tomorrow." Danny was with her. A long silence followed where she imagined the young couple kissing. "Let's do it. We can figure out the details later."

It had been almost six months since Kate's last visit, and Giselle noticed differences in her this time. Her steps, usually brisk, were slow and measured, feet staying low and close to the ground. And her hands were shaking, mostly her right one but sometimes the left one, too. Was she drinking again after all those years? Giselle didn't want to say anything, but she was worried. Her friend was not well.

"How was Ireland?" She had heard from Danny that Kate had spent a couple of weeks there over the summer.

"It was wonderful," Kate answered. "I've always wanted to go there . . ." Her voice dropped off.

"Excuse me. I didn't hear the rest of what you said."

Kate cleared her throat and began again. "I always wanted to go there. My family is from Limerick."

"I understand that, wanting to go back to your roots."

"I wish I could convince Tieina of that."

"Yes, I know that concerns you."

There was a loud bang and then glass breaking.

"Kate, what happened?" Giselle stood to go to her.

"Stay, Giselle. I bumped into the table. My glass broke."

"Are you all right?"

"Yes." Was her friend crying? She heard her sweeping the floor and then something else fell, maybe the broom? "No, I'm not all right. I'm sick. I'm terribly sick and I'm getting worse."

Despite the risk of stepping on broken glass, Giselle went to her friend and found her sitting on the floor. She knelt beside her and held her trembling hands. "Then you must tell me about it and tell me what I can do." Kate had always been so brave and stoic; Giselle ached to comfort her as Kate had comforted her so many times.

As Kate confided, there was a lot Giselle could not understand about the disease called Parkinson's. But she understood enough to know that there was no cure and the medicine Kate had been taking for the last two years was working less and less. She was fearful for her friend but also for herself. Her parents, Max, her dear aunt and uncle were all gone. She didn't want to lose anyone else in her life.

"I don't know how I'm going to do this. I'm only forty-eight years old. What am I going to do when I can't take care of myself? How will I survive?"

"*Siviv sou fos kouraj.* You will you know—survive on the strength of your courage." She sat back down. "When I first started losing my vision, I had such terrible headaches. The doctor told me I had a brain tumor. I thought I would be dead before Natali finished high school."

"Yes, I remember."

"But I didn't die and the headaches went away. I always

wanted to ask you—why did that happen? Why did I live? Why didn't I die?"

"Sometimes, tumors just die. They do their damage but then they die."

"Like a storm that comes and goes?" Giselle asked her friend.

"Sort of. This disease isn't like that though." Kate sounded so certain. "Do you miss it?"

Giselle waited for her to say what the "it" was.

"Not being able to see things?"

"Every minute." She remembered the moon spells. "Well almost. They're talking about getting married, you know?"

"Dan and Natali?" There was surprise in Kate's voice.

"Yes."

"I didn't know. They told you?"

"There are some times when having a keen sense of hearing is invaluable."

"You know what that will make us?"

"Mothers-in-law!" they answered at the same time, and laughed like a couple of schoolgirls.

The splash of water on the front porch was immediately followed by the smell of bleach and the sound of a scrub brush. Giselle threw on her robe and went outside.

"Natali?"

"Yes, Mother." The girl's voice came from beneath her feet.

"Why are you scrubbing the porch?"

"Because it's dirty." Natali continued scrubbing.

"I can't believe someone would do this." Yvonne was there, too.

"Do what?"

"Someone painted a *djab*—wild spirit—on your porch last night."

"Why would someone put a Vodou curse on us?"

"My best guess is that Josephine did it."

The scrubbing finally stopped.

"Josephine? You went to school with her when you were little girls. You danced together in church. Why?" Giselle asked.

"She and her solidarity group defaulted on their loan. I know it's a difficult season for many people but it's their second default. I had to ask them to leave the program. It's only fair to the others," her daughter answered.

Natali sat beside her and continued. "It's too much for me to manage alone. We have ten offices now and three hundred clients." She sounded exhausted. "I haven't told Dr. Kate yet. But last month we were short two hundred dollars. Someone is stealing from us. And now this."

She touched her daughter's arm. "Remember why you are doing this. When there is great poverty and money available, there will always be jealousy and corruption. But it doesn't have to destroy the program and you don't have to do it all alone. Talk to the women in the program. Let them work with you on a solution."

"Thank you, Mother." Natali kissed her on the cheek. "I'm not giving up on this. I'll see you this evening. Remember we want to talk to you later."

"Danny said he and Natali want to talk to us before we leave tomorrow. They're coming over in a few minutes." Giselle lowered herself into a chair.

"Yes, I received the same invitation." Kate laughed.

"Do they really think we don't know?"

"I think they're so much in love they don't notice much else."

"We have to act surprised."

"I agree."

Danny opened the conversation. "Natali and I have been talking. You know we love each other." He paused so they could acknowledge their agreement. "We've decided to get married."

Giselle felt Natali kneel in front of her and then grasp both of her hands and kiss them. Despite being forewarned, Giselle cried.

"I love you, Mom," Danny said to Kate, his words choked as he joined in the tears. "I never would have found all this." Danny gathered them all in an embrace.

"We want to live here at least for two years," Danny began.

"Dan is going to help me with managing the program. I told him about what happened this morning," Natali continued.

Giselle had already filled Kate in on the Vodou curse and missing money.

"Mom," Natali continued, "I took your advice and we spoke with the women's groups today. We're going to put more safeguards in place to protect the program and our clients."

"What will you do for money, Dan?" his mother asked. Giselle had to smile to herself. Kate was always one for details. She loved her for it.

"A few months ago, I applied for a grant. You remember the McHenry Foundation?" Danny answered.

"Yes, you wrote a proposal for the microcredit program—the health education component—right?" Kate asked.

"Well, I just got an e-mail and we're getting the grant and they're willing to pay me a stipend to live here and oversee the implementation. I'm going back to turn in my notice at the school and wrap up some things at home. I'll move here in three months."

For the first time in years, Giselle imagined herself dancing and dancing—at her daughter's wedding no less! Danny was a wonderful man and with Danny and Natali living in Mirebelais, Giselle would have her daughter close. But Natali would also have the chance Giselle never had—to leave Haiti if she wanted. And soon there would be grandchildren. She would hold them in her arms and smell their sweet baby smell and comfort them when they cried as she had Natali. True, her vision was forever gone, yet these images did more to lift the darkness from her heart than a thousand suns could.

CHAPTER

42

KATE

UNITED STATES
MARCH 2007

Kate did not feel like running; she hardly felt like walking. But that's what she and Danny had to do, run with their carry-ons banging against their thighs and backs after their flight from Haiti arrived late. They ran to customs and from there, to the security area at Miami Airport where they would have to pass through screening again before boarding the plane home.

Danny kept turning around. "Hurry, Mom. We're not going to make it."

Finally he relieved her of one of her bags and took off, promising to save her a spot. The haste was hardly necessary. Slow as a snake on its belly at the North Pole, the airport security line crept along. It had been like that ever since 9/11.

Her shoulders ached from the weight of her backpack even though it was only half-full this time. More than anything else she longed to lie flat on the floor and stretch out the muscles in her back and neck and shoulders, and it was nearly time to take her medicine, too. But she would have to dig through her bag and Danny would ask questions. She had never taken medicine before the last two years and now it was two pills every four hours, and even then the effects wore off and she was literally paralyzed in place. If she anticipated this on-off phenomenon of her disease when her muscles seized up, she could give herself one of the pre-made syringes in time to try and prevent it. She threw a couple in her knapsack before they rechecked their luggage for the flight home. No, she would wait until they got to the gate and make a quick visit to the ladies room before they boarded. She had to go anyhow. The Parkinson's was also playing games with that. Sometimes she couldn't get it out and other times she peed her pants with no warning. It was the hallmark of her disease. One minute she couldn't, the next minute she couldn't wait.

Danny was already removing his laptop and Ziploc bag of liquids to pass though the X-ray and metal detector machines.

"Next." The unsmiling man in the TSA uniform reached from behind his security podium for her documents.

She couldn't move.

It was only a few feet. But suddenly her feet were like lead and the ground a magnet. She could not lift her legs. She stared at the yellow strip on the ground that marked the line behind which passengers were instructed to wait.

Her body refused to move.

"Ma'am. You're next." The agent waved at her to come.

How could she explain to this man that she just couldn't move?

A woman behind her touched her gently on the shoulder. "Do you need help? A wheelchair?" The kind stranger started to take her arm and lead her forward. That was all her muscles needed. They were ignited again with enough momentum to get her past the podium with a stern look from TSA.

She struggled to lift her bag on the belt. Danny was already through security and searching the lines for her to follow. She stood in front of the metal detector.

"You have to remove your shoes, ma'am."

She had forgotten. Forgotten to remove her shoes and forgotten that sometimes doorways were like brick walls to a person with Parkinson's disease. Unfortunately, the metal detector looked like a doorway and this was one of those times. To make matters worse, the security guard confiscated her bag from the conveyor belt and nodded to his co-worker at the metal detector.

"Remove your shoes before you pass through the metal detector." The order came again.

"I can't," was all she could get out. How many times had she jumped out of bed to check on the kids, jogged for miles in the park, or trekked up the mountain path in Ti Mirebelais like a goat? And now as hard as she tried she couldn't even bend down to take off her shoes. She felt so helpless.

"Mom, what is it?" Danny looked at the contents of her bag displayed on the stainless steel metal table. "What are you doing? What are the syringes for?"

They grabbed her arm. "Come with us. You can stay there." One of the guards motioned for Dan to sit on a bench.

"Hey, wait."

The guard gave no acknowledgment to her son's remark. He started after them, but was stopped by a third guard.

"She's a doctor," Danny explained. "She works in Haiti. That's why she has needles."

Less than two months had passed since she had the run-in with airport security on her way back from Haiti. Kate took inventory of what remained after the Goodwill truck removed all the items she would no longer need. There were close to a dozen boxes, packed light so she could lift them—if it was a good day. They were labeled with a big black sharpie—*Books, Pictures, Kitchen Items, Christmas Decorations,* and *Important.* In the last box, she had packed all her journals. Leather-bound, spiral notebooks—weathered and worn like herself—she leafed through them one last time, pausing to smile or cry from time to time. She had had quite a run of it for sure. Danny was marrying Natali. They were so in love, nothing else mattered to them. Only with one promise had she failed. Her promise to get Tieina back to Haiti to see her grandmother and to feel the love and beauty of the world Kate had taken her from as a child. It had taken Kate years to really feel the joy beyond the poverty. She had no regrets for the taking, only for not showing her that there was more than misery.

Scattered around the four-bedroom house where she had raised her children were a small couch, a dinette table with chairs, a TV, her desk, a bed, and a chest. That was all she would have room for in her new home—the Home, as she referred to it.

She had brought the luck of the Irish back with her from her trip to Ireland. She called a real estate agent, listed the house, and before the "For Sale" sign was pounded into the ground, she had accepted a cash offer and signed a long-term lease for a one-bedroom apartment in an independent-living community. Independent-living community—how many different euphemisms were out there these days?

It was time to move on while she still could. The only consolation she found was that her children didn't have to make the decision for her. She would never put them through that, the guilt of having to place their mother in a nursing facility. No, at least she had spared them that. She tapped her cane on each of the boxes.

"Hi, Mom." Danny appeared with a U-Haul rental truck and Jen. "Are you ready to get going?"

"In a minute." She wanted one more meal with her children

in their home of the last fifteen years. "Let's have something to eat first." She pulled up one of the four remaining chairs to the small table that would fit in her new little dinette area. "I ordered a pizza. It should be here soon."

Jen looked at her watch but Danny had already grabbed a soda. "Good idea. I'm starved."

"What else is new?" Jen looked around at the empty rooms and shrugged herself into a chair as well.

Kate finished one slice of pizza in the time her children ate four. Danny looked around and asked the same question he had asked so many times since she announced her decision to sell the house and move.

"Mom, are you sure about this? I can move in and help out. Natali will understand if I don't go to Haiti for a while."

Jen stared at her plate.

"Thank you, honey. But no." She covered his hand with hers. "And thank you both for helping me with the packing and move today." She looked around. It was just a house and stuff. Right? "I actually feel good about this. I can focus all my energy on other things now."

"But it's only one bedroom. You'll be alone. Aren't you afraid?" Danny asked.

Jen gave him a swift kick under the table.

"Dan and Jen." She added her daughter's name because Jen had the same concerns; she just couldn't get them out there as easily as her brother could. She chose her words carefully. "Yes, I am afraid of being alone. But my greatest fear is not to be alone. If I saw you here every day or every week or even every month that would mean you're not living *your* lives. You—" She grabbed both of Jen's hands and kissed them. "—that would mean you aren't curing cancer or some other disease."

"I wish you would have told us before you did all this," Jen said.

"I had to do it my way." Kate smiled sadly at her daughter.

Jen returned the smile and nodded. Of all her children, Kate knew Jen understood about doing things on her own terms.

"And you." She turned to Danny and ruffled his hair. "Danny, if you're here, you aren't kicking that ball around and doing flips and showing the kids in Haiti that there is something else out there for them. And your sister Tieina, she's not off somewhere racing to or running from whatever it is she's got to figure out."

"She wanted to be here to help, too. But she had a deadline on a story about child slavery in Ghana," Dan said.

"Visit me when you can and think of me often, but smile when you do. You'll do that, won't you?" She pushed back her chair, rocked back and forth, and with considerable effort, she raised herself from the chair. She reached for the metal tripod cane to steady her walk. "We better get moving. This really is a new beginning for me, you know." She prayed this demon, her disease, would stay at bay long enough to see Danny and Natali marry, to see Jen finish her PhD, and to get Tieina back to Haiti as Kate had promised her grandmother when she took her from their village fourteen years ago.

43

KATE

MARS
SEPTEMBER 2008

"I guess our mother ran out of words before she ran out of time." Jen's words woke Kate from her late-morning nap. The rumble of the cafeteria cart announced lunch at St. Vincent's, the skilled-care facility that became her home six months earlier when she could no longer manage independent living.

"I can't believe you just said that," Danny whispered.

Still Kate heard him loud and clear. She heard them both.

"What I mean is, that Mom was always the one with the voice in the family. She was always so focused. I really miss that. I always felt there was more we needed to say to each other."

"She would like it if you would come for our wedding in Haiti," he said softly.

Oh, how Kate wished she could be there.

"You could get married here," Jen proposed.

"Natali's family can't come to the U.S. Even if we could afford to buy the tickets, it's nearly impossible to get a visa if you're Haitian."

"I guess that makes sense," Jen said while she paced. "Do you think Tienia will go?"

"Doubt it. Mom has tried to get her to Haiti for years. She refuses."

Yes, the one thing she still hadn't been able to do. But she held one last hope. Edward and she had worked out a plan, even if she wouldn't be around to see it happen.

"It doesn't look like she's going to wake up. You might as well drink the milkshake, Dan."

Her son always brought a chocolate milkshake for her. But even the effort it took to suck from the straw and swallow was too much lately. Some days, like today, Kate pretended to sleep. It was easier that way. She didn't have to see the worry and fear on their faces every time she struggled to answer a question. She was their mother; she wanted to comfort them, but her body wouldn't cooperate. The words wouldn't come out and there was no key to unlock the stiffness and tremors that had become her prison. But if she just listened, she could still hear and find out what was going on in their lives.

Dr. Owens entered Kate's room. "Good afternoon. How is our lady today?" she asked.

"She hasn't woken up since we got here," Danny reported. "It's been like this the last three times I visited."

"I'm sorry. Maybe we can make an adjustment in her medication."

If only there were a new magic pill that could unlock the darkness of her disease. Perhaps it was time to consider the alternative. What else did she have to lose?

"Doctor, there's something I've been wanting to ask you." Jen's concerned voice interrupted Kate's thoughts.

"Yes, Jen. What is it?"

"Do you think my mother's Parkinson's disease could be genetic? She's so young. Could I, I mean, could we be at risk to get it, too?"

The apprehension in her daughter's voice beneath her clinical inquiry nearly broke Kate's heart.

"Jen. What are you talking about?"

With the alarm in Danny's voice, Kate's eyes instinctively popped open. She shut them again before anyone noticed.

"Look, Dan, I'm sorry but Dr. Owen can confirm that in early-onset Parkinson's, there's an increased chance that it can be inherited. There are some pretty good tests to determine that."

"This isn't one of your research projects. This is our family!"

Kate hated what this disease was doing to her body. She hated even more what it was doing to her children.

"Yes, I'm thinking about our family. I'm not having children. But you and Natali are getting married and talking about having them."

Grandchildren? Kate should have considered that.

"Maybe I don't want to know. Tests can be wrong. Isn't that right, Doctor?"

"Yes, tests can be wrong and even if the genetic abnormality is there, it's not 100 percent that the disease will manifest itself. There are other factors involved," Dr. Owen answered. "At this point, I think we should leave the decision up to your mother. I'd need her permission before we do any testing."

"What if she can't give it? Like Dan said, it's been weeks since she's been able to talk to us," Jen said.

"She still has good days when she's alert and we can talk a little. Unfortunately, today is not one of those days," the doctor said. "I'm sorry."

Kate was, too.

Dan and Jen kissed her goodbye and told her they loved her. That was hardest of all, not saying it back out loud to them. When she was sure they wouldn't see her, she let herself open her eyes just enough to watch them walk out the door, Danny's arm encircling his sister. She couldn't continue to act like she wasn't there when she was. If there might be a chance—yes, it was time. As afraid as Kate was, afraid of what might happen if she went through with it, she was more afraid of not trying.

Her eyes leaked a lot even when she wasn't crying. It was another trick of this disease. Nothing about Parkinson's disease made those around her believe she was anything except suffering. Thank goodness the kids left before the floodgates opened. Her pillow was soaking wet from the tears and the drooling. But she had another purpose for seeking help than simply a change in linens. She moved her hand a few inches and watched her finger find the call button.

"Yes, do you need something?" the voice on the intercom said.

"I'd like to talk to the doctor please."

"Yes, do you need something?"

The nurse hadn't heard her, but she didn't attempt a second time. Someone would come in to check in a few minutes when they had the time. She would save her voice for talking to the doctor.

"Your children were here, Kate. Were you listening?" Dr. Owens asked.

She nodded. The doctor and she had talked about Kate's tactic to stay silent sometimes when she was having an especially bad day.

"Your daughter asked about genetic testing. What do you think?"

Dr. Owens leaned over her bed so that her ear was just inches from Kate's mouth as she said, "Do it. But tell me first."

"Of course. I'll order the tests immediately. We should have the results in a few weeks."

She reached out for Dr. Owen's arm. "The other treatment, too." Kate couldn't bear to say the words. She was terrified at the thought of someone sticking a needle into her brain, into her mind, into the one part of her body that hadn't yet been damaged by her disease.

"The deep-brain stimulation?"

She nodded.

"You want to try DBS—deep-brain stimulation?"

"Yes. There are things I need to say. I am not finished."

"You remember what we talked about. It's a fairly new treatment. There can be serious side effects. I can't promise you'll be better than you are now and you could be worse."

"I have to try." She closed her eyes and her head collapsed back onto the pillow. It's all she could get out before her voice failed her again.

Ironically, it was one of those pretty good days. With the help of an aide, Kate brushed her teeth, combed her hair, and was able to sit in the chair for a few minutes. What a shame she couldn't eat breakfast. She may have been able to swallow something more solid than the pureed slush they fed her three times a day. Baby food, she called it, though never to the staff or her children. But today was her surgery and Jen would be there soon to sit with her until the ambulance came to transfer them to the hospital. A few wires would be threaded into her brain and a battery implanted under the skin of her chest. She'd be awake for the whole procedure so they could check her responses. She would rather have been asleep, deep under the dark, unknowing, unfeeling of anesthesia.

"I hear we both passed our tests," Kate said to Jen when she sat down to wait with her.

"Dan wouldn't have it done. But I'll tell him now that you and I don't have the gene for Parkinson's. He doesn't have to worry." Jen smiled a protective smile.

"You look good today, Mom. Are you sure you want to go through with this?" Jen asked. "I'm checking the Internet every day for new treatments. Stem cells are promising. But it's going to be at least a few more years, between science and politics." Jen had that fiery look in her eyes and that dogged edge in her voice that reminded Kate of herself when she was back in San Francisco fighting for her AIDS patients.

"And once a week, I make myself the biggest pain in the butt for those guys in Washington. The potential for stem cells to help people with diseases that we thought were incurable is incredible. Diseases like spinal cord injury, MS, and Parkinson's." She stopped short. "I'm so sorry, Mom."

"Please don't ever apologize for your passion. It makes me . . ." She couldn't finish for the joy and sadness that fought inside her. She placed her hand over her heart and smiled through the tears.

Jen came to her and kneeled in front of her, taking her hands. "Mom, I'll be here when you wake up."

"Work?" She struggled to get the words out. There was a deadline coming up for Jen's latest grant.

"I'm just taking two days. We're close, Mom." Jen got that excited look she wore when she talked about her research. "I think we have the right strains for the vaccine. It'll take some time for the approval process. But in five years we should have a better vaccine to prevent cervical cancer for the millions of women in the developing countries."

She had so many questions she wanted to ask her daughter about her research, about the guy she just started dating, and all the other things that went on in the life of a twenty-three-year-old woman. But it was too hard. After the procedure, they would have plenty of time to talk. Yes, they would have plenty of time for conversations, after the procedure. If it worked.

"Sometimes I wish I was more like Dan or Tieina. They never seem afraid to travel to places like Africa and Haiti. I just sit in the lab and in front of the computer. But this vaccine, it's a good thing, Mom."

She motioned for Jen to come closer and brought her face to her lips. She kissed her cheek and so many memories flooded her heart. She recalled the day her daughter was born, her stubbornness so like her own that manifested in everything from taking her first step, to straight "A"s on every report card, to remaining steadfast in her decision to move in with her father when she was nine. All along, this child, her daughter, had known what she wanted and how to make it happen.

"I'm so proud of you." With all the strength Kate had left, she grasped her daughter's hands within her own. She marveled at the strong and courageous young woman who sat in front of her ready to take on the world. And when they came to wheel her away, she let go with no regret or fear left in her heart.

4

ECHOS
(2008–2009)

For last year's words belong to last year's voice

And next year's words await another voice

And to make an end is to make a beginning.

—T.S. Eliot

44

TIEINA

SAN FRANCISCO
OCTOBER 2008

"Nobody wants to hear about Haiti! The place is a goddamn disaster. Why are you doing this to me?" Tieina asked her boss as she tried to speak into her cell phone while straddling a mountain bike and brushing a damp strand of hair from her eyes. "Look, I know I was born there, but I haven't been back since I was eight years old and I'm not interested in going there now." She lowered her voice slightly in response to a startled pair of young female joggers. "I've played by the rules—spent last summer at the WHO HIV/ AIDS conference in Africa and I loved that." Even though she knew she didn't need to remind her boss, for emphasis she added, "And I not only nailed that story, but I also learned every orphan drug name—chemical and generic—and in case you forgot, contracted fucking malaria and dysentery." She shuddered to remember how sick she had been. If one of her co-workers hadn't checked on her in her tent that night, she probably would have died. At least that's what the handsome Ugandan doctor told her at the medical outpost when she woke up with IVs in both her arms. Dr. Mangu

Ubeku was his name and she couldn't wait to get back to Uganda to see him.

It was useless to argue. Mel, her boss, had made it clear when she signed on with the magazine two years earlier that his decisions were not to be questioned when it came to handing out assignments. Tieina sighed, anxious to get back to the trail and finish her fifty-mile ride before dark. Although just this once she wished she was sitting at her desk instead of answering from her cell phone. Right now she longed to express her displeasure with an immature physical gesture like slamming down the receiver. Clipping her BlackBerry onto her waistband just didn't have the same effect.

But why was she so angry? She was damn lucky to land a job with a well-respected international organization at only twenty-three. She loved covering the story on child slavery in Africa. It got to her. It was why she went into journalism. Being able to speak for those who couldn't—those who didn't have a voice, like the AIDS orphans in Africa, or those who had lost their voice, like the women who were raped and had their tongues cut out so they couldn't identify their attackers. She shuddered at the memories of what she had seen.

So why did covering UNICEF's work exposing child slavery in Haiti feel like a jail sentence rather than an opportunity? Probably because her mother was always pushing her to go back there. Some day she would; it just was not at the top of her list.

On the other hand, she'd like to meet the women who wrote the book on *restaveks*, as domestic child slaves were called in Haiti. So maybe an interview in Pittsburgh wouldn't be so bad. But going to Haiti to follow up with the other journalists on the investigation there, she was not into that. She could get what she needed from the Internet for now to supplement the interview and write a killer story like she had been doing with every assignment the last two years since she graduated from NYU.

Maybe a week back East wouldn't be totally unbearable. And she really wanted to see her mom. It had been almost a year, and that had been a short visit wedged between trips to Africa and conferences in San Francisco. Jen had called and said that after the DBS procedure their mom was moving and talking almost like the old days. But Tieina sensed there was more her sister wasn't telling her. Yes, she needed to get back and see for herself.

She mounted her bike and redirected her energy and frustration to climb up an especially steep section of JFK Drive. She executed each pedal stroke with the same exact precision as her investigative journalism. By the time she coasted out of Golden Gate Park, she was finished mentally packing for the morning flight.

There was something between the lines that dared her to keep reading and something in the words that compelled her to stop. Perched on a stool at a La Guardia Airport bar, Tieina switched from coffee to wine with the second flight delay and with the second chapter of *Restavek: Haiti's Hidden Secret*. She sipped the spicy Shiraz and read, "My childhood ended the day my mother died and for all intents and purposes, I was sold into child slavery for the price of a goat."

The author's mother died when she was eight and desperate for food; her father sent her to live with relatives, who promised to send the child to school. The goat was actually a gift. But after eight years of cooking, cleaning, and washing for the family, little food, and not a single day of formal education, the exchange of animal for slave rang truer for the writer. At age sixteen, after enduring two years of repeated rape from the sons and father of the family, the girl escaped. She ran straight to the doors of a Catholic convent and never looked back until she decided to write her book years later.

So this was the woman Tieina would interview in Pittsburgh. She glanced at her BlackBerry—8:00 p.m. and another two hours before her flight was rescheduled to depart.

"Yes," she replied to the bartender's inquiry for a second glass of wine. Why not? The airport shuttle was picking her up. She'd go straight to the hotel and stop by and see her mom in the morning.

Her BlackBerry hummed and danced on the bar counter.

She looked at the number and caller ID. It was Jen.

"Is everything okay?" Tieina didn't even wait for the hello.

"Well, good evening, Tieina. Thank you, I'm fine. And how are you?" Must not be too serious if she has time for sarcasm. "Mom would like to talk to you."

"Tieina," Kate said. Her mother's voice sounded strong and clear like she remembered.

"Mom, you sound great. Everything okay?" That was a stupid question to ask someone in a nursing home.

"I just wanted to call you. I'm feeling better. I had a procedure a few weeks ago. They put these electrodes in my brain and there's a little battery that controls the electrical pulses. The doctor is still adjusting all that. But I'm doing well."

"I'm coming to town tomorrow, Mom. The journal wants me to do an interview." Tieina was surprised her mother didn't remember talking with her after the surgery, but decided it was probably the sedation that made her forget.

"Will you stop by and see me?"

"Of course I will. I can't wait to see you."

"You, too, honey. Have a safe trip. When are you coming again?"

Tieina waited in the rental car, finishing e-mails on her BlackBerry. Jen's car pulled into the parking lot.

Jen had called her that morning. "I want to talk to you before you go in."

Tieina hated the place. She had only been there once. The Home, as her family called it. There was nothing homey about it. From the heavy metal doors and multiple alarms to the stained linoleum and air that never seemed to quite lose that urine/excrement/Lysol smell. But the care was supposed to be the best. She never understood that corollary, like one had to choose between the two.

Jen pulled up and they walked in together. "Listen, she looks good. Her voice is strong and the tremor is almost completely gone. And the stiffness is already much better. They weren't expecting that to happen."

"But . . ." Tieina sensed it coming and from what she read online, there were definitely some potential "buts" with DBS.

"She's writing in a diary. I don't know what that's all about. When I ask her, she just smiles and says, 'My memories.'" Jen shrugged. "But that's the thing. Her memory is not always there. Sometimes it's perfect and then it's gone—like a light switch going on and off. As many physical limitations as Mom had, I never noticed that before the procedure."

"Maybe it's her medication or she's adjusting to the electrical stimulation?" Tieina also knew, from what she read on the Internet, that memory loss could be progressive.

"I don't want to make a big deal about it. I just thought you should be aware of it."

"My sister, the doctor. You always were the smart one." It may not have come out that way, but Tieina was proud of her sister.

"You know, Tieina, when we were growing up, I always wished I was the brave one." Jen hugged her. "Like you. I'm going to get some coffee in the cafeteria. That'll give you some time alone together. I'll see you in a bit."

For once, Tieina was at a loss for words.

The woman sleeping in the bed looked like a red-haired Snow

White dwarfed by the pillows that surrounded her. Her mother's reading glasses had slid down her nose. A leather-bound book was opened on her chest, pages toward her heart.

Tieina tiptoed into the room and arranged the roses she brought in a vase on the dresser. When she turned around, her mother's eyes had opened and she was looking at her, like she was out of focus.

"You're awake." She went over to kiss her.

But her mother pulled away and closed the book.

"Mom?" She thought of what Jen had said. "It's me, Tieina."

"Tieina, what are you doing here? I thought you were in Africa?"

"I'm here to cover a story." She kissed her this time. "And to see you."

"What kind of story are you working on?"

"Actually, it has to do with Haiti. Do you know what a *restavek* is?"

"Yes." Her mother removed her glasses. "Why?"

"Well, that's the story I'm covering. A woman whose mother died when she was young was given to relatives who abused her." As she articulated the words, they sounded more familiar than just something she was reading.

The question that had been brewing the last few days finally surfaced in Tieina's consciousness. "Mom, was I a *restavek* when you adopted me?"

"There's a lot I don't remember. I've been going through the journals I wrote in over the years. I tried to talk to you a few times before I got sick." Her mother motioned for her to sit on the bed beside her. "Yes, I do think you were a *restavek*. Do you want to know more?"

"I'm not sure." She had so little memory of her life in Haiti.

"In the closet, there's a box. When the time is right for you, I'd like you to read the diaries." Her mother looked wistfully out the window as if she was remembering a time in the past where she believed, like Tieina did most days, that anything and everything was still possible. "I just wish I could have done something to help her, your mother. But then I got sick and things happened and . . ." She paused and her face brightened when she looked at Tieina. "But look at you, a journalist. She would have been so proud of you."

"Thanks, Mom." She wanted to stay longer. Her mother looked good, yet she was different, still loving and concerned, but detached. "I'm sorry, Mom. I have that interview. But I'll be back tomorrow. We can spend the day together." Tieina reached up on the closet shelf and removed the box with the books. By the time she turned around, her mother was sound asleep again. Tieina didn't have a clue what secrets and treasures she carried away with her that day. But she decided it was time to find out.

Tieina sat through the presentation taking copious notes and afterwards had a fifteen-minute interview with the author. She went straight to a nearby coffee shop with her laptop and pounded out a 1,000-word article for the next day's deadline. By four o'clock she had hit the "SEND" button and was on her way back to the hotel with two takeout containers of Thai food.

Her mother's journals were scattered on the bed. She pulled them close like they were her children. Some were spiral notebooks, others leather-bound and engraved with different designs, but all had a start and end date specified on the first page. She began at the beginning.

Tieina knew some of what was recorded by the bits and pieces of her past that her mother had shared with her. But there was so much she didn't know that it felt like she was reading someone else's biography. As she turned the last page of one volume, she found a faded drawing of a rose and something written beneath it—

pa bliye m. She did not know what it meant except for the English words beneath it, which apparently were the translation: "don't forget me." At the bottom, in cursive, was her name, "Tieina." How many years ago and under what circumstances had she written this?

She picked up her cell phone. It was midnight in Pittsburgh, but only nine o'clock on the West Coast.

"Mel." She threw the last four journals into her duffel bag. "Can you still get me on that flight to Haiti tomorrow?"

Tieina couldn't wait to tell her mother she was finally going back to Haiti after all the hassle of trying to get her to go there for the past fifteen years. They would have so much to catch up on when she returned.

When she saw her mother making her bed, she felt like crying. It was a simple task, but one she hadn't been able to do for several years. She really was doing well, and Tieina thought maybe it was a good thing her mother had decided to go through with the procedure.

"Can I help you with that?"

"Yes. Thank you. I never was much of a housekeeper."

"You always say that."

"I'm sorry. They tell me I repeat myself a lot." Her mother picked up the pillows that had fallen to the floor and gave her a puzzled look.

"I didn't mean that." Tieina scooped up the last one. Her mother was studying her like she wanted to ask something important but wasn't sure how.

"I was a doctor, you know? I worked in Haiti for years. I delivered a baby there once."

Tieina nodded. She had read about that in one of the journals.

"I wonder how she's doing now." Her mother looked at her like it was the first time she had seen her. "Are you from there?"

"Yes, a long time ago. But I haven't gone back since I was a child." Her mother really didn't know who she was. Her flight would leave in two hours, she needed to leave or she would miss it. "I'm on my way to the airport now. I just wanted you to know that I'm going back to Haiti today."

"The people are so poor there. It'll be difficult for you to see that again." Her mother sank to the chair like it really had taken all her energy to make her bed. "Maybe I can go with you next time, when I'm feeling a little stronger."

Tieina, never easily or comfortably moved to tears, found herself choking to keep the sobs from escaping. "I hope so. I truly hope so." She kissed her mother and hurried off to catch her plane.

45

TIEINA

HAITI

The Hotel Montana was as nice as any she had stayed in anywhere in the world. The rooms were spacious, clean, and had all the usual bells and whistles—cable TV, hairdryer, and even wireless Internet. The menu included international and local options and enough top-shelf booze to satisfy an upper Manhattan gig. Tieina sipped a beer on the expansive circular cement overlook and gazed at the bay, the mountains, and Port au Prince, all shrouded in a hazy smog, but enchanting nonetheless. This was not what she expected when she agreed to come for the UNICEF Conference on child servitude in Haiti. It was not like the Haiti she read about and the only memories she had from when she was a child were those she had soaked up from her mother's journals in the last three days.

She finished her beer and made her way into the conference room along with the other hundred or so attendees. She was one of a dozen journalists who had been snatched up from the airport in an air-conditioned van and transported to this palatial hotel with barely ten minutes to glimpse the shantytowns and garbage heaps along the way. Being one of the few who had not been to Haiti recently, she had little to say. She did not mention that she was Haitian born. Others would expect her to have some knowledge of the customs and be able to speak the language.

The conference was informative but too long. Her butt was numb, and she fidgeted so much the guy next to her glared. There were lectures and panel discussions and small group meetings, separated by coffee breaks with huge platters overflowing with French pastries and fresh fruits. Lunch and dinner buffets were laid out around a huge ice sculpture of three children reading a book. For two days she ate, sat, listened, fidgeted, and took notes, naps, and more notes.

Haitian translators were scattered throughout the audience. They all spoke Creole, French, English, and Spanish. Dominique, his nametag labeled him, was different. Tieina pondered that during the meeting when she was bored. His shirt was clean and perfectly pressed, but in contrast to the other translators, it was too big. He kept pushing up the sleeves, like he had borrowed it from someone else. He did not have a black vinyl flight bag for his belongings, but a knapsack that he kept hidden under the table while they ate. He wore tennis shoes, and not the freshly polished loafers of his colleagues. And while almost everyone piled their plates full of food from the buffet table, he quickly made a cheese sandwich that he wrapped with a few pastries in a napkin and put in his knapsack. His English and French were flawless. She couldn't really judge his Creole or Spanish.

"Dominique?" She approached him after lunch. "I'd like to get out of here for a while. Can you be my guide for the afternoon?"

"Okay, but don't you want to change your shoes?" He looked disapprovingly at her sandals. Strapless and with four-inch heels, they brought her almost to eye level with most of the other journalists.

"Nope. These are fine." She checked her bag for her camera

and grabbed a couple of bottles of water from the table next to the ice sculpture. "Let's go."

Nothing looked familiar to her. Yet the chaotic movement of the people and the closeness of the air, hot and heavy with charcoal and diesel fumes, touched something in her memory. By the time they reached the Petionville Square, her water bottle was empty, her handkerchief soaked, and she regretted dismissing Dominique's advice about her choice of shoes.

They walked in a few art galleries that didn't charge admission and stopped to listen to a Rara band as it marched by them.

"McDonald's and Pizza Hut!" she proclaimed. "I can't believe it. Do you eat there?

"No, ma'am. *Tres cher*," Dominque answered, slipping back into Creole. "Too expensive."

"Yeah. I got that."

"You speak Creole?"

"Oh, no." Did she?

She noticed some of the children wore uniforms of solid-blue pants or skirts and blue-and-white-checkered shirts. Others were dressed in rags. A few of the youngest boys had only shirts, their uncircumcised genitals exposed. She pointed to a group of teenagers in jeans and T-shirts. "Aren't all the kids in school?"

"Some." He kept his answers short, frustrating for the journalist in her.

"Where do you live?" She tried again.

"Over there." He pointed vaguely in the direction of some of the nicer homes and a Catholic Church that rose above everything else as far as she could see.

"I was born in Haiti, you know?"

He looked doubtfully at her shoes and jeans.

"I lived in a village called Ti Mirebelais." That she had learned from her reading. "I was adopted by a doctor from the U.S. when I was eight."

"Do you remember anything?"

"Not much." She was starting to, though.

"Be careful. The memories can be powerful in a place like Haiti. They'll swallow you up like the earth does and make you a zombie." He did a little imitation that looked like something out of Frankenstein and they both laughed.

"So you live over there?"

"I live with the Brothers. They took me in off the streets when I was ten, sent me to school, helped me to find work as a translator. It's a good job in Haiti. There is always work with all the international organizations trying to fix our poor little country. "

She nodded, ignoring his sarcasm for now. They walked along in silence through the market. She had to grab Dominique's arm several times to keep from stepping on mounds of produce that were heaped up on mats on the ground. A younger boy dressed in a shirt and tie and a woman in a stylish suit were piling fruits and vegetables into a basket on top of a young girl's head. She had no shoes and her shirt was worn so thin that Tieina could see the outline of her breasts beginning to develop.

While the woman, who she guessed was his mother, paid the vendor, the boy gave orders to the girl, who clearly looked older than he.

"*Alle! Alle!* Go! Go!" He wagged his finger in the girl's face. "*Si ou vole*—if you steal . . ." He slapped his hands together so hard the girl winced and backed away.

"*Wi*, Monsieur Jacques. *Non*, Monsieur Jacques." She darted off sideways as if to escape a blow she knew would eventually find her.

"She's one of them, you know?" Dominique discreetly handed the girl the sandwich he had put in his backpack.

"A *restavek*?"

"Yes, she stays with that family. I see her often. Sometimes she has bruises." He lowered his voice even though the boy and the woman were a block away gnawing on ears of roasted corn.

"Can't you get her a place with the Brothers?" She would offer to pay for that.

"No, they only take boys."

"Is there nowhere else for her to go?" Alarm crept into her voice, leaving the most unsettling feeling in her stomach.

"The people at the meeting. They are trying to help. They find a few. But there are so many of us." He gave her a knowing look. "It is Haiti's biggest secret. Parents who give their children away are ashamed and the people that take them, well—they have reasons, as you see." He pulled her out of the way of a motorcycle that jumped up the broken sidewalk to get around the crowd. "Come, let me show you something you'll like."

At the far end of the square was a small grassy area. Vendors were set up on the fringes, and in the middle children were gathered and making something with sticks and plastic.

Kites! The children were making kites. One boy scraped twigs with a razor until they were bare of bark; another cut them into equal lengths. With a piece of string, they tied them together so the sticks radiated out like six-point stars. The frames were covered by flimsy plastic fashioned from dry cleaning bags. Some were painted with colorful flowers; others were cut around the edges in intricate designs. Rags were formed into a tail, and a plastic water bottle, like the one Tieina had just discarded, served as a spool to hold the string.

After they finished the construction, one child held the homemade kite and another ran with the spool, letting the string out as the first child let go and the kite gained altitude.

"*Monte kap*," Dominique explained.

She watched in fascination. She had never flown a kite before.

"It means to be lifted up—our word for kite."

"I need to get a picture of this." Tieina took her camera and snapped one of a girl running toward her. She pointed her camera up and searched for the corresponding kite. The sun was bright and her eyes teared from the smog. She struggled to focus the kite and keep it in view as it jackrabbited up and down around the church steeple in the smoky sky. "I got it!"

Just then the girl collided with her. Tieina fell off her sandals. Her camera fell to the ground, and she crashed into one of the vendors' stands. The last thing she saw before she hit the ground were beans and kernels of corn being scattered in the dust beneath the adjacent stalls.

"*Ti zawzo* okay?" a voice called in the darkness.

"*Wi m'ap okay, Mama,*" came the answer. It had come from her. When she opened her eyes, the young girl with the kite was being comforted by the *ti machann* whose stand she had just demolished.

"You! You *Blan*—white person." The woman came at her, clutching her tearful child as Tieina raised to her elbows. "You should be more careful. You could have killed my daughter and this is my business." The woman spread her arms to the scattered produce.

Others were already reassembling her stall.

Blan. She called me *Blan*?

Dominique ran over to her. "You okay?"

Tieina stood up and retrieved her camera and sandals from Dominique. "She called me *Blan*. She called *me Blan!*"

He smiled. "Your skin is dark, that's true." He looked her up and down, from her designer sunglasses and jeans, expensive camera, and totally impractical shoes. "But, to most of the people you'll meet in Haiti, you are American. That's all it means. It is not a bad term. Come on. Let's go. Your driver will be at the Montana to take you to your village."

The crooked wooden sign tilted uncertainly at the fork in the road and read, PETIT MIREBELAIS 5 KM.

"You can let me off here." Tieina jumped out of the car with her duffel bag and handed the driver the agreed upon $100 U.S. for the trip from Port au Prince.

"But it is far," he argued after counting the cash.

"It's okay. I like to walk." Since her tumble in the Petionville Square, her Creole was coming back. It just came out, like Dominique said it would.

"I'm looking for Yvonne Delva," she said to a man scraping dirt off his boots.

He pointed down the road. She walked slowly the rest of the way, still undecided what she would say when she finally saw her grandmother again after more than fifteen years. The door was open to the house the man had designated.

"*Bonswa. Bonswa.*" She knocked on the wall outside.

"*Wi.*" A white-haired woman with stooped shoulders came out the door drying her hands on her apron.

"I'm looking for Yvonne Delva?" Tieina knew her by her eyes, tired as they were. They were so similar to the ones she saw each morning in the mirror.

It took only a second longer for the older woman to recognize her. "Praise be to God! I have been waiting for you to come, my granddaughter." A broad smile spread across the woman's face and tears filled her eyes. "How did you know where to find me?"

"My heart reminded my feet." She took the old woman in her arms. It was the closest she felt to the truth in many years. "I don't want to forget anymore, Grandmother. Can you help me to remember?"

"How is your mother?" Giselle inquired over coffee the next day.

"Better, at least physically. She had a procedure. Her voice is back and she's writing in her journal and she's walking pretty well again. Sometimes she's a little forgetful." Tieina refused to let herself think that she would be anything but okay.

"Give her our love," Giselle said.

Yvonne nodded agreement.

A beautiful tall woman dressed in a blue skirt and white blouse introduced herself. "I'm Natali. You probably don't remember me."

"You're *the* Natali? Danny's Natali?" Tieina asked, reaching out.

"Yes, and you and I used to hide in the bushes and spy on the women's group." Natali returned the hug. "I'm glad to see you. Our paths were destined to cross again. Dan told me you are a writer and very talented."

"Really? He said that?"

"Of course." Natali was lovely and gracious. She could see why her brother was so in love. "Why don't you come with me today and I'll introduce you to our microcredit group. Your mother's organization has been our main supporter. I'll show you the village, too. If that's okay with you, Yvonne."

"Yes, please. It is hard for me to get up and down the road these days." Her grandmother rubbed her knees. "Later, I have some things to share with you, Granddaughter. Things that belong to you."

As they walked up the mountain, she and Natali talked like they had never been apart. They shared stories about work and men and what they hoped to accomplish with their lives. They laughed at the idea of them being sisters-in-law, and Natali managed to get all the details of Danny when he was younger. He would kill her when he found out.

"I hope our children are just like him," Natali confided.

"Are you pregnant?" Tieina asked.

"Not yet. But soon, after we get married. We hope."

"What is that sound?" Tieina asked.

"The drums?"

"Yes, and the singing."

"That is our *Sanba*. He tells us stories." Natali reached an arm around her waist. "Like you, I think."

"Funny." She linked arms with her future sister-in-law. "That's what my mother said one time." She couldn't wait to see her mother again and tell her how she regretted not coming back to Haiti sooner.

"How do you want to spend your last day here?" Natali asked.

The week had passed so quickly.

"Well . . ." Tieina had been thinking about this since the conference. "I saw some children in Port au Prince making kites. I've never flown a kite before. Can we do that today, Natali?"

"It's been a long time since I have. But yes, let's do that. It will be fun. Like when we were children."

Giselle stripped the sticks of their bark. She did it so quickly the rest of them had to hurry with their tasks to keep up. Natali held the frame together while Tieina lashed the sticks in place with some yarn Yvonne gave them. Rags were easy enough to find. But plastic bags required more innovation until Tieina remembered that she had thrown a few dirty clothes bags from the Montana in her duffel. They were opaque, white, and thicker than what the children used when she watched in Port au Prince. She didn't remember whose idea it was to paint bright yellow birds on the plastic. In two hours, from start to finish, they had an authentic Haitian kite.

All agreed Natali would hold and Tieina would run and launch. It was more challenging than she anticipated to keep the string taut as she ran downhill. But the wind was with them and their birds took flight. When the string could go no farther, Tieina carefully made her way back to the other three women. She offered the spool to Giselle. With both their hands in control, the kite ascended and descended the clouds.

"How does it feel?" Natali asked her mother.

"I feel like it wants to soar high above the clouds. And I feel like I don't want to let it go," Giselle answered.

Natali placed a hand over her mother's to feel the forces she described.

"Will the string break?" Tieina asked.

"Maybe, but sometimes strings can be very strong." Yvonne added her hand to the others on the spool.

"What does it look like?" Giselle's face was turned upward.

"It looks like our little birds are dancing in the sky," Yvonne responded.

"Yes, that is exactly how I see it, too," Giselle confirmed.

One by one, from first born to last, the women let go and released the kite into the wind.

46

TIEINA

MARS
DECEMBER 2009

Tieina watched as Jen tried again to straighten the angel falling off the tabletop Christmas tree that was the sole sign of the impending holiday. Danny was pacing the floor waiting for Natali to call from Haiti. It was the first time in over a year that the three of them had been together. Their mother, her hair now more silver than red, was deep in sleep when the doctor arrived for the family conference Jen had requested.

Danny stopped pacing and gently rubbed their mother's shoulder. "Mom, Mom, the doctor's here to talk to us."

"Shouldn't we wait until our mother wakes up?" Tieina asked the doctor.

"I think what the doctor is going to tell us—" Jen responded, still fidgeting with the angel, "—is that she's not going to wake up." She bit her bottom lip as if that would be reinforcement enough to keep her from crying.

"Is that true?" Tieina knew that Jen was concerned when she had called her in San Francisco, and Danny in Haiti, the week before and suggested they come home as soon as possible.

"Yes, she's deep in a coma and she has been for about ten days now. This happens in a small percentage of cases after the DBS," Dr. Owens explained. "More often a slow progressive dementia sets in. I'm sure you noticed the memory loss."

They nodded.

"Your mother knew the risks. It was a good year for her. I'm sorry it couldn't have been longer."

"I don't think that thing has been straight since I was little." Danny placed his hand over Jen's and gently removed the angel from the tree.

"What do we do now?" Jen asked. "An IV? Feeding tube?"

Edward looked at Dr. Owen, who spoke first. "Your mother didn't discuss this with you?"

All three of them shook their heads. Only Edward didn't seem surprised.

"Actually—" The doctor showed them a legal form on the front of the chart. "Mr. Rose has the healthcare power of attorney."

They all turned to stare at this man they barely knew, yet whom their mother had entrusted with her final wishes.

"She didn't want any of you to feel responsible when the time came." Edward spoke softly but clearly.

"Your mother has requested in the event of her losing consciousness, that no further measures be taken to keep her alive. Specifically, no IVs, no feeding tubes, no CPR, no hospital." Dr. Owen filled in the details.

Again they nodded in silence.

"How long do we have?" Tieina could not take her eyes off her mother.

"A day or two; a week at most." The doctor closed the chart. "If there is anything you need, please just let us know. Would you like us to have hospice come in?"

"No. We'll stay with her," Jen answered, and Tieina pulled up a chair and sat beside her sister.

Danny's cell phone vibrated in his pocket. He checked the number. "It's my wife, Natali. I'll call her back."

"Can we take her home, to Jen's house?" Tieina asked. She thought her mother would prefer that.

Her sister scanned the doctor's face and then their mother's. "I don't think we have that much time," she said, again answering for the doctor.

Tieina was sorry for Jen being the smart one this time. She must have known how bad it was for the last few weeks and neither she nor Danny had been there for her.

Danny returned from his phone call with Natali shaking his head yet smiling.

"What is it, brother?" Tieina asked, trying to guess why he was grinning. "Did Natali get a travel visa?" Her sister-in-law desperately wanted to come with Danny, but the U.S. Embassy in Haiti was months behind in issuing the visas for Haitians.

"No, better. She's pregnant," he plopped down in a chair shaking his head again in disbelief. "We're pregnant!"

"I can't believe it." Tieina said. She thought of how pleased their mother would have been to know the news. "So we're going to have a little Danny running around."

"No," he answered, looking only at their mother now. "A little Katherine. Natali is completely convinced the baby's a girl."

"Come they told me. . . Pa rum pa pum pum."

Tieina's first thought was that the Sanba had come to take their mother. But then the voices came closer and louder and continued with the familiar Christmas carol. Her mother had to be the most beautiful dying person ever.

She pulled up a chair to the other side of the bed and held their mother's hand. Her eyes met Jen's across their mother's failing body. The silence between each labored breath had grown throughout the afternoon since the doctor talked with them.

"*M konprann mama*—I understand. *M regret*—I'm sorry. *M renmen ou*—I love you," she repeated over and over again in her native language that she had denied for so long.

"I've got coffee for everyone." Edward, like a gentle giant bearing gifts, stood in the doorway.

It was easy to see why their mother had confided in him.

"There's no good time to tell you this. But I think you need to know your mother's other request," Edward spoke again. "When the time comes, she wishes to be cremated. And . . ." He paused. "She would like her ashes spread in Haiti."

Jen took in a sharp breath like she had been wounded in some way.

Tieina looked at Danny and it was like they were kids again doing soccer drills. She knew what he was thinking, what his next move would be. She nodded to him. It was his shot.

"I know it's short notice. But Mom really would have liked for all of us to do this together. What do you say, Jen?"

"Okay, you guys win. I'll go." Jen brushed a stray lock of hair from their mother's face. "Okay, Mom. I'm in, too, this time."

Tieina picked up her mother's hand. It was warm despite the gray veil that had descended over her face. Jen was right. One last sunset was all they had.

"Well then, Haiti in January?" Danny's sideways grin ever so slightly brightened the dark circles that had lived under his eyes this past week. "It sure beats winter in Mars."

Tieina stood up and Danny took her place at the bedside.

"I feel like we should pray or something." Jen dabbed her eyes.

"I don't remember Mom praying very often," Danny responded.

"She did," Tieina said.

They both looked at her like she was crazy. She opened the top drawer of the bedside table and pulled out the last of the thick leather-bound journals her mother had been keeping for the final year of her life.

"Did you guys know that Mom kept a journal for the past twenty years?"

"For twenty years?" Jen echoed.

"There are pieces of each of our stories, and my mother and grandmother and Natali's family, too. I found out more when I was in Haiti last year." Tieina handed her sister the latest journal.

"I thought you were there on an assignment."

"I was." She held hands with her brother and sister. "At first, but then . . ." She started to say that her journey had become a mission. But that didn't seem quite right either. Later, there would be time to explain.

The carolers appeared in the doorway to deliver their message. *"Come they told me . . . Pa rum pa pum pum . . ."*

The Beginning

It has been said that something as small as the
flutter of a butterfly's wings can cause a typhoon
halfway around the world . . .

—CHAOS THEORY

PORT AU PRINCE, HAITI

(CONTINUED)

. . . The short soccer woman seemed to know first. "Earthquake!" she shouted.

It was the woman with the glasses who got up before the others. That would have surprised me, if I had not been so disturbed myself. Ordinarily, she was the least steady on her feet. She started to run toward the guesthouse, toward her brother, her shattered glasses left behind.

"Oh no! Danny!" she cried.

The other two sisters reached her just in time. Their arms locked around her like a terrible nightmare around an awakening child. They held on, no matter how she screamed and fought against them.

"Let me go, Tieina. Let me go, Natali. I need to help him. Oh, Danny. Oh, Danny."

He'll feel no pain, I wanted to tell her.

"No, Jen." They repeated over and over again, disregarding their own grief.

Three levels of cement collapsed down, one upon the next.

He was in the middle.

Dust darkened the dusk.

And the three sisters did the only thing they could do when

the earth opened up and the world above came crashing down. They held onto each other and prayed.

And their voices joined the millions of others in a collective gasp of horror.

Many lamented for sins of a lifetime.

"Surely the world is ending!" the Haitians shouted.

But it wasn't the end of the world, not the way they feared. No one noticed the sky stayed clear, so the light would last a little longer. And no one noticed the sign I sent to them, a single and perfectly ripe mango that held onto its tree.

It was nobody's fault. It just happened.

I felt many knees in the days and weeks that followed. The Haitians understood better than the others. There are times when a man should pray on his knees with his hands folded. And there are times when he should pray on his knees, his hands working with anything he can find—a knife, a spoon, a shovel, a broken window pane, even bare bleeding hands. January 2010 was one of those times. They prayed and they dug and they dug and they prayed.

The dining room table at the guesthouse was salvaged and pulled into the soccer field. Transformed into an operating room table, its perfect mahogany finish was stained with blood and hesitation marks as legs and arms were sacrificed to save lives. There were no doctors or surgeons in those first days and only a sip of rum and a splash of Clorox water to ease the pain and lessen the stain.

The soccer field . . . became a hospital.

No one counted the number of people who were rescued before more help arrived. I know it was tens of thousands. Many worked alone in small groups because everybody knew somebody who was buried under the rubble. The cries turned to whimpers turned to unspeakable smells, and the buzz of the flies and the squeal of the rats was the only closure many people had that their sons, their daughters, their friends, their parents were among the reported 316,000 dead.

In the weeks, then months, that followed, many came from all my other places. It was like a parade—not a happy one, of course; but not exactly a sad one either. Humanity loved a cause and this little country was the cause to love. It was a strange parade, though. The reporters arrived before the doctors, and the cameras before the water and medicines. They came by air, by bus, by boat, and on foot. Everyone wanted to "do something."

The doctors marked the injured with colored tape on their heads—red, yellow, green, or black. It didn't take long to decipher the code. The ones marked with black came to me first.

The soccer field . . . became a hospital . . .
became a cemetery.

The soldiers brought tents in camouflage-green and gray. Wearing bulletproof vests, they bled bullets of sweat. Brightly colored handkerchiefs were swabbed with Vicks VapoRub and hastily tied round their faces.

"The smells," they gagged as they dug pits for latrines and set up water and food stations.

"Temporary," they declared. "Three months at most."

Long past three months they handed out rations as people stood like patient beggars. They lined up for miles in the hot tropical sun for water and rice and oil and cookies. Babies were born and died. Birthdays and holidays passed. The news surged and faded. The blame shifted.

People forgot to remember why they came.

The soccer field . . . became a hospital . . . became a
cemetery . . . became a refugee camp.

Then the rains came. People held what little they had over

their heads as the flood of mud climbed up their legs, and tents and tarps were ripped apart in the wind. They thought the world was ending again.

But it didn't.

Less than a year later, the second plague arrived. It was the water this time that brought the deaths. Did it really matter where it came from? People remembered again.

The blame shifted.

It wasn't long before the brightly colored T-shirts descended from the planes.

"Pray with us," they implored.

And yes, prayers were good. But so were jobs.

Most people think it was one of the big organizations with millions of dollars and big initials that made things happen. But I would tell you a different story.

This is how it began, with one little girl with one lone leg; the other was lost on that January day. She needed to do something to try and forget. Forget that she waited beneath the rubble crying and praying. And for what did that five-year-old pray while she was buried?

She prayed for rocks. Rocks that would be close enough for her to reach and small enough for her to throw. The rats bit at the fingers and the nose of her baby sister, lying not five feet from her. She yelled at them to stop and she threw rocks for hours and hours into the dark then into the light and then the dark again. But they didn't stop and after a while, she stopped throwing the rocks. She was so tired and thirsty; she didn't want to hit her sister and hurt her. Finally, she had only one rock left. She sensed her sister was gone and she would soon be, too. So she kept the last rock for herself—just in case. That was the last thought she remembered until she woke up many days later and her right leg was missing.

". . . below the knee," the woman in the blue outfit said. "She should do well with a prosth . . ."

She didn't understand until later that it was an artificial leg they were talking about. She got one from an organization that came into the camp. It was pink plastic, not like her real one at all. Still, she went to therapy every day for a month. She wanted so much to take the sadness from her mother's eyes. But it was easier to balance on the crutches. The leg was put under the bed with a few things her parents saved when their house collapsed. She didn't care much what was there. All that she really longed for could not be salvaged.

So, many months later, the little girl with a single leg began the task of rebuilding her country. Without even knowing it, that's what she did. One morning, balanced on her crutches, too big for her tiny frame, she came out of her family's tent and kicked a soccer ball with her only foot. It was a half-empty ball, the air had leaked out into the dust long ago. She didn't know the ball had been stitched by children in Pakistan and she didn't know it had found its way to her by the red-haired man who loved to play soccer and who loved to teach the Haitian children to play soccer. She just kicked the ball as hard as she could.

It didn't go far. But it was far enough. Her hands burned from blisters that burst where she gripped her crutches. Still, she accepted the challenge. She stepped forward to meet the ball and kicked it again and again. When the night came, she picked up the ball and vowed to forget many things. But she also vowed to always remember the words that remained in faded red on the dusty, spent ball: *Roses for Haiti.*

The next day another child joined her and then another. Soon, an adult watching saw them laughing and took down a few of the tents. With a rock, he pounded four posts into the ground, in two pairs only twenty feet apart. Now they had goals. In the next weeks, more children and a few adults joined in the game. Before too long, a little corner of the field, which had once been a soccer field, then a hospital, then a cemetery, and then a refugee tent camp, became a soccer field again.

The laughter and joy spread all over the country, and the children made kites like those the children have who come today, five years after the day the earth quaked, for the dedication of the soccer field . . .

"Monte kap!" the Sanba calls out . . .

The short Haitian woman in the blue T-shirt lines up facing the now ten-year-old Haitian girl, yellow shirt—one thick leg balanced on her crutches. Both are smiling as the American woman with the glasses drops the ball into the circle and the tall Haitian woman on the sidelines, holding her little girl, called Katherine for her grandmother, blows the whistle. For just an instant, I feel the girl's weight shift to the crutches and then with a powerful force, her leg connects and the ball sails down the field to her teammate in yellow.

"Monte kap!" the children answer.

Baby Katherine, along with the others, releases her kite into the wind. The crowd cheers. Their voices echo as one against the hospitals, businesses, churches, schools, and homes that have modestly risen above the rubble. Much has been accomplished.

But for the three sisters and two little girls, it is only the beginning . . .

—"When the Earth Trembled,"
from the *Sanba Diaries*
by Tieina Delva Rigando Ubeku
Pulitzer Prize, International Journalism, 2015

Acknowledgments

"Mesi Anpil," Thank You . . .

- My beta readers—when I didn't even know what a beta reader was—Bridget Ray and Ralph Simeone, for their encouragement and friendship.

- The muses who accompanied me through the ups and downs of life, who inspired me to be a more compassionate and authentic writer and person.

- The talented editors, designers, and marketing team at SDP Publishing Solutions, especially Lisa-Akoury Ross, for all your advice and patience.

- My friends, co-workers, and fellow board members at Partners in Progress, Outreach to Haiti, Hospice St. Joseph, the Association of Peasants of Fondwa and the University of Fondwa in Haiti, especially Sister Betty Scanlon, RSM, Dr. Richard Gosser, and Father Joseph Philippe, CSSP, who introduced me to Haiti and guided me through those initial and sometimes traumatic "life-changing experiences." Much joy and a few tears have paved the way to our mutual understanding and accomplishments. May our journey together continue in the realization of our dreams.

- Most especially, the victims and survivors of the January 12, 2010 earthquake in Haiti, and those who came to assist in rescue and recovery efforts—we must never again forget all that day compelled us to remember.

ABOUT THE AUTHOR

ROSEMARY HANRAHAN (EDWARDS) is a physician specializing in Pathology and Public Health. She has volunteered and lived in developing countries, including Haiti, for more than a decade. She has published articles and literary works in peer-reviewed medical and non-profit journals and has enjoyed dozens of speaking engagements with a broad range of audiences about her experiences in Haiti. The mother of two adult sons, she currently lives, writes, and practices medicine in western Pennsylvania, and is a board member and consultant for several international and U.S.-based non-profit organizations. *When Dreams Touch* is her debut novel, which is published under her pen name Rosemary Hanrahan.

www.RosemaryHanrahanEdwards.com

When Dreams Touch

Rosemary Hanrahan

www.RosemaryHanrahanEdwards.com

Publisher: SDP Publishing

Also available in ebook format

TO PURCHASE:

Amazon.com

BarnesAndNoble.com

SDPPublishing.com

 SDP Publishing

www.SDPPublishing.com

Contact us at: info@SDPPublishing.com